1 MONTH OF
FREE
READING

at

www.ForgottenBooks.com

By purchasing this book you are eligible for one month membership to ForgottenBooks.com, giving you unlimited access to our entire collection of over 1,000,000 titles via our web site and mobile apps.

To claim your free month visit:

www.forgottenbooks.com/free178336

ISBN 978-0-267-46935-2
PIBN 10178336

For support please visit www.forgottenbooks.com

The
Curious and Diverting
ADVENTURES

OF

SIR JOHN SPARROW

BART.

OR, The Progress of an Open Mind

By Harold Begbie

"*Nihil est ab omni parte beatum.*"—Horace

With Frontispiece by L. RAVEN HILL

LONDON
Published by METHUEN & CO.
36 Essex Street
Second Edition

First Published . . . . *September 1902*
Second Edition . . . . *October 1908*

THE BOOK OF SIR JOHN SPARROW
TO STEPHEN GWYNN, CRITIC

At last I'm born, and, Zeus be praised, the Fit
  Of Parturition, though it leaves Me weak,
  Hath mercifully spared Me Breath to speak
A Word the Author never would have writ ;—

Poor miserable Hack ! behold him sit
  Propping with languid Hand th' unblushing Cheek,
  And musing easily :—"Soon Men will seek
At every Stall this Offspring of my Wit."

Critic, what little Virtue I possess,
  Of Force and Faculty what little Store,
Are neither Mine nor His.   Let Me confess :—

My Strength, by pale Lucina's Torch, were less ;
  My faults, by the Three Sisters' Loom, were more ;
  But for the Touch of your maïeutic Lore.

From My Lord Chesterfield
To the Author of Sir John Sparrow

How fine a Thing is this Exalted Rank
    When Genius such as thine is proud to take
    The Hand stretched out for Learning's darling Sake,—
The Hand from which that monstrous Mountebank

Who knew not *pastern*, very vilely shrank.
    Above my Name, Great Genius, thou dost shake
    Blossoms of Immortality, each Flake
Fragrant with Sweets of which the Muses drank.

Let us thank God for Patrons, and rejoice
    That there are Noblemen who turn away
        From all the damned Refinements of the Smart—

From Bridge, from Baccara ; and of free Choice,
    And careless of the Thing that Jockeys say,
        Permit their Names to be commixed with Art.

SIR JOHN SPARROW
TO HIS LITERARY EXECUTORS

WHEN forth from crematory Fires you bear
   The Ashes once my negligeable Frame,
   Carve lightly on th' enfolding Urn my Name,
Duly append the Day, the Month, the Year,

Which saw my Star uprise and disappear ;
   Then afterward subscribe :—" From God he came,
   To God he went ; There, haply, he shall claim
That safe Perfection which he found not Here."

And thou who shalt my History unfold
   To Ages yet beneath the Wings of Birth,
   Prithee, be sparing of too easy Mirth,

And in my troubled Pilgrimage behold
   An infant Lesson for a blundering Earth :—
Perfection is not cast in fleshly Mould.

CONTENTS

CONTENTS

CONTENTS

THE CURIOUS AND DIVERTING
ADVENTURES OF
SIR JOHN SPARROW, BARONET

CHAPTER I

Concerning the Gentleman whose Adventures the Reader is invited to follow

ABOUT as many years ago as the middle-aged reader will care to remember, there lived in the north of England that worthy and honourable gentleman whose curious adventures are at once the theme and inspiration of these pages. Sir John Sparrow, for such was the gentleman's style and dignity, had inherited from his father a dozen years before the opening of our chronicle an amiable disposition, a baronetcy, and a poor twelve or fourteen hundred pounds a year. He resided in a modest cottage, kept a butler, entertained the parson to dinner some three or four days in the week, and drank tea with the ladies of his neighbourhood as persistently as any gossip in the four corners of England.

In appearance the baronet was of a rather insignificant description. His inches beyond five feet were scarce worth mention, and his features could boast none of those graces and refinements which are popularly

B

supposed to be the heritage of aristocracy. He was short, then; he wore moustache and whiskers, he had a clumsy nose; his shoulders were rounded; he held himself slackly. But our baronet was a dandy. The moustache was trimmed carefully, the spreading whiskers clipped close to the skin, and his thick dark hair—anointed daily with oil—was combed and parted as if that operation were the day's chief matter. He wore an eyeglass—a large glass which had the effect of sending one of the thick eyebrows higher up into the wrinkled forehead than its fellow on the other side—and his eyes were of a sad and tragic cast, gazing out upon a perplexing world with as wearied and inconsolable an expression as the gentle reader can possibly imagine. There was no petty spleen in this tragic look, simply polite boredom; there was weariness, not disgust; for, as Maeterlinck has well put it, the large aversions are unknown to the sage. Our little gentleman further intensified this expression of intellectual weariness by carrying his head on one side, letting it droop forward from the shoulders as a sunflower from its stem.

But there was no hint of a weary mind in the baronet's dress, which was of a sporting rather than a philosophical kind. He wore, winter and summer, a white billycock hat cocked over the eye with the big monocle, suits of a white-grey cloth, white gaiters on his boots, and he dangled from his coat-pocket handkerchiefs with elaborate borders. His manner of walking was characteristic of the man. With his white billycock over his brows, his head on one side, his big monocle shining dazzlingly under the hat's brim, Sir John struck up through the village street, legs swaggering to left and right, a thick malacca cane tight under an arm, his hands—in lemon-coloured kid gloves—clasped rigorously in the middle of his back. A little figure, but an important figure. A man conscious of his own dignity, yet humble before the inscrutable dispositions of that Providence which, among other and more universal inexplicabilities, had done so badly by him in the matter of inches. And in these walks Sir John would oft pause to exchange a word with farmer or housewife, speaking always in his low, carefully subdued voice; now and then pulling up to lay a sad hand on the sunburnt curls of a village urchin, gazing pathetically through his eye's window into the young face turned sheepishly from his mournful and philosophic glance. A popular man, one who could bow from his pedestal without loss of dignity; a good man, a kind man, a sympathetic man. To everybody in his own parish a great gentleman, *sans peur, sans reproche.*

Now Sir John Sparrow had two foibles: The first and least important was a passion for pretended romance. He hung his walls, for instance, with pictures of women he had never met—women, perchance, who had never existed; and Tom Shott, the parson, and Tiplady, the butler, had oft seen the little baronet gazing dejectedly at these portraits as though bound to them heart and soul by the tenderest and sacredest of ties. When he discoursed with ladies, too, it was the worthy gentleman's habit to assume as woebegone an expression as you shall see in the eyes of the greenest Romeo. Particularly was this so in the case of the widow FitzGerald, who lived at the Hall, childless and forlorn, a dashing lady with a merry eye, a musical voice, and an income of dimensions staggering in that quarter of the world. In her society the baronet was as sad and subdued as a mouse mesmerised by a round-eyed cat; and so many people had heard his sighs in the widow's presence, so many people had noted the lingering manner in which he paid his adieux that for

the past year it had been freely gossiped in the dale
(to the misery of other spinsters before whom Sir John
languished) that these two, the little baronet and
the beautiful widow, were trembling on the verge of
matrimony.

Thus we dispose of the first foible. The second was
of another character, and demands more thoughtful
consideration from your honourable worships. Be it
known, ladies and gentlemen, that Sir John Sparrow
rated above all other possessions the preservation of an
open mind. He had sooner be a fellow in mean rags
with an open mind than the possessor of millions
wedded to any single definite idea. This passion for
impartiality, as you may suppose, led our little baronet
into a thousand intellectual extravagances; but as his
only male friend was Tom Shott—a gentleman who
rested for six days from the labour of utterance on the
seventh—and as the ladies in that part of the world
were neither great readers nor deep thinkers, our hero
never met with such opposition (save from his own
butler, with whom he was gracious enough to discuss
the affairs of the world) as should force him to realise
the incongruity of his theories on the many problems
it was his great pleasure to discuss. He was no more
a Tory than a Whig, no more a Churchman than a
Dissenter, no more a Pessimist than an Optimist. He
had eyes for the good of each and the evil of each;
no mind to determine which was nearer the truth.
"I hope," he once said to Tom Shott very reverently,
"to go to my Creator with an unbiassed mind." Here
you see the gentleman's ambition. *He died with an
open mind:* such would he have chosen his epitaph.
There could be, he held, no higher praise bestowed on
mortal man than this recognition of strict, inviolate
impartiality. "Noisy fellows," said he, "are always

wedded to their own opinions; weak fellows to the opinions of others. The perfect man, conscious of his intellectual finitude, is content with aspirations. Don't you think I am right?" And he passed the decanter with a deep sigh.

Here, then, is Sir John Sparrow when we first meet him. A quiet, self-contained gentleman, living in a remote corner of our island, entertaining the parson to dinner, drinking tea with the ladies, discussing social problems with his butler, and playing patron in a grand manner, albeit on a small scale, to the farmers, tradesmen, and labourers of his little world; a gentleman with a mournful eye for pretty women, a passion for impartiality, and a particular fondness for the sound of his own polite voice.

The events which violently altered the even tenor of Sir John's way, luring him from his haven of peace into the stormy billows of life's open sea, are set forth, faithfully and truly, in the following chapters, which the historian begs your honours to peruse, if not with sympathy, at least, for the sake of our hero, with an open mind.

"I would go fifty miles on foot, for I have not a horse worth riding on, to kiss the hand of that man whose generous heart will give up the reins of his imagination into his author's hands—be pleased he knows not why, and cares not wherefore."

You remember?

CHAPTER II

In which Sir John Sparrow receives a call

ON a warm June evening, the French windows being wide open, a bowl of roses on the table, Sir John sat at dinner with his friend the parson—a red lobster-faced gentleman, with pale blue eyes and white hair ; as broad-shouldered, deep-chested, and ample-paunched as his host was dapper and insignificant. Over the comforts of the two diners hovered Tiplady. This vigorous and active person was of portly dimensions. His body, from the double chin—exposed to full view between the wide opening of his collar—to some few inches below the beginning of his legs, described the arc of a circle. He had a military carriage. He was white of face, pudgy and humorous in the features, and possessed two protuberant black eyes, heavily bagged, and capped by almost vertical eyebrows. Above his ears, sticking out on either side, were wings of black hair, the bushy whiskers on the fat cheeks having the appearance of mere overflow from these wings. The crown of Tiplady's head was flat, white, and polished.

While the scarlet visage of Tom Shott was bent over his plate, the fork working at a great pace, and while Sir John Sparrow, with his head on one side, was discoursing to his own great satisfaction on the frightful problems pressing on the world, there came upon the still air over the smooth lawn of the baronet's garden

6

the faint click of the drive gate, followed by the slow crushing of heavy boots on the gravel. It was an un-usual hour for callers, and Tiplady resented the discord in the pleasant harmony of the evening over which he ranked himself as presiding god. Dish in hand, he approached the window (it was odd to see so heavy a man move so briskly), and stood there glaring across the garden, prepared to withstand the invasion of tramp or French soldiery.

"Who is it?" asked Sir John; just the suggestion of annoyance in his "soft and irresistible *piano* of voice."

The butler did not answer for a minute; then he turned his head, not his body, and made the following answer, spoken in a brisk, vigorous fashion: "It is a labouring man, Sir John—a stranger in these parts, a peculiar-looking vagabond; and unless I am consider-ably out in my reckoning, a person with malicious in-tentions. But a more ridiculous-looking fellow, Sir John, I really never did see before. His coat, if I may be allowed to say so, is a regular porcupine of common flowers, weeds, and all manner of straw!"

"Dear me!" said the baronet.

"Don't be alarmed, Sir John," replied the brisk butler; "I'll defend the house. He won't get further than the windows, not while I'm about. If he attempts to force his way——"

"Hit him on the head with a spoon!" grunted the parson over his plate.

Tiplady, who was of an affable nature, acknowledged the jest with a broad smile. "I'd back my spoon against his knife, sir," he said modestly, squaring fat shoulders.

"Good-gracious!" cried Sir John; "you don't mean to say he's armed with a knife! What?"

"Only my way of putting it, Sir John; but you never know what these ruffianly tramps will whip out of their pockets when they're confronted and dared to come on. And he's got upon the lawn now, and he's coming straight over here, Sir John! Well, I never did! Excuse me talking so much, Sir John, especially at dinner; but in all my born days I never saw such a queer old stick as this vagabond. Why, he's a lunatic." Tiplady drew back. "The Lord save us, Sir John; I do believe he has escaped from a menagerie or a lunatic asylum! I'll send one of the maids for the constable! I'll get your gun, Sir John! It isn't safe for you to be left undefended. He's mad, Sir John; I'm sure of it—clean, raving mad!"

"Tell him," said the baronet very calmly, "to go to the back door."

"Or to the devil!" grumbled the parson, waiting for the replenishment of his plate.

Before the butler, who had now retreated several feet from the window, could make any reply to this unpleasant order, there rose on the air, loud and long-drawn, the crow of a cock—once, twice, thrice; then there was silence. The three men looked at each other in blank amazement.

"It's him!" cried Tiplady, "and it proves my words that he's a freak or a lunatic. He's a crower—a two-legged human crower!".

Sir John was irritated, both by the interruption of his conversation with Tom Shott and by the unseemly garrulity of Tiplady in the presence of a guest. "You are too much given," he said seriously, addressing the butler, "to jump to conclusions. I have so often warned you against the danger of hasty opinion. The crowing may very possibly be the only means this peculiar person possesses of clearing his throat, or in the country from which he comes it may be the natural method of announcing one's arrival. Pray don't be insular. Cock-crowing is by no means an infallible proof of lunacy. Oblige me by going to the window, and directing this stranger to the back door. After that you will perhaps give Mr. Shott some more jelly."

In the face of such an order disobedience was impossible. Tiplady squared his shoulders again, and moved, but very slowly, to the window. By the time of his arrival there, however, the stranger having finished his crowing, there was no time for the deliverance of this message; for there, two feet from the window, stood the cause of all this commotion at the baronet's dinner table—a lusty old fellow, with small, deep-sunken eyes, a tangle of grey beard, and dressed in the cumbrous corduroys of agricultural labour. All about his person the old man had stuck wild flowers, grasses, stalks of corn, even wisps of hay. His conical-shaped wideawake was decorated in the dust-stained broad band by thickly massed poppies and cornflowers, and every buttonhole, pocket-hole, and rent of his coat was stuffed with meadowsweet, honeysuckle, sticks of straw and leaves of vegetables, while weeds and grasses nodded out of the straps that bound his heavy legs below the knee. He wore a satchel slung on his back, carried a staff in one hand, and clutched to his breast with the other an old leather-bound Bible. From head to foot he was weather-beaten and dust-grimed.

"Go to the back door, please," said Tiplady. "It's round there to the right, just past those rhododendrons; follow the gravel path. You can't mistake the door. A dark green door, and a scraper at the side. To the right there, just past the rhododendrons! It's quite easy to find. To the right——"

"Chut—chut—chut!" drawled the old fellow slowly. "'Ave doon, 'ave doon! You're an immartal soul, for all you stand an' wait at t' table."

Tiplady staggered back. "He called me an immortal soul!" he gasped.

"You said he was mad," grunted the parson.

"An immortal soul!" repeated Tiplady, rolling terrified eyes on Sir John Sparrow.

The stranger had advanced and now stood at the open window, filling the breadth thereof with his clumsy, flower-tricked body. Behind him was the sunset and twittering of birds.

"What do you want?" asked Sir John, trying to frown very dreadfully.

"Thee soul," answered the old fellow in a pleasant voice. He chuckled good-humouredly, and came a step forward, dragging his staff lazily after him.

"May I ask who you are?" said the baronet politely.

"The Messiah," said the stranger. His eyes glittered.

The only calm person at this announcement was the parson. He had helped himself to jelly, and sat at his end of the table as cool and unmoved as Mount Ararat in the flood. Tiplady's jaw fell, and he gasped a "God bless my soul!" as he backed to the door. The eyeglass dropped from Sir John's eye.

"A'm the Messiah, I tell 'ee!" chuckled the old man, leaning on his staff. "The Lard 'e du zend me aboot the country tellin' the glad tidings, don't 'ee zee, that the wurrld's coomin' to 'n end. Ah, 'tis zure! The Lard 'as chosen me, 'e 'as, an' a'm goin' to 'bey this Maäster, whatever a may ha' doon wi' t'others who pay by t' week. So, *whoop! whoop! whoop!* repent 'ee ov your zins! The wurrld's goin' to pieces 's fast as ever it can, an' thar's little toime left fur gettin' on t' right roaäd to Glary. Zo, a tell 'ee—repent! baronet and parson and the manservant whaät is within thy gaätes, all three ov 'ee. And doänt 'ee never go an' zay as a 'aven't towd 'ee, now!"

At the end of this speech Sir John Sparrow had screwed the big monocle under its bushy eyebrow. "You're a very interesting person," he said enthusiastically.

"Eh! a'm that fur certain zure!" answered the veteran, with a deep chuckle. "The A'moighty 'e doan't choose no fules fur jobs o' this kind. 'E maun ha' the best, the salt o' t' earth. Thar's a many to choose from, bishops an' lards an' gentlefolk, but 'e maun ha' the best."

The baronet rose, dusting crumbs with his napkin. "Come in," he cried. "Come in and sit down. I'm delighted to make your acquaintance. Tiplady, draw a chair to the table, and bring a wineglass. You'll drink a glass of port? Let me take your stick. Come in, do. This is a very great pleasure. Really, I'm delighted."

The Messiah, as he called himself, looked shrewdly at the little baronet for a minute, and then, with a grin slowly and painfully overspreading his stolid, weather-beaten countenance, suffered himself to be dispossessed of staff and Bible, and conducted to a chair at the table. His glass was filled, a dessert plate set before him, and in a few minutes he was as much one of the party as if he had dipped a spoon into the soup and followed the dinner through all its courses to this its fruitarian conclusion. Tiplady retired, pondering the staggering fact that over and beyond being a butler he was an immortal soul, and that his master had offered a glass of port to the Messiah.

The doings of the "Messiah" had been reported about the country for several months, but this was his first entry into that particular neighbourhood, and the first time Sir John Sparrow had ever seen him in the flesh. The baronet was overjoyed. Like all lovers of peaceful days, he was glad to welcome startling diver-

sion when it came of its own accord to break the quiet
monotony of a well-regulated life.   And the coming of
this old labourer was something delightfully fresh and
novel. Sir John waited upon the strange fellow as though
that worthy had been his sovereign lord. He plied him
with food, he plied him with questions, he kept his glass
as full as the parson's—who had a decanter to himself.
Nothing that his natural urbanity could suggest for
making his guest feel at home and at ease was left undone
by our solicitous hero.

"And so you really believe in this mission?" said he,
as softly as lover in his mistress's ear. "You interest me
intensely. I don't for a minute, you know, doubt the
truth of your conviction, but it seems to me—it does
really, you know—that the great number of prophets
who have appeared on this globe with a message identical
to yours vitiates in some degree the assertion you make,
with perfect sincerity, that you are the chosen instru-
ment of the Creator. You see my position, don't you?
Any number of people have appeared and foretold the
incontinent destruction of our planet. They have
appeared, died, you know; and now, while they are
mouldering in the silence and darkness of earth, the
world is going as strong as ever. You see? I hope
I make myself quite plain? (Let me give you a
banana.) That there have been other Messiahs, of
course, is by no means conclusive evidence that your
message will suffer the same contradiction as theirs;
not at all, you know. But the fact that there have
been these other people prophesying exactly the same
thing, all through the tragical history of our most unfortunate race, persuades me, constrains me, I might
almost say forces me, to preserve on this question a
perfectly open mind until such evidence is presented
to me which is overpowering either for your case or

against it. At the same time—do try some more grapes, then—I listen to what you say with profound respect, conscious that your mission is above the mere ephemera of life, and anxious, you know, to get light on that great and awful mystery which haunts the son of woman from the cradle to the grave. What?"

It was a perplexed yet half-amused face turned to Sir John during this oration. The Messiah had that familiar habit among old people of forcing his eyebrows, as if by the most laborious and painful effort, from their place above the eyelids to the centre of the forehead. Innumerable wrinkles radiated from his small, sunken eyes, and while the brows quivered in their elevation, the little grey eyes blinked and smiled deep down in their depths as though the mind—an infinity of miles behind the eyes—were being slowly tickled by some laborious crowbar.

At the conclusion of Sir John's speech the old fellow passed a fat, wrinkled hand over his shock of touzled iron-grey hair, gave his broad shoulders a humping shrug, and replied, saying, " The Lard 'e du zend me t' most amaäzin' visions! When I beä sleepin', the Lard coom to me, 'e du, an' all t' cocks start a-crawin', an' 'e zay to me—Josey, 'e say, 'tis gettin' near t' end; a few more zunrises, a few more zunsets, a little more wind, an' a wee bit more rain, an' then *whoop!* t' whole wurrld will pop oot, clean oot, Josey, an' nothin' left ov it savin' t' smell. Zo, Josey, 'e says, beä you oop, an' tellin' folk whaät a tell 'ee; tell 'em straight, Josey; hit 'em haärd, lad; don't 'ee be afraid; t' angels are wid 'ee; zo hit 'em just as haärd 's ever 'ee can, fur a'm willin' to gi'e 'em all a chance. An' then t' Lard, doan't 'ee zee, 'e shaw me angels an' devils, heaven an' hell; an' a 'ears the zingin' ov t' angels an' t' terr'ble screams ov t' others, an' a waäkes oop all in a sweaät, a du, wi' t' cocks crawin', and t' zun shinin' bootiful, zame as if nawthin' had happened in t' night. Eh! 'tis wunnerful fine visions the Lard zend me!"

Sir John, in his most confidential voice, made answer, "Now, may it not be possible—I don't say it is, you know—that these dreams are the effect of which something or other taken with your supper is the direct and predisposing cause?"

"Cheese," grunted the parson.

"Yes, it might be cheese," went on the baronet very seriously. "A mere fraction of over-ripe Wensleydale might very easily induce visions of the most wonderful, absorbing, and even sacred character. A pipe smoked too low is also a frequent cause of these miraculous and baffling visions that visit the midnight pillow, and bead the forehead of the unconscious sleeper with the dew of terror and physical apprehension. Isn't it so?"

The Messiah rubbed his nose. "Mightn't t' A'moighty," he said, "wurrk by a bit o' cheese or a thread o' tobacco? Du 'e despise the small things o' t' earth, fur confoundin' t' wisdom o' t' greaät? What's more, I beän't t' only one who goes aff to zleep arter cheese an' tobacco, don't 'ee zee; but a'm t' only one who zees the Lard an' talks confeedential wi' un!" He chuckled, and passed the back of his hand over his mouth.

"Well, then," said Sir John, waving his napkin very grandly, "let us grant that you *are* sent by our Creator, by the inscrutable providence in whose tremendous purposes lie hid the destinies of our miserable race; let us grant that. Now, tell me, what do you propose doing? For instance, you come to me, you know. You come here, you sit down, you talk to me. Don't you? Now, what have you got to say to me? What is the message that celestial inspiration puts into your mouth for delivery to my ears?"

"Repent!" said the Messiah. "An' a'll trooble 'ee fur an opple, if ye'll beä zo koind."

The eyeglass nearly dropped a second time from the baronet's eye. He regained his composure, smiled very affably, and drew his chair nearer to his guest. "Don't think me self-righteous, my friend — you won't, will you?—but what are the sins of which you think I should repent? Of what unpardonable enormities am I guilty? To tell you the truth, preserving an open mind on all these great questions, I cannot altogether see the force of that cry, repent. I mean, speaking generally of the human race, we are none of us hopelessly bad; we earn our bread, go about our business, and only in the few minutes left between sleep and necessary daily toil do we get any opportunity of falling into those sins and wickednesses which war against the spirit. We are toilers first, and free agents next. In the circumstances I am rather inclined to hold, you know, that 'repent' is too big a word for the matter. We are more fools than sinners; more blockheads than evil-doers. You mustn't be too hard on toilers. Don't you think there is something in what I say? Don't you, now?"

Josey shook his head.

"Thar's good an' thar's evil; thar's heaven an' thar's hell. Zo, a tell 'ee, *repent!*" The old fellow paused. "But," he added, raising his glass, "a doan't moind tellin' 'ee a bit more. When a coom into this village a axes who lives heer. Sir John Sparrer, they tells me; a kind gentleman. Kind gentlemen, a says, are like to go to hell, fur they'm mostly do-nawthings; a'll gang oop an' tell un zo. An' oop a cooms, an' you treat me like a gentleman, tho' the paärson's at t' table. Zo I'll tell 'ee a bit more. Coom Joodgement Day, Sir John, t' Lard will zay to 'ee—John Sparrer, 'e'll zay, a gave 'ee a title an' mooney an' **t'** gift·o' t' gab, 'e'll zay, whaät did 'ee du wid 'em? Did 'ee gang oop to Lunnon an' taäke a part in t' big foight, whar t' devil is 'avin' things all 's own waäy; or did 'ee zit drinkin' port wi' t' passon in a wee bit o' a plaäce whar 'ee warn't waänted no more than a owl in a bee-hive? Tell us, John Sparrer, 'e'll zay; téll us straight oot, mon; fur you're no fule, an' you've got tongue inter 'ead, fur a've 'eered it clackin' over t' dinner-table this lang toime, 'e'll zay."

Sir John grew thoughtful. It struck him, slowly but convincingly, that he was, as this old blunt fellow said, guilty of an almost irremediable wrong. He had neglected those great qualities, of which no one was more conscious than himself. He had wasted his powers. He had buried his talents in a napkin. Sir John was never more startled in his life.

"Friend," he said solemnly, "I thank you for teaching me my duty; I do really. I believe that the Word is with you. I express no opinion on the speedy dis-solution of the world—that's another matter—but I say again, and emphatically, that I believe the Word is with you."

The parson started.

"Eh, that's a fac'!" chuckled Josey. "A'm not one o' them who taäkes a text o' Scriptur' an' hammers un on a pulpit-desk fur twenty minutes till he's flat 's a penny, an' good to nawbody. Whaät a du is to zit still an' let t' tongue speaäk accordin' to wisdom. A zee things as they are, an' a just zays whaät a zee. A gi'es a zinner naw room fur squeezin' oot o' ma cleft-stick. A holds 'im faäst, a du, an' a zays you're a zinner, an' you caänt get away from it, doän't 'ee zee! A cleft-stick, a tell 'ee, is better 'an all t' sarmins; an' a'll trooble 'ee fur anawther opple, Sir John Sparrer."

When one has cultivated an open mind for a long time—taken elaborate precautions to keep the gateways of the brain always wide open—it is astonishing how many and how queer ideas will flock unquestioned and undisputed into the chambers of the intellect, and there, for the nonce, make themselves thoroughly at home. It is the more reasonable theories, the more popular beliefs, that are challenged at the gateways, held in long dispute by the sentinel posted there, and finally turned away empty. And so it came about that with the first approach of Josey's idea—his testimony to Sir John's power and talents, his accusation that the baronet was wasting his genius—our worthy open-minded hero found himself embracing, with all the enthusiasm in the world, the startling project that he should set out to London, see the modern world with his own eyes, and, if he found it so wicked and perverse as it was declared to be by all philosophical reformers, take steps to make it a great deal better.

It was a pleasant idea. Sir John liked himself in the rôle of universal reformer. Other people, he felt, had bungled the matter by coming to it with ancient theories and illogical prejudices. He would attack this question with an open mind.

He was not in the least surprised by the suddenness of his determination to visit London and play the part of philosophical reformer. Not in the least. His only thought on this head lay in a contrary direction; he would have liked to pack his bag on that very instant. No time was to be lost. And London—the wonderful London of the modern world—was so far off! What a long time must elapse before he could set foot upon its roaring stones! Sir John, you see, was not a slow mover when conviction occupied his mind. That is what ever happens in the case of the unprejudiced; when they

c

have decided on a definite path, made up their fastidious minds which way to take, they go like the very——

"You have taught me my duty," said the baronet. "I shall go to London."

"What!" cried the parson, jumping in his chair. For you must understand that Tom Shott not only loved Sir John, but that his ambition was to see the baronet happily married to the rich widow, and in fitting state presiding over their village world. So he jumped in his chair, exclaiming, "What!"

"I shall go to London," said Sir John.

"Don't," said Tom Shott quietly.

"But why not, my dear fellow?"

The parson shook himself together. "Because I don't want you to."

The Messiah chuckled aloud. "Eh!" said he, "'tisn't whaät t' parsons want; 'tis what t' Lard wants. Them two be direct contraries, they be."

Tom Shott eyed the old labourer with those staring blue eyes of his for many silent seconds, his upper lip—as red and shining as the rest of the face—thrust well out under the nose; and then he spoke. "If I thought," said he, "that the Almighty worked by such means as you, I'd turn atheist to-morrow." He ended with an explosive "Faugh!"

Josey grinned deep in his eyes and slowly over his wrinkled face. "Hasta never heerd, parson, that t' Lard moves in a mysterious waäy His wunners to perform?"

"Mysterious, not ridiculous!" burst out the parson.

"Tom," cried the baronet, "my mind is made up. I will go to London, with an impartial mind, and see for myself if it is the abominable Babylon that some people declare it to be. 'Tis more than twenty years, Tom, since I walked down the shady side of Pall Mall, and then"—with a sigh he glanced at the picture of a woman on the wall—"I was young and self-centred. Now I shall see things with larger, other eyes. No longer distracted by passion, no longer tortured by amorous despair, I shall pass through the throbbing thoroughfares of the empire's capital, an unimpassioned spectator, an intellectual observer, a meditative philosopher."

"And mind 'ee call out as 'ee go along, REPENT! REPENT!" said the Messiah, rising to depart. "If 'ee doän't do that 'ee moight as well bide heer an' die in idleness wi' t' parson an' t' pigs."

Oddly enough, at the conclusion of this speech the parson uttered one of his deepest grunts. The Messiah, putting on his hat, smiled good-naturedly at his theological rival, and then with a nod of his head moved away.

"Farewell, my friend," said the baronet, accompanying Josey to the window. "I hope I shall see you after my return from London. You will give me the opportunity, won't you? Come here as often as you can, then we shall be able to carry our discussion a point further. The saddest thing in life to me is that the brevity of its duration permits of arriving at no definite opinions. The most we can do, alas! is to advance a point or two from the prejudices we imbibed with our mother's milk. It is very sad. But we will meet and discuss this matter again. You won't forget me, will you?"

"A'll pray for 'ee," said the Messiah, moving laboriously off. "An' a wish 'ee a good-night, Sir John Sparrer."

The parson leant forward in his chair and screwed his scarlet face round to the window. "Don't you dare to pray for me!" he bellowed, quivering with indignation.

"A never waästes me breath!" answered Josey from the lawn, and he shuffled off humming a hymn.

Sir John brought a serious face back from the window "Now, Tom, you call that fellow rogue and vagabond. You are wrong. It is impossible for us to say definitely what he is. We can only say, my dear fellow, what he is approximately. Is he nearer honesty or roguery? Is he——"

"He's a confounded humbug!" cried the parson.

Sir John shrugged hopeless shoulders. "Of course, my dear fellow, if you will persist in giving your pre-judices—what I might almost call your undigested opinions—the full weight of mature and reflected judgments, it is impossible for me to argue with you."

Tom Shott, loading a big pipe, unstalled himself from his chair; and breathing like the elephant he was, stumped over to his host. "Harkee, Jack," said he, very red and fierce, "that fellow's a rogue or a lunatic. That's plain!"

Then he stood looking down with troubled eyes on the spruce little baronet fidgeting at his white tie.

Sir John smiled. "For the sake of peace, my dear fellow, I yield to you. Let us say he's a rogue or a lunatic."

"That's good!" said the parson, striking a match. "And now you won't talk any more nonsense about going to London. The idea of it!"

"Oh, that's another matter!" said Sir John. "I have made up my mind to go there."

"Stuff! You're better here. Don't go, Jack."

Sir John, very sad and dejected, was gazing up at another portrait of a fair woman. "I must, Tom," said he in a strained whisper.

"What!" bellowed the parson, the white smoke curling about his scarlet face, the pale blue eyes shining like stars through the wreathing mists. "What! you really mean to tell me you're going to London?"

Sir John nodded.

"Then you're a damned fool!" thundered Tom Shott, and lumbered out of the room, grunting and puffing, before Sir John could believe his own ears.

CHAPTER III

Which tells of Sir John Sparrow's obstinate departure

ON the morning following upon the appearance of Josey the Messiah, Sir John Sparrow took an early walk up the village to pay a few brief calls of farewell. Tiplady remained at the cottage busy with his master's and his own portmanteau.

It was a glorious morning; a radiant earth, a radiant sky, laughter and ringing voices in the hayfield, the whole air tremulous with the music of the larks; a murmurous humming in the hedges, a deeper note from the village schoolhouse, the iron clangour of the smithy, the rumble of wheels and the sharp striking of iron hoofs on the hard road. Old men pottering with toddlers in fragrant cottage gardens; brisk matrons polishing and scouring at cottage doors. Life everywhere; happiness and labour pulling in double harness the little village world; and the sun shining with all his might.

It was not the sort of morning that tempts one to set about reforming his fellows. Sir John felt it was good to be alive, and that was all. The sun beat cheerfully upon his white billycock, and there was sunshine in our gentleman's heart for all the habitual gloom in his sorrowful eyes. He drank the sweetness of the scented morning, the fresh breath of the young day-break.

Now, it chanced that Mrs. FitzGerald was driving early to the market town that morning, and so it came about that she and Sir John met in the village under the shadow of the church tower. The widow pulled up her stout ponies, and the groom hopped from his seat behind the little phaeton and went to their heads, while Budge and Toddy, her two terriers, came pawing at the baronet's legs. Sir John therefore, leaning against the edge of the dashboard, had Mrs. FitzGerald almost to himself.

Now Mrs. FitzGerald is worth your honour's attention, if, as I pray it be, your honour never finds it a trouble to pay the tributary glance to beauty. If when you take your walks abroad, you have an eye for a pretty lady, and can find joy in a moment's contemplation of a face you may never fondle or caress, prepare now to yield your adulatory glances, to shoot the eyes' testament of admiration, before the shrine of this lady leaning from her phaeton (how gracefully she leans!) with white reins in her white-gloved hand. And what a pretty hand it is! How perfectly it tapers from the narrow wrist, swells again as if to regain once more the arm's full glory, and then, pathetically yielding to anatomical destiny, shrinks sadly and beautifully away to the fine points of the finger-tips! Ah, dear sir, could I persuade Mrs. FitzGerald to take off that white glove and show you, in the full sunshine of the morning, the real narrow hand beneath, the little hand of human flesh, white as ivory, little, but no skeleton, mark you, white but warm, and with such pretty nails tipping each finger—if I could do this, I should have you pushing my hero from his place beside the carriage (necessary to this history), and seizing up the soft white hand to salute it before all the world.

Which warns me I must be careful when I bid you look at the lady's face. Now I hate those old romancers who could sing no pæan to their heroines when they had tripped with a silly girl's giggle across the teens, who would make all their women past twenty coldly virtuous and respectably dull, as if romance for them had ceased to be. These are not the notions of the world in which we move, and the world will not call me fool for answering boldly to all whom it may concern that the widow FitzGerald's age was—— But let each reader fix it for himself. If, respectable patriarch, you must love seventeen, and only seventeen, say she was seventeen, and had been widowed as many of those seventeen years as you choose to consider romantic. If, ingenuous youth, you cannot abide simple girls of your own age, and love only the matured woman, say that she was anything from four-and-twenty to—the Fates know what. · And while you are quarelling about the right age (how you settle it I care not a jot), I will set about drawing the lady's picture, which (let me tell you) is a thousand times more to the point than the tale of her years. Is it not the case, madam?

I draw an oval, a perfect oval; but genius leaping atop of my chalk at the right moment gives expression to the chin ere one touch of colour has been added. The chin lives even in outline. You can see the laughter breaking out there. The line trembles with the humorous blood beating beneath the yet unadded flesh. And now, while genius is so close to me, I make hurry to dip my brush deep into joy and merriment, and, *presto!* I have splashed the oval outline into quivering life. What warm, soft flesh! Ah, the warmth of it, the softness of it! And pray, sir, observe the dimples in the cheeks. What the curl is to the roseleaf, what the ripple is to the wave, what the sparkle is to the diamond, what the brook is to the glen, so are those wicked dimples to my lady's face! And mark well the smile curling the red lips into secret laughter, parting those pretty gates just wide enough for you to see the strong white teeth shining in their shadow. What a delicate nose, yet not narrow enough to be chilling and sculpturesque; curved nostrils vibrant with breath quick-drawn and careless, neither Roman nor Greek in form, but English, with the finishing Irish touch that gives courage and bewitchment to the tilt of the tip. But behold my brush has done better work than all this. The eyes! The eyes! Open as the sea, generous as the sky; round, brave eyes! Grey, with violet fighting to shine there; but fighting, mark you, with laughing rivalry, half in love with the grey, as the grey is all in love with the violet. Large eyes, but above all things merry eyes; merry as a May morning; merry as a Spanish dance; merry as a tumbling summer sea; merry as freedom. Laughter leaps out of them, forcing the long dark lashes into that beautiful curve you noticed before I could speak of it, holding them there because he is for ever leaping in and out. Come, now, madam, on your honour, did you ever see outside your own looking-glass such eyes as Mrs. FitzGerald's?

And the dark cluster of hair, lustrous as the coat of a bay horse (if the simile smack not too much of the stable), and wound at the back of the head into a coil that looks so enticingly easy to unprison. What rich hair it is, and what small wonder that it participates in the merry humour of the eyes, nose, lips, chin, and those wicked, twinkling dimples! If the lady would but re-move her hat——

Come, sir, you have already clamoured for the glove, and now you are at the hat. I must put a stop to this. Bear you in mind that the lady whose portrait

I have painted is sitting in a phaeton, in the midst of a village, with a gentleman leaning against the dashboard and languishing at her through his eyeglass. Pray you, keep to the footpath.

"You are early abroad," she says, and all the silent birds take to singing in a chorus, for she has spoken, and they have been waiting quivering for that on a hundred branches ever since she came out to the world.

The lover sighs. "I was just coming to bid you a hurried good-bye," says he, very sad, stroking Toddy's smooth head.

"My dear Sir John!" she exclaims, serious for a second, the red lips parted. You see the breath drawn in.

"I am going away," he says. How softly he speaks!

"But has anything happened? No one has told me a word!" The lady is wide-eyed.

He looks at her despairingly through his glass. "I think it better that I should go away."

"But we shall miss you so! Oh, the place won't be the same! Down, Budge; down, sir!"

"If I could think that," he says, smiling ever so sadly.

"You must think it! Why, we shall weep for you; we shall talk of you at tea, and say that the sun has set behind the hills for ever and ever. Who will hand the bread and butter so charmingly? Toddy is making your trousers so dreadfully dusty! Down, Toddy; down!"

Sir John fixed her—for we must get back to the past tense lest we slip into the region of tragedy—and there was in his sombre eyes at that moment all the agony of a stricken deer. "It is a comfort to know that the people here will sometimes remember me," quoth he. "But if I could know that my absence would really make any difference to you—I mean, if I knew that you would miss me, condescend to notice that I was absent from your festivities; if I knew that——"

He sighed and drew slowly back from the dashboard gazing at her. Mrs. FitzGerald—what could she do? —bent her pretty face so that the merry chin was smothered in the cloud of cream lace that flowed from round about her neck, ending in a careless bow over the swelling bosom. Her eyes were hidden under the nodding brim of her wide hat.

"Good-bye!" cried Sir John, in a voice of suppressed tragedy.

She gave her little hand into the lemon-coloured glove.

"But you are not really going away for ever and ever?" she cried. "It is too impossible! I never heard of such a preposterous thing in all my life. You don't mean that you are deserting us for good! You are only going away for a season, for a week or two; you will come back. You will come back, won't you?"

"I hope I may be brave enough," he said, gazing mournfully into the churchyard. "Some day, perhaps —when I have been able to forget. Good-bye."

"You make me horribly miserable," said she. "You have wrapped ·yourself in a most irritating mantle of mystery; and you're not a bit like your real self."

"Don't you think one has perpetually to conceal one's real self, always to be hiding one's most passionate feelings under the tweeds and homespuns of pride and prejudice? Don't you think so?"

Mrs. FitzGerald blushed. On my word of honour, sir, she blushed a rosy red—"You are a great mystery," said she; "and I give you up."

"Ah!" sighed Sir John; "you give me up!"

"And so must everybody else if you persist in leaving

us so tragically and mysteriously," said the lady, smiling
reproof at the baronet's naughtiness.

" Everybody else doesn't matter," he said very softly.
" Good-bye."

Again she gave him her hand, and then, while the
groom hopped back into his seat and the ponies trotted
off, he stood there leaning dejectedly on his cane, his
white billycock still swept from his head, and watched
her go. Toddy stayed to lick his glove a moment, and
then bounded after Budge and the phaeton.

The next minute our lovesick hero was swaggering
along in much the same fashion as we saw him before
Mrs. FitzGerald flashed upon the scene with her pretty
eyes, her roguish dimples, and the white reins in her
white-gloved hands.

But his adventures had not ceased. Hardly had the
young, middle-aged, or ancient widow—which you
please, ladies and gentlemen—flashed out of sight to
the accompaniment of trotting ponies, before that
leviathan, Tom Shott, loomed upon the scene, heavy,
morose, and gloomy. Now, the parson was in a great
state of anxiety as to the effect of his explosion on
the previous night. He loved Sir John with all his
heart, and he had rather a hundred times undergo
physical torture than lose the friendship of the loquacious
little baronet. So he came along awkwardly and
sheepishly, hands thrust deep into his pockets, shoulders
about his ears. Sir John, on the other hand, who valued
his dignity more than all the friendships in the world,
and who never in his whole life had been damned for a
fool until last night, held himself very erect, assumed
a more portentous carriage than ever, and even took
his malacca cane from under his arm, to swing it carelessly and dashingly as he swaggered, humming an air,
towards the elephantine person.

The nearer they approached each other the more intense waxed their diverse emotions. The parson's head hung forward and his eyes sought the ground; the baronet kicked up his feet, twiddled his cane, and looked straight ahead of him as nonchalantly as a parvenu cutting a poor relation in the Park. He hummed desperately hard.

So they approached each other, the big man and the little man, old friends of over twenty years' standing, on this bright June morning. When they were within a pace of each other, both stopped and stood looking at the other's waistcoat buttons. Then, at the same moment, they both cleared their throats.

The parson was the first to find his voice. "Beautiful morning," he said.

"Beautiful," said the baronet, as haw-demme as you please.

"Beckwith's getting his hay in, I see," said the parson, kicking up a cloud of dust with a mighty boot.

"Yes," answered Sir John, withdrawing his legs from proximity to the whirling dust.

"Umph!" grunted the parson.

So they stood a space in silence, and then the baronet held out his hand.

"Good-bye," he said. "I'm going to London in an hour's time, and we may not meet for some time. I hope you will keep very well."

The parson drew a deep breath. Alas! his conscience smote him. He saw now, in the cool morning air of reflection, that his angry opposition to the baronet's decision on the previous night was responsible for this sudden departure.

"You're really going then?" asked the parson, lugubrious and humble, taking the hand in a dazed, half-hearted manner.

"By the twelve o'clock train."

There was nothing more to be said. "Well, good-bye," said the parson; "I hope you'll take care of yourself."

"I'm taking Tiplady with me."

The parson nodded. Just as the baronet was passing on, Tom Shott pulled up. "I think it's a mistake, Jack!" he said in a burst.

"You mentioned that opinion last night," said Sir John icily.

"Umph! I believe I swore at you too." This by way of apology.

"I imagined you had forgotten it," quoth Sir John, caressing the pin in his black tie.

"Well, Jack, what I think is this. You're happy here; you're the life and soul of the place; everybody loves you, particularly Mrs. FitzGerald—why you don't marry her I can't for the life of me understand—and yet you go and throw us all on one side just because a confounded, crack-brained hedge-preacher tells you that you ought to be chasing the devil through the streets of London. 'Tisn't sane, Jack, and 'tisn't kind."

This was a long speech for the parson, and he pulled up, breathing hard. Sir John regarded him for a moment in chilling silence, and then made answer.

"You are exceedingly kind to take so much interest in my affairs," said he, "and believe me I am correspondingly grateful. But whether it is possible for one who has called his friend a coarse and an opprobrious term to take a beneficent interest in his doings, is a question which finds me, I am sorry to say, with no very definite answer. I wish you good morning."

The parson watched him go in silence. His heart was very sore, and the retreating figure of the baronet seemed with every step to leave a larger and more aching void there. He tried to follow, tried to call out; but legs would not stir, voice would not come. He simply stood in the centre of the dusty road and watched his little friend swagger out of his life. After that he shuffled away to the baronet's cottage, and there pledged Tiplady to keep him well posted with the affairs of Sir John Sparrow. "Telegraph if he's ill," said the parson, lunging out of the house.

As for Sir John he was saying to himself, "Why doesn't Tom come grunting after me? Why doesn't the dear fellow say he's sorry for insulting me? What a foolish old bear it is, confound him!"

Then he went on, and turned in at the rectory to bid Mrs. Shott farewell. He found her, as usual, surrounded by the family. One seldom saw a full-length Mrs. Shott; it was almost invariably a head - and - shoulders Mrs. Shott who greeted her friends over a ring-fence of little Shotts. Now, dear reader, the Shott children were a company of professed wits, with their grinning mamma for perpetual audience. There was Master Anthony Shott, cynic and sayer of smart things to be reported over other tea-tables; Master Dick Shott, clown and acrobat; Master Tom Shott, imitator; Miss Emmy Shott, partner with Tom in the imitation department, but with a line of her own; and Miss Nelly Shott, a round-faced infant, with big eyes, whose special genius was for saying uncomfortable things before strangers, and making everybody, save her mamma, exceedingly unhappy.

Sir John, approaching the tree under which this company were assembled, received his first greeting from Nelly.

"Dwawes, dwawes!" said she, and pulled up her frock to a bunch round her chin that the baronet might observe her promotion from the diapers of infancy.

Mrs. Shott, her face suffused with laughter, made a dash for the child.

"Wonderful things, kids!" said Anthony. "Always thinking the whole world takes an interest in them. Fancy making a song about what-you-may-call-ems!"

Master Tom Shott, who would presently convulse the family by an imitation of Sir John's manner, was busy at the baronet's back, critically and ostentatiously studying the little gentleman's carriage and deportment. Emmy — whose imitations took the form of singing songs like Mrs. FitzGerald, or walking, talking, and smiling like other of her mamma's friends — studied Tom with the careless indifference of a haughty rival. Dick Shott was now making funny faces at the baby, hoping that Sir John was admiring him.

In the midst of this interesting family stood the baronet, announcing his departure. He was going to London; his nephew, the heir, lived there. He thought it better he should go. Why? Oh, there were many reasons. Ah! many, many reasons. He hoped to find Mrs. Shott and the family in excellent health on his return.

His fingers went to his waistcoat pocket and fumbled for half-sovereigns. He must leave a reminder of himself with the young people, or they would forget him during his absence. He had been young once himself. He hoped Anthony was not too old for a tip. Anthony, forgetting cynicism, grinned painfully. The children formed a ring round Sir John.

In the silence of that moment Nelly toddled whimpering to her mother. "'Oddidmun, 'oddidmun!" she said, expressing repellence for our hero. Sir John gazed at her solemnly through his glass.

"Strange, strange!" mused he, being unversed in baby language. "No doubt she has expressed in those inhuman words a wish none of us can fathom, but which, nevertheless, seriously disturbs the peace of her mind. And the words—are they of a language that an ourang-outang would perhaps recognise, just as we recognise our own language when it is spoken by a foreigner? I wonder what she means? None of us, for all our wisdom, can say. The limits of mortality! Ah, we are a poor, finite lot!"

The children began to giggle. "I think," said Mrs. Shott, "I think she had better go indoors."

"But on such a lovely morning!" exclaimed Sir John. Then he bowed himself to the child, and gently patted the contorted cheek. "Does little Nelly want to go indoors, does she? Doesn't little Nelly love the flowers, and the pretty sun, and the nice cool breezes?"

Little Nelly stamped with rage, repeating, "'Oddid-mun, 'oddidmun. Beast man," amid incipient sobs.

The baronet, however, had infinite patience. "Nelly mustn't be crossy-crossy!" he exclaimed; "she mustn't, really. Shall I take Nelly in my arms and give her a nice ride, eh?"

"I shouldn't advise you to," said Anthony; "she kicks like winky."

"Strange, very strange!" sighed Sir John. "How little do we understand the emotions of the infantile mind; how little do we appreciate the wants and require-ments stirring the depths of baby intelligence. And yet 'tis but a few years ago that we too uttered baffling words to those who stood about us uncomprehending. What does she mean? What did we mean? No one understood us, no one! No one!"

"She makes queerer noises than that!" said Anthony, which set Tom and Dick laughing so heartily that Mrs. Shott was obliged to join in. Then with the swearing Nelly in her arms she bade Sir John adieu, and while

D

the baronet, accompanied by the other children, walked towards the drive gate, made her way as hastily as possible to the nursery, where Nelly soon ceased to whimper.

In this simple, homelike manner Sir John Sparrow bade farewell to his friends in the sleepy village where he had lived so many quiet years, and set out with an open mind on his momentous journey to the seething capital of the British Empire.

CHAPTER IV

*Wherein it is recounted how Sir John Sparrow
took a Walk down the Strand*

"AND this is London!" Sir John thus soliloquised, taking his first walk down the Strand. "Here the individual is merged in the mass, the personality sucked into the great tidal river of humanity." A porter carrying a tray of fish bumped into the little baronet, and sent him stumbling towards the gutter. Here a boy thrust a newspaper into his hand, and a flower girl, ere he had quite recovered his equilibrium, began sticking a nosegay into his buttonhole. Sir John thanked them both for their attention, inquired of them his indebtedness, and having discharged that liability, set his hat right, pulled his coat down, and continued his walk and his interrupted soliloquy. "A Shakespeare or a Milton might walk as I am walking now, and be as little an object of veneration, or even of momentary interest, as I myself. A girl would offer the creator of *Lear* a rosebud ; a boy would offer the poet of Beelzebub an evening *Star.* Here and there one would turn and say to himself, 'Why, there goes Will Shakespeare!' and then straightway proceed upon his business. Oh, strange, wonderful, and perplexing little world! What is it that thou seekest with such painful and intense assiduity ? Oh, race of man, cradled in doubt, nurtured on hypothesis, certain of nothing! what is it that drives

35

thee forward at such lightning speed, jostling thy fellows, treading down thine own children, as though the object of thy labour, the destiny of thine existence, were clear and certain before thine unhappy eyes? Here every man is for himself, here every man is intent upon the acquiring of riches; and here is perpetual unrest, ceaseless misery, unending toil! How shall I make myself heard in the midst of this Babel?"

At this point in the simple gentleman's moralising, he became aware of an interesting figure some few feet away from him. This was a middle-aged man, in frock coat and tall hat, with an umbrella thrust under his arm, who stood against a shop-window under the shade of an awning, briskly distributing little pink tracts to the passers-by.

He wore a military moustache, and in spite of an unbrushed coat and a somewhat seedy hat, had the appearance of one well used to more or less prosperous circles in society. He was tall and thin, a long scraggy neck rising like a column from his sloping shoulders, and supporting a head that widened at the brows to an abnormal breadth. There was a fire in the small eyes, but a fire more of cheerful alacrity than of fanatical zeal. He was quick and brisk in his movements, and the sentences wherewith he adjured the rushing crowds were delivered in a bright, sharp, staccato manner, suggesting a salesman crying his wares, or an auctioneer disposing of other people's goods. Sir John was particularly struck by the fellow's cheerful voice, by the entire absence of any burning anxiety to obtain a hearing. This strange being merely pushed the leaflets into people's hands, pushed them at a great rate, constantly moistening his thumb at his lips, and with something like a smile in his bright eyes repeated the words that had arrested our gentleman's moralising.

"Are you saved, sir, are you saved?" he rattled.
"Now is the time of salvation. Not to-morrow, next
day, or Tuesday week. Now, sir, now. No time to be
lost; not the fraction of a second. Don't waste time.
You, sir, are you saved? Glad to hear it. Death is
certain. Judgment is certain. Fine day for considering this question. Don't delay. Most important matter.
Now is the time of salvation. You saved, sir? Ah,
you won't laugh later on! Advise you to think about
it now. You, sir, are you ready for the next world?
Good, good. That's one at least. Now is the time of
salvation. Repent, repent. It will pay you. Ten to
one on Repentance for the Eternity Stakes! Time's
slipping away, sir. It is indeed. Don't miss your
opportunity. Salvation is to be had, sir, for the asking.
Too late soon. Don't neglect it. You saved, sir? Now
is the time of salvation. Read it when you get home,
sir. Never mind who wins the three o'clock race. Save
your soul, sir, and save your money. Now is the time
of salvation."

While Sir John Sparrow stood listening to the quick,
jerky utterance of this reformer in frock coat and silk
hat, standing under an awning in the Strand, he was
approached by a woman who edged towards him in the
crowd with a friendly smile and an amiable bow. Sir
John, much surprised, whipped his white billycock from
his head and offered the woman his hand.

"Isn't it warm?" said she.

"Very hot indeed," said Sir John, wondering where
he had met the lady before.

"Are you out for a walk?" she asked, smiling.

"Yes," said he; "I only arrived in town yesterday.
This is my first view of the town since my arrival."

"Oh, I never!" said she.

Sir John was a little puzzled. "I forget where we

met before," he said after a pause; "and I am sorry to say—you must really forgive me—that I have forgotten your name. It may even be possible—I hope you won't think me rude — that you have made a mistake, and that we are not acquainted with each other at all. Such mistakes do occur, don't they, especially in big cities; what?"

The woman laughed. "Go on!" she said, with great good nature. "You're making fun of me, you are."

"On my honour, no!" exclaimed Sir John.

She looked at him critically. "Aren't you going to stand us a drink?" she said.

Before the startled, the astounded baronet could reply, he felt his arm touched, and turning about found himself face to face with the reformer whose ministry had first arrested his peregrination.

"A word with you, sir," said the reformer.

"Certainly, with pleasure," said Sir John; and turning round to make his excuses and adieux to the woman, he found that she had disappeared.

"Don't look back, sir," said the reformer. "Remember Lot's wife; pillar of salt; a warning to all ages! Glad to put a pinch of salt on your tail, and save you from brimstone in another world."

"I should like a word with you," said Sir John, perplexed and interested.

"That shows you're not wholly lost to good," said the reformer. "You have stopped in time. You have drawn back at the pit's mouth. Better late than never. Come with me. I'm just shutting up the shop for a minute. Can give you two minutes."

He stuffed his leaflets into the tail pockets of his coat, and taking the umbrella from its place under his arm, walked briskly down the street, his head high in the air, and the same half-amused light in his small, brisk eyes. Sir John trotted after him, and presently followed him into a bread shop.

The stranger strode at a great pace up the shop, selected an empty table at the far end, and sat down with a tradesmanlike " Phew!" as he pushed his hat to the back of his head and mopped an unpleasantly damp forehead with a crimson pocket-handkerchief.

" Hot work!" he exclaimed. " Bound to be; saving souls from hell fire. And it takes it out of one. But it's my business. I make it my business. It don't pay, but I'm content to wait for profits. Next world's dividends good enough for me. Well"—he turned suddenly and half looked at Sir John—"aren't you ashamed of yourself?"

" I beg your pardon?" said our hero.

The reformer was smiling genially, while he studied with bewildering alacrity the faces of the various customers drinking their tea and coffee. He seemed a great deal more interested in them than in Sir John.

" You ought to be ashamed of yourself," he said in an abstracted way, tapping the marble-topped table with his fingers. " Nothing worse than to see an old cock like you serving the devil. Hullo, here's the girl at last! Large glass of milk, two ham sandwiches, piece of seed cake, and a bun in a bag. What's yours? Tea, wishy-washy; coffee, indigestible; cocoa, too hot. I advise milk. Small glass, penny; large, three-half-pence. Take your choice. Everyone must decide for himself. It's like the other little matter. Heaven or hell?—choose for yourself."

All the time the stranger was speaking he rattled with his finger-tips on the table, smiling quietly to himself, his eyes roving over the faces of the other customers with an expression of amused interest. While Sir John was ordering his tea the reformer—

Mr. Spill, to give the gentleman his name—hummed quietly to himself, smiling in the same secret fashion as before.

"My advice to you is this," said he, as the girl withdrew; "follow my example, and make a business of religion. It's the only thing that will save you. It's an idea of my own, and I can tell you it's been pretty successful with me. I was just like you once; just like the rest of the world. I didn't care a pin about religion. Never gave my soul a moment's thought. But, by Jove, sir, when my eyes were opened—when I read Tompkins's tract, *Don't be a Fool*—I saw my mistake. I pulled up sharp, jolly sharp, I can tell you. No more glasses of bitter, and half-crowns on Captain Coe's 'Nap' for me! No, sir, no! I jerked myself back on my haunches, and took a good look into the pit, a look that'll last me all my time. Confound the girl, how slow she is! Wonder if she's saved! And then I set about saving my soul, and I found the best way to do that was to save the souls of others. Not like the parsons do it, once a week with a choir and a collection afterwards; no fear! I make a business of it. First thing in the morning, up I get; dash off a tract or two; rush round to the printer; leave it there; then on to Cheapside or Ludgate Hill, just when the clerks are streaming into London; offer every one salvation and one of my tracts; then down into Whitechapel or Bethnal Green for the workmen's dinner hour; then back Into the Strand or Regent Street in the afternoon; tea at a bread shop; then off to Hyde Park to deliver a lecture—ah! here she comes at last, and spilling half the milk!—then back home to correct proofs, write my memoirs, and address letters to so-called religious papers."

"A very busy day," said Sir John politely.

"Not more busy than a pork merchant's or a publican's. I give myself up to saving souls; they to making money. It's just a matter of business. I don't press it on you, but I advise it. Give up your sins; don't mix yourself up with public women; and then set your whole mind on the next world. This sandwich is as stale as a bishop's sermon. It's a cheat and a fraud. The company expects to go to heaven on sandwiches like this! You see, people don't regard the matter from the point of business."

Sir John interrupted. "You are labouring under a misapprehension as regards myself," he said gently. "I was spoken to, and merely returned what I hope was a polite answer. I had no idea that the——"

"Oh, yes, I know all about that! I used to say the same thing. It's unpleasant having to own up. Confession isn't good for the pride. But I'll believe you when you give up wearing a white hat, and cocking it over your eyeglass in that fashion! You can't take me in, old fellow. I've been there myself. I'm a Londoner, born and bred."

Sir John tried in vain to shake Mr. Spill's conviction that he was a scamp. Mr. Spill wouldn't believe it. "I'm not taking any," he said briskly. And so, accepting the inevitable with a good grace, the curious baronet drew Mr. Spill out on the subject of himself and his ministry.

"Do you make much headway?" he asked, setting down an empty cup.

"I hope so; I believe so," replied the stranger genially. "Impossible, of course, to tell. Since I took to authorship I have written something like five hundred tracts, and distributed millions of them. My words on the question of religion have been read by millions of people. They won't be able to say they haven't had a chance, even if they don't repent. I don't whine to them, mind you; I simply say, 'Here you are; heaven on this side, hell on that; it's for you to decide as a commonsense man of business which it will pay you best to take. Don't bother me with questions and confessions and all that; simply take your choice.' That's how I do it. No hocus-pocus. Simply a plain, honest, downright matter of business."

"And London, you think," said Sir John, "is a very wicked place?"

Mr. Spill laughed. "Well, I should say it was, considering that according to my calculations four millions of its inhabitants, making due allowance for children, are as certain to be damned as *that!*" He smote the table jocularly with his bun in its paper bag. "One of my tracts, an improvement on Tompkins's, is called *Don't be a* Damned *Fool.* It goes into figures, and shows a fellow exactly how things stand. He chooses for himself, after that, whether he will be damned or not. London! London!" he exclaimed, laughing pleasantly, "why, it's about as bad as they make 'em. There's not only sin and wickedness and atheism— that's bad enough; but there's humbug and laziness on the part of the clergy, non-con's and all, which is worse. Bless your soul, they don't care a hang whether you save your soul as long as their churches are full, and the money-bags too. That's all they care about. They're idle all the week—reading the paper, going out to dinner, stalls at the theatre; yes, bless you, they're as given to the devil as the rest of the world; I know my London. I tell you, and I tell you straight, that in its heart (not on the surface, mind you) this city is as black as Sodom, as godless as Jerusalem, and as devilish as the hot-place itself."

"Really?" exclaimed Sir John.

"It's as rotten as a rotten apple, sir! There's no godliness in church, senate, law court, or drawing-room. It's all feasting, and dancing, and laughing, and **revelry**. Make a business of religion? Why, they'd laugh if you proposed such a thing. Religion's an incident in their lives, like a pin in a lady's dress — like yesterday's dinner or to-morrow's breakfast. That's all!" He laughed good-humouredly.

"You must despair sometimes," said Sir John, full of sympathy.

"Not in the least," said Mr. Spill cheerfully. "My own soul is perfectly safe, and as long as I give them the chance of getting on the winning horse, my conscience isn't uneasy. No, it don't trouble me in the least. I do my work, let them do theirs. We shall soon see who was right. Mind you, I'm giving 'em all a chance. That tract of mine, *Don't be a* Damned *Fool*, I'm sending to every bishop and clergyman in the kingdom. Make some of the old boys sit up, eh! And I've done *you* a good turn, I hope; made you think of other people's souls as well as your own. Don't thank me; it's all in the way of business. I'm always at it; it's nothing unusual, not in the least. You're only one in a million. That's all."

He seized up his ticket, grabbed the umbrella from the rack, and rose from his seat. "Sorry I can't spare you more of my time. No time to be lost in this business; competition pretty strong, I can tell you. I've got to think over my lecture. Good-bye. Stand firm; fight the devil, and keep your eyes fixed on eternity. If possible—make a business of it."

Sir John ordered another cup of tea, and pondered the words of this bustling reformer. He struggled hard to preserve an open mind, but the more he cogitated the more convinced did he become that England had lost all her old sobriety and solid righteousness—that she was, in fact, tottering on the precipice of everlasting destruction. London overwhelmed him. The young men chaffing the waitresses, the waitresses ogling the young men, seemed in his eyes representative of that giddiness and lightness which belonged by right to the French, a people, as he had always held, long ago sold to the devil. It was just possible, however, that the glamour of the reformer's eloquence had thrown a spell over his judgment, whereby he was unable to see this weighty matter in the true perspective. Therefore, the good gentleman, finishing his second cup of tea, determined to call forthwith on his nephew and heir, Reginald Sparrow, and discuss the matter calmly and dispassionately with that sober and intelligent young man.

This Reginald Sparrow, the eldest son of Sir John's dead brother, lodged in the Temple, and thither the baronet bent his steps after he had paid for his tea at the cashier's box near the door of the bread shop. He walked painfully through the laughing, noisy, pushing crowds, and turned with a sigh of relief, spiritual and physical, into the slumbering seclusion of the Temple. Here he seemed nearer to the peace of heaven. He stood still, breathing gratefully the cool air, and studying with moody interest the people sleeping or reading on the benches. "I wonder," said he, "if all these people are among the four millions of Londoners doomed to destruction?" The figures appalled him. Four millions! Wiping his brow with a gaily-bordered handkerchief, and setting his hat at the right angle, Sir John wandered on until he reached a doorway where the name of his nephew stood out familiarly on the board at the side.

Now just as Sir John reached the landing upon which his heir resided, such a noisy clamour broke forth from

the room bearing Reginald's name that the poor gentleman's heart sank within him. Loud, reverberating
laughter; the sound of warring voices; the jingle of
glasses! "Good heavens!" sighed the baronet; "I had
always thought that Reggie was such an upright young
fellow!"

There was more laughter, then a strong voice rising
above the clamour, and after that a very Babel of
tongues. Good heavens! what hell lay behind the
door? In the midst of this storm Sir John half turned
to make a descent of the stairs, but suddenly remembering the reformer's adjuration that he should stand firm
and fight the devil, the conscientious little dandy returned to the door, smote a commanding summons
with the knocker, and stood there ready to confront his
nephew with a face as accusatory and rebukeful as any
Teutonic chromo-lithograph of the prophet Elijah.

When the door opened, Sir John found himself face
to face with Reggie Sparrow, a young gentleman of
muscular build, with fair ruffled hair, and a clean-shaven
face of considerable intellectual strength. "Very greatly
improved," said Sir John to himself, and the rebuke
faded from his eyes.

"Hello, Uncle John!" exclaimed the nephew. "Why,
who ever dreamed of seeing you here? Come in, come
in. I hope you don't mind a bit of a racket? What
luck this is! How awfully glad I am to see you!" All
this very soberly, with no guilty consciousness.

The baronet found himself in a room with six or
seven young fellows smoking cigarettes, each smoker
armed with a tumbler. He was introduced, choking
from the smoke, and made his bow with that awkward-
ness difficult to shake off when one is conscious of
interrupting a merry proceeding.

"And what will you drink?" said Reggie. "There's

ginger-beer, and there's lemon-squash. We don't allow anything else."

Sir John turned to the table and saw that his nephew was not jesting. "Thank you," said he; "I have just had some tea, and will not drink anything at present. Perhaps you will let me smoke a cigar in self-defence."

The young gentlemen all laughed, swore that the atmosphere of the room was beastly, and then sat in silence studying the polite little baronet with open interest.

"I heard such laughter while I waited at the door," said Sir John amiably, "that I am really bewildered to see only temperance liquor upon your table. How do you manage to keep up such good spirits, Reggie, on such very wholesome and nutritious beverages?"

Reggie smiled. "Alcohol, sir," he said quickly, "is anathema maranatha in these chambers. Before your eyes, my dear uncle, are gathered together a company of men whose ambition is to make crooked things straight. Alcohol plays the deuce with character; indeed, alcohol is probably the chief cause of crime, degradation, and misery. Therefore we, as reformers, have banned it sternly and relentlessly."

Before Sir John could express his keen interest in this statement of his nephew, one of the men, a good-tempered fellow, with fat face and spectacles, broke into the discussion.

"You must bear in mind, sir, that we are not bigots in this matter. We are not a temperance society. The exclusion of drink from our gatherings is a mere incident. Our ideal extends several leagues beyond the mere sobriety of England. To make England sober is not our aim, but we would have England sober that we might the more easily achieve our aim."

Sir John nodded a thoughtful head. "You are work-

ing, then," said he, "for the regeneration of a people
hopelessly given to the devil ? "

" The devil ! " cried one of the youngest ; " the devil !
Why, who on earth believes in a devil ? "

" My uncle was speaking figuratively," said Reggie.

" Oh dear me, no ! " exclaimed the youngster. " He
pronounced the word as though he was afraid of it !
There was no don't-care-a-hang about it. Not a bit
of it ! "

" You don't believe in the devil ? " murmured the
baronet. " Now this interests me very much. Your——"

" You do believe in a devil, then ? " demanded the
youngster, interrupting.

Sir John looked at the point of his cigar for a second
before he made answer. He did not love interruptions.
Then, very slowly and deliberately, he replied as follows:
" On the subject of the existence of a personality of
evil I preserve an entirely open mind. I do not assert
that there is such a being ; at the same time no
argument has ever been laid before me which proved
beyond all possibility of contradiction that the devil
is a myth of superstitious creation. I hope you appreciate my position ? On matters of this kind I hold
very seriously that it is most unwise to dogmatise—
either one way or the other. The faith of one century
is the folly of the next. The most we can do is to
preserve an entirely impartial mind, and wait for
spiritual development in other spheres—don't you agree
with me ?—for the solution of the mystery."

A great gloom settled upon the society. Men
smoked their cigarettes in silence, looking at their
own boots or the boots of their fellows, and giving
no sign of continuing the conversation. Reggie came
to the rescue.

" Perhaps, my dear uncle, I ought to explain to you,"

said he, " that we are a small body of Christian Socialists. I hope I don't shock you. We found our socialism on our Christianity; we keep ourselves severely aloof from the vulgar party politics of the day, and preach a socialism that is not political, but simply and purely spiritual."

" As a matter of fact," said another guest, " we don't preach at all. That's only Reggie's way of putting it. We aren't vulgar reformers, you know. We don't stand in the street and ask people if they're saved ! "

" Christian Socialists ! " murmured Sir John, very perplexed; " but how can one combine the two things? I had an idea that all Socialists were atheists; and my idea of Christians has always been that they are— I exclude Dissenters, of course—hotly Conservative. I confess that you puzzle me."

Then one by one, sometimes all together, the company began to explain their creed to the perplexed baronet. But in the defining of their religion there was so much argument, so much assertion, so much contradiction that the poor little gentleman couldn't for the life of him see how they stood, or what they were driving at. One was for this, another for that; one held such-and-such dogma, another the very opposite, while a third was for no dogma at all. Eyes flashed, voices rang harshly, and ratiocination clouded the minds of the speakers as much as tobacco smoke clouded the atmosphere. The Bible was torn into a thousand fragments between them. There was not one single premiss on which these philosophic reformers could agree, not one, indeed, round which they did not wage a battle of uncompromising words. For every assertion there were half a dozen flat contradictions, and every contradiction brought a shower of counter-contradictions upon the perspiring debater. At last when the war of words abated something of its fury, Reginald Sparrow turned an apologetic countenance to his bewildered uncle.

"It is always difficult," said he, "to hit on a definition that exactly suits all parties."

"But you are of one party," objected the baronet, mopping his brow.

"There must be intellectual freedom in such a society as ours," said Reggie, with great self-satisfaction. "That is one of our main positions. We are all agreed in our object, the reformation of the world by means of a socialism which is purely Christian; and that, of course, is the great thing."

"But," said the baronet, "I understand that you don't preach these doctrines. How, then, do you expect to secure the reformation of the world on the lines you advocate, even if you could agree upon the details?"

The good-natured man in spectacles undertook to illumine the slow-witted visitor on this head. "Reform, sir," said he, "never came by Act of Parliament. I mean, of course, moral and spiritual reform. Rather does it come by the spirit of the age, a force generated by active intelligences bent upon the problems of humanity. The views we hold, for instance, are not proclaimed by means of periodic literature, by lecture, or by platform debate. But we are confident that in the fulness of time, the ideas we discuss among ourselves will, by that very means, slowly, gradually, and enduringly permeate the great masses of the people, till the entire world suddenly awakes to find itself Christian Socialist, without being aware of the processes by which such a result has been obtained. There's no need for us to preach. The thing is right, and so it's bound to come."

"Of course," said the eager youngster with a contempt for the devil, "if we could find a financier to

E

back us we might start a weekly journal setting forth our principles."

"Of course," said half a dozen voices.

"You wouldn't care to finance us?" said Reggie, half in jest, to his uncle.

"Frankly, I should not," said Sir John. "In the first place I must plead guilty to a natural aversion from socialism, and in the second my mind at the present moment is a complete blank as to your principles. I don't see, 'pon me honour, what you are all driving at." Here a number of chairs were drawn nearer to Sir John, and everybody began to speak again. But Sir John held up his hand. "At the same time I am very deeply interested in the subject of reform, being convinced that this city is very far from righteousness; and all that I can do to fight the dev— to bring about a better state of things, I shall endeavour to do to the best of my ability. Therefore I hope you will allow me to cultivate your society, in which as a humble listener, perhaps as occasional speaker, if you will permit it, I may learn in what direction you are moving, and together we may agree upon some concerted action for the moral regeneration of the people."

Hardly had Sir John completed this fine sentence when everybody in the room was at him with suggestions. Your honour never heard such a clamour in all your life! Each man, contradicting the other, protested that they were agreed on this point or that point; and this point and that point, according to the several protesters, was the only point that really mattered. If Sir John would start a journal, each protester was ready to act as editor without emolument of any kind, and each protester assured him that such a journal would take London by storm. The little baronet was the centre of another tempest. In the midst of the clamour he gradually realised that these Christian Socialists aimed at sweeping away all abuses, all injustices, all wickednesses, and all cruelties, simply by making people good Christians. But as Sir John considered that the Church was provided with a better equipment for securing this objective than any possessed by the young gentlemen about him, he decided to preserve an open mind on the subject, and to lend neither his sympathy nor his purse to this discordant society of philosophic reformers.

At the same time Sir John was greatly troubled in spirit. He was convinced that something must be done to rescue London from her perilous position of wickedness and sin, but for the life of the poor gentleman he could not discover any channel for these sympathies and energies which with every hour of his stay in London more and more occupied and incommoded his mind. He must do something ; he felt that he was "called" to do something—but what ? He had as little stomach for distributing tracts in the Strand as for sitting over a glass of lemonade and talking philosophy till the millennium appeared. What should he do, then ?

That night ere he went to bed he called Tiplady to his side.

"What is your impression of London?" said he gloomily.

"It's a dirty hole, Sir John," answered the brisk servant ; "a place where a white shirt gets soiled and tarnished quicker than I could have believed. But its bustle, Sir John ! its merry faces ! its happy people !— why, it makes one glad to be alive !"

"The people, you think, are happy?" said Sir John, disappointed.

"Happy? Why, they don't seem to have a care, sir. And the foolish persons always trying to seduce 'em into nonsensical sects and parties — why, Sir John, they simply brush 'em aside like flies. They're too big for such ridiculous busybodies and peace-breakers; too big and too happy. Oh, they're a fine people, Sir John; there's no doubt about that."

"How did you hear of these reformers?" inquired the baronet.

"Our landlady's son, Sir John—begging your pardon for mentioning him—is a trial to his mother, being addicted to Radicals and other low company. This foolish young person, it seems, is always attending these vulgar meetings. He wanted me to go with him to-morrow to a place he calls St. Martin's Hall, where there is to be, so he gave me to understand, a sort of carnival of Radicalism. But I put him in his place, Sir John; I did very quick. The idea of me attending any such impudent affair as that."

Tiplady, the fat, brisk Tiplady, smiled contemptuously.

"Where did you say the meeting was to be?"

"St. Martin's Hall he called it, Sir John."

"Oh, St. Martin's Hall! Very well. You need not wait."

And the weary little baronet went to sleep that night, dreaming of a carnival of Radicalism, wherein Mephistopheles and Mr. Spill, in frock coat and tall hat, danced arm in arm round a circle of applauding Christian Socialists, all drinking lemonade and smoking cigarettes, while Tiplady, astride of a giraffe with its nose in the air, and led by Tom Shott, rode slowly among the people distributing little pink tracts.

CHAPTER V

In which Sir John Sparrow takes the first step

"I MUST put this matter right," said Sir John, flinging down his newspaper.

The worthy gentleman, having eaten a good breakfast, had spent the best part of an hour studying the police intelligence provided by his journal for its readers' entertainment. Every case drove the wedge of conviction deeper into his open mind. He was painfully shocked. For not only were the cases horrible in themselves, but the magistrates' humorous comments filled him with what the faithful historian must call a desperate despair. Was a man charged with drunkenness, the magistrate had his jest on the subject of temperance. Was a woman accused of cruelty to her children, the magistrate convulsed a sycophantic court by his two-penny-halfpenny facetiæ. Was a breach of promise considered, the counsel made sport of the sacred passion. Was a merchant brought to justice for knavery, the judge had his quip on sharp practice which produced the inevitable "loud laughter" of newspaper reporting.

"I must put this matter right!" cried Sir John.

He sent Tiplady to buy a Liberal newspaper, and spent the time of waiting in pacing slowly up and down his chambers, considering the awful state of national life.

"Have we become a light people?" he exclaimed.

53

"Nowhere do I find seriousness. Everyone is a jester. Our judges administer the laws of this country with a pun on their lips; magistrates punish wickedness with a smile on their faces. And England—England, the country of sobriety and religion—joins in the hellish laughter that rings unnaturally through her solemn courts of justice! It is really, it is indeed, a very terrible state of affairs. Women illtreat their children; husbands murderously attack their wives; clergymen are charged with abominable offences; merchants plot the ruin of poor trusting shareholders; and ladies who thieve from shops are excused on the scientific ground that they cannot help themselves. And this is the England of Alfred and Arthur! How great a change from the England of twenty years ago! Let me pray the Almighty that it is not too late for me to take such action as shall convince this people that they have deserted the paths marked out for them by Providence, and have entered upon that broad and perilous way which leadeth to destruction."

Tiplady, smart and brisk, entered with a Liberal newspaper.

"Plenty of these to be had, Sir John," said he, with a cheerful smile. "For in this quarter of the town, which is occupied only by the quality, papers of such a vulgar nature have no more sale than whelks or monkey-nuts. When you've finished with it, Sir John, I'll burn it; it won't do to leave such rags about in case of friends calling."

"Tiplady, my good fellow," said the baronet, sinking into an armchair, "I fear you are still a prey to illogical prejudices. You have lived so long in a peaceful corner of the world that you are unaware of the vast evil and wickedness of our generation. You do not appreciate, therefore, the efforts of those who war with sin. London,

Tiplady, is inhabited by knaves, rogues, scoundrels, and wicked people."

Tiplady smiled incredulously. "What about the upper ten, Sir John?"

"A drop in the ocean," sighed the distressed baronet. "A mere Lot's family in this Gomorrah of iniquity; and even among them I fear there may be more than one Lot's wife. Alas, Tiplady, that it should be so! But I intend, God helping me, to consecrate the remainder of my days to the giant's task of rousing from spiritual slumber a nation in whose destiny I imbibed with my mother's milk an interest that cosmopolitan tastes can never shatter or obliterate."

Tiplady's face during this speech was a study in pity, amusement, and perplexity. He stood before his little master, large and imposing, his hands idle at his side, his shoulders squared, his head slightly bowed, and in his dark eyes the expression of one altogether persuaded of his own intellectual supremacy, but doubtful of the means to convince a fool of his folly. At the conclusion of the speech, his good-natured fat face melted into a broad smile.

"They've got the board-schools, Sir John," he said argumentatively; "what else do they want?"

"They want rousing from sleep," answered Sir John gloomily.

"We pay the Church of England to save their souls," said Tiplady firmly; "we do all that for them, and still they go on asking for more. There's no satisfying the democracy, Sir John: They're like the Israelites, and always will be."

"The awful peril is," replied our hero, "that they do *not* go on asking for more. They are content with their spiritual darkness."

"Oh well, then," said Tiplady briskly, "if they aren't

asking for anything why bother about 'em? Let us leave them to a merciful Providence; and if I was you, Sir John, speaking respectfully, I shouldn't mix yourself up with any of these low people; for never was truer saying outside the Bible than that about the pitch. If you mix with these people, Sir John, you'll suffer in mind and person, I'm sure you will."

The baronet fixed his servant with solemn eyes, and before that strong gaze Tiplady visibly quailed. He felt he had gone too far. At last, shuffling towards the door, his hands setting one or two things straight on the table as he backed away, the servant found his voice.

"I hope I haven't said too much, Sir John," quoth he, with deferential smile. "But when a gentleman's servant is sent for a Radical newspaper, he feels wound up to deliver himself of free speech. I should be sorry to see you even a Liberal Lord Chancellor, Sir John, I should indeed, sir, for I take that pride in your blood and family that I feel sometimes as if I myself am almost a little twig on the family tree."

"Pride in aristocratic birth has its dangers, Tiplady," said the mollified baronet. "But put your mind at rest, I shall not become a Liberal politician. I intend to work for the nation through the Liberals, but not with them. This paper"—he unfolded the journal— "will inform me on many points of which at present, I regret to say, I am wholly and inexcusably ignorant. I wish to see"—he raised his voice—"how many evils and injustices demand the lopping axe of the reformer; how many sorrows and afflictions grind the poor of this stony-hearted city into the mire of the gutter. I will ascertain that; then I will move."

He ceased abruptly. Tiplady, at the door, made a little bow. "The Radicals are pretty sure to make them worse than they are, Sir John. That's what they're paid for."

"I shall study their arguments critically," said the baronet. "My mind, under the mercy of Providence, is too impartial to be swayed by any *ex parte* statements."

"Ah, you're right there, Sir John!" cried the servant, grinning with great good humour. "For it is an ex-party true enough, just as all its old leaders are ex-leaders. A most ridiculous pack of quarrelling humbugs they are!"

And with that Tiplady bowed himself out, and left Sir John alone with his newspaper.

Having sighed over the prejudice of his faithful servant, our hero, with considerable excitement, turned his attention to the columns of print before him, and began to read. Eagerly did he begin this study, but by degrees the frown deepened on his forehead. The sheets were turned more and more petulantly, and at last the paper was cast contemptuously aside, and our baronet sprang up from his chair to pace restlessly up and down his chamber.

"Where must I look for help?" he exclaimed. "Has Providence decreed that I should stand alone in this matter, that I should be the *fons et origo* of national reform, the initiator, builder, and upholder of a new and better era? For here"—kicking the paper at his feet—"these Liberals are engaged in vilifying themselves, fighting an internecine battle, while the hosts of Satan swarm over the land and desolate the little cots and homesteads of righteousness. And here, too, is this dreadful spirit of levity; column after column of cheap raillery; paragraph after paragraph of foolish buffoonery. Not one word of the sorrows of the people, of the evil of this generation, of the moral and spiritual blindness of the entire nation! Am I to stand alone? Is it my destiny to sound single-handed the trumpet-call that shall rally to one banner all those who hate iniquity? I tremble like the leaf of an aspen in the strong wind of responsibility!"

This was merely an oratorical hyperbole. In reality, Sir John was rather pleased than otherwise at the prospect before him of figuring in history, and possibly on the coinage of his country, as another St. George driving the lance of reform into the agonised jaws of the dragon of evil. He pulled down his coat, rearranged his tie before the mirror, smoothed his glossy hair, and studied his features with new interest. Of course, it was a difficult task, and he was sore puzzled as to making a beginning; but he had no manner of doubt that he was the elect of Providence for the express purpose of awakening the nation, if not the entire world, to the magnitude of its unrighteousness. That conviction firmly engrafted in his mind, all the rest was a matter of detail.

In the meantime he would attend the Liberal Conversazione, and judge for himself what that political party was really engaged about in the counsels of the nation. After that he would begin—he had not the least idea in what manner—his own crusade, and in the words of the Strand distributor of tracts, make a business of the salvation of souls.

Sir John was walking towards St. Martin's Hall in order to obtain a ticket for the evening's entertainment, when he ran against an old college friend whom he had not seen for something like fifteen years. This gentleman was one Captain Chivvy, late of the 13th Lancers —a middle-sized, well-groomed man-about-town, with as winning a face as ever acquired the set expression of polite boredom. He had large, full eyes that shone on the least excuse with heartfelt laughter; he wore a small, dark moustache, carefully brushed, and his whole face expressed, despite its fixed expression of impending calamity, an inclination for laughter as unmistakable as his high-bred and distinguished appearance.

After the two gentlemen had exchanged the warmest of greetings, to the amusement of the casual among the passers-by, the light and the laughter suddenly faded from Captain Chivvy's face, and thrusting an arm through his friend's as they walked along, he delivered himself in this fashion :—

" My dear Sparrow, there is something tragic in meeting my oldest friend at this moment; for, my dear fellow, there is nothing before me but suicide. I don't want to bother you with my troubles, for I suppose you have plenty of your own—everybody has; but you wouldn't like me to take my leave without telling you that this is probably the last time we shall meet on earth. My dear old fellow, I'm in the devil's own mess. It's my own fault. I've got no one to blame but myself. I don't ask anyone for sympathy. But I should like to warn you if I can against the dangers of betting. My dear Sparrow, it's a mug's game. It's ruined my life, and it's brought me to within close range of a bullet. If you want to save your peace of mind, chuck it. Chuck it, my dear chap. For the love of heaven chuck it. The only people who make it pay are the men who make a business of it. If you can't make a business of it, chuck it."

Captain Chivvy paused in his speech and in his walk at this moment, and drew his friend towards the gutter, where a villainous-looking blackguard was selling some sporting prophet's racing selections. Sir John remarked how the fellow's face instantly lighted up at the sight of Captain Chivvy's smiling countenance; there was so much humanity in the soldier's face that it made even the beggars feel happy.

"Well," said Chivvy, "what's the hot thing for to-day?"

The man whispered confidentially in his ear.

"A friend of Tom Cannon told me the same thing," said Chivvy. He gave the fellow a sixpence for his penny card, and continued his walk.

"You often get a good thing from those poor beggars," he said. "By George! Sparrow, what a hell of life, eh? I tell you, my dear fellow, I'm an anarchist, I am really. I'm hanged if I see why these brutes should drive about in their carriages with their confounded display of wealth while others are shivering in the gutter, hungry for a meal." He stopped suddenly. "I say, what a pretty girl! Isn't she nice? By George! what a sweet little thing!" He was turning round, staring after the pretty girl. "But as I was saying," he resumed, walking forward again, "one often gets a good thing from those fellows. Now look here, Sparrow, just look down this list of horses like a good fellow, and tell me which you fancy, which one strikes you as a likely winner."

Sir John protested that he knew nothing about horse-racing; but altogether in vain. Captain Chivvy begged him to select any name that struck him in its appearance as looking like a winner. "For," said he, "I believe a fellow often spots a winner by the mere look of a horse's name, I do really. You've no idea, my dear chap, what a tremendous lot of mystery there is in gambling. That's what makes it so devilish fascinating. It isn't mathematics, by Jove, not by a long chalk!"

So Sir John looked on the racing-card and selected a horse—for no reason that he could explain to himself —whose name was Chopsticks. Captain Chivvy, slightly disappointed, said he rather fancied that horse himself, but his tobacconist had told him that Moorhen was a certainty, and the hall-porter at his club had heard from the owner that Whimple the Third was a real good thing, so that really he didn't quite know what to do.

"By George, look at that!" he cried suddenly, pulling up dead, and pointing across the road.

"What is it?" asked Sir John excitedly.

"A straight tip, a straight tip!" quoth Captain Chivvy. "A Chinaman! don't you see? Chinaman; Chopsticks! It's a tip, by George!"

"He's a Japanese, I think," said Sir John, greatly interested.

"Same thing! By Jove, that's a stroke of luck. I'll have twenty pounds on Chopsticks. I'll plunge on it. It's a rank outsider; I daresay it'll start at twenty-five to one. By George, Sparrow, I'm thundering glad I ran up against you this morning! You've saved me, old fellow; you have really."

And after inviting Sir John to lunch with him on the following day, the excited Captain Chivvy hailed a hansom, asked the driver whether he fancied anything for the races that day, and then directed him to drive to the office of his commission agent. The last glance Sir John obtained of the amiable soldier was through the side window of the cab, Captain Chivvy smiling at him with great happiness, and waving the racing-card in affectionate farewell.

This episode had a marked effect on our hero. His mind was once more overwhelmed by the magnitude of the task set for him to do by that Providence which overrules the affairs of men; for in Captain Chivvy he beheld a representative of thousands of good-natured people, living utterly foolish and selfish lives, without an inkling that their lives are thus frivolous and wicked.

"And how in the name of fortune," exclaimed the baronet, "can I start preaching to such a fellow as Chivvy? Spill says, 'Make a business of religion.' Chivvy says, 'Make a business of racing.' Chivvy is the pleasanter person of the two. I couldn't preach to Chivvy. Really, this is a very delicate mission. I shall have to exercise, I can see, considerable tact. I must begin gently. But in what way? Dear me, this sort of work is very distressing."

It was in this perturbed frame of mind that Sir John Sparrow found himself announced at the Liberal Conversazione by a blundering steward as "Mr. John Barrow," and had the honour of shaking hands with a distinguished Liberal statesman. The speeches that followed soon after this greeting only deepened the baronet's feeling of loneliness and difficulty. What to him were party differences and family squabbles, when the world was going to the devil at the rate of four millions in London alone? At the conclusion of the speeches he wandered about the room as unhappy and friendless as a Chinese mandarin would be dumped suddenly down in the middle of Regent Street.

But as he moved about in the crowded room Sir John espied a lady who awakened in his chivalrous bosom all his old love of amorous conquest. To be sure she was nothing much to look at, certainly not to be compared with the dashing Mrs. FitzGerald; but Sir John was often attracted by faces which your honour, or any man of fine taste, would pass without a remark of any kind. In this case the lady was moderately tall, thin to the point of bones showing, and could boast no more grace or distinction of carriage than you will discover in the movements of an ostrich. She wore a dress of faded yellow brocade, low in the neck, loose in the waist, and heavily flounced about the skirt. Her head was small; her features thin; her eyes as bright and sharp as needles. She walked about the room, her head thrust forward, her eyes restless, as if searching for acquaintances. Somehow or another she appealed to our moody baronet.

Sir John got in her way and languished. The lady's little eyes played about him for the fraction of a second, and then continued their restless search. Sir John followed the lady, passed her with a long-drawn sigh, and then, his arms pathetically folded over his breast, again awaited her approach. The lady once more flashed her eyes over him and walked on. Sir John, taking a few steps, overtook her, sighed heavily as he went by, and once more faced about to meet her glances. This time she looked him fully in the eyes, and then made her way slowly and carelessly to a lounge. As she sat down (there was room for two on this settee) the lady raised her eyes to our gentleman, and immediately dropped them with virgin modesty. Now, Sir John (who can explain these things?) at that moment ceased to care any more for the lady, and a certain fear that he had been playing with fire overtook him in his innocent gallantry. But he was too much of a chivalrous knight to leave the lady without his favourite and invariable explanation in such circum-stances; and so he walked sadly and slowly towards the lounge where Dulcinea sat bolt upright, fanning herself with a soiled yellow fan, and stood before her for a minute with wrinkled brow and sorrow-laden eyes. Then, with a sigh, sad and heartbreaking, intended to explain that a cruel destiny prevented him from throw-ing himself then and there into the arms of the only woman he could ever love, our baronet was about to move moodily away, when the lady flashed upon him such a look of anger and withering contempt that his lingering steps were incontinently hurried into a hasty and undignified retreat. He shot off like a cat with a terrier at its heels.

So Sir John found himself once more friendless and alone, without distraction of any kind to take his thoughts from the contemplation of his solemn mission. He wandered on, half inclined to go, half hopeful that something might happen if he remained. The room was thronged with garrulous, well-dressed people, and over the whole gathering there was that air of cheerfulness and self-contentment which one usually associates with church congresses or a bishop's garden - party. There was none of that frank sympathy, that open and unaffected spirit of brotherhood, for which our poor little gentleman was hungering and thirsting with all his soul. He moved pathetically about the room, or stood against the wall gloomily surveying the company, as dissatisfied as one could imagine an angel roaming through the lounge of a music-hall.

But salvation was at hand. Little did our hero reck that in entering that room he was taking the first step in the series of adventures destined to immortalise his humble name, and bring instruction to all the generations to come. It was here in this stuffy hall, surrounded by smiling chatterers, and as disheartened as he had ever been in the whole course of his existence; it was here, I say, that Sir John Sparrow, without preparation or warning of any kind, came upon the great, the soulful, the only Simon Peace. Thus it is, most honoured reader—if you will permit me the luxury of a moment's moralising—that we chance upon those tides in our affairs, which take us at the flood off our unprotesting feet and sweep us forward to the great ocean, where, amid its buffeting billows, we all ultimately find our grave. How little was your honour thinking of domestic felicity when you first met the blushing maid who now wears your honour's gold ring, and sends your bank balance floundering in confusion with the single stroke of a milliner's bill!

It was while Sir John stood morosely against one of the walls, studying through his gleaming eyeglass the moving throng of people, that Mr. Simon Peace, on the look out for an audience, sauntered up and dropped into conversation with the agreeable baronet. Mr. Simon Peace presented to the world a large, flat face of dazzling, almost transparent whiteness. His appearance was one of contradictions. His iron-grey hair grew luxuriantly, and was brushed helter-skelter over the crown of his imposing head, presenting a savage and unhandselled appearance eminently in keeping with the coarse, iron-grey beard and rough moustache that flowed incongruously from the ascetic whiteness of his flesh. The eyes under the beetling brows were of a sad, far-away blue, as pathetic as the tint of forget-me-nots, and as dreamy and super-sensual as stars in a sunlit sky. The rest of his long body was not imposing; the shoulders sloped away as abruptly as the apex of a triangle, and there was no more flesh on his staring bones than would supply a healthy cannibal with a *hors-d'œuvre* for a ten-course dinner. One striking feature in the appearance of Mr. Simon Peace was the large round Adam's apple that swelled and moved monotonously upwards and downwards in his inordinately long and fleshless throat. Mr. Peace was evidently proud of this feature, for he wore one of those turn-down collars that leave the neck as naked from the chin to the chest as the ears or the nose.

After a few words on unimportant matters—Mr. Peace speaking in a high falsetto voice as weak and

F

trembling as a girl's—the two gentlemen found that they were of one mind concerning the meeting.

"I came here," said Sir John, "in the hope of finding guidance in a matter of much moment to me—the best way to reform mankind."

Simon smiled. It was a beautiful smile; one that stirred the depths of his savage beard while it illumined the surface of his meditative eyes; even the Adam's apple in his long neck seemed to glow under its genial influence.

"They're well-meaning," he piped in his thin voice; "they think they're honest; but of all the blind leaders of the blind these politicians are the blindest. It is strange that they do not know that they are blind."

He was leaning against the wall, and Sir John stood before him looking up into the serene countenance of his newly found friend with the profoundest attention. "It is very difficult," said our hero, sighing; "I have met a religious reformer who moved me somewhat, but whose methods did not commend themselves to me. I have also met some Christian Socialists, but in their propaganda I could see no animating influence likely to achieve a wide and universal triumph over sin and wickedness. I come here to a meeting of political reformers, willing to fling myself"—Sir John pronounced this grandly, with a swing of his arm— "into the work of political reform, but I find myself chilled and repelled. It is very distressing."

All through this speech Simon smiled, a long-suffering, much-enduring smile. "Are you a vegetarian?" he said simply, at its conclusion.

"A vege——? I beg your pardon?" asked Sir John.

Simon leaned more negligently against the wall, letting his feet slide forward till his fine tousled hair was nearly on a level with the well-brushed head of our little hero. "A vegetarian," he repeated, pronouncing it 'vegetahrian.'

"Ah, I know what you mean," said Sir John. "Of course, of course. People who eat vegetables for the sake of their health. No; I am thankful to say the Creator has endowed me with a very vigorous and successful digestion. I eat heartily."

You should have seen Simon's face! He smiled and smiled, till his great long teeth stood clear of moustache and beard from the upper gums to the lower. A pale flame crept into the transparent whiteness of his cheek; a moisture dimmed his eyes. As for the Adam's apple, it indulged in a wild St. Vitus' dance for nearly a minute.

"A vegetarian," said he very quietly, very tenderly, very tolerantly, "is one who loves. A vegetarian is one who would make life beautiful. He loves as no one else can love."

There was something very provoking in all this. What in the world was the nexus between Love and Vegetables? Sir John felt that Simon was keeping back a great mystery, and begged his new acquaintance to go into details. Simon only smiled.

"I never proselytise in conversation," he said. "One knows that the most highly developed minds must gravitate towards us, and that for the ordinary man vegetarianism must ever remain a foolishness. But briefly our religion is this. We will not kill. We will not blend our pleasure or our pride with sorrow of the meanest thing that feels (Wordsworth). He prayeth best who loveth best all things both great and small (Coleridge). We will not fill our mouths with the slaughtered flesh of sentient creatures. We will not be partakers in the inevitable demoralisation of butcher and slaughterman, red with the blood of suffering beasts. We will not hurt nor destroy in all God's holy mountain (Isaiah). We will live purely, eat purely; keep our tables sacred from smoking flesh; make our kitchens as beautiful as our gardens. That is our religion. And with this diet comes bodily and spiritual peace. The brutal passions die down; and the spirit's vision becomes clearer. That is vegetarianism, briefly."

For the first time in his life Sir John Sparrow had something definite to live for. Beloved reader, do you understand? He has been longing all this time to make a martyr of himself; he has been seeking for some altar whereon to sacrifice himself. And behold, it is here! Give up, give up! cries Goethe; and that is just what Sir John, without quite knowing it, has been longing to do. When once we get off the beaten track we must set about searching for thorns and brambles whereon to hang up the habiliments of Use and Wont, so that we may go naked to our martyrdom. Give up, give up! Deny thyself! Be different from the rest of the world! In other words, go and hang thyself.

"Good God!" cried Sir John very reverently; "and I have been eating dead animals all my life!"

"You have an open mind," quoth Simon, smiling triumphantly.

He could have uttered no more clenching argument if he had been the most zealous of proselytisers.

"It has been my greatest ambition to sit loose to the opinions of the world," said Sir John proudly. "My mind has been an open house to all honest wayfarers in the realm of intellect. And even now, when I gladly make room at the table of my brain for this great thought of yours, I am constrained to put a certain restraint on my welcome lest I find on examination that the theory is not congruous with my master of ceremonies, my supreme major-domo, Logic. But there is so much grace and courtesy of manner in your thought that I profess myself utterly charmed with it, and for the introduction I am most profoundly grateful to you. Eating dead animals! How horrible! And it never struck me before! Good God, how awful!"

"I must introduce you to my wife," said Simon very sweetly. "She will convince you more quickly than I can in the matter of detail—about which I never bother—for she leaves no man, woman, or child alone till she has forced them to see the convincing naturalness of our religion. And here she comes. Let me introduce you."

Sir John turned about, and there approaching him was the lady in faded yellow brocade who had so suddenly and dramatically resented the blandishment of his eyes. It was an awkward moment. Quiet as Simon had seemed to him during their conversation, it now became apparent to Sir John that there was a very lion slumbering behind that calm exterior. The savage hair bristled with ferocity. He did not like the shifty character of the Adam's apple. Our hero wished that the vegetarian was not quite so tall; not quite so long in the arm. Anything in the nature of a brawl was distasteful to him; he wished himself devoutly out of the room and (it must be confessed) Mr. and Mrs. Peace at the devil. But, like the true Briton that he was, our little baronet braced himself to bear the consequences of his gallantry, and faced the lady with as humble a boldness as his disquieted feelings could put on at such short notice.

"Priscilla," said Simon, "this gentleman is very anxious to make your acquaintance."

"So I imagined," snapped Mrs. Peace, her eyes glittering.

"So you imagined!" quoth Simon. "My dear Priscilla, what on earth do you mean?"

"I mean," said Mrs. Peace, "that he has been following me about the room, ogling me in the most insolent manner, and behaving himself like a perfect little monkey."

Sir John saw the Adam's apple in Simon's throat come suddenly to a dead stop. Our hero shuddered.

"It is possible you may be mistaken," said Simon very calmly.

"Mistaken? Fiddlesticks!" cried the lady. "I could have picked him out from a pailful of tadpoles."

"Madam," said Sir John, "let me assure you that—quite unintentionally, I am sure—you have misconstrued my glances."

"You take me for a fool," said the lady.

"That would be a worse insult than the other," quoth the baronet on the spur of the moment.

"I must ask you," said Simon, tapping the baronet's shoulder, "for an explanation of your conduct."

"Oh, bother his explanation!" said the lady. "Let him go his way, and cut him dead when you meet him again. We can't waste our time on such little imps as him."

"Allow me to judge," said Simon, righteous indignation flaming in his eyes. Then he turned to our gentleman. "If I had not devoted myself to calming my baser passions," he piped, his voice quavering, "I should take you by the scruff of your neck, run you to the porch of this hall, and then kick you from the doorstep into the middle of next week. As it is"—his voice got higher and higher—"I tell you in plain language that you're a cad, that you're no gentleman, that you ought to have your head punched."

"Hush, hush!" said Mrs. Peace, laying a hand on her

lord's arm. "Curb yourself, Simon. People **are** looking this way."

"Let them look!" cried Simon grandly, his hair waving like turnip-tops in a breeze.

"You really must allow me to speak," said Sir John, turning round to verify for himself what the lady had said. Yes, people really were looking at them.

"Would you make my wife a liar?" cried Simon, shooting himself up to his full height, till the agitated Adam's apple passed like a comet out of Sir John's vision.

"I beg you to be cool," whispered Sir John, glancing over his shoulders at the spectators of this painful affair.

"Who are you to tell my husband how to behave?" demanded Mrs. Peace, withering the baronet with a look of scorn.

"Dear lady," sighed Sir John, recovering, "it is in my power to afford both you and Mr.—Mr.——"

"My name is Simon Peace," said the outraged husband very grandly.

"Come, we are getting to know each other a little better already," said Sir John, beginning to swagger.

"What about your own name?" snapped Mrs. Peace. "My husband's name is well known; I daresay you've heard it more than once in your life. But what about your own name? Oh, you've got a card case; how very imposing!"

Sir John produced a card. "I am desirous that we should be better acquainted," said he, handing it to the lady.

She looked haughtily and contemptuously at the name, then gave a little start. Sir John saw the lower lip drawn in, and the colour mount to her cheeks; he lowered his eyes. After a pause she passed the card to her husband. Mr. Peace studied the name with knitted brows, and after he had mastered his surprise, turned the same wrathful face upon our hero, but addressed him in a much softer tone of voice.

"Sir John Sparrow," said he, "I am willing to listen to your explanation."

Then the gallant baronet told them in a few well-chosen phrases how he had come into that hall lonely and sad; how he had wandered about the room seeking for sympathy; and how, struck by the intelligent and reposeful face of Mrs. Peace, he had looked—but with no idea in the world that she was conscious of his attention—at that smooth, broad brow, those bright spiritual eyes, the firm, resolute lips, and longed to make her acquaintance, feeling sure that from such a noble soul he would receive light and guidance in his great necessity. Strangely enough, light and guidance had come from the lady's husband, and he now professed himself anxious to cultivate a deeper acquaintance with Mr. and Mrs. Peace, not only that he might learn more of that form of diet which he felt sure must exercise a beneficent influence upon the passions and weaknesses of the mortal mind, but for the pleasure of a more intimate acquaintance with Mr. and Mrs. Simon Peace.

At the end of this speech Simon turned to his wife. "Priscilla," said he, "are you satisfied with the explanation given by Sir John Sparrow?"

"Quite," said Priscilla. "It is a most gentlemanly and reasonable explanation"

"Sir John Sparrow," said Simon, "I accept in my wife's name your explanation. I shall be pleased to make your further acquaintance. I don't happen to have a card with me, but if you will accept this envelope, for which I have no further use, I shall esteem it a favour. Any time you care to drop in at 5, Clematis Grove, Canonbury, we shall be pleased to see you. Our tea hour is six o'clock."

So they parted. And in this way Sir John Sparrow took his first step on the road of reform, which led him whither your honour shall be most truly informed ere the word "Finis" uses up the last drop of moisture in your servant's inkpot.

CHAPTER VI

*Which returns to Sir John's Village, and shows
how sincerely his departure was missed by
Tom Shott and the Widow*

YOUR honours are here asked to pause for a happy
moment in following the history of Sir John
Sparrow that your honours may see how sorely our
worthy gentleman was missed in the village from which
he set out on his notable journey. God never puts
his finger on a country gentleman without thinking
twice about it. Death strikes monarch or minister, and
the world, after that it has doffed its cap, goes merrily
forward; but when the squire is carried to his last
long home there is a countryside weeping at his grave,
and at a hundred humble firesides the village keeps
his memory green for a generation. So it came about
that the sudden departure of our talkative little baronet
from the dale's life was the cause of much cackle and
lamentation. It was as though the church tower had
fallen, as though the finger-post at the cross-roads
pointed in an opposite direction. The village world
could not get used to his absence. And of all that
little world none felt it more than honest Tom Shott.
Not only did he hunger for our hero's chit-chat and
mightily yearn after those neat little dinners in the
cottage dining-room, but he went guiltily about his
work, in secret upbraiding himself for that he was the

cause of the baronet's departure. But in his blackest moments of gloom the honest parson would lumber up to the manor-house and for comfort "talk Sparrow" —as the lady called it—to the bewitching Mrs. FitzGerald. For he had got the idea into his head, because of the lady's sympathy and because of her admiration for Sir John, that the widow was in love with the baronet, and he nursed no dearer dream in his elephantine mind than the romantic idea that one day Sir John would come merrily homeward and marry the charming lady of the manor. It was to him, this consummation, as natural a climax as a pipe of tobacco after dinner. He never doubted it.

So we find him—for a brief moment—sitting on the colonnade with the widow, "talking Sparrow." The lady, your honours will observe, has Toddy upon her lap, and is stroking the ears of Budge sulking with his front paws on her knee.

"No news from Jack," says the parson.

"London—that horrid whale!—has swallowed him up," she answers; "but it is ungrateful of Sir Jonah not to write at least to you; he must know how you miss him."

"I do," answered the parson, folding his big hands; "we all miss him. *You* miss him: of course you must."

"The dale isn't the same."

He looks at her gratefully. "It isn't, is it?"

"Why, I mourn for him night and day. There was no one who could talk so prettily and so learnedly about books and pictures and china and dogs and horses. He was our one breakwater against the waves of village gossip. And now, oh, we are becoming so dreadfully parochial. Really, I shall have to fill the house with smart people, and ask all the village to come and hear them chatter about theatres and books.

And Toddy misses him, too—don't you, my darling, and Budge as well—naughty little Budge, who goes and rolls in the dust directly he's been tubbed!" And the wicked Budge, blinking repentance, is stroked with the hand of merciful forgiveness.

"He'll come back soon, he must," grumbles the parson.

"And then you'll be quite happy?"

"We shall all be happy."

"Never did hero have so faithful a disciple," laughs Mrs. FitzGerald; "I truly believe you think of nobody else. And you haven't told me yet about poor old Mrs. Gathercole."

"She's better," impatiently.

"And Croxton?" She is smiling.

"He's better too." The parson gets upon his feet, restless.

"When will he go back to work?"

"Next week."

"I sent his wife a few things yesterday, but oh, dear, she's such a fool of a manager one might just as well have sent a recipe for a fruit salad to the Cannibal Islands."

"I wonder he hasn't written," murmurs the parson.

"Who?"

He jumps. "Little Jack Sparrow. Oh! you were speaking about Mrs. Gathercole; she's better, gout's gone, quite."

Mrs. FitzGerald here tumbles Toddy from her lap, and rises laughing. "You should really employ a 'local demon' till Sir John returns. You're unfit to look after the parish in your present state of mind, indeed you are. But come in for a minute, and I'll give you a cup of tea before I report you to the bishop."

He follows her with his hands in the big side-pockets of his shooting coat. But as he enters the room he starts, and then with a great frown strides over to the photograph of a cavalry subaltern standing on a table.

"Who's this?" he asks, with suspicion.

"A brave boy," she answers lightly. "Mr. Drayton, with a Guy before it, though his godfathers and god-mothers, if they had been good Christians, would surely have called him Apollo. He's so nice, too. I met him last week at my cousin's in York."

"Very young," says the parson critically.

"Oh, quite young!" says the widow, with enthusiasm.

After a pause he blurts out, "Don't ask people here —not yet."

"Why not?" She turns laughing; but the parson does not notice that her eyes rest for a moment on the photograph of Guy Drayton.

"Not yet."

"But why?"

"Wait till he comes back—I should."

Mrs. FitzGerald puts her hand through his arm, and leads him to a big chair by the tea-table. "Now listen to me," she exclaims in mock seriousness; "if you don't take care you'll go melancholy mad; you've got Sir John on the brain, and you can think of nothing else!"

The parson laughs. "Oh, he's a good little chap!" and sits down with a bump.

Budge springs upon his lap, and Toddy follows his beautiful mistress to the tea-table.

In some such manner as this—day by day—was the memory of our errant baronet kept green in the village he had abandoned for London, that great whale.

But the photograph of Mr. Guy Drayton caused our parson an anxious hour.

And what was it, this photograph of a dandy soldier, to the pretty widow?

Well, it was a hope. The tragedy of a loveless marriage had been played out, and emerging from the shadow-house, romance had met her with promise of love and days of delight. As bravely as she kept a merry face to the world she strove to put the dear idea away, but her heart was hungry for romance, and the picture fed the flame. It was that to Mrs. FitzGerald; just that—hope and a temptation.

CHAPTER VII

Of a Carnivorous Lunch, a Vegetarian Tea, and the question of Canine Teeth

THE more Sir John Sparrow thought of it the more revolting it appeared. Eating dead animals! Breeding, fattening, and murdering poor uncomplaining sheep and oxen, to gratify the base lust of the stomach! How cruel, how hideous! To think how often he had sat with a leg of sheep smoking under his nose, or with ribs of beef filling a civilised dining-room with ungodly odour, unconscious of the horror, the barbarity of such a diet! No wonder the world was at sixes and sevens. What hope was there for the religious zealot distributing his millions of tracts, for the Christian Socialist idly dreaming of a millennium, or for the political reformer beating at the forts of Folly with crumpling Acts of Parliament, while all of them, in the intervals of business, sat down, like so many cannibals, to the flesh of living, breathing, sentient animals? Could the blind lead the blind? Sir John's æsthetic soul rocked in its tenement of clay when he considered how oft and how thoughtlessly he had placed in his mouth, bitten with his nice white teeth, and despatched viâ his gentlemanly throat to his patrician epigastrium, the bodies of animals that had once snuffed the morning air, chewed the fragrant cud, and lain peacefully drowsing in the comfortable grass of English or Argentine pastures. I say, Sir John shuddered at the thought. Henceforth he would keep himself clear of this contamination; henceforth he would spend all his energies in persuading the world to forsake its blood-guilty feasts.

The morning post had brought Sir John an invitation for tea from the gracious Mrs. Peace for that very afternoon, and with this encouragement in his coat pocket, he set out after a vegetarian breakfast to take lunch with his friend Captain Chivvy at one of the famous Service clubs. He found the gallant soldier in low spirits. The eyebrows were high in the forehead, a dull misery brooded in the full eyes, and the lips were forced forward in a weary mutiny against the decrees of circumstance. But he was as charmingly polite as ever. He greeted Sir John with deep affection, as one might greet a dear friend standing under the shadow of bereavement, and after seeing to his guest's hat and stick, led him into the smoking-room. Chivvy rang a bell, and the two gentlemen sat down.

"You saw that Chopsticks won?" he began lugubriously.

"No, I did not," said the baronet, suddenly interested.

"Yes, it won at a hundred to eight; but, of course— just like my infernal luck—I went and plunged on Pretty Polly for the last race, and the beast was beaten by a short head. My dear fellow, I don't complain. I know it's my luck. Nothing will alter it. Other fellows do thundering well by it; there's Barton, a member here, who makes six hundred a year by it, never does anything else; but I——!" He shrugged his shoulders, with an expression on his face which seemed to imply that for some occult reason or other the great Dispenser of men's affairs had so ordered the laws of chance that Captain Chivvy should never make a fortune out of the bookmakers.

A waiter appeared, and Sir John could not help remarking with what cheerful willingness the servant went about Chivvy's order for sherry-and-bitters, and how pleasantly he waited upon that distressed warrior.

"Oh, it's a mug's game," went on Chivvy. "I wish to heaven I'd been born an agricultural labourer, with a cottage in the country, a few chickens and a pig, and all that sort of thing. They're the happy people!" Then, with sudden energy: "My dear fellow, what's our life? Isn't it, after all, a damnable misery? How many hours of real happiness do we get in a day? What does our civilisation do for us? What avails all our culture and refinement? Not a d——n!"

Under the influence of sherry and bitters, the spirits of Captain Chivvy revived. "But I mustn't bore you with my troubles," he said, smiling cheerfully. "I hope you'll like the lunch I've ordered. I didn't quite know what to get for you; but I've ordered some salmon mayonnaise and curried prawns to begin with, some lamb cutlets, roast beef (it's awfully good here—best in London), fruit jelly of sorts, and calf's brains on toast to wind up with. Is that what you like? It's a very simple lunch; but if you're like me, my dear fellow, that's the very thing you'll feel inclined for during this confounded hot weather."

Sir John leant forward in his chair. "Since I accepted your invitation, Chivvy," he said very gravely, "I have embraced vegetarianism." He expected to see the soldier jump in his chair, but instead of that Captain Chivvy became tremendously interested.

"My dear fellow, I believe you're quite right. I believe that half our satiety and despondence and nearly all our vices are due to eating animal food. I've often thought about turning a vegetarian myself. By Jove, Sparrow, I believe you're quite right!"

G

"So you will understand," said Sir John, greatly pleased, "that while I am very grateful to you for your lunch, I must content myself with the vegetables."

"Oh, damme, no!" cried Chivvy. "My dear fellow, you really mustn't talk like that. I'm a vegetarian in theory as much as you are, and I'm quite sure if we all took to vegetarianism, we should be ever so much better in health. But there's no need to be bigoted about it. Hang it all, my dear fellow, it isn't a matter of conscience."

Sir John was greatly perturbed. "I hate to disappoint you," he said in his winning way, "but really my horror of consuming animal food is so intense that I could not possibly swallow a morsel of your lunch, except the vegetables and the sweets; I couldn't really. I hope I don't offend you, my dear fellow; but from last night I made up my mind never to touch flesh of bird, beast, or fish again, and even to oblige you, for whom I entertain feelings of the warmest friendship——"

"I know you do," said Chivvy, with all his heart.

"I couldn't bring myself to eat salmon and lamb and beef."

"Now look here, Sparrow," began Chivvy, "I want to talk to you very seriously. I see your point; I know exactly how you feel. But, my dear old fellow, if you rush on a change of diet in this hot-headed fashion you'll be deucedly ill. You must begin gradually. You must get your stomach used to the change. You must cheat your digestion into the belief that things are going on just as usual, so that it doesn't notice that the meat supply is lessening and lessening every day."

"I don't quite like that idea," said Sir John.

"In any case," said Chivvy jovially, his human face lit up by Olympian smiles; "in any case, be mortal for to-day. Have a thundering good flare-up before you send in your papers to butcher and fishmonger. Do, like a good chap! To oblige me; in memory of the old times, do! Just this once. Come along. We'll go and eat our lunch and drink a bottle of Perrier Joüet together, and then we'll come back here and argue about vegetarianism till midnight."

"I have an engagement this afternoon," said Sir John; "a vegetarian tea."

"I'll go with you."

"Will you?"

"If you eat my lunch."

"My dear Chivvy, you oughtn't to press the point."

"My dear Sparrow, don't for heaven's sake go to a vegetarian tea on top of a vegetarian lunch!"

Just at this point—such things will happen, though it requires a bold historian to note them in an age of idyllic refinement — one of those protesting gurgles which empty stomachs utter when they want something to grind issued tragically and mutinously from the abdomen of our hero. In vain did he cough to smother it; in vain did he straighten himself up to prevent a repetition. Again and again did that slow, insistent rumble run up the gamut of its remonstrance—bobble-bobble-bobble-bobble-gr-r-r-r!—and each time did the radiant Chivvy point triumphant finger at the discomfited baronet, exclaiming with each stomachic remonstrance, "There!" ending finally with, "And, by George, you had a vegetarian breakfast this morning; I'll swear to it!"

"I did," said Sir John.

"That settles it," said Chivvy, and taking the arm of the unprotesting vegetarian he led him to the dining-room. "My dear fellow," said he, "you must be starving. A vegetarian breakfast! Good Lord!"

Now, to tell the truth, Sir John was quite willing to be persuaded. He felt hungry, horribly hungry; and it chanced that in Chivvy's menu there were many of the honest baronet's favourite dishes. And besides Chivvy was such a good fellow; such a dear, dear fellow. Sir John noticed how the steward approached him with beaming face directly he entered the room, how the waiters brightened at his table, and how pleasantly he was saluted by other members. He knew the steward by his. name, the waiters by theirs; he inquired after the steward's baby, after the waiter's fortune in a cricket match; and his manner was so pleasant, so high-bred, so very sincere. Chivvy was a good fellow, however far he might be from the kingdom of grace.

So Sir John ate his lunch and enjoyed it. He returned to the lamb cutlets, he returned to the beef ("Excellent beef here," said Chivvy, with no reference to vegetarianism), and he returned, I blush to confess it, even to the calf's brains on toast. Then followed cheese, and with the cheese port—excellent port. More port? Sir John wagged his head knowingly. A very good glass of wine. More port. A wine that couldn't hurt anybody. A very sound port. One more glass? Yes, just one. One more each, and then the smoking-room for coffee and cognac? Very well, then. Such a very good glass. Ah, it stirred the deeps of memory! Those old Oxford days! Did Chivvy remember that dinner at the Mitre? By Jingo, what a saddle of mutton that was! And the lark pie! What youngsters they were in those days! Good days; good days! Poor little Stuart was killed in Egypt the other day. That famous song of his, "One more bumper"! Poor little Dick Stuart! Ah, it is sad work, growing old! Excellent port; a clean drinking wine. And that run up to town from Oxford with Tommy Lumsden. Dead, dead! What a wild fellow he was! Good heavens, that night he broke a policeman's jaw in Carfax! The visit to Evans's supper-rooms in Covent Garden. Old Paddy Green's "dear boy" to everyone, his wig and his snuff-box. What a jolly old fellow of the ancient world! And poor Lumsden dead. A fellow who might have been anything. Clever as the very——

Come, come, let us go into the smoking-room. Sir John's heart was aglow. He smoked a huge cigar, drank his coffee, sipped his brandy (sixty years old— finest in London), and talked of Oxford and the men of their time who were now ruling provinces beyond the sea, or voting like gentlemen at Westminster, or lying under the cool sod smiling up at the stars. And Chivvy, whose generous heart was no less stirred than the baronet's, talked just as keenly of those far-off days, moralised on the uncertainty of life, swore he was a Socialist at heart, cursed bookmakers, jockeys and horses, vowed that the best life was to be found in a labourer's cottage, and swept away all Sir John's objections with a "My dear old fellow, I know it."

So they sat and talked, ladies and gentlemen, sinking deeper and deeper into the comfortable chairs, speech becoming slower and slower, eyelids heavier and heavier, cigars smouldering between their fingers, till at last a discordant snort from Captain Chivvy brought them both back with a jump from the borderline of slumber.

"By George!" said Chivvy; "I was nearly asleep. My dear fellow, I'm most awfully sorry. I hope you won't think me rude. The truth is, I was awake half the night with neuralgia. I'm most frightfully sorry."

Sir John was on his feet. "It is time I went," said he; "I've got an engagement this afternoon——"

"Oh, the vegetarian tea!"

"Yes, the vegetarian tea."

"Need you go?"

"I really must."

"Then I'll come with you."

"Would you really like to?"

"Nothing I should like more. My dear fellow, I'm as certain as anything that vegetarianism is the best thing in the world for a man. If we only gave up meat, we should be better in health, purer in life, and a hundred times happier. We should indeed. I'm certain of it. I remember a fellow in India telling me that——"

It was very pleasant to come out from the somnolent atmosphere of the smoking-room into the fresh air of a bright July afternoon, and the drive in a cab to far-off Canonbury shook sleep off the eyelids of our gentlemen and put them in the best of spirits with themselves and the whole world.

But when they got out at 5, Clematis Grove, a sudden horror took hold of them, for, behold! the heavy knocker on the little, blistered, brown door was swaddled in thick flannel. Somebody was ill.

"Ah," said Chivvy very knowingly, "that's the worst of vegetarianism! You go under suddenly. No stamina."

"Had we better go in?" sighed Sir John, very unhappy.

"Better knock and inquire," decided Chivvy.

After some moments the door was opened cautiously, and a little maid-of-all-work eyed the visitors with stupid interest.

"Is Mrs. Peace at home?" whispered Sir John.

"Yes," whispered the girl.

"She isn't ill, I hope?" he whispered.

"No," whispered the girl.

"Mr. Peace quite——"

But at this point the daughter of the house, snub-nosed and spectacled, with her shoes in her hand, came rapidly down the stairs immediately facing the door, and approached the visitors with a broad grin.

" Ma's in the drawing-room," she said.

" Shall we come in, then?" asked Sir John, still whispering.

"Oh, yes, of course. Miss Vince is in there. But you'd better come in quietly if you don't mind. Very quietly, please."

" I hope no one is ill?" whispered Sir John, crossing the threshold.

A door at the side opened, and the face of Mrs. Peace shot round the corner. She smiled pleasantly, beckoned Sir John in, and then disappeared. The two gentlemen entered.

" No one ill, I trust?" asked Sir John.

"Shut the door quietly, Izzie," murmured Mrs. Peace to her daughter. When the door was closed, she turned to the baronet. "So sorry to receive you in this way, Sir John Sparrow," she said, smiling good-naturedly. "But Mr. Peace is just now writing a letter to the papers, and we have to be so very careful not to make the slightest noise. I'm so very glad to see you. It is so very good of you to come."

"It was kind of you to ask me," said Sir John. "And I have taken the liberty of bringing a friend of mine—Captain Chivvy—Mrs. Peace—who is interested in vegetarianism."

Mrs. Peace received Captain Chivvy very graciously —what woman ever received him in any other way?— and then presented the two gentlemen to Miss Vince, Miss Jane Vince.

A large, comfortable lady was Miss Vince. Her fat, slightly florid cheeks had an unmistakable air of self-

satisfied repose, in which the little brown eyes, the little
white nose, and the little smiling mouth all participated.
She wore a bonnet of last year's fashion on the top of
her big head, and a mantle heavy and bright with jet
over her ample shoulders. She gave each gentleman a
little patronising nod, accompanied by a humping of
the shoulders, from her place at the head of a horsehair
sofa. She murmured something—it might have been
"how-er-er-er," or "good-er-er-er," in a musical voice
that sounded very good-natured.

"Miss Vince is a great lady in the movement," said
Mrs. Peace. "She's the life and soul of all our meetings, and one of our most generous subscribers."

"I think," said Miss Vince, smiling broadly, "that we
all ought to do our best. I'm not like my poor uncle—
a Scotchman, he was—who said with a sigh on his return to Edinburgh that he hadn't been in London five
minutes before bang went saxpence!"

Everybody laughed. "Oh, was that your uncle?"
asked Captain Chivvy, hugely delighted.

"Yes, my mother's brother, Andrew MacDonald,"
said Miss Vince. "Oh dear, what a funny man he was!"
she added, chuckling, while the fat shoulders shook like
a blancmange.

"Why, surely he was the man who sent that 'Don't'
joke to *Punch* wasn't he?" asked Chivvy. "I'm almost
sure it was the same man."

"Indeed it was!" exclaimed Miss Vince. "Fancy you
knowing that, now! How very interesting, isn't it,
Mrs. Peace?"

"Oh, I've often heard of him," answered Chivvy very
solemnly. "Haven't you, Sparrow?"

"I'm afraid not," answered Sir John quite seriously.

Jane Vince gave all her attention to Captain Chivvy.
"His sister was very witty too—my aunt Matilda.

I remember her once, on re-entering a shop about some wrong change, being asked by one of the commissionaire people with rosettes whether she had been served by 'a gentleman with a black moustache.' 'No,' said my aunt Matilda, and you really should have seen her face; I declare it was as good as any play. 'No,' she said, 'it was by a nobleman with a bald head.' Oh dear, how I laughed! 'No,' she said, 'it was by a nobleman with a bald head.' Wasn't that good?"

Chivvy's laughter was not loud, but Jane Vince's voice was rising in scale with the Captain's appreciation of her wit. So Mrs. Peace said that she was really very sorry, extremely sorry, but she greatly feared that Mr. Peace, who was writing in the room above, might be disturbed by their merriment. Would they mind being a little quiet until Mr. Peace descended from his desk?

This led the conversation away from Jane Vince to the labours of Simon Peace. "Does your husband write regularly for the papers?" inquired Sir John smoothing the back of his head.

"Pretty regularly," answered Simon's lady, beaming. "Of course you've seen his name?"

"Oh, yes," answered Chivvy, with a will.

"He writes on all subjects," said Mrs. Peace. "Foreign politics, cruelty to animals, street nuisances, religious questions (he's very good on religion), and anything that may be occupying the public mind. His writing is very fine—isn't it, Miss Vince?—marked with a wide culture, expressed in the most impassioned rhetoric, and distinguished by the closest logical reasoning."

There was a pause after this eulogium. "Does he write—er—leading articles?" asked Sir John, after a deep silence.

"Oh, dear me, no!" exclaimed Mrs. Peace contemptuously. "He's not a journalist, you know! He writes letters to the editors!"

"Yes, rather," said Chivvy, taking the hint. "Haven't you seen his name, Sparrow, in the correspondence columns? I always read the correspondence. Best part of a paper, I always think. Mr. Peace's letters are excellent, quite excellent."

"I'm so glad you like them," said Mrs. Peace. "Did you see the answer to Huxley in the *Islington Gazette* some years ago? On the question of the Gadarene swine, you know. It was crushing, quite crushing."

"Huxley didn't reply?" asked Chivvy.

"Not he," laughed Mrs. Peace proudly.

"That reminds me of one of my cousins who was standing for Parliament," said Jane Vince, beginning to shake. "He was very young-looking, quite a boy, in fact; such a good-looking young fellow he was; and at one of his meetings a man cried out—one of those coarse interrupters, you know. 'Does your mother know you're out?' he cried. 'Yes,' said my uncle—my cousin, I mean—did I say cousin?—it was my second cousin, the youngest son of my eldest brother. 'Yes,' he said, 'and she soon hopes to know that I'm in.' *In*, you see! In Parliament. Wasn't that clever? On the spur of the moment. There was no answer to *that!*"

"And was your cousin a vegetarian?" asked Sir John, with his head very much on one side.

"No, he wasn't," chuckled Jane Vince. "None of my relations," she added quite proudly, "are vegetarians. Oh, dear me, I don't know what they think of me! They've quite given me up. I hardly see any of them now."

"You keep very well on vegetarianism?" asked Sir John, very solemn.

"No need to ask that," answered Chivvy briskly. "Miss Quince looks the picture of blooming health."

"Vince is my name," said the lively Jane, beaming all over her fat face. "Yes, vegetarianism suits me very well, I'm glad to say. I've never had an illness of any kind since I gave up eating butcher's meat."

"Oh, don't, Miss Vince!" cried Mrs. Peace, with a pretty affectation of horror. "'Butcher's meat' sounds so horrible. Isn't it a dreadful name, Sir John Sparrow? Izzie dear, you might just run and see if tea's ready. Go quietly, darling."

Izzie, grinning very hard—she was about fourteen years of age and very nearly fourteen stone—galumphed across the room, and passed out on tiptoe.

"There are drawbacks in clever husbands," said Captain Chivvy.

"Indeed, yes," Mrs. Peace replied. "Sometimes when he is on religion, really one's life is a perfect burden. I assure you the whole house has to stand still and hold its breath. No scrubbing of floors, no sweeping of stairs, no blacking of grates. The slightest sound in the middle of a sentence is fatal. He's so fastidious about his adjectives, you know. And sometimes when he's got a splendid one, a great big one, on the tip of his tongue, Izzie drops baby on the floor above his head, or the girl kicks over a pailful of water (you know what a dreadful noise a metal pail makes on a stone floor), and then it goes clean out of his head, and nearly drives him frantic. So we have to be so careful. You know how fastidious Mr. Peace is about his adjectives, don't you, Miss Vince?"

Before Jane could corroborate the wife's interesting allusion to Mr. Peace's fastidiousness in adjectives the door opened—slowly and tragically—and Simon himself appeared. There was a wild yet patient look in the great author's eyes; his hair was tossed about his head in a very frenzy of intellectual stress; and he walked slowly and laboriously, as if his whole apparatus physicus were exclaiming, "Out of me! Out of me!" It was a very striking appearance — what one may describe as a dramatic entrance. A silence that might be felt (someone, I fear, has said that before me) descended upon the cheerful company. Even Captain Chivvy felt the intensity of the moment.

Simon lounged over to the horsehair sofa, gave Miss Vince a slack hand, and, as if it were wrung from his very soul, asked in his lowest falsetto how she was. Without waiting for an answer, however, the weary Titan shuffled over to Sir John Sparrow, looked him long and earnestly in the eyes, and then with a terrible suddenness shot out his right hand. "How d'oo?" he exclaimed, with a lazy emphasis on the interrogation. As if the exertion had been too much for him, the great author paused at this point, passed his hand weariedly through his distracted hair, and sighed deeply. Mrs. Peace approached him and laid a hand upon his arm. He looked at her as though striving to recall her features. "Sir John Sparrow, dear," she said, as one speaks to an invalid, "has brought a friend with him— brought a friend to tea, dear." He listened uncomprehending.

Captain Chivvy approached, an expression of great solemnity on his face. "One, sir," he said, offering his hand, "who is very proud to have the pleasure of meeting so distinguished a writer for the papers."

A pale smile flickered over Simon's face. It was a smile that said as plainly as these words that while he, the great author, acknowledged the compliment, he was amused by the thought that one with Captain Chivvy's intellectual limitations could possibly appreciate the full depth and profundity of his literary achievements. Having shaken the soldier's hand, Simon swung moodily to the thick, white hearthrug, and turning wearily right-about face there, leaned his back against the mantel-piece, his head sunk meditatively upon his breast. One looked in vain at that moment for the restless Adam's apple.

Mrs. Peace made a gallant attempt to revive the conversation. But in despite of all her efforts, Captain Chivvy would persist in sitting with his face turned squarely to the brooding author, his big eyes fixed reverently and ecstatically on the great man's coun-tenance; while Sir John Sparrow, the memory of last night's brawl unpleasantly fresh in his mind, was so overcome by the omnipresence of Simon in the little parlour that he could do nothing but sit with his eyebrows high in his forehead, his eyes firmly fixed upon the author's footgear. As for Jane Vince, she did little else but smile, for at this moment her mind was full of the pleasant thought that she was sitting there in the company of a baronet and an officer, and that she was on equal terms with both of them. So poor Mrs. Peace had to rattle on by herself, and the only response she got was from dear Jane Vince, who smiled vacantly all the time and occasionally bobbed her head.

It was not very long, however, before the door burst open with a good healthy bang, and Miss Izzie—grin-ning across her fat white face, her eyes bright behind their spectacles—bounced into the room. She went over to her father, breathing hard and grinning hard, and expressed her great delight at seeing him down. " I've just been up to your study," she panted, "and I found you had finished it, and I came rushing down the stairs three at a time——"

Simon smiled paternally. He stretched out his long arms, laid his hands gently on the shoulders of his daughter, and holding her thus at arm's length stared luxuriously, but still a little wearily, into her spectacled orbs. Mrs. Peace beamed delightedly at them from the other side of the room. Then there was a pause; for it was seen by everyone that the author was about to speak. His lips moved for a minute, the eyelids flickered. He let his head droop to one side.

"Good Izzie!" he exclaimed affectionately. Then he drew her to him and kissed her brow.

"It isn't good of me," said Izzie, mightily pleased. "I like to look after you. It's to please myself I do it."

"Good, good Izzie!" said Mr. Peace.

"And tea's quite ready," went on the blushing and the gurgling Izzie; "and I've put a footstool for your feet, and a cushion on the chair, and I've put your plate next to mine!"

He pushed her from him. "You spoil me, Izzie," he said. "Come, let us go to our simple meal."

And, like a funeral procession, they went.

Now tea was served in the parlour, a small, stuffy room in the basement, reached by a dark, narrow, and perilous staircase. It was occupied almost entirely by a big table. One had to squeeze between the chairs and the wall in getting round to one's place. What furniture there was in the room was of the heaviest description, such as a great, gloomy, glass-covered book-case in one alcove and a swollen, frowning sideboard in the other. The two armchairs beside the fireplace were of horsehair, and their serious-looking backs were covered with woollen antimacassars. (In getting past one of these armchairs to his place at the table Sir John Sparrow barked his shins on the coal-box.) The ornaments on the mantelpiece were protected by glass cases, and stood on woollen mats. There were one or two prints on the walls, and innumerable coloured mottoes. "God Bless our Home," for instance, on one wall was squeezed between "Man wants but little here below" and "All Flesh is Grass."

It was in this little room, this little modest parlour of suburbia, that Sir John Sparrow ate his first real vegetarian meal; and that, most worthy sir, is my excuse for bothering your honour with a catalogue of the furniture. For, surely, to us looking backward there must be something almost sacred, certainly something very precious, in the least antimacassar that occupied part of that room in which Sir John first saw the delicious prospect of vegetarianism opening out before his eyes in the full plenitude of its allurement. One likes to think of the very humility of the apartment, the simplicity of it, the homeliness of its texts, the stuffiness of its atmosphere, the tight fit of its colossal furniture. Be sure that if ever Mr. and Mrs. Simon Peace have to offer their household gods to public auction (which heaven forfend), every article of furniture in the parlour will be eagerly purchased by the great-hearted British public.

We must not forget to say that on entering the parlour our guests found some five or six children, all white-faced and spectacled, sitting at the table in clean bibs and tuckers, with the maid-of-all-work standing guard over them from behind. The table itself was loaded with plates of sandwiches, odd-looking biscuits, weird-looking cakes, and any number of pots containing vegetarian delicacies. There was a teapot of abnormal size and a Brobdingnagian urn at the head of the table, whither Mrs. Peace made her way with charming pride. Izzie, with a proprietary air, set a knife right here, smelt critically one of the vegetarian pots there, and gave the decorative parsley on one or two of the dishes a somewhat more artistic pose. Then she turned all her attention to pa.

"Now, Sir John Sparrow," said Mrs. Peace, " I'm not going to let you select your own dishes; you must eat exactly what I tell you! In the first place, begin with a nuttose sandwich. Miss Vince, may I trouble you to pass Sir John Sparrow the nuttose sandwiches? Captain Chivvy, you must really try a nuttose sandwich. No, no; those are the lentil tartlets. They come after the sandwiches, you know." All the time she was rattling away in this manner, the lively Mrs. Peace was stirring the tea with a big wooden spoon, occasionally peeping into the steaming pot with an excited eye to see how the brew was faring.

There was soon a pleasant clatter of plates and forks. The children began to stuff, the little maid-of-all-work to dash about with dishes in her two hands, while the indefatigable Izzie vacated her seat by Simon to confer with her mamma over the teapot. Miss Vince told some capital stories of her relatives—no lady ever was so rich in witty relations—and Captain Chivvy laughed with the best will in the world as the radiant Jane gave to all the anecdotes of his childhood a local habitation and a name. As for Sir John Sparrow, he helped himself to a second nuttose sandwich.

" These sandwiches are really very good," said he.

" I'm so glad you like them," Mrs. Peace replied. "Dear little Izzie cut them herself."

"Oh, hush, ma!" said dear little Izzie, swinging nervously from side to side.

" But, of course," went on Mrs. Peace, "the food itself is a manufactured product, one of the thousand and one excellent vegetarian food-stuffs which render the consumption of—you know what I mean!"—she shuddered prettily—"quite inexcusable. Isn't it really quite nice?"

"One of the nicest sandwiches I ever ate in my life," said Chivvy enthusiastically. "It's really quite as good as foie gras."

"Ah!" The cry was from the silent Simon, who fell back in his seat, his eyes reproachfully set upon the gallant soldier.

"I beg your pardon," said Chivvy.

"We never mention things like that at meal times," said Mrs. Peace, with a gracious, pardoning smile. "We don't mind them in the drawing-room."

"I'm so very sorry," said Chivvy, and looking up he caught the eyes of Izzie studying him from behind their spectacles as though he were some frightful and disgusting monster.

"Have you ever tried grasserine, Mrs. Peace?" asked Jane, changing the subject.

"No, Miss Vince, I haven't. I don't think I've ever heard of it."

"It's an improvement on grass-paste. Not quite so sticky, you know."

"Oh, really; I must get some. Fancy, how very nice! And now, Sir John Sparrow, I am going to give you your tea."

The baronet's hand went forward with all the grace of courtesy to receive from the trembling hand of Mrs. Peace a large breakfast cup filled with a pale green mixture that rocked like a miserable sea in the circling china. Sir John bowed his head, thanked Mrs. Peace, and set the cup at his side.

"Tell me what you think of it," said Mrs. Peace, smiling confidently.

Sir John, dusting crumbs from his moustache with one of his neat handkerchiefs, cocked an eye on the

H

liquor, slowly slipped his finger into the handle, and then raised his eyes to Mrs. Peace.

"It is not ordinary tea?" he asked, a little anxiously.

"Oh, dear me, no!" replied the lady.

"How very interesting!" said Sir John convincingly.

"Try it," said she.

"I will!"

He lifted the cup; sipped the liquor; sipped again; very gently smacked his lips; sipped again; then took almost a long draught, and with the cup still in his hand looked up to his beaming hostess. "Excellent!" said he, with great decision.

"Isn't it good?" cried the lady. "It's our own invention—Izzie's and mine. Just a herbal tea, nothing more; quite simple to make. I must give you the recipe, Sir John Sparrow; you'll find it excellent for brain work. My husband always has a cup when he's in the throes; don't you, Simon?"

"Nearly always, Priscilla," said Simon.

"I must try it," said Chivvy gravely, his eyes on Simon.

"You are a brain-worker, sir?" asked Simon.

"In a small way. A thinker, at any rate."

"You are interested in vegetarianism?"

"Greatly."

"Vegetarianism," said Simon, sitting well back in his chair, and a great hush fell on the gathering, for it was seen that he was about to break his long silence. Mrs. Peace touched Sir John's arm and whispered, "Now, you listen"; Izzie pushed her chair on one side so as to obtain a good view of the author's placid face and ferocious hair; Chivvy leaned deferentially forward; the children suddenly stopped eating and gazed at their plates, each holding his breath. "Vegetarianism," said Simon, speaking very slowly and emphasising every syllable, "is the magnet of fine souls. It attracts the sensitive mind, the pure heart, the aspiring brain. It strips life of all barbarity, all hideousness, all unworthiness. It sweetens the bitter waters of existence. The vegetarian passes an ox without guilty shuddering; looks into the deeps of the little lamb's eyes without the blush of shame; holds up clean hands, innocent of blood——"

"Do try a haricot puff," whispered Mrs. Peace to Sir John.

"——hands innocent of blood to that Creator of ox and lamb, when with the first flush of dawn and the last flickering ray of the night's candle he addresses himself to the great Author of humanity——"

At this point in Simon's eloquent exposition there was a dull thud from the flannel-enwrapped knocker, and the maid-of-all-work—who all this time had been looking at Captain Chivvy, not at her master—flew hastily out of the room. It seemed hardly a second (certainly the silence remained unbroken) before the parlour door swung open, and a young man with a felt hat in one hand and a tall hat in the other shot himself into the room. He stood at the door, bowed to Mrs. Peace, waving the felt hat in that lady's direction to emphasise the respect of his salutation, and then turned to Simon.

"The guv'nor wants to know," he said, breathless, "whether you've taken his hat by mistake." Izzie rushed from the room. "He's been cussing you like old winky; says all this comes of goin' early! Sorry to interrupt the 'armony of a party, Mrs. Peace, but the guv'nor's rampagin' like a mad bull, he is!"

Izzie returned with the hat.

"All right, Mr. Peace," said the young man; "don't you worry. I'll make it all right with the guv'nor.

By-bye. Good evening, Mrs. Peace." And with a
second obeisance with the felt hat, and exchanging silk
hats with Izzie, the young man disappeared as suddenly
as he had come.

The interruption, trivial as it was, had a disquieting
effect upon Simon. He relapsed into his old silence,
only raising his eyes to frown occasionally upon the
children. Jane Vince came to the rescue. She related
anecdotes of a brother who always called the Atlantic
the "herring-pond"; stories of a cousin who had tele-
graphed in reply to an invitation from royalty, "Sorry
can't come: lie follows by post"; adventures of her
dear father—oh, dear, what a handsome old gentleman
he was!—who said to his mother one Sunday after
church, when he was quite a little fellow in pinafores
(such lovely golden curls he had!), "What did you get
out of the plate, mamma? I only got a fourpenny
piece."

But while Jane rattled on, to the delight of Captain
Chivvy and the diversion of the maid-of-all-work, Mrs.
Peace talked vegetarianism to Sir John Sparrow. And
she talked so earnestly, and Sir John listened so attentively—they had to put their heads close together because of Miss Jane's rattling tongue—that Simon at
the other end of the table (having nothing else to do)
began to grow jealous. He saw Sir John take a pocket-
book from his pocket, open it secretly, and scribble
down something whispered to him by Priscilla. His
blood began to simmer on the hob of jealousy. He
recalled last night's adventure; the story of his wife;
the confession of Sir John Sparrow that he had looked
with admiration on Priscilla; he recalled bitterly his
wife's sudden forgiveness on learning that her insolent
admirer was a baronet; her eagerness on their arrival
home to get Sir John to their tea-table. Simon looked

up, and opposite to him on the wall he read, "God Bless our Home." The words infuriated him. They mocked him with the perfidy of Priscilla. When Izzie inquired of him whether he could not possibly manage just one more protene biscuit, he brushed her rudely aside. Then he coughed loudly, and glared at the all-unconscious Priscilla. He coughed again, more loudly than before. Mrs. Peace went on smiling and talking, bending closer to the attentive baronet as her eloquence more and more won him to "the cause." This was too much for Simon. His blood boiled over. He rose suddenly from his chair, glared furiously at his startled wife, and then stalked noisily out of the room, amid a dreadful silence from the tea-table. Lord, lord, how he banged the door!

Shortly after this extraordinary action on the part of the great author—excused, of course, on the ground of the eccentricity of genius—Sir John Sparrow took his departure, promising to come again, and receiving a ticket from Miss Vince to attend a great Vegetarian Fête to be held in the ensuing week.

He left the house delighted with its inmates, in love with vegetarianism, and most agreeably surprised by the queer food he had eaten. He had never dreamed, worthy soul, that the martyrdom of vegetarianism could be made so pleasant to the palate. But our hero was to receive a still greater surprise, for as he walked away from Clematis Grove, that good-hearted man of the world, that tender-souled weakling, Captain Chivvy, swore by all his gods that he had never met such nice people in his life, and that he had never eaten a more glorious or satisfying tea. "My dear fellow," said he, very seriously, "*those* are the people who are happy. Good people, simple people, domestic people! What is our existence worth to theirs? Who gets most happi-

ness out of life? By George! Sparrow, if only I had
been born in their sphere what a different man I should
have been!"

Sir John Sparrow worked the conversation round to
vegetarianism and found Captain Chivvy equally enthusiastic. The honest baronet could hardly conceal his
delight.

"My only fear, Chivvy," said he, taking the other's
arm, "lies in the argument concerning man's natural
diet. It has just occurred to me that we are armed
with canine teeth."

"So we are," said Chivvy. "But you don't mean to
say that vegetarians expect people to believe that
vegetables are man's natural bill-of-fare?"

"Oh, yes, I assure you so. Mrs. Peace was very
strong on that point."

He stopped short. "Do you know, Chivvy," said he,
"I think I'll just run back and mention the matter to her?
I wish I had thought of it at the time. It's worrying
me a good deal. Don't you see, Chivvy, the whole
matter turns on whether the Creator intended us to be
carnivorous or the other thing? Therefore, my dear
fellow, the question of canine teeth is a crucial point.
I really think I must go back. I shan't get a wink of
sleep till I settle it. Do you mind?"

Chivvy didn't mind the least bit in the world, and so
back the two gentlemen turned and made their way
to No. 5, Clematis Grove.

Now it so happened that Simon had angrily watched
their departure from the front parlour window, and to
all Mrs. Peace's questions, after their departure, had
returned no answer at all, keeping his face to the window, his back to his wife. Mrs. Peace, after giving the
sulky author a rather vigorous admonishment for his
boorishness, flounced out of the room, and rejoined Jane

Vince at the tea-table. Hardly had the door slammed upon her, when Simon, boiling with rage and half-fearful that his jealousy was ill-founded, espied the cause of all his misery arm-in-arm with Captain Chivvy, actually returning to the house whose happiness he had wrecked. This was too much for Simon, a great deal too much. He strode from the room, took one step from the parlour door to the hall door, and as Sir John's hand reached the knocker, swung the door open and confronted the astonished baronet with looks of the most terrifying ferocity. So dreadful, indeed, was the vegetarian's countenance, so threatening his agitated hair, so baleful the fires in his light eyes, that for the very life of him Sir John could not explain the reason of his return. He stood there, his head on one side, his brow caught into fifty wrinkles, glancing up at the towering Simon, with as confounded and guilty a look on his face as the most exacting of jealous husbands could desire or deserve.

"Well?" said Simon, and glared even more furiously.

"I—er—I hope I——" Sir John stopped, How the deuce could he talk about canine teeth to a fellow with a face like a hungry tiger?

"Well?" said Simon, very tragic.

"I hope I don't—er—I hope I haven't disturbed you at your writing?" cried Sir John desperately.

"Well?" said Simon, growing angrier every minute of this prevarication.

"I merely came back to ask a question," said the baronet, looking hopelessly at Chivvy.

"Yes," said that gallant fellow, taking up the conversation, "we merely came back to ask a question, a very interesting question."

Simon kept his eyes fixed upon the guilty face of Sir John. "Ask it," said he very calmly.

"The question," quoth our hero, swinging his cane unhappily, "is—er—hardly one for the doorstep. Forgive me for saying so, won't you? But it isn't really."

Simon trembled with rage. "No," said he, "but it's one for the boudoir, I suppose, and to the boudoir you do not go!"

Sir John looked helplessly at Chivvy, and the glance maddened the jealous Simon. "Ask your question!" he challenged. "Ask it, ask it, ask it!"

"Yes, ask it," said Chivvy. "I don't care for kicking up my heels on a doorstep; I'm not used to it, damme."

So Sir John Sparrow pulled himself together, and looked boldly into the fierce eyes of the trembling vegetarian. But ere he could speak Mrs. Peace came running upstairs with a "What's the matter?" on her parted lips. Simon wheeled round. "Go back!" he cried fiercely. "Go back, and leave this matter to me."

"What matter?" demanded Priscilla, brindling.

"Go back, I say!" shouted Simon, beside himself with rage.

"Fiddlesticks!" said Priscilla, advancing. "I insist upon knowing what this matter is."

Then Captain Chivvy, standing tiptoe, looked over Simon's shoulder and spoke down the passage. "The matter, Mrs. Peace," said he, "is a question bothering my friend, Sir John Sparrow; and he came back here to ask you that question in an ordinary civilised manner, but found Mr. Peace barring the way——"

"Well, I never!" cried Priscilla.

"What is the question?" shouted Simon, whiter than ever. "Why don't you ask it, instead of standing there with guilt written all over your face? Ask it, ask it, I say. Why don't you ask it?"

"Good gracious me!" gasped Priscilla. "What on earth is the matter with you, Simon?"

"Ask it, Sparrow," whispered Chivvy encouragingly.

Sir John once more pulled himself together. "The question I returned to put to Mrs. Peace," he began in his low, calm voice, "was on the matter of——"

"Quite so," said Chivvy ; "quite so."

"I wanted to know," said Sir John, in great distress, "something more about vegetarianism."

Simon advanced threateningly. This was blasphemy.

"Don't prevaricate," he cried, very fierce. "Speak the truth, Sir John Sparrow."

"We came back," said Sir John stoutly, "although it certainly seems absurd to say so now, to ask about— about——"

He paused, and then, as such things will happen, both he and Chivvy came out simultaneously with the two awkward words—

"Canine teeth."

"You—you—you!" Simon could get no further. He stretched forth a trembling hand, and pointed tragically down the road. His hair shook, his lips twitched, his Adam's apple bobbed like a float on rough waters. Then, in a voice hoarse with passion, he managed to ejaculate, "Go, go! Never return. Go!"

The door banged so that the knocker was jerked high into the air. They heard husband and wife scuffling in the passage.

"The fellow's mad," said Chivvy. "What in the dickens was he raving about?"

"Dear me!" sighed Sir John. "This is very sad. Come, let us get away, Chivvy. Dear me, dear me ; this is very distressing. No answer to that question. I fear there may be none. They dare not answer it. I shan't get a wink of sleep to-night."

CHAPTER VIII

*In which Sir John takes another step, and finds
himself in a hole*

FORTUNATELY for our hero, Mrs. Peace was not
a lady to sit quietly under the displeasure of her
husband, and the next morning brought him a long
letter from the energetic dame, together with a bulky
packet of vegetarian literature capable of converting
the most devoted cannibal to the rigours of a Pytha-
gorean diet. Sir John read the apologetic letter hastily,
and then settled himself down to a long, careful, and
luxurious study of the pamphlets. By lunch time he
was intellectually stuffed with vegetarianism.

"Tiplady," said he, when the butler made his appearance, "I intend to take you out with me this morning,
and to give you lunch at a restaurant of which I heard
yesterday"—he produced his pocket-book—"a restaurant
where only vegetarian dishes are supplied. My object
in this is to educate you in vegetarian catering, for from
this time forth I shall never again pollute my body with
the flesh of animals. Will you get your hat?"

On their way to the restaurant Sir John discoursed
volubly on the joys and delights of pure living, ex-
patiating with all the eloquence at his command on the
horrors of carnivorous feeding, and the brutality of such
a diet. He had a great and burning desire to convert

106

his servant; for did not Mahomet begin thus humbly?
Tiplady smiled quietly and confidently.

"What you say, Sir John," quoth he, "is very strong
in the parts; but, if I may be allowed to say so, it is
weak in the whole. For what does it come to, Sir John?
It comes to this, that the world is all wrong, and a few
vegetarians alone are in the know. Which seems to me,
Sir John, like saying that Little is more than Much."

"I shall be very pleased to answer that argument,
Tiplady," said the baronet graciously. "You must know,
then, that there are in the world an infinitely greater
number of vegetarians than flesh-eaters. The limitless
inhabitants of India, the innumerable millions of China
and Japan, are for the most part almost entirely strict
vegetarians. The number of flesh-eaters compared with
these millions is insignificant. You labour under the
delusion, excusable enough, that vegetarianism is a
modern invention, the fad of a few miserable dyspeptics.
'Tis nothing of the sort. As old as the world, as natural
as the flesh that clothes us, vegetarianism is the most
ancient diet of the race, and, moreover, the only way
to true bodily health and peace of the spirit. It is, in
short, man's natural diet."

"I must admit, Sir John," said the butler, still confidently, "that I am staggered by the thought that there
are more vegetarians in the world (although a poor lot)
than there are people who eat after the custom of this
enlightened and progressive country. I admit that
freely, Sir John. But when I raise my eyes from earth
to heaven, Sir John, your argument—I say it with due
respect—seems to vanish into thin smoke. For what
was the Creator about, Sir John, when He gave the ox
its ribs and quarters, the sheep its legs and saddle, the
pig its beautiful ham bones? Why does the pheasant
and the partridge and the quail taste delicious? Why do

the fish that swim in the ocean cook and carve so
naturally? Was it all for nothing, Sir John? Was
there no reason for all this elegance in flesh and all this
refinement in meat?"

"I am very glad to find that you take so intelligent
a view of the matter," answered the baronet; "for there
is much in your argument that is reasonable, nothing
that is mere ignorance and bigotry. However, I am
in a position to clear away from your mind all its doubts
and perplexities, so that your reason will find nothing
illogical or irreverent in the diet which—after much
reflection—I have adopted for my own. The Creator,
Tiplady, has done everything well, but He is not
responsible for the mistakes of His people. In the
beginning He gave Adam his diet, and that diet was
vegetarianism. You will find in the very first chapter
of Genesis—I forget the verse—that God said to Adam,
'Behold, I have given you every herb bearing seed,
which is upon the face of all the earth, and every tree,
in the which is the fruit of a tree yielding seed; to you
it shall be for meat.' That was the Edenic diet. Fruit
and herbs; a pure and bloodless diet. There was no
slaughter-house in Eden. But it was necessary for the
whole world to be populated, and in the race's migra-
tions across the globe it was impossible for mankind to
obtain an uninterrupted supply of fruits and vegetables.
Therefore the Creator, in His wisdom, suffered, but did
not command, the children of Adam to hunt, slay, and
consume all those creatures mentioned by you as the
possessors of delicate and palatable flesh. But it is
obvious that when the peopling of the world was once
accomplished, the Almighty would desire His people
to return to the primeval and natural diet which
He laid down for man with the foundations of our
sphere. And that is the *raison d'être* of modern

vegetarianism. We no longer adopt vegetarianism as a diet; we exalt it into a religion, a religion whereby the salvation of the world is to be secured. For unless men return to this their natural diet, sickness and disease, vice and madness, spiritual sloth and blasphemous irreligion will continue to degrade the human family beneath the level of the beasts that perish. That to me is plain and indisputable."

At this point in their conversation the baronet and his butler arrived at the vegetarian restaurant recommended to Sir John by Mrs. Peace over her tea-table, the writing of whose address in his pocket-book had whipped the jealous Simon into fury and rebellion. It was a modest establishment, prettily decorated, and served by a bevy of neat girls, whose appearance was certainly an attractive recommendation for vegetarianism.

The lunch ordered by Sir John proved a great deal more convincing to Tiplady than all the arguments of his master. It was a very pretty meal. Vegetables were battered out of all recognition, spiced out of all their natural flavour, and caught up into such cunning and enticing shapes that the butler found himself falling more and more in love with the fad of his enthusiastic master. And not only was the meal savoury and delicious; it was satisfying.

Tiplady, who was fond of fruit, found when the dessert appeared that he could eat neither grape nor banana. As he expressed it to the delighted baronet, he was "quite blown out."

"And mark another argument in favour of vegetarianism," said Sir John very calmly; "the economical argument. This lunch, my good Tiplady, will cost me no more than three shillings — eighteenpence each! And there are other vegetarian restaurants in the City where people can obtain a three-course dinner for sixpence. Think of it! Is it not clear that in vegetarianism we have the solution of the problem of poverty? . I confess that the more I think of it, Tiplady, the more do I become convinced that vegetarianism is the one and only panacea for all the social problems of the world. Don't you agree with me?"

"I've enjoyed my lunch, Sir John," replied the careful butler, "and I'm more in favour of vegetarianism than when I first sat down. But that's another thing to throwing the butcher overboard. I don't see now what meat was made for except for eating. No, Sir John, I can't really. Why, think of a round of beef! Could anything be more natural? An ox isn't made for grace or beauty; his shape isn't pretty; he can't do anything useful; but he's made, so it seems to me, expressly for eating. Drop him with an axe, and he falls natural into joints for the dinner-table."

"Think, Tiplady, I implore you, of the man who does that killing! How can the spiritual graces flourish in a life red with slaughter? Did the Creator, in your view, ordain that this man should spend his days in the murdering of animals, blunting all his sympathies, freezing up the genial current of his soul, and learning to bear unmoved the pitiable moan of ox and lamb, the silent reproof in those large, patient eyes? You can't think that; you can't really!"

Tiplady leaned nearer to the baronet. "The truth is, Sir John, a man gets fairly flummuxed when he sits down to talk about God. We can't understand Him, Sir John, and we never shall in my opinion until we get to heaven—if then. For you see, sir, if He's love on one hand, He's very near what we poor worms would call cruelty on the other. There's a devil in every cat. If we had ears fine enough to hear, Sir John (you've told me so yourself), we should be driven crazy in taking a walk through a pretty greenwood by the shrieks of murdered insects and other things of that nature. And so, Sir John, if God made the weasel and the spider, I don't see why He shouldn't have made the butcher also. And it certainly isn't for you, me, or anybody else to say that He shouldn't have made one nor the other."

Sir John sighed sadly, as all good men sigh when forced to contemplate the suffering and travail of creation. "The mystery of pain," said he, "is a very great one. We beat our hearts out striving to break through its web. Better, then, to leave it alone, and take all the more care to avoid causing needless pain ourselves. You wouldn't kill a butterfly, would you? Why, then, should you kill—by proxy—an ox, a lamb, or a bird? Why should you?"

"It seems to me, Sir John," answered the butler, "that if we didn't kill them, they'd very soon put an end to us. They'd overrun the world; they'd eat up all the vegetables and all the grass, and they'd drive us off our own land without a thought of gratitude for the abolition of the butcher. There's no appealing to an ox's better nature, seeing that the Creator hasn't provided him with one, which is another reason why we should eat him."

"Nature will see to that," said Sir John. "Animals will decrease slowly, for vegetarianism will not come with a leap, but gradually, very gradually. Enough for us is it to know that flesh-eating is not our natural diet. I daresay, Tiplady, you are thinking in your own mind that flesh-eating is our natural diet, since we are provided with canine teeth, and that therefore my contention falls to the ground. But there is a mass of scientific evidence to prove that man was originally frugivorous, and I can quote to you the opinion of more than one professor to the effect that our teeth are not the teeth of the carnivora."

"Sir," said Tiplady, "what a professor says or thinks can't upset the habits of humanity. Those sort of people are always argufying, forgetting that the world can't live on argument. The stomach of the people turns against argument; and fortunate it is for us that it is so, seeing that the professors are always changing their opinions, making nonsense to-day of what they said yesterday was the truth and nothing but the truth, so help them Evolution! The people remain steady and conservative under all the arguments of professors, thank God for it! And so, Sir John—knowing that you would wish me to state my opinions honestly—I say that if our teeth are vegetarian, knives and forks are flesh-eaters, and if God put it into men's heads to build churches, I suppose He put it into their heads likewise to make knives and forks."

"One thing alone we know, my good Tiplady," answered the baronet, "man is the creature of aspirations. He must seek improvement or die. To him progress is more necessary than flight to the bee or motion to the sea. And you have only to think—as I hope you _will_ think, very seriously—whether the eating of fruits and vegetables is not a more perfect diet than the eating of dead animals' bodies to perceive that if man is to progress towards perfection he must discard the latter and adopt the former. Come, let us go."

In paying the bill Sir John expressed his pleasure and satisfaction with the meal he had eaten, and asked the neat girl behind the counter how she found her health on a vegetarian diet.

"Oh, I'm no vegetarian!" said she, with a pretty toss of her head; "I'm only vegetarian while I'm here, because I have to be. I eat a good meat breakfast before I start, and I eat a jolly big meat supper when I get home."

"Oh!" said Sir John, and went out of the restaurant with Tiplady at his heels.

Although at the end of an hour both the baronet and the butler found themselves rather more hungry than when they first sat down to their meal, our worthy hero grew deeper in love with vegetarianism as he swallowed larger doses of vegetarian literature, until the day of the great vegetarian fête found him as convinced and as enthusiastic on the point as any ox or ass.

The fête was held in the Martyrs' Hall, a gloomy building in the middle of London, where the Vegetarian Universal League had their offices, held their meetings, and quarrelled among themselves from morning till night. It was to the main hall in this building that Sir John was directed, and there he found himself in the midst of all the storm and stress of a busy bazaar. Stalls ran round the entire hall, on which were stacked specialities in vegetarian foods and drinks, specimens of vegetarian cloth, piles of vegetarian boots, vegetarian soaps, and vegetarian butter. The centre of the hall was filled with chattering people, all moving slowly to and fro under a roof of gaudy-coloured flags, while a string band on the flower-decked platform discoursed sweet music to inattentive ears. Sir John had no time to study either the stalls or the people before he was pounced upon by Miss Vince, and carried off to be introduced to some of the great people in the vegetarian world. He shook hands with innumerable ladies and gentlemen, who first talked about the weather and then asked him with great enthusiasm if he had seen the new vegetarian boot. How many times he was taken to

examine this boot, made of no animal's hide, neither
our hero nor his historian can dare to say; but so often
did he go to and fro on this errand that he might have
imagined his conductors to be the agents of this new
invention, for his own boots were in danger of being
worn clean through in the process.   But at last he
found rest for the sole of his foot, the lively Jane Vince
introducing him to a very famous and eloquent member
of the Vegetarian Universal League, who cared no more
for the vegetarian boot than Mercury himself, and who
was by the same token keenly disposed for conversation.

This gentleman was one Alexander Fontey, and his
appearance was of a very striking and dramatic kind.
In the first place his legs were bare, and if that were
not enough to attract public attention, these legs were
thickly covered with curling red hair.   His feet were
shod with sandals.   He wore a deep purple tunic, cut
low at the neck, and falling gracefully to some inch
or two above the knee; it was slackly girdled at the
waist and boasted but a pretence at sleeves, leaving two
thin white arms to flourish before the world.   Mr.
Pontey's face was of an equally dramatic description.
His thick red hair grew luxuriantly, and was combed
back into a lion's mane over his humped shoulders; the
upper lip was covered by a thick red moustache clipped
close to the mouth; the eyes under fierce red eyebrows
burned with a fierce penetrating light in deep sockets,
guarded by short, shining, sandy lashes.   He spoke in a
splutter, at lightning speed.

"So—so—so—so you're a vegetarian? Very well,
that's all right.   Just converted, good!   But take care!
Mind how you go.   Eh?   Don't play the fool with your
health.   Health's everything.   If—if—if—if—if you don't
look after your body you'll go to pieces.   Sure as a gun.
Health must be first consideration.   What?   Attend to

your body. Study your foods. Ex—ex—ex—ex— experiment with yourself, and get back to Nature as quick as you can. Stick to Nature."

How long, ladies and gentlemen, you have taken to read these remarks of Alexander Fontey I cannot say, but I can swear on the honour of a poor Christian that they have taken more than a minute to record. In utterance, good sirs and madams, they went with the flight of a single second. As an express train flashes past your window as you fret in a local, so rushed out these sentences of Mr. Fontey, and were gone on the instant. There was no stammering over hard syllables, but every now and then he would repeat a single word over and over again, like the popping of a Maxim gun, as if by that means he got a good start in firing off the remainder of a sentence.

"Mr. Fontey," said the amiable Jane, "is our man of science; he knows more about the values of food than anybody in the world. But he's too advanced for me!"

"No—no—no—no, I'm not," flashed the eager Alexander. "Anyone can follow where I go. I follow Nature, that's all. Nature's the only guide. Follow Nature and you can't go wrong. It's only be—be—be —be—because we've deserted Nature that we're suffering, that's all. What? Stick to Nature; don't try and improve on her. You can't do it."

"That reminds me," said Jane, beginning to shake, "of two tradesmen in my old village. Dear me! what funny fellows they were! One of them printed on his bags a Latin motto, 'Mens conscious rector'; and the other to outdo him—a funny little grocer he was— printed on his bags—dear me! I can see those bags now, little yellow things with a great sheaf of corn in the centre—'Men's and Women's conscious rector'———"

"You—you—you—you can't improve on Nature," in-

terrupted Alexander Fontey. "Give up eating animal
food, and you're very little nearer the truth, a long—
long—long—long way off Nature."

"Good gracious!" cried Sir John.

"Man's natural diet," went on Mr. Fontey, "was not
vegetarian, couldn't have been vegetarian. Man's
natural diet was fruitarian, must have been fruitarian.
All—all—all—all cooking is unnatural, and therefore
wrong, utterly wrong. Man's natural diet was fruit,
pure fruit, nothing but fruit, and raw fruit. If you want
to follow Nature, eat fruit."

"You interest me a great deal," said Sir John in his
calm, slow way. "Do I understand, sir, that you yourself eat nothing but fruit, raw fruit?"

"Certainly," answered Mr. Fontey; "I follow Nature
and nothing else. Who else should I follow? Nature's
good enough for me."

"Mr. Pontey's school has a great contempt for us,"
explained Miss Vince, with a genial smile. "They
declare that we are neither one thing nor the other—
'mermaids,' as one of my brothers always used to call
people of that kind."

"You—you—you—you do me an injustice," said
Alexander carelessly. "I have no contempt for
vegetarianism; I merely see its limitations, see how
far it falls short of Nature. Man in his natural state
ate fruit. Eh? Nothing but fruit. Man in his natural
state was not troubled by gout, madness, vice, tuberculosis, or social problems; and until we get back to
Nature we shall suffer from all these evils. Of course
we shall."

"Would you advise me, then," asked Sir John, "to
adopt a fruitarian diet? I am certainly anxious, let me
tell you, to reach the highest point of perfection that
my development will permit of, extremely anxious."

Mr. Fontey shrugged his shoulders. "Just as you please," said he. "If you want perfection, you must follow Nature. You can't go outside Nature. That's all."

"But from motives of health would you advise caution in adopting a diet exclusively fruitarian?"

"If—if—if—if——" began Mr. Fontey, but Jane interrupted.

"You stick to vegetarianism, Sir John," said she in her kind motherly fashion. "There's plenty of time to think about fruitarianism, and you haven't made quite sure yet that even vegetarianism will suit you."

Sir John, very serious, listened thoughtfully to this caution, and then made answer. "Unless I reach perfection I shall be unhappy. Dear lady, there is not, unfortunately, plenty of time in this matter. I awoke only a few days ago from a long sleep of wicked self-satisfaction and idle brooding over the problems of the age. I am no longer a young man. Now I am hungering and thirsting after the Ideal. I cannot stop short of it. Every obstacle in the path of my progress must be removed. If vegetarianism is only a stepping-stone, I will go on to fruitarianism, and if fruitarianism prove only a stepping-stone, I will go on to other heights. For it does seem to me, since I have conversed with Mr. Fontey, that vegetarianism cannot by any possible means be accepted by any open mind as man's natural diet. Originally there were no means of cooking food. Originally man could have known nothing of gardening, nothing of vegetables. But it is very obvious to me that our first parents would have turned instinctively to the beautiful fruits swaying in the air, and gathering those with their hands, have eaten them with no thought of cooking."

"I—I—I—I—would advise you," said Alexander carelessly, "to begin gradually. Eat a pound of Brazil

nuts, some almonds and raisins, and six or seven
bananas for breakfast; more bananas, half a dozen
apples, and a fruit pudding midday; with a milk pudding
and as many apples, pears, and raisins at night as you
can eat.   You can drop the puddings as you get on."

Sir John produced his pocket-book. "Would you be
so very kind as to repeat the—the——?"

"The prescription!" chuckled Jane.

"Very slowly, please," said Sir John, beginning to
write.

Just as Mr. Fontey ceased to dictate, and just as Sir
John was replacing his pocket-book with a very grave
air, someone came up to our little group and took
Miss Vince aside.   Alexander Fontey drew closer to
Sir John.

"You—you—you are interested in this matter?" he
began. "You—really are?   You see, do you, that the
great thing is to get back to Nature?   Well, I'll tell you
something more.   I've got—got—got—got a scheme—a
great scheme.   Only it wants money; it wants money."

"Very much?" asked Sir John.

"No—no—no—no.   A thousand pounds or so to
start with."

"You may confide it to me," said Sir John, with all
the assurance of a capitalist.

"I—I—I—I want to found a colony, a great nature
colony," proceeded Mr. Fontey.   "It's the dream of my
life.   A colony of vegetarians and fruitarians, men and
women, cultivating the land, living by their own labour,
wearing natural clothes like these that I have now got
on, and getting back to Nature in every possible way.
We should sleep out of doors in summer, hold debates
in the evening, and welcome everybody who would give
up all their money and join our brotherhood."

"A glorious idea!" cried Sir John, with enthusiasm.

"Isn't it? We—we—we—we should be the light of the world. It's the only way of converting mankind to true socialism. No—no—no—no revolution required, no Act of Parliament; simply a quiet and orderly return to Nature. The dream of my life!"

"I'll see it accomplished!" cried Sir John.

"You will?"

"As soon as you please."

"You—you—you—you shall be the first president!" quoth Fontey generously.

"If you think me worthy."

"I'll call on you to-morrow with plans. Where do you live?"

Our hero produced his card-case. Then he paused. "Excuse me, will you, for mentioning a little point? Er—er—your clothes. Would you mind—people in my neighbourhood are so bigoted—would you mind coming——?"

"That—that—that—that's all right," answered Mr. Fontey. "I only wear this costume at fêtes. The police won't let me go about the streets in this suit. Police are the enemies of Nature. I'll wear trousers. That's all right."

Jane Vince returned, and Mr. Fontey retired.

"Let me introduce you to Miss Frisby," said the beaming Jane. "She's the great apostle of sun-baths, you know. She's going to cure us of all our liver complaints, all our rheumatism, and all our neuralgia, aren't you, Miss Frisby?"

Miss Frisby wore pince-nez, through which she studied Sir John's face with consuming interest. She was tall, thin, extremely fair, and but for a flat figure, not at all ill-looking. She cultivated a foreign manner of speaking, thrusting her face into the faces of those with whom she was speaking, while eyebrows, eyes, lips, nostrils, hands, arms, and shoulders emphasised in their several ways the general alertness and animation of her manner.

"Sun-baths?" asked Sir John doubtfully.

"The body," said Miss Frisby quickly, "requires the sun. Oh, sun and air are so essential to its health! Clothes rob it of both. Cruel, cruel clothes!"

"I see," said Sir John thoughtfully; "and it is quite evident to me without going any deeper into the matter, without further investigation of any kind, that what you say is true. It is, in its way, a return to Nature, isn't it? Yes, very true, very true. One ought to bathe in the sun. But—but how? We can't all live at the seaside, can we? And here in London it would be so very difficult. I don't quite see——"

Miss Frisby was equal to the emergency. "Ah! but Miss Vince has the sweetest, dearest little field at the back of her charming cottage. She will let you dip in the golden waters there! Won't you, dear Jane? It's quite private, oh, so private! She and I often go there —often, often! A little green field full of sunshine— charming, charming! You and I bathe there, dearest Jane, don't we? Oh, often, often!"

Jane began to chuckle. "I really don't think you need have told Sir John that!" cried she, with amiable animation. "He's quite welcome to try a bath in my paddock at any time; to-morrow afternoon, if he will. But you needn't have told him that I disport myself there!"

"All you need to bring," said Miss Frisby, "is a pair of bathing-drawers. Just the simple bathing-drawers. No more. We will lend you the rest—all the rest."

"The rest?" asked Sir John.

"A rug, slippers, and a dressing-gown. To walk from the garden to the field. Do come! Oh, but I shall be breathless till you have tried it!"

So it was arranged that the enthusiastic baronet should make the journey to Chorley Wood on the following afternoon, and there make his first experiment in sun-bathing. He bade the two ladies farewell, bestowing a stricken-deer glance upon the animated Miss Frisby, and turned to leave the hall. But the enthusiastic little gentleman had scarce taken three steps before he came face to face with Simon and Priscilla Peace, the couple standing in his path obviously to intercept his progress. Our gentleman stopped dead.

"Well, Sir John Sparrow," exclaimed Priscilla in a tone of reproof, "I really think you might have found a minute to spare to us. Miss Vince, I know, has a gift for chatter, and Miss Frisby is supposed by some people to be entertaining; but after all they have their limitations! And it has really been very amusing for me to watch Jane Vince trotting you up and down, introducing you to the President and the Secretary, showing you off, in fact, to the whole room as *her* friend, when it was Mr. Peace who converted you, and I who introduced Jane Vince to you at my own tea-table. Oh very amusing! Mr. Peace and I have had a good laugh over it; we couldn't help it. It wasn't uncharitable; we simply couldn't help it."

Now all this was very unkind, and not a little acrimonious; but as Mrs. Peace was talking to Sir John for no other purpose in the world than to convince the entire audience that she was on the friendliest terms with the baronet, she delivered herself of this acerbity with a thousand smiles, an infinity of friendly gestures, and all those little swayings of the body, inclinations of the head, and softnesses of the eyes that are the property of a loving and a tender spirit.

"Are you jesting with me?" asked Sir John, confused by all this.

"Oh, dear me, no!" cried Priscilla. "It was Jane Vince who was making a jest of you, dear Sir John Sparrow! And I'm not in the least jealous; Jane Vince is a friend of mine, and will remain a friend of mine so long as she doesn't overstep the bounds of decency and decorum. But I really do think, I really do, that you might have made some effort to speak to your earliest vegetarian friends before the conclusion of the fête."

"I am so sorry," said Sir John gently.

"Don't apologise, Sir John Sparrow," said the smiling Priscilla, "for I daresay my husband's treatment of you—though I hope you know that other authors beside Mr. Peace often act without quite knowing what they are about—I daresay, I say, that the treatment you received on our doorstep was enough to make you feel chilly in approaching us. So please don't apologise. But remember that, however charming other folks may be, it was Mr. Peace who converted you, I who asked you to tea, and that it was at No. 5, Clematis Grove that you met the lady whom gossip says is to be the future Lady Sparrow."

"Good God!" cried Sir John, jumping.

"People will talk," went on Priscilla. "There's no stopping clacking tongues. But we can at least prevent ostentatious behaviour likely to set gossips chattering. People talk about me, but they can't get further than the price of a new hat, or the age of a jacket, because, Sir John Sparrow, I take very good care never to give them cause!"

At this point Izzie Peace, in a large, flopping hat stuck all over with red poppies, came leaping towards her mamma. She was smiling, and her eyes behind their shining spectacles were big with a surprise. Without looking at Sir John, save for the briefest of seconds, she pushed her face against Priscilla's ear, and whispered something that made Mrs. Peace catch up her two hands, glance angrily at Sir John, and exclaim, "Well—I—never!"

"Isn't it too awful?" said Izzie, and went over to whisper the same thing into Simon's gloomy ear.

"Well, Sir John Sparrow," cried Mrs. Peace, "if Izzie hadn't told me I never would have believed it. Really, I wouldn't!"

"What is it?" asked Sir John, his head beginning to spin.

"Oh, Sir John Sparrow, this is dreadful!" said Mrs. Peace, with a shocked face.

"Priscilla," said Simon, interrupting, his hand grasping Izzie's as though to protect her from danger, "this is no place for you. Kindly leave Sir John Sparrow to his new friends and accompany me to the further end of the hall."

"Oh, Sir John Sparrow," went on Priscilla, taking not the slightest notice of her lord, "to think that you should have gone so far in so short a time!"

"Please tell me, dear lady, what all this trouble is about," said our hero desperately. "I really cannot guess what your complaint is. I can't, really!"

"Why, the whole room's talking about it; everybody in the place is shocked and scandalised. Don't you know you're the talk of the room? *To think of you and Jane Vince taking a sun-bath together!* Oh, it's dreadful, dreadful! And you who might have married anybody!"

Sir John's eyeglass slipped from his eye, and his whole face expressed the utmost horror and consternation. "It is not true," he said jerkily; "I assure you it isn't. I am to take a sun-bath, but not with the lady. Of course not!"

"Priscilla," cried Simon, "I must insist upon you moving to the further end of the hall."

"Well, good-bye, Sir John Sparrow," exclaimed Mrs. Peace, smiling more graciously than ever, and extending the friendliest of hands; "good-bye, and I do hope, most sincerely, I am sure, that if it comes to marriage you will be happy and comfortable. She's a very worthy soul, very simple, homely, and kind. She deserves a good husband. Of course I never thought of the dear old thing marrying above her station; such an idea always seemed utterly preposterous to me, and I often used to laugh at the very thought of such a thing, oh, many a time; but still some unequal marriages turn out comfortably, and I am sure that I wish yours may be an addition to the list. Good-bye, Sir John Sparrow, good-bye. It has been such a pleasure to see you again. Good-bye!"

And with that Mrs. Peace smiled more amiably than ever, gave Sir John the most patronising of little nods, and then swept off to give the genial Jane Vince a piece of her mind.

CHAPTER IX

*Of the Sun-bath taken by Sir John Sparrow in the
Paddock behind Miss Vince's Cottage at Chorley
Wood*

IT is to be feared that Alexander Fontey was disappointed in our hero when he presented himself,
in trousers, at Sir John's chambers with plans for the
foundation of a Nature colony. The enthusiasm of the
bazaar had departed. Our little gentleman wore an
expression of gloom, he spoke in an abstracted manner,
he fidgeted with his hands and feet. The more Mr.
Pontey raved, the more our baronet sighed. There was
no encouragement in his manner of listening; rather
the reverse. But just as Alexander rose with frowning
brow to take his departure, Sir John suddenly jumped
to his feet, a smile chased the heavy gloom from his
visage, and he exclaimed in a voice of the utmost
cheerfulness, "I have it! Of course, of course. Good,
good!" And with that he dismissed the astonished
and perplexed Mr. Pontey with a promise that he would
look into his plans, loaded him with thanks for the
trouble he had taken, and then called Tiplady to his
side.

"One of the reasons of our physical weaknesses and
distempers," he began in a lively manner, "is to be
found in the clothing we wear, which shuts off the body

from the precious and essential benefits of sun and air. The body, Tiplady, requires the sun as much as the rose or the lily. Air is as necessary to the body as water to the fish. Therefore it becomes us to expose our bodies as often as possible to the unsheltered rays of the sun, which is the source of life, and to the gentle breezes which carry God's blessings over the round earth. This afternoon, Tiplady, I take my first sun-bath, and I regret that circumstances will not permit of my giving you the same opportunity; but later on I will make arrangements for you to participate in all the blessings of my discovery. And so in asking you to go out and purchase for me a pair of ordinary bathing-drawers, I will request you to provide yourself with a larger pair at the same time, in order that you may be fully prepared to join me on the next occasion."

Tiplady received the money for the purchase of these bathing-drawers with a blank face. "Shall I pack your bag, Sir John?" he asked, very glum.

"Pack my bag? Why? I don't follow you."

"I supposed you were going to the seaside, Sir John; I don't know where else a gentleman may expose himself."

The baronet smiled. "There are places nearer London where a man may go as nature clothed him, and very shortly I trust to have an establishment of my own within a gunshot of the four-mile radius. No, do not disturb my wardrobe. But I will ask you to go as quickly as possible for the bathing-drawers, and at the same time to inquire at Captain Chivvy's club if that gentleman will be disengaged at one o'clock. May I trouble you to go quickly?"

The servant departed, Sir John paced to and fro in his room, and in half an hour, armed with a small brown-paper parcel, and cautioned by Tiplady to be careful, he set out to call for Captain Chivvy.

It was the sudden idea that he should take Captain Chivvy to Chorley Wood which had so miraculously changed our hero's mood of despondence into one of cheerful enthusiasm. To go alone to the house of Miss Jane Vince after the alarming remarks of Priscilla Peace was beyond the baronet's courage. He had lain awake through half the night, shaken by a thousand terrors, tortured by a thousand fears, and had awakened in the morning to the same terrible thought which had chased sleep from his pillow through so many silent hours of the night. Was he being caught in the toils of matrimony by Jane Vince? Would he be forced into marriage by that genial old spinster?

With all the burning zeal of a proselyte he longed to plunge his jaded body into the rays of the sun, longed to feel the soft wind of heaven playing over his weary frame; but much as he craved for this bath, he had no wish—as the phrase goes—to put his foot in it, no desire to get into hot water. Sir John loved his bachelorhood with a force that manifested itself only when he found that darling of his soul perilled by the subtlety of scheming woman. But with the thought of taking Captain Chivvy as a protection from the attacks of Miss Vince and Miss Frisby, our hero cast fear behind him, and went forth to his sun-bath as gaily as troubadour to the war.

During the journey to Chorley Wood, Captain Chivvy —who was once more on the verge of self-destruction— vowed and declared that sun-baths were the only possible means of dispersing the cholers of the body, swore by all his gods that clothes were the invention of the devil, and begged his dear friend Sparrow to stick to sun-baths all the days of his life and never,

never, never to go in for gambling. A mug's game!
"By George," sighed he, "if only I had taken sun-baths
all my life, what a different fellow I should be now!"

The two travellers were greeted with much courtesy
by the ladies in the cottage, and Sir John Sparrow,
after being shown the way through the garden to the
paddock, was conducted to a bedroom where he might
divest himself of his garments, don his bathing-drawers,
and wrap himself in a blanket for the purpose of passing
through the house and garden. The ladies then retired,
accompanied by Captain Chivvy, and shut themselves
in the drawing-room, with the blinds down.

Sir John's troubles on this momentous day began
early. For when he had stripped himself, and stood
up in Miss Vince's bedroom in all the nakedness of
nature, he found on undoing his parcel that Tiplady
had purchased not the old-fashioned, elastic-bound
bathing-drawers, but a one-legged puzzle in flaming
red, which might have been anything from a sun-bonnet
to an infant's chemise. Our hero held this mysterious
object up to the light; turned it this way and that;
pulled a string here, another there; considered it from
this angle, studied it with knitted brows from that
angle; laid it on the floor; spread it on the bed; and
finally—after loading Tiplady with a few pointed reproaches—took his courage in both hands, and gingerly
inserted one leg through the single opening of the
puzzle. This, as it happened, was the wrong leg, and
it took the nervous and angry baronet several minutes
before he arrived at the conclusion to try the other.
And even when he had pulled the drawers up the right
leg he was for some little time under the impression
that he was wrong again, for the costume was an utter
and hopeless failure in the all-important matter of fit.
So Sir John tried to get both legs in the hole, but

failing here again, it struck him all at once with a shock that brought an unuttered d—— to his lips, that his blundering blockhead of a servant had packed the larger pair of drawers intended for himself, instead of the smaller intended for his master!

But it was such a burning July day, such a steaming summer afternoon, that our gentleman determined, by hook or by crook, to make these Gargantuan drawers serve his own Lilliputian purpose. So he tugged the strings here, drew them there, crinkled up the rebellious scarlet linen into a hundred creases, and then setting his right leg into the hole, drew the flimsy thing about his body and tied it in a great knot over his thigh bone. Now all this pother, as your worships may well imagine, had taken a considerable time, and Jane Vince—anxious to see that her distinguished guest had found everything to his comfort in the bedroom, and being convinced that he must by now be bathing in the paddock— ascended the stairs and opened the bedroom door at the very moment when Sir John was struggling into his scarlet garment for the last time, as described above.

Lord, lord! what a moment that was!

For both the lady and the gentleman were so genuinely surprised by the appearance of each other that they stood for many long seconds face to face, like a couple of idiots, gazing point-blank into one another's wide eyes with looks of the blankest astonishment, and uttering not a single word. Then Sir John, clinging desperately to his drawers, his head very much on one side, murmured an incoherent apology and—like an ostrich—turned his back. The lady started, banged the door to, and when it was quite shut, called through the screening wood that she was *so* sorry, that she had *no* idea that Sir John was still in the room, and that she *earnestly* hoped he would forgive her.

K

After this misadventure it required no little courage on the part of our hero to slip his feet into woollen slippers with pink ribbons, to wrap a blanket about his person, and thus arrayed to emerge from the comparative security of the bedroom, with his eyeglass in his eye, to all the terrible possibilities of the staircase and garden. But, as the faithful historian has already recorded, there was delicious temptation in the warmth and gladness of the afternoon, and soon the sultriness of the day overcame the flutterings of timidity in Sir John's bosom. Opening the door, with a preliminary cough he stole out into the publicity of the house. His ears were saluted by the laughter of Chivvy and the clatter of the ladies in the drawing-room. He heard a maidservant screaming to a cat in the kitchen. The banisters creaked sinisterly. Otherwise the house was still, painfully still, with sunbeams fast asleep on the stair-carpets, and dust-motes dancing in a golden light. He descended the stairs, coughing hard, shuffled his feet noisily down the little stone passage, opened the garden door with a great clatter, and unmolested passed down the gravel path (where he began to whistle), and opened the little green door in the creeper-clad wall which stood between him and his bath.

The paddock was no more than a couple of acres in extent. Its only occupant when Sir John entered was a bony white horse, who lay in a sleeping condition under a group of elm trees at the far corner of the field. On all sides, with the exception of Miss Vince's wall, the paddock was bounded by a high hawthorn hedge, a rickety gate on the opposite side opening into another field, which sloped abruptly down to an invisible valley. Far away on the opposite side of this valley Sir John could descry through his eyeglass a few sleepy cottages, so small and indistinguishable that they might have been beehives. A soft mist veiled upland and wood. There was a sense of loneliness in the scene, a conviction of privacy in the little field. Not a human sound reached his ears. Birds sang in the trees and flashed across the field; the wailful gnat buzzed and danced in the clear sunlight; butterflies flitted languidly across the enamelled mead; the shadows of the trees lay prone upon the grass.

Sir John put off his blanket. Then, with his eyeglass in his eye, the woollen slippers on his feet, and holding on to the uncomfortably loose drawers, our noble gentleman walked slowly out of the shadow of Miss Vince's cool wall, until he stood in the open, exposed to the full blinding splendour of the summer sun.

"This is glorious!" cried Sir John. "Until this moment I have never tasted the intoxicating cup of freedom. What do they know of liberty who sing only of political freedom, whose bodies are mewed up in the wools of sheep, and whose one glimpse of Nature is the brief moment when they shiver in a stuffy bathroom? This, this is freedom! This is Nature! My soul takes on the glory of youth, and my body responds to the gladness thereof. Henceforth I shall advocate on all occasions the taking of sun-baths. I will subsidise a paper for the advocacy of this glorious discovery. I will preach of it from a hundred platforms. In my colony we will dip day and night in the sparkling rays of the great source of life, the Almighty's ministering agent, Apollo the healer, the far-darting Apollo!"

Saying this to his own soul, our hero cast himself ecstatically upon the soft sward, and lay with his nose in the grass snuffing the sweet savour of the soil. In this position there was no need to cling to the ill-fitting drawers, and so Sir John stretched his arms straight out from the shoulders and let the sun beat down upon his back. After some five minutes he rolled slowly and luxuriously round upon his scorched back, and lay with his breast to the sun, his eyes blinking straight up into the tremendous vault of heaven.

"What a worm is man!" exclaimed Sir John in this position. "What is our globe but a speck of dust whirling through zoneless space? And man, what is he amid the myriad spheres, the rush and roar of the planets, save an insect too small for God to behold, too insignificant for outraged deity to crush? In this very position, but beneath the cool sod, I shall one day be laid to sleep—the eternal sleep of death. I shall gaze up, but with sightless eyes, to the overhanging dome of heaven, where the stars will still shine, and the dews still gather; and above me the grass will grow, the daisies drink their meed of dew, and the birds sing as they sang in the Garden of Eden. Ah! what a thing is man! A breath! A little puff of wind! Nothing more. A breath!"

I know not, ladies and gentlemen, whether your worships have ever lain upon your honourable backs in a green field and gazed into a cloudless sky, quivering with the heat of a summer sun; but if you have, you will bear me out in this—and if not, you must take it on trust—that whatever be the effect upon the mind, the effect upon the eyes is to turn the green of the grass and the green of the leaves to a dull blue, and to blur every other object on the landscape out of all recognition. Now, when Sir John had done moralising in the face of heaven, and feeling that his head began to ache from the heat of the sun, he turned himself about, sat upon his haunches, and gazed on either side of him with a confused and chaotic mind. At that very moment it chanced that a shaggy Old English sheep-dog broke through the hedge, and seeing what it had never seen before, and in the middle of a paddock, it put nose to the ground and bore down upon our hero with incredible fury. Sir John, with his eyes still dimmed and blurred, incontinently mistook this dog for a mad bull, and springing to his feet he made with all the speed he could muster for the rickety gate on the opposite side of the field. Fortunately the gate was not far, and being incommoded by no clumsy clothing, our worthy gentleman was able to reach it without receiving any impetus from the horns of a maddened bull. Which means that Sir John clambered over the gate just as the dog butted into it; but awoke, poor gentleman, to the terrible knowledge that in reaching the further field he had by no means reached safety. For a sheep-dog can go where a bull cannot, and though for some minutes puzzled by the gate, the dog showed not the slightest sign of abandoning pursuit; on the contrary, he rushed at the bars, stormed at the posts, leapt up to the top rail, and thrust his snout ferociously under the bottom. Then he dashed to this side of the gate, then to that, charging into the hedge so that the twigs for half a dozen yards shook and rattled as though a nor'-wester were blowing. Sir John took to his heels. He ran, poor little gentleman, as he had never run in his life before. The gradient of the field helped him. He spun over the sward. Clutching at his scarlet drawers, his eyeglass dangling over his back, gasping and perspiring, he shot down the sloping field, while the pink ribbons of his woollen shoes whistled in the air.

The furious dog, of course, was not long in forcing a passage through the hedge, and, with four legs against our baronet's two, it soon came charging down the field at a pace compared with which Sir John's velocity was the progress of a London omnibus. And to add to our

hero's discomfiture—if indeed it were possible to do so
—he discovered that a busy hamlet lay in the valley to
which he was bounding at this unstoppable speed.
Behind him was a furious dog ; before him an unknown
village—human habitations, men, women, and children.
He struck off desperately to the right hand, and the
dog shot past him. He rushed to a tree; the dog,
tumbling upon its nose, doubled round and followed
him. Sir John fell against the tree with outstretched
hands, and clambered to the other side. The dog was
there at the same moment.

" Good dog, good dog ! " panted our spent hero.

" Bow-wow-wow ! " returned the dog in an agony of
fury, and made a dash at Sir John's calf.

From motives of self-preservation the baronet kicked
with all his might at the animal's jaws, sending one of
the woollen slippers flying over the creature's head,
while the loose drawers shot down and clung limply
about his feet. The dog made for the slipper, and
Sir John—seizing his opportunity—with a great jump
sprang up to the lowest branch on the tree, caught it
by his two trembling hands, and after swinging backwards and forwards two or three times—while the dog
jumped about his dangling legs, inflicting innumerable
scratches and one or two skin-deep bites on those
tortured limbs—he managed to swing himself up to the
branch, and out of all reach of the dog's fangs.

While the dog howled at the foot of the tree Sir
John, panting hard, with the blood bumping painfully
in his head, looked about him. On one side of the
field was a broad road leading to the village ; on the
other lay the paddock in which he had taken his
bath, where the bony horse still drowsed under the
trees. The other boundaries of the meadow in which
he now found himself were a young plantation and a

river creeping sluggishly through innumerable green
fields.

"Go away!" gasped Sir John to the dog, and stooping forward to give force to this dismissal, the baronet
let his bathing-drawers slip quietly over his feet into the
moist jaws of his pursuer. For some minutes he had
nothing more exciting to do than watch the sheep-dog
tear those scarlet drawers into a hundred shreds,
occasionally raising his eyes to look hopelessly towards
the cool, creeper-clad wall surrounding Miss Vince's
cottage. Against the wall, a dim white speck, lay the
blanket he had worn about his shoulders.

The dog, having tickled his appetite with the drawers,
set up once more a horrible clamouring for the flesh
and blood of the vegetarian baronet. And such a
passionate howling was this that it attracted the attention of the rector's two daughters and their governess,
who were at that very moment ascending the steep road
from the village. Seeing a dog, well known in the
neighbourhood, raving like a mad thing at an apparently
empty tree, the girls and their governess determined
forthwith to investigate the mystery. They crossed
into the field, then, and made their way, all unknown to
the baronet, to the scene of this unnatural clamour.
The howling of the foaming dog prevented Sir John
from hearing the voices of these intruders, and the
spreading, heavy-bunched leaves of the trees prevented
the intruders from seeing Sir John. So it came about
that all the parties became aware of each other at the
same moment, and with an equally balanced surprise.

The ladies screamed, and dragged each other a pace
back.

Sir John, doubling himself up on his branch to
modify his nakedness, implored the ladies to withdraw
themselves altogether from the scene, waving frantic

arms to emphasise the words which the howling of the ferocious dog almost completely drowned.

"It's a tramp!" said one of the girls.

"It's a madman!" said the other.

"It's a naked gentleman!" said the governess.

They called the dog away from the tree, and seizing him by the collar dragged him off with them, hurrying with all the modesty in their natures to the road they had so rashly forsaken. Now, Sir John, as we have already pointed out, could not from his perch command the whole of this road, and therefore he was no more aware of the ladies' departure from the field than he was of their entrance into it. Therefore he sat cursing his fate, and making no move, while one of the girls, at her governess's beck, ran down the road at top speed to tell her father that a naked man was up a tree in the hillside meadow. The rector on hearing this jumped to his feet with a face expressive of all the righteous indignation in the world.

"I know who it is!" he exclaimed, very stern. "It's one of those confounded vegetarians taking a sun-bath —atheists and lunatics, all of them—one of that Vince woman's friends! I'll put a stop to this. I'll have him locked up, and I'll drive that woman out of the parish. Give me my hat, Jinny!"

So it happened that just as Sir John Sparrow screwed his courage to the sticking-point, and dropped tenderly upon his feet, there came into the field, with a clamour infinitely more terrifying than the howling of sheep-dog, the rector, the constable, a dozen yokels, men and women, a score or two of children, and an innumerable tribe of small, yapping dogs.

"There he is!" cried the rector, flourishing his walking-stick. And with that all the dogs flew forward yelping and snapping in a frenzy of excitement.

Sir John would have made a dash back for the protecting branch of the tree, had not the presence of several women in the noisy crowd driven all thoughts out of his distracted head save that of instant flight. He turned his back on dogs and mob, and with only one woollen slipper between his two feet, and with no drawers at all, started to run up the hill as fast as his legs would carry him. The shouts of the people drove him frantic; the yelps and snaps of the curs at his heels maddened him. His world had left its orbit and was spinning to destruction. Nature had torn up her Magna Charta, and all was chaos and anarchy. Blindly, with arms outspread, the eyeglass dancing a tattoo on his naked back, the panting baronet struck up the field, and made, with despair in his heart, for the green door in Miss Vince's wall. His feet plunged through thistles, he stumbled, his legs were scratched and torn by the yelping dogs, and nearer, ever nearer, came the shouts of the pursuing villagers. He could hear the loud voices of the men, the shrill anger of the women, the piping, uncontrollable laughter of the children. Oh, reader, be not angry with those heartless urchins. Thou thyself, seeing a naked little gentleman with moustache and whiskers, dressed only in a bedroom slipper adorned with pink ribbons, an eyeglass dancing over his shoulder —thou thyself, seeing such an one running for dear life up a sloping field under a sweltering sun, wouldest have held both thy sides—nay, have rolled upon the grass in an ecstasy of laughter. For of all the comic things in this world of comedy, nothing is more humorous, no-thing so risible as a naked white man running heartily under his Maker's blue sky. Which would seem to prove the contention that white people are degenerate descen-dants of black; for there is nothing comic in a naked black man, and we do not laugh when we see one.

But Sir John has been running while we have been moralising; he has even scrambled over the rickety gate, and is once more in the paddock; so, too, are his pursuers. On he went, panting hard, his heart pumping rebelliously in his bosom, the sweat of labour pouring from his brow, dripping from his chest and limbs; and behind him, pressing ever harder, parson, constable, yokel, virago, hobbledehoy, and urchin.

But, ladies and gentlemen, you are saying within yourselves, "What is Captain Chivvy about? What is Miss Vince doing all this time?" Let me tell you. Surprised by the duration of the baronet's bath, Chivvy had been sent out to reconnoitre at the very moment when the timorous Sir John hopped from his tree in the valley below. Seeing nothing in the paddock save a drowsing horse and a tumbled blanket, Chivvy returned hastily to the cottage and rehearsed his tidings. The ladies jumped to their feet, and stared blankly into each other's faces. Something had happened! The baronet had either lost his reason or he had been kidnapped.

In an instant the three of them were rushing down the garden path.

So you see, ladies and gentlemen, I knew as well as your worships that our old friend Chivvy and the two ladies in the drawing-room ought to be doing something in this matter; and, by your worships' leave, I bring them upon our stage, through the little green door in the creeper-clad wall, just as Sir John, naked but for Miss Vince's slipper, makes a dash for that very entry.

The sight of the two ladies at this moment was too much for the poor baronet. It was the last straw on the camel of his nakedness. With a shout that might have brought tears to your honours' eyes an you had heard it, our worthy gentleman flung up his arms, fell flat upon his face, and lay there crying hysterically;

while the infuriated mob—the constable was stout, and moved slowly—surged about him, beating him with sticks, spurning his aching body with their big boots, and urging all the terriers and curs that pushed between their legs to attack his quivering flesh.

Into this mob, like a true hero of romance, broke the redoubtable Chivvy, and wresting a cudgel from a yokel's hand, laid about him in such vigorous fashion that the attackers were obliged to give way before him. "Infernal cowards!" cried he. "You infernal cowards!" And then seeing the parson among them, "You're a damned blackguard," says he.

Up came the perspiring constable.

"Saunders," said the clergyman, "arrest this person," pointing to Sir John, flat on his face. "I charge him with indecently exposing himself. Arrest him!"

But Saunders, the constable, his face radiant with smiles, was standing with feet together, the toes at an angle of forty-five degrees, shoulders squared, his hand at the salute; and Captain Chivvy was saying, "Hullo, Corporal Saunders!" to the utter confusion of the parson and everybody else in the group.

Then came forward Jane Vince with the blanket, and flinging it gently over the body of Sir John, immediately departed, calling back from the little green door that Captain Chivvy should bring Sir John into the cottage.

Chivvy whispered to Saunders, Saunders whispered to the parson, and while the last not ungraciously bade the villagers depart, Chivvy assisted Sir John to rise with the blanket about his person, and escorted him with womanly tenderness through the green door into the cottage. And thither, in a minute or two's time, followed the frowning parson and the beaming constable.

CHAPTER X

Which treats of more than one Religion

WHILE Captain Chivvy assisted the broken baronet to Miss Vince's bedroom, Saunders, the constable, enlarged upon that officer's merits to the rector, Mr. Paul Orviss. "I was his bâtman once," said the policeman proudly, sticking the fingers of his right hand between his belt and the tunic; "so I know all about the captain, I do. Eh, sir, if all officers were like him there'd be no bother about recruitin'! Why, the men fairly worshipped him! It wasn't that he didn't flare up when occasion demanded, you must understand; but he treated the men like men, took an interest in them, didn't rag 'em for nothing, and was always ready—ay, that he was—to get a fellow out of a hole. That's his point. Nothing was too great a bother for the captain when it came to getting a chap out of a hole."

"But all this is beside the present question," said the rector, from the deepest chair in Jane's room. "What we have to decide is whether this baronet—what's his name?—is to be arrested for indecently exposing himself."

The parson, ladies and gentlemen, was tall and spare, small-headed, sharp-eyed, with long limbs and a humorous mouth. The hair on his little, round head, where it had not fallen under the scythe of Time, was grey, and the close-clipped whiskers on his otherwise clean-shaven face were grey also. If there was humour in the long, thin mouth, there was the heart's own merriment in his small, deep-sunken grey eyes. But all the merriment in those eyes of his could be frozen into hard sternness when occasion demanded.

"As for arresting the baronet," said Saunders, squaring his shoulders, "I'm prepared to do my duty at all costs. But I am of opinion that we shall hear something from the captain when he comes downstairs which will render such a step as that what you might call a bit ultra. For the baronet being a friend of the captain, there isn't no hole too small for the baronet to get into, but what the captain will get him out of it if he puts his mind to it."

"We can't have naked men running loose about the parish," said the parson, crossing his legs.

"Excuse me, sir, you don't know what you can have when the captain's in a business," answered the constable firmly.

At this point Captain Chivvy entered the room, wearing a troubled look, his large eyes heavy with anxiety, his eyebrows higher than ever in the wrinkled forehead, his lips close set. But it was noticeable that he had brushed his hair during his absence, and that he had given a careful twist to the ends of his little black moustache.

Saunders clicked his heels together, and stood at attention. The parson watched the soldier under his eyebrows.

"My friend Sir John Sparrow is much shaken, sir," said Chivvy in his politest voice; "but he insists upon coming downstairs to explain his conduct *in propria persona*. In the meantime, may I offer.you anything?

I am sorry to say there is no wine in the house, for my hostess is a vegetarian, which also means a teetotaler; but there is tea or milk!"

"Your hostess, sir," said the parson, his eyes twinkling, "is something more than a vegetarian. She's a public nuisance."

Chivvy smiled. "In what way, sir?" said he.

"She comes into my parish," said the parson, sitting up in his chair, "and she goes from cottage to cottage with vegetarian tracts, dosing my sick with vegetarian remedies which nearly kill them, and advocating fads and crotchets which might very easily undermine the body politic. If this were not enough, the good lady has lately taken it into her capacious head to indulge in what she calls, I understand, sun-baths, an amusement which consists in exposing her naked body to the rays of the sun and to the gaze of anybody who happens to be passing by the fields in which she thus disports herself. This last fad, sir, has scandalised the whole neighbourhood, and I have determined to put a stop to it. One faddist, sir, shall not be allowed to play hankey-pankey with a whole community."

"I see exactly what you mean," said Chivvy, smiling all over his face. Then he laughed softly. "By George!" said he, "a lady with Miss Vince's notions must be the very devil in a village. Lord! what a firebrand! Something like a barrack-room lawyer in a regiment." He looked at Saunders.

The constable slapped his leg, and chuckled till his face grew purple.

"I am glad you appreciate my position," said the rector, twinkling.

"My dear sir," rejoined Chivvy heartily, "I see exactly how you are placed."

"I must put a stop to Miss Vince's eccentricities,"

said the parson, "and this is my opportunity. Your friend must go before the magistrates for indecently exposing himself. I am sorry for him, but I must save my people."

The door opened, and our hero, clothed and in his right mind, entered the drawing-room.

"I should hardly have recognised you," said the parson.

"Clothes," said our hero, "as Carlyle has pointed out, either add to or subtract from our dignity; they either magnify the man or they humble him. But the philosopher did not go deeply into this matter, did not arrive at the logical conclusion to his thesis, which is that clothes, being contrary to Nature, and in many subtle ways injurious to true spiritual development (as in the notorious case of vain women), ought to be discarded altogether, or, where climatic conditions render this consummation impossible, cut down to the very lowest necessity. For hygienic reasons, too, it is essential that the body be exposed to the sun and air as often as possible, and I was making my first experiment in this matter, when a series of unlooked-for eventualities forced me into the predicament which, for all its distressing nature, has had one pleasant feature, in that it has given me the pleasure of your acquaintance."

"You are a vegetarian, I presume?" said the parson. Sir John inclined his head. "I need hardly ask you that question," said the parson, turning to our friend Captain Chivvy.

"I am not a vegetarian in practice, sir," answered the soldier, "but I really do believe that we should all be very much better if we gave up eating so much animal food. For people with the gout——"

"You miss the point, my dear Chivvy," put in the

baronet, sitting down. "For it is not only to secure an immunity from bodily afflictions that we adopt a vegetarian diet, but far. rather to aid and abet that growth in spiritual development without which man would be no better than the animals he so mercilessly slaughters for his daily food. But this is not the occasion for a protracted argument, and I am somewhat shaken by the events of the day; therefore I will confine myself to an explanation of these unhappy events, as I understand that I have rendered myself liable to pro-secution on the ridiculous grounds of going as my Maker fashioned me among my fellow human beings."

The shrewd parson saw from all this that Sir John Sparrow took himself so seriously that he could by no possible means be taken seriously by anybody else. "Put your mind at rest, sir, on the score of prosecu-tion at least," said he, "for I am quite certain your explanation will render so drastic a step unnecessary. Nevertheless, I am curious to hear your story, and if you feel well enough to relate it, you will find me a greedy as well a grateful listener. As for the constable, his presence here must be something of a menace to you, and I have no doubt he will gladly be relieved from further attendance."

"I'm so frightfully sorry," said Chivvy, jumping up and going to his old friend the corporal, "so frightfully sorry that I can't offer you a drink, Saunders; for, as I told you, these confounded vegetarians are always teetotalers as well! But——" And here the gallant officer put something into the broad palm of the constable, and wringing his hand, inquired tenderly after Mrs. Saunders, asked how many children there were, and followed the corporal out of the room to show him due honour at the doorstep.

In the meantime Sir John, with a very solemn face,

related to the merry-eyed parson how he had been chased from Miss Vince's paddock by a fierce dog; how he had sought refuge in the branches of a tree; how three ladies had discovered him there; and how—thinking that these ladies were departed—he had descended from the tree, only to find a yelling mob rushing up the hill to do him grievous bodily injury. "The rest of my painful story," said Sir John very sadly, "is, I believe, already in your possession."

Captain Chivvy, who had returned during the baronet's narration, here informed the rector that Miss Vince would be glad to make his acquaintance if he cared to see her. Parson Orviss—the serious baronet having put him in excellent conceit with himself—expressed his willingness to discuss matters with Miss Vince, adding cheerfully that if he succeeded in persuading her to leave the neighbourhood, it would be the best day's work he had done since he had taken Holy Orders. So Chivvy went for the lady.

Miss Vince entered the room with a beaming face. The parson jumped up from his chair and stood, tall and erect, with his back to the mantelpiece. Miss Vince bestowed upon him a little pleasant nod, and made her way with rustling skirts to the sofa. The parson watched her under his eyebrows.

"This has been an eventful day!" exclaimed Jane cheerfully.

"It has," said the parson.

"I really think," went on Jane, "that dogs ought to be chained up. People have no business to let them go running about loose."

"I suspect, madam," said the parson, "that the sheep-dog in question did not find his way into your field unaided."

"Good gracious!" cried Jane, her little eyes wide

open; "you don't mean to say that dog was actually set upon Sir John Sparrow?"

"I mean," quoth the parson, "that people in the village object strongly to the sight of naked men and women in the neighbourhood."

"The rural population," put in Sir John, "are always behind the times."

"It would be as well," laughed Parson Orviss, "if vegetarians would get behind something, even the *Times*, when they go naked into open fields. And as for a backward rural population, sir, you will find, I think, if you try a sun-bath in the middle of Trafalgar Square that the population of London is no whit behind them in this matter."

"Very true," said the baronet seriously.

"The world is not ripe for us," said Jane. "As a brother of mine always used to put it, we are 'before our time.'"

"Pardon me, madam," said the rector, "but how can it be that you are in advance of your time when one of your ambitions, as I understand it, is to return to the conditions of the Garden of Eden?"

"There are some backward steps," said Sir John, "which, though they seem backward, are in reailty strides forward. Thus when we see an evil person forsake his iniquity, we say that he has *returned* to virtuous ways. Or when a mortal takes that greatest of all strides forward, the step across the river of death, we say rightly that he has *gone back* to God. And so in our endeavour to return to the age of innocence—in our struggle to regain the old simplicity and natural-ness of our first parents—we are in reality taking such a step forward as the world has never known."

"Reculer pour mieux sauter!" quoted Chivvy, pronouncing the words in such a manner as prevented anyone from recognising the phrase.

"You hold, then," asked the parson, "that the whole world has blundered into a wrong diet?"

"The few flesh-eating nations of the world's myriad population," answered the baronet gravely, "have come to think that a diet adopted under special circumstances, and permitted by the Creator for His own excellent reasons, is their one and natural means of supporting mortality. But this is not so. And our faith is that God would have us return to Edenic fare, in order that we may shake off all those ills of the body which are the result of wrong feeding, and which monopolise much of our attention to the great detriment of higher and nobler aspirations."

"Our blessed Lord, sir," said the parson, "made no reference to this subject."

"Our blessed Lord, sir," rejoined the baronet, "belonged to the sect of the Essenes, and the Essenes, we are given to understand, were vegetarians. But I do not wish to labour that point. Sufficient is it for me that our blessed Lord commanded that we should love one another, for on that direction I found both my religion and my vegetarianism. I could not now eat meat, however much I desired it, because I have learned to care for dumb animals, and because my sympathies extend to the slaughterman and the butcher. It is in no vaunting spirit that I make this boast, for I can assure you that the cultivation of this spirit of love— the development of the power of sympathy—brings one a thousand heartaches and soul-tortures of which hitherto one was blissfully ignorant."

"I honour you, sir, for these sentiments," said the parson. "But forgive me if I express my surprise that you should speak reverently of the Catholic religion, for I have always understood that vegetarians deny the salvation of Christianity, and are never weary of doing all that in them lies to hinder the work of the Church." Here the parson regarded Jane Vince with unblinking directness.

That good lady smiled all over her rosy face. "We cannot all think alike, can we?" said she, looking from the parson to the baronet, from the baronet to the captain. "And we must be loyal to our convictions, even when our convictions disagree with our neighbours'. Let us, whatever else we are, be just. As my sister's eldest son said of his headmaster at school, 'Temple is a beast, but a just beast.' That is what we should all be; for it is quite certain that every man is more or less of a beast to his neighbour. A bachelor uncle of mine often used to say that he had never yet met the man he would wish to call his son; and yet, of course, many of the men he had met were their mothers' darlings, or their wives' ideal. And so, I hope"—here Jane beamed again—"that I may expect toleration for my views, which are not altogether the views of the people in this neighbourhood."

"You are not a Christian?" asked Sir John, with much interest.

Jane shook her head a little sadly. "Not quite in the same way as Mr. Orviss understands the term. In principle, yes; in detail—well, not quite. We should only quarrel over the names, I expect. I am like a cousin of my brother's wife," she added, beginning to shake, "who on the subject of names often used to say that he could not understand why a family which spelt its name C-h-o-l-m-o-n-d-e-l-e-y should pronounce it Marshbanks! Oh, dear! What a witty fellow he was! He used to tell the story of how he once went into a music-shop and asked for 'Moses in Egypt,' and the man told him that he was out of 'Moses,' but could supply him with 'Ehren on the Rhine'! I don't suppose it was really true, you know; I expect he made it up himself; but it was very clever of him, wasn't it? Aaron on the Rhine!"

"Do I understand," asked Sir John, who had preserved a perfectly grave countenance through these remarks, "do I understand that you are a Roman Catholic, or a Dissenter?"

Jane laughed. "I am all that, I suppose, in a way; because my religion teaches me to regard with favour all things that work for good; but in reality I am a theosophist!"

"A theosophist!" exclaimed Sir John. "You interest me a great deal. Pray, will you tell us the principles of this religion, for, I am sorry to confess it, I know nothing of its teachings, nothing at all?"

The parson went over to Miss Vince, extending his hand. "I must bid you farewell," said he, smiling good-naturedly. "Believe me, I would be a just beast if I could, and listen with the enthusiasm of Sir John Sparrow to your definition of theosophy; but, madam, time is short, and one religion is enough for a man who has work to do in the world. And so, believing my religion to be a very serviceable one for making people happier and better, I stop my ears to the attractions of Buddha, and bid you good-bye."

"Good-bye," said Jane, rising from her sofa with a merry face. "And whatever you think of theosophy, I hope you will at least think more kindly of vegetarianism."

"I must tell you," said the baronet to the parson—he had risen with Miss Vince, "that vegetarianism, strictly speaking, is not the best nor the natural diet. The form of eating which I practise, and which I intend to advocate in the future—a diet undoubtedly best fitted for man's growth in purity—is not vegetarian, but fruitarian. I advise fruit—pure, uncooked fruit. For a little reflection will convince you that the primeval diet of our race could not have included such things as beans, haricots, cabbages, potatoes, and brussel sprouts; but that it must have been obviously confined, solely and entirely, to the fruits which grew and ripened in the sun without cultivation or any adscititious aids from man."

"I will go," said the parson, "ere you reduce me still further. For if animal food is wrong, and vegetarianism is wrong, fruitarianism—ere we get to the end of your arguments—may be wrong also. The protoplasm, I opine, sucked nutriment from fogs and vapours. Good-bye."

"Truth," said the baronet in a tone of reproach, "must be sought painfully."

"You take a gloomy view of the Creator!" smiled the parson.

"Ah, I agree with you, sir," said Chivvy, striking in with enthusiasm. "Why should we make this life a penance? Why should we deny ourselves this, that, and the other thing? We didn't ask to be born. We didn't form our own natures. We are not responsible for the appetites of the body. Look what a man inherits from his parents! Confound it all! our wills are formed before we can say Yes or No; we are what we shall be at eighty when we are sucking a coral or dribbling on to our bibs! I agree with you entirely. I don't believe God wants us to be so mighty sad. I believe—I say it with reverence, for no man in the world can hate irreverence more than I do——"

"Ah!" interrupted the lively Jane, "that puts me in mind of my dear old uncle, the clergyman. He used to say of irreverence, 'It's worse than wicked, it's vulgar!' And really when one thinks of it, it is, isn't it? Worse than wicked; it's vulgar."

Chivvy took the interruption good-naturedly. He stopped short in his passionate tirade, smiled at the right moment, and then looked helplessly towards the parson.

"Yes?" said the clergyman encouragingly. "What is it you say with all reverence?"

"Why," quoth Chivvy, in a quieter voice, "that the Almighty smiles oftener than He frowns when He looks on this ant-heap."

"Perhaps He does," said the parson, smiling for his part cheerfully enough. He turned to Miss Vince. "One word in farewell. Remember that a small village is not prepared for revolutionary ideas. Convert the cities first if you must convert anybody, and then come to us. While the cities remain indifferent, leave the villages in peace. For—I must tell you, madam, at the risk of paining you—the notions you scatter among my people, while they do not win them to vegetarianism, stir up in them a bitterness and a scorn that are not Christian, so you see we are both losers. You do not make them better; you make them worse! And, for pity's sake, give up sun-baths!"

Then he went, with Chivvy to see him off.

"There goes a good man," said the baronet, as the door closed on the parson; "a good man, but blind."

"He is fulfilling his mission," said Jane comfortably. "In his present stage of development he cannot do more."

The baronet drew his chair closer. "And now tell me," he said very earnestly, "about theosophy."

Before Jane could reply to this eager request the door opened, and the fair and fluffy Miss Frisby, with Captain Chivvy in attendance, entered the room. "Ah,

I am so sorry!" said she, all in a flutter; "so sorry that your first sun-bath was this terrible fiasco. But you must not let it prejudice you against the theory. Of course you cannot hope to derive the great benefit from it, after having taken oh, such dreadfully violent exercise in the hot sun, and having received such a great number of unpleasant shocks——"

"I fear," said Sir John, "that I must have given you a shock."

Miss Frisby smiled and blushed. "Oh, please don't think about me; ah, no, please do not; though I must confess I was a little horrified, alarmed, shocked—all that—on opening the wall door to see you——"

"Yes, yes," said the baronet self-reproachfully; "you must have been. Most unfortunate!"

"To see you in your own skin like that," said Chivvy, smiling, "very nearly made me jump out of my own, I can tell you!"

"Oh, you! you were splendid!" exclaimed Miss Frisby, with enthusiasm. "The way you set about those horrid villagers was heroic, glorious. And when you called the clergyman a dreadful word, such a dreadful word—I could have kissed you. Oh, I could really. It was superb, magnificent. I hoped that you would knock him, I did really; I could not help it."

"Come, come, this is shocking," Jane commented, with deep chuckles. "And here is Sir John Sparrow longing to know all about theosophy, the religion of love and sympathy! My dear Eleanor Frisby, you will make him think we are as great hypocrites as the Christians themselves. Pray do not be so intensely human!"

Miss Frisby had wheeled round on her chair to where Sir John sat long before Jane had made an end of her admonishment. She thrust her face into Sir John's her eyes expressing the most sincere interest, her little eyebrows caught into a pucker of mental concentration, and thus addressed him: "Oh, ·this is charming, perfectly charming! You really feel drawn towards the religion of the East? You really—ah, but this is magnificent! Is it not what I always declare, dear Jane, that the vegetarianism breaks up all the old prejudices, all the old ideas, and makes of the mind a clean sheet for the pencil of the Truth? It is superb, it is glorious! Another convert, another disciple! And now that you have come to the light, ah! you must bring the gallant Captain Chivvy as well. You must not leave him in the dreadful darkness. He must share your good fortune, must he not? Oh, Captain Chivvy, you will come too, will you not?"

These last sentences were uttered with the lady's face not a hand's breadth from the countenance of Captain Chivvy; for in reaching that part of her speech where his name was mentioned Miss Frisby had jerked her chair round, dragged it a foot or two forward, and sat with her knees touching the knees of Chivvy.

"I shall have much pleasure," said he very politely. "It's awfully good of you to take such an interest in me. I always have said, ever since I went with my regiment to India, that there's a great deal more in theosophy than people think. Take the case of our own missionaries."

"Yes, yes?" cried Miss Frisby, drawing her chair closer.

"Well, from what I saw of them——"

While Captain Chivvy and Miss Frisby dropped into this tête-à-tête, Sir John Sparrow turned his head in the direction of Jane Vince.

"Will you tell me about theosophy?" said he very earnestly. "At present I know nothing about it."

"Oh, dear, you mustn't ask me!" cried Jane, laughing. "I'm only a beginner, and it takes a lifetime to understand it."

"That's rather a drawback in a religion, isn't it?" said Sir John.

"Exactly what I thought at first," answered the beaming Jane, "but in reality it isn't at all. For you must know, my dear Sir John, that all the parts of it you don't understand in this life you will understand perfectly in another incarnation. It seems that theosophy is so true a religion that it will last us in other states of existence as well as in this; we go on learning more and more about it through all our incarnations, until at last we understand the whole thing."

"And then what happens?" asked Sir John.

"Why, then, of course, we are swallowed up into Nirvana, don't you see, and the whole thing comes to an end."

Sir John considered. "What are the beginnings of this creed?" said he critically. "It sounds to me a very natural religion, and I find myself strangely predisposed in its favour, but I should like to know something about it before I commit myself to it entirely. Will you, then, tell me its elements?"

Jane smoothed her skirts and smiled in a state of collapse. "I'll do my best," said she, "but really it's an awful task. For, to tell you the truth, I don't think I quite understand the beginnings myself. You see one can enjoy bits of a thing without caring very much about the rest. Like a dear nephew of mine who used to say when he got a difficult egg at breakfast that 'parts of it were excellent.' You see what I mean? I can assure you that parts of theosophy are excellent, without knowing anything about the rest. But according to my notions the religion is really something like this. Each person, to begin with, is a part of the divine——"

"I hold that," said Sir John.

"And each person has been living for ever and ever. We have existed in ants and bees, in dogs and cats, in sheep and oxen, in horses and giraffes, and goodness knows what else beside, before ever we existed in human shape. And we have been human beings over and over again. You, for instance, have very likely been a Roman senator, a Greek poet, an Italian noble- man, a French king, perhaps even a London Lord Mayor. Isn't it wonderful?"

"It is, it is," said Sir John. "Pray continue!"

"Well, then, having been all this, we are taught to regard life in any form as sacred. We mustn't hurt or kill anything that has life. We must love everything on earth more than we love ourselves, and we mustn't love our fellow human beings more than we love our 'little brothers,' the animals. Isn't that a beautiful idea?"

"Beautiful, beautiful," said Sir John, with suppressed enthusiasm.

"It makes a kind of brotherhood of all the inhabi- tants of the world," went on Jane, "though it is really a little difficult sometimes to think that we have any connection with beetles and—you know what! Some- times quite unconsciously I kill an insect, and then——"

Sir John shuddered.

"Oh, it is dreadful," went on Jane; "for you see I put that poor little life back in its gradual evolution towards Nirvana—it may be millions of years. It has got to begin all over again! Isn't it dreadful? But that's what I say about all religions; if they're com- forting one moment, they're a nuisance the next." ·

Sir John nodded his head sympathetically. He was profoundly interested.

"But, mind you," said genial Jane, "I haven't told you a *fraction* of the real thing! You must go and see Mr. Skyler; he'll tell you everything, and *so* clearly. He's reached Kâmaloka, you know, which is the astral plane, and he can, of course, see the spiritual world just as clearly as you and I see trees and hills. Isn't it wonderful?" .

Sir John had pulled out his pocket-book. "Mr. Sky——?" he asked, pencil in hand.

"Skyler," answered Jane. "S-k-y-l-e-r, Mr. Caraway Skyler. You'll find him at the Martyrs' Hall; he's the manager of the literary department of the Vegetarian Universal League."

Sir John thanked the lady, replaced his pocket-book, announced very gravely that he would call upon Mr. Skyler on the following day, and then rose to depart.

Miss Vince at this point told Miss Frisby how she had recommended Sir John Sparrow to call upon Mr. Skyler, and Miss Frisby swimming towards the baronet began such an eulogy of this great Mr. Skyler that the head of our poor baronet began to swim.

He heard a confusion of such terms as Manas, Kama, Kâmarûpa, Devachan, Dûgpas, Nin-mâ-pa, Gelûgpa, Nir-mânakaya, Chela, and the Lord knows what else beside. He laid his hands upon the back of a chair. The lady rattled on at express speed. Her eyeglasses blinded him. He closed his eyes. His knees began to tremble. Still she rushed on. A dew started suddenly from his forehead. A great shudder passed through his body. On, on went the enthusiastic Miss Frisby. Then he collapsed upon the floor in a heap.

"Ah, the sun-bath has been too much for him!" cried Eleanor.

"Brandy!" said Chivvy.

"Not a drop in the house!" exclaimed Jane. "Oh,

dear me, what can we give him? There's some soda-water." And out she flew from the room, her good-natured heart in a flutter.

Captain Chivvy loosened Sir John's collar, fanned him with his handkerchief, and sent Miss Frisby—who remained perfectly calm—for water and sponge.

In the end, after bathing the poor gentleman's forehead, and holding smelling salts to his nose for five minutes—without one single soda-water bottle being opened—he came to, sat up, and looked about him.

"He must sleep here," said Jane.

"No, no," whispered the baronet, clinging like a frightened child to his friend Chivvy.

"Oh, but you must," said Jane affectionately; "you're quite unfit for a railway journey. You shall have my room, and be quite quiet."

"Take me away, Chivvy," whispered the baronet.

"Don't you think you'd be better here?" asked Chivvy, as tender as a woman. "Don't you think you would, dear old fellow?"

"No, no!" whispered the baronet. "Take me away. For God's sake take me away. I won't be caught. It's a trap, Chivvy, a trap! Take me away; stick to me, Chivvy; don't leave me!"

"Ah, that sun-bath has affected him!" cried Miss Frisby. "It was a terrible fiasco. What a thousand pities! Oh, to think of such a beginning! I am so sorry, so very, very sorry! Ah, it was terrible!"

And the end of this adventure was that Sir John Sparrow, fainting and swooning all the way, returned to town under the tender guardianship of Captain Chivvy —who informed him in his rational moments over the evening paper that had he, Chivvy, been at his club he would have won twenty pounds over the Jessamine filly, a horse he had always meant to back the next

time it ran—and was handed over to the remorseless
Tiplady.

"Ah!" said the butler, with acerbity, "this is what
comes of bathing-drawers where there isn't any water!"

"Give me an apple," said Sir John.

CHAPTER XI

Wherein it is told how Doctor Eaves disputed with Sir John Sparrow, together with the troubles encountered by our Hero at Margate

FINDING himself on the following morning too weak to leave his bed, the worthy baronet sadly relinquished his intention of paying Mr. Caraway Skyler a visit at the Martyrs' Hall, and even permitted Tiplady to go forth in search of a doctor. The butler, faithful to the true interests of his deluded master, gave the physician a full account of the baronet's eccentricities, and counselled him to insist in his prescription on a more natural and sustaining diet.

"Leave the matter to me, my good fellow," said the doctor, "for unless your master wants a certificate for Bedlam he shall eat a pound of beefsteak before Big Ben strikes two this afternoon."

On entering the baronet's bedroom, followed by Tiplady, Doctor Eaves—for such was the physician's name—went briskly to the bed, and without salutation of any kind seized upon the baronet's wrist, laid his fingers on the pulse, and jerked a large gold watch out of his waistcoat pocket, all in a single moment of time. But this was not all; for while he held the wrist in one hand and the watch in the other the doctor bent upon the startled baronet such a frightful and terrifying look as might have driven the stoutest nerves into a very frenzy of alarm. And as by nature the doctor's face was of a ghostly and saturnine character —his complexion being grey, his cheeks hollow, and his eyes deep sunken—this fixed, frightful and penetrating expression was all the more disquieting to the nerves of our invalid.

After a long silence, during which Sir John could hear his own heart struggling to outrace the quick ticking of a carriage clock on the mantelpiece, the doctor dropped his patient's wrist as suddenly as he had seized upon it, and popped the watch into his pocket.

"Have you made your will?" said he, taking up his hat.

"I beg your pardon?" cried the baronet, breaking into a cold sweat.

"Have you made your will?" repeated the doctor sternly.

"You don't mean to say——"

"You had better summon your friends," said the physician, making a move to the door.

Sir John considered the matter for a moment, and then raised himself upon his pillow. "This is very sudden," said he, in his level voice, as polite as possible. "I had no idea, the thought had not even crossed my mind, that the end of this mortal experience was at hand. It is a little startling; but I am sorry if I should appear to you in any way upset by the intelligence. For to the true philosopher there can be nothing either terrifying or unwelcome in drawing the sword-soul from its corporeal sheath in order that one may fight the spiritual battle in other spheres ; and in a few moments, when I have recovered from the somewhat abrupt manner in which you have conveyed to me this really unimportant matter, I shall be in a position to discuss the question with you in a quiet and rational manner. I beg you to be seated."

The doctor sat down.

"Oh, my dear master!" exclaimed Tiplady, coming forward so suddenly that the baronet jumped in his bed. "If you had only gone on eating like an ordinary Christian gentleman this would never have happened! Whatever shall I say to Mr. Shott and Mrs. FitzGerald? What will they say to me, who sat still and saw you slowly committing suicide with haricots and lentils, which fill the body with wind and the brain with delusions? Oh, if you had never left the village where you were loved by man, woman, and child! To think of you dying in middle-age, the best gentleman in England, the kindest master in the world!—going out like a candle, with no warning to speak of, and leaving me and Mr. Shott and Mrs. FitzGerald alone in the dark! It's a tragedy, and all owing to common beans and vegetarian messes."

"I beg you not to distress me, Tiplady," said the baronet. "Your grief, I am sure, is sincere, and it is pleasant for me to reflect on my deathbed that we have been something more than master and servant; but in relations of this kind, my good fellow, there are limits which must not be overstepped, as I have been always careful to point out to you; and though I have encouraged you to speak openly with me on the problems of the world—thereby, I like to think, broadening your mind and enlarging your sympathies—it is not seemly that a servant should load his master with reproaches at the moment when that master is preparing to meet his Maker."

"If you have taught me to broaden my mind, Sir John," replied the butler, very grave, "you have also

M

taught me to love you—at a distance, of course, and with due respect to your position; and it is this love which makes me bold to say that it would have been better for you, better for me, better for Mr. Shott and Mrs. FitzGerald if you had never got your knife into the butcher, and taken up with this vegetarianism."

The doctor jumped to his feet.

"Go," said he to Tiplady, in a voice of stern command; "go instantly to the butcher and bring back two pounds of beefsteak. Cook it half through, and bring it here instantly."

"Any vegetables?" said Tiplady at the door.

"Not a pea!" said the doctor.

"My dear sir," said Sir John, as the door closed on the butler, "if you are counting upon my eating the flesh of any animal, you are making, I must inform you, a vast mistake. The one thought torturing my pillow at the present moment is the reflection that it was only in middle life I learned to appreciate the horror and barbarity of a carnivorous diet; that for so many years ate without pang of any kind the dead flesh of poor sentient animals, thereby participating in the cruel act of their destruction, and in the inevitable demoralisation of the red-handed slaughterman."

The doctor listened with a perfectly grave face to all this, and so soon as the baronet had ceased speaking, remarked in a matter-of-fact voice: "You must eat it nearly raw, taking care to masticate it well. Don't bolt it. Let it mix freely with the saliva before it finds its way into the digestive organs."

"Forgive me," replied Sir John gently, "but you do not seem to have understood my meaning."

"Beefsteak," said the doctor, "is usually spoilt by over-cooking. In order that its beneficent juices may be preserved, it is of the first importance that it should be grilled as lightly as possible. But this necessitates slow and deliberate mastication. Are your teeth in good order?"

"I am at a loss to understand you," said Sir John wearily. "I have told you as plainly as I can that I do not eat animal food. I am a vegetarian, or rather, I should say, a fruitarian. For while vegetarianism is to be preferred before kreophagy, fruitarianism—since it is obviously man's natural diet—is to be preferred before vegetarianism.

"Some doctors," said the physician dryly, "believe in chicken. They like the white flesh, and they consider that the more delicate flavour tempts the invalid to go on eating. But, for my own part, I believe that an invalid can feed on nothing better than beefsteak, under-done beefsteak; for his very weakness is stimulated by the sight of the rich red flesh, while its full, deep flavour creates in him an insatiable craving for strong meat, which is fifty times more to the purpose than a mere tickling of the appetite. The logic here is irresistible. Offer a bankrupt the opportunity of making a shilling, and you do not move him from the depression of mind into which his circumstances have thrown him; you cannot entice him with delicacies; but set before him the chance of making three or four millions, and he throws off his lassitude and becomes as keen a money-maker as he was before his failure."

"I do not appreciate the force of your reasoning," said the baronet, beginning to sit up; "and I can show you where the fallacy lies without making any great call on my strength. Now, if your bankrupt is a moral man, whose very failure has been brought about by discovering that both the shilling and the three or four millions are objects of no real and eternal value, the opportunity you give him of acquiring all the wealth of the Indies will merely serve to disgust him. In any case, animal food—

chicken or steak—appears to me something so horrible and revolting that the very thought of eating it fills me with nausea, and even if I knew that the consumption of a mere spoonful would save my life I should refuse to do so."

"Mind you," said the doctor, greatly interested, "I am not altogether opposed to chicken, but I hold and affirm that in ninety-nine cases out of a hundred beef-steak—as raw as possible—is likely to prove fifty times more efficacious. I stick to fifty times."

"You may possibly be thinking," put in the baronet, leaning on an elbow, "that my contempt for death is assumed and unnatural. But I assure you, sir, it is very real and sincere. I will tell you why. When the soul has once realised that its existence on this earth at any given time is only one in a long series of incarnations, there can be no sorrow or regret in speeding through the brief passage of death to further and greater experiences. For instance, I do not regard myself as John Sparrow, an English gentleman, but as an Ego who for the time being is merely playing that trivial part. In other incarnations I may have been a Roman senator, a Greek poet, a French king, an Indian rajah——"

"The last lunatic I met," said the doctor, "told me that he was Emperor of China."

"And no doubt there was some foundation for that belief," answered the baronet. "It is ridiculous to suppose that the human mind could harbour such an exalted idea without cause of any kind whatsoever. Very possibly, millions of years ago, the lunatic of whom you speak was an Emperor of China, and in his madness he passes back over his thousand and one incarnations and confuses with his present existence that dim existence in the eternity behind us."

"I gave him beefsteak," answered the doctor, beginning to walk up and down the room.

"Your extraordinary mania for beefsteak," replied Sir John, "convinces me that in a very recent incarnation you were either a slaughterman, or perhaps even an ox. Beefsteak seems to be the sun of your intellectual system, round which all your thoughts revolve in as narrow an orbit as a soup-plate. I should endeavour, if I were you—in order that you may speed your spiritual development in future incarnations —to exclude from your mind rigorously and firmly all thoughts that touch at the fringe of beefsteak. Try to think of something else. Cultivate a hobby. There is fretwork, or beekeeping, or stamp collecting—anything that will keep your mind off beefsteak."

The doctor drew a chair to the baronet's bedside and sat down. "You are beginning to interest me," said he, fixing Sir John with a searching look.

"If your mind had not been monopolised by beefsteak I might have interested you sooner," replied the baronet tartly.

"For although you are as mad as a hatter——" went on the doctor.

"Sir!" cried the baronet angrily.

"Ah, that's a bad sign!" the doctor sighed. "I don't like to hear you contradict that statement. It's a bad sign, a very bad sign."

"I must request you to discontinue your attendance," said Sir John, turning away his head.

"Try and talk as little as possible," said the doctor. "I want you to nurse and husband your remaining intellectual strength while I speak to you frankly and fully on the cause of your breakdown. Now, my dear sir, like all people who have temporarily lost their wits, you are convinced that you are sane, and that I am

a lunatic. I want you, then, to get into your mind
this premiss—I am sane, you are a lunatic! Fix that
firmly in your mind.   I don't ask you at present to
decide whose notions on the question of diet are the
right ones; I merely request you to convince yourself
that you are demented, and that I am as rational as
Euclid or Plato.   And now let us carry our discussion
a point further.   Your madness takes the form of
desiring to return to one of the earlier forms of diet.
(I don't mind your keeping your head turned away
from me if you are listening.)   Such a desire is illogical
and impractical.   For while there was a time when man
undoubtedly was a vegetarian, so many thousands of
years have elapsed since that period—during which
time he has adapted his physical apparatus to a wider
and more comprehensive diet—that his body is no
longer capable of assimilating sufficient nourishment
from fruits and vegetables alone.   He can't do it.
Imagine to yourself a scholar who has taken a first
in Greats, suddenly remembering that he learnt his
alphabet by means of bricks, and insisting in all his
future studies on acquiring knowledge by those same
infantile means."

Sir John turned on his pillow.   "Your incapability of
detecting the fallacy in such an argument," said he, "is
strong presumptive evidence that your first premiss
requires to be inverted before we can carry our discussion
further.   For it is very evident that *you* are demented,
and that I am as rational as Plato or Euclid."   Then he
turned round again.

"Animal food," said the doctor, "in some form or
another, is essential to man.   If you refuse beefsteak—
raw beefsteak—then you must take animal food in some
other form.   I notice on your table, for instance, a glass
of milk, and milk is an animal food."

"It is an animal product," said Sir John, turning round.

"It is obtained from a cow," went on the doctor, as the baronet rolled over on the other side; "and before the cow can deliver her milk, she must first of all produce a calf. Now all calves that are born into this world of pain and trouble are not cows; some of them, a very large proportion, are bulls. From the bull-calf you can obtain no milk, and if you wish to support the world on vegetarianism you will need all the fields for the growing of corn, vegetables, and fruits, so that you will have no grass to spare for these bull-calves. What, then, do you, who hold it is wicked to kill, intend to do with them?"

Sir John rolled slowly over. "I had not thought of that," said he.

"It is obvious," went on the doctor, "that these bull-calves should be fattened generously and kindly, and converted, with as little loss of time as possible, into beefsteak."

At this point Tiplady entered the room.

"And those beefsteaks," the doctor continued, "should be carefully cooked; the natural juices should be preserved."

"I have ordered it to be lightly grilled, sir," said Tiplady.

"Dear me, dear me," sighed the baronet to himself, "I really had not considered that point."

"So you see, sir," said the doctor, "vegetarianism breaks down at the outset of our inquiry."

"Very distressing," murmured the baronet. "Yes, yes, these bull-calves are a nuisance. I don't see how to get over them."

"I have convinced you, then," went on the doctor, once more taking up his hat, "that your amiable theory is an impractical dream. Eat your steak slowly, mix each mouthful with saliva, and take care to insist in future that all your meat is lightly cooked. I will call again this afternoon."

As the door closed upon Doctor Eaves, Tiplady went quickly to the baronet's side. "And is it really true, Sir John," said he, "that the doctor has convinced you at last that all this vegetarianism is a fudge?"

"He has convinced me," said the baronet slowly and sorrowfully, "never to drink milk again."

And having uttered this resolution, our worthy hero called for all his vegetarian books, journals, and pamphlets, and began a careful search through them to see if this question of bull-calves had been faced by vegetarian disputants. He found no mention of it, but in turning the pages of his weekly journal he came across an advertisement of some lodgings in Margate where vegetarians were carefully catered for by one Mrs. Hogg. No sooner had Sir John beheld the advertisement than he was seized by a great longing for a sight of the ocean, which was accompanied by as powerful a craving for sea-salt breezes as ever possessed dipsomaniac for strong waters. He yielded instantly to this inclination; bade Tiplady pack their boxes; himself searched for a train in the time-table; and in another hour both the master and the servant were driving in a cab to the railway station. Dr. Eaves—far too shrewd a man to suppose that the baronet had eaten his beef-steak—arrived at Sir John's lodgings to resume his disputation just as the cab deposited baronet and butler at the station.

"I am glad, for one thing," said our hero to Tiplady, "to escape that doctor you brought me; for of all the lunatics jostling the shoulders of sane men I should say your physician was the greatest. Like all such unfortunates, he has his lucid intervals, and one of his arguments was not at all unworthy of a rational mind; but to be attended in sickness by such a crackbrained practitioner is a supposition so dreadful and terrifying that I am glad this good train is putting swift miles between him and me."

"All the same, Sir John," answered the butler, "he gave you the best prescription any doctor could have invented when he sent me out for the beefsteak."

"How can the cause of all our physical ailments," replied the baronet, "produce good effects in the body of a vegetarian?"

"I can't answer that, Sir John," the servant rejoined, "but I can see with my eyes that you are wasting to a shadow with the natural food!"

"The system," replied Sir John, "for so long groaning under bad treatment, demands a certain time in adapting itself to so great a change in diet. But it is wonderful how clear and strong my mind has become, even while my body languishes for the moment. For a thousand thoughts are crowding in upon me, which never before suggested themselves even to my sub-consciousness. I am tortured, Tiplady, by every cracking whip that descends upon a horse's back. If I hear a mother call roughly to her little one I shudder at the thought of a flogging to come. In each case it is as though I was the subject of chastisement."

. "Which seems to me, Sir John," interrupted the servant, "a poor substitute for a sound digestion and a stomach at peace with all the world."

"Would you, then," cried Sir John sadly, "rather have bodily satisfaction than spiritual development? My good Tiplady, I tell you I would sooner be burned by fever, racked by rheumatism, tortured by dyspepsia, and shrivelled by paralysis than lose these faint be-ginnings of a wider sympathy which are now opening

out illimitable worlds to my spiritual vision. There is
no pain in the world but I feel it; no suffering but
I endure it. I lie on my bed at night and think of
the sobbing children, the drunken parents, the reeling
harlot, the cheating tradesman, the groaning horse—
till all nature's travail racks my single heart, and in
my person I make protest to the God who made us.
It is this feeling of thus utterly sharing the load of
humanity which makes me trust, my good Tiplady,
that ere that death comes which your doctor promises
me I may discover some byway to the millennium
of which at present neither philosopher nor Christian
has any knowledge."

After this manner the master and servant discussed
the subject uppermost in their minds, and so passed
away the time in the railway train till they arrived at
Margate. After fighting for their luggage in a noisy
crowd our two travellers secured a fly, and drove away
to the lodgings of Mrs. Hogg. To the baronet's chagrin
and the butler's annoyance they discovered that these
lodgings were situated in a mean street in a suburb of
the town at a considerable distance from the sea. The
house was dirty, with dirt grimed upon the windows,
and dust whirling with scraps of paper on the steps
leading to the front door. Not a window was open.

"This won't do at all, Sir John," said Tiplady firmly.

"It is not what I expected," replied the baronet;
"but I daresay it is better inside. We will try it."

"There are plenty of decent hotels in the town,"
grumbled the butler.

"But not vegetarian," replied the baronet.

So they knocked on the door, and were received—
with considerable astonishment—by Mrs. Hogg. This
good creature had her hair in curling pins, wore a dirty,
coarse apron, and had her sleeves tucked up. She was

of a faded prettiness, with a weak, smiling face, large, gentle eyes, and two hectic splashes on the cheeks. Seeing the character of her callers, she grinned nervously, rolled her sleeves down, and led the way . into a parlour.

"Pooh!" said Tiplady indignantly, and stamped over to the window, which he opened with a bang.

"Yes, the room do feel a bit stuffy, don't it?" said Mrs. Hogg agreeably; "but, there, it's next to impossible to keep a window open here, for the dust do blow in something dreadful, and there's nothing like dust for getting into carpets and antimacassars and spoiling all the furniture, is there? It ain't so bad on the other side, but we have to keep 'em shut there just the same; for the smell of the drains—well, there, it's awful, it is reely! It seems to come right up into your nose, you know; and I'm sure with children about it's dangerous, though I'm thankful to say that none of my nine has suffered this summer, though it never does to boast, I'm sure, does it! No, I'm sure it don't!"

Sir John listened to this dissertation as politely as possible. He was picturing to himself the hard, sordid life of Mrs. Hogg; the nine children clamorous for food, the housework to be done, the rent to be paid, the weekly bills to be discharged, the clothes for the family. Ah, what a travesty of life! And here was the poor woman's opportunity of making a little money. How high that poor heart must be beating! He could not disappoint her; no, not even though Tiplady gave notice on the spot.

"You advertise rooms for vegetarians?" said Sir John softly.

"Years ago I did," returned Mrs. Hogg, smiling. "Half a crown for three insertions they charged me, but nothing ever came of it, and half-crowns aren't to be picked off clothes-lines, are they?—no, I'm sure—and so I said to my husband when they wrote for more half-crowns to go on with the advertisement, I said, 'Well, Alfred,' I said, 'if there's a half-crown to invest,' I said, 'better spend it on a nice brass plate or a new card for the window,' I said, 'for here they'll be before our eyes, and we shall know what we've got for our money,' I said, 'but spending money on advertisements in a London paper is like sending it abroad without knowing the post office at the other end,' I said. And so we give it up," she said resignedly. "Yes, we give it up."

"The advertisement was in the paper last week," said Sir John.

"Lor'! was it, now?" exclaimed the astonished Mrs. Hogg. "Well, there; it's by no orders of mine, so it's no use them coming to me for any more half-crowns, and I can tell 'em so. I suppose what it is they're so badly off for advertisements they're glad to make a show with old ones. Yes, I'm sure."

"You are a vegetarian?" asked Sir John.

"I was once," returned Mrs. Hogg, with a very broad smile. "And once is enough for me. Oh, never again; not if I know it! Of course, it's cheap, and for children, as I always say to Alfred, it's very good, *very* good, I'm sure; but there, the way it makes you sick of a milk-pudding, and takes all the heart out of a basin of porridge. Why, as I said to Alfred, I could eat far more vegetarian food when I took a bit of meat, and enjoy it. Yes, I'm sure. And so," she concluded in the same resigned air, "we give it up; yes, we give it up."

"I," said Sir John, "am a vegetarian."

"Well, there," said Mrs. Hogg, "it suits some, and no doubt of it. But all stomachs aren't built alike, are they? No, I'm sure. What one body can eat and enjoy makes another fairly retch to look at it, don't it?"

There was no protestation of ability to provide Sir John with vegetarian cookery. The absence of all endeavour to secure lodgers struck him as something pathetic.

"Do you think," said he gently, "that you could provide me with the food I require? I am in reality a fruitarian, for I am persuaded that a fruit diet is the most natural, and therefore the best; but I am not very well just now, and I feel it would be wise to temper my usual fruit meals with a few vegetarian dishes—lentils, haricots, macaroni, you know. Do you think you could manage that?"

" I've almost forgotten how to cook the special dishes," replied Mrs. Hogg, looking with a weak smile into the glaring visage of Tiplady; " but I daresay I can rummage out the cookery books somewhere, if the children haven't torn them to bits. I'll go and have a look, if you'll excuse me, and will sit down a moment. I'll show you the bedroom after. Five shillings is what we charge by the week, but if you share the sitting-room, I daresay we could make it seven-and-six for the two. Of course, the bedrooms aren't very large, but they're comfortable, and gas is included, and I'm sure the air up here is just as good as the sea front, though the other's more fashionable. So please sit down, will you? and I'll just pop downstairs and see what I can find of the cookery books."

When the woman had left the room Sir John turned to Tiplady and explained his anxiety to do the poor thing a good turn. Tiplady suggested that he should pay her a week's rent and take his departure without delay. But Sir John, objecting that this would infallibly hurt the poor thing's feelings, announced his intention of staying in the house, and offered Tiplady the opportunity of boarding out if he wished it. The butler, however, resolutely refused to leave his master, and so it was finally decided that the couple should make trial of Mrs. Hogg's cooking for at least a week.

The landlady managed to find a cookery book; and when Sir John had seen his bedroom and made arrangements for supper to be served at eight o'clock, one of the nine children was despatched for a carriage, and baronet and butler took a drive through Margate.

The supper, we are bound to say, tried Sir John very severely. For the plates were yellow and cracked; the cloth was hard and coarse; the knives were stained, the spoons and forks were of tin, and the tumblers were as thick as a wash-basin. Then the cooking! Poor Mrs. Hogg's macaroni and tomato pie was as choking as gruel, as tasteless as water, and ill-looking as pig's wash. The apple pie was little better; and even the dessert, set out on flat pudding-plates, had for Sir John as forbidding an appearance as an Irish stew or an Indian curry.

Unhappy in mind and weary in body, then, our hero retired early to bed, and there gave himself up to meditation. When he blew out the candle which had lighted him to his room the little chamber was instantly filled with a diabolical smell, and in hurriedly snuffing the reeking wick our philosopher burned his fingers. But even this failed, after the first moment of pain, to interrupt the delicious flow of his meditations. In as clammy a feather bed as you can imagine, with the wind rattling the loose windows and shaking the flimsy door, our admirable baronet lay with open eyes dreaming of a millennium when there should be no sordid labour, no poverty, no idle drones, no suffering, no cruelty—nothing save perfect peace, contentment, and philosophy. The walking of someone overhead set his jug rattling in the basin, and all the toilet requisites a-jingling; but he did not heed it. He was threading the delightful ways of his vegetarian colony which had suddenly grown from fifty acres or so till it overspread the entire globe.

Sir John, with these thoughts in his mind, was just dropping off to sleep when he became suddenly aware of a slight irritation on the calf of his leg. He reached down his hand and scratched the spot. Something very lightly, almost imperceptibly, touched his wrist; he imagined it to be the bed-clothes, and, after rubbing the place, once more settled himself down to sleep. But now a sharp irritation on his forearm, and a fiercer pain in the calf of his leg, drove slumber from off his eyelids. His whole body began to creep. Not only the calf of his leg, but the thighs, the ankles, the feet; not only his arms, but his chest, his back, his stomach, and his neck—all began to tingle and itch as though possessed by some all-conquering pins and needles. Sir John began to scratch and rub with a vengeance. He scratched till, as Tennyson once said, he could have shrieked for glory. He scratched, he rubbed, he tore, till his body was in a flame of fever. And still he went on scratching, rubbing, and tearing, feeling all the time as though a million ants were swarming over his body. Then, with a sudden sense of horror, he reached out for the matches, struck a light, and set fire to the wick of his tallow candle.

Standing on the floor, our hero pulled up his night-dress, and in the wavering light of the candle looked over his body. It was all a bold pink; a raw, angry pink, with swellings at every three inches or so. He dropped his gown, and with the candle in his left hand dragged back the bedclothes and peered down upon the rumpled sheet.

"Good gracious!" cried Sir John.

Now in such circumstances as these the natural impulse of man (God-planted, as we suppose) is to wage.

pitiless war upon the enemies of his peace, and by opposing end them. Sir John, at the first sight of his bed, yielded to this impulse, but ere he had put it into effect he drew back with horror, and once more exclaimed, "Good gracious!"—this time, however, with a far greater emphasis.

For to kill even the least of creatures was murder in the eyes of the spiritually awakened baronet. "Are not these," said he to himself, "even these, man's little brothers, sharers with him of the burden of mortality, the mystery of existence, subject like him to all the changes and chances of this mortal life? Let the fool say that they exist for no purpose! To me, do they not wear the livery of God? are they not marked with the impress of creation's finger? and have they not some destiny to work out which now thrills and excites the watching hosts in heaven? I could as well believe that the worlds exist for nothing, as that these little creatures sprang from God's brain for no purpose at all."

The wind stormed at the window, rattled the sash as though a hundred devils were beating at it, lifted the carpet in a great heave from the floor, and blew shrewdly against the legs of our moraliser. The door shook noisily, the wick in the candle fluttered and danced, the curtains swung inwards. It began to be very cold.

Sir John looked longingly at the bed. "If only I could coax them on to the carpet!" said he, shivering.

He wrapped himself in his dressing-gown, got into slippers, hung his eyeglass about his neck, and drew a cane-bottomed chair to the bed. "After all," said he, "by watching these little creatures may I not learn something of their destiny? Darwin gave more than thirty years to earthworms; shall not I spare one night in my life to these?"

So Sir John sat on the cane-bottomed chair, and the fleas occupied the bed. With the candle at his side, his glass in his eye, our philosopher watched with the intentness of a man of science the movements of these little interrupters of his slumber.

"It would almost seem," he sighed, after an hour of this watching, "that they have nothing else to do but hop. Strange! What is the mystery that God has hidden from our eyes beneath this tiny body? Perhaps, even in these wonderful hoppings, these miraculous jumps into the air (for does not the flea spring some hundreds of times its own height?) we may discover a consuming desire for a higher and more exalted place in the scale of creation. For there is nothing more certain than this, that aspiration for something higher and beyond ourselves is the driving force of all humanity, and it is only a sordid and contemptible anthropomorphism which would exclude the flea from the all-embracing purposes of the Creator. When I have acquired the—the astral vision, I will go deeper into this matter."

Then Sir John's thoughts went off to Mr. Caraway Skyler, and he longed with a mighty longing for the acquaintance of that wonderful man. He determined to quit Margate on the following morning, and to go so soon as he set foot in London direct to the Martyrs' Hall. His mind became flooded with the idea of theosophy, and under that soporific influence our gentleman blinked lazily at his "little brothers" in the bed, nodded his head, dropped the monocle from his eye, and gradually fell into an easy slumber, while the tallow candle "burned down in its socket and——"

N

CHAPTER XII

Of Mr. Caraway Skyler and the "Wisdom Religion," with an account of Mr. Spill's pitiable condition *

WITH what feelings of awe does the historian approach this period in the curious and diverting story of Sir John Sparrow! It has been fool's work to follow the aspiring baronet from meat-eating to vegetarianism, from vegetarianism to fruitarianism, and to hint as we went along at that broadening of the sympathies which so quickened his compassion as to make him cudgel his brains day and night to devise some short cut to the Golden Age. 'Twas fool's work, and we did it bravely.

But now——

Oh, reader! Oh, posterity! how shall the historian lead ye from these trivial beginnings into that vast, measureless, ghostly and awful morass whither the intrepid hero of this chronicle is moving at such horrid speed! While he clung, however slackly, to the common God and the Catholic faith, we felt no terror in following him from the highway of life into its queer turnings, its little

---

* To avoid prosecution for the infringement of copyright, the historian must put it on record that much of Mr. Caraway Skyler's exposition appears to be taken *word for word* from well-known theosophical works. The gentleman seems to have been an omnivorous reader, blest with a retentive memory. .

zigzags; while he expressed no antipathy for his native country and the government of this realm, we felt that he did but sport with the unimportant details of existence; but now that he flies with his open mind into a wilderness of disembodied spirits, into a morass where human laughter is never heard, into a bog of chaos, anarchy, and communism, how shall we follow him?

Let us at least go warily.

Sir John did not call upon Mr. Skyler on the first day of his return from Margate, but contented himself with writing a letter to that theosophist, announcing his intention of calling on the following morning. He also addressed a letter to Mr. Alexander Fontey, concerning the immediate foundation of a nature colony.

The next day, after a fruit breakfast, our hero stepped into a hansom cab, and ordered the driver to proceed to the Martyrs' Hall.

Nothing of moment occurred on the journey, but it must be recorded that every time the driver touched his horse with the whip the baronet drew in his breath, muttered an exclamation of pain, and made up his mind never to take cab again.

It was a dark morning, with drizzle in the air; and the Martyrs' Hall, when Sir John entered it, seemed filled with a choking fog. Gas flared with a hissing sound from every bracket in the gloomy corridors. The people pouring through the building—some this way, some that; some whistling, some talking—made the stone floor resound with a hollow tramping of feet disquieting to anyone who had drifted out of the ranks of humanity. Sir John felt unaccountably timid and unhappy. He became conscious of a chilling sense of loneliness. Our little gentleman climbed the stairs slowly and sadly, making way for every charging errand boy and clerk who passed him, with ostentatious politeness. He felt that he must evince an interest in their work. At length, breathless and very unhappy, our hero reached the floor whereon Mr. Caraway Skyler had his offices, and after winding down three or four dark and narrow passages he found himself before a door bearing the name of that theosophist.

Sir John rapped on the door. "Come!" boomed a deep voice from the inside. Sir John opened the door.

Inside the room, seated at a little table, with his back to the window, his face to the door, sat as remarkable a looking man as you shall meet in a life's travel. But not to lead thee, my honoured and well-beloved reader, to expect all the eccentricities and absurdities of Mr. Fontey, let me at the outset explain that what was chiefly remarkable in Mr. Skyler was an almost unearthly calm. Where this calm lay, in what particular feature it reposed, the historian is unable to decide. But it was there, smoothing the whole face and overspreading the entire countenance; and so I may hazard the conjecture that this marvellous calm resided in the mind. Let us say it was in the mind.

Mr. Skyler was the possessor of a gigantic head, a brow so enormous rising from his solemn, sunken eyes as would have put Shakespeare to shame, had he beheld it. The dark hair upon his head was neatly parted and brushed carefully back. His complexion was sallow, the face almost devoid of flesh; and he wore moustache, whiskers, and small, pointed beard. On the bridge of the nose, pressed close to the eyes, and under the shadow of his enormous forehead, Mr. Skyler wore eyeglasses, and it is interesting to note that these glasses did not shine and twinkle with all the liveliness of white glass, but that they appeared to be smoke-coloured, so dull were they, and so darkly did the calm black eyes of their owner show through them.

When Mr. Skyler rose Sir John Sparrow was surprised to see a man no taller than himself, a little man, with square shoulders, puffed chest, and neat little legs. From the head he had expected a giant.

Without saying a single word Mr. Skyler took Sir John's hand in his own, and stood facing him for several seconds with slightly knitted brows, the eyes gazing calmly through their glasses into the large, solemn orbs of our hero. Then he opened his mouth and spoke.

"You have an extremely interesting auric egg," said he, with conviction.

"I beg your pardon?" said Sir John.

"You have an extremely interesting auric egg," repeated Mr. Skyler slowly and solemnly.

"That is something in my favour?" asked Sir John anxiously.

"It is."

"I am very glad to hear it," said Sir John, much relieved. "To tell you the truth, until you told me, I had no notion in the world that I possessed such a thing. May I sit down? These stairs are very trying."

Mr. Skyler allowed Sir John to relax his hand, and the gentlemen seated themselves.

You must picture to yourself Sir John Sparrow, very dapper and polite, with one leg carelessly swung over the other, his eyeglass in his eye, his white billycock hat, malacca cane, and lemon-coloured gloves in his right hand, seated upon a little chair beside a little table, with Mr. Skyler in a big chair, leaning one elbow on the table, gazing thoughtfully, calmly, and withal passionately into the eyes of the baronet as though striving to mesmerise him. That is the picture.

"It would be passing strange to me," said Mr. Skyler slowly, "if I was not aware of man's astounding ignorance of himself, to hear you say that you did not know of your auric egg. Sir, your auric egg is yourself. When I look at you I see not only your physical body—that's a small part of you!—but"—here Mr. Skyler began performing conjuring tricks with his right hand—"I see an oval mass of luminous mist, exactly co-extensive with your physical matter, circulating in a rosy light, expressing by its vivid and ever-changing flashes of colour the varying desires which sweep across your mind."

"You astound me" said Sir John.

"I knew that by a flash of this same aura," replied Caraway Skyler very calmly. "And this aura, or auric egg, you must know, is the true astral body. It is the Ego which thinks, hopes, strives, and desires. It is the Ego that in its passage from birth to birth acquires fresh experience, wider knowledge, holier aspirations."

"And you can really see this auric egg as you look at me?" asked Sir John. "A sort of shield in front of me? You can see it?"

"I can."

"Why cannot I see it in you?"

Caraway Skyler arched his brows. "You look at me," said he slowly, "with physical eyes. That is the reason. I look at you with the astral vision."

"But—pardon me for mentioning the point; I am only seeking for information—you look at me through eyeglasses?"

"With my physical eyes, yes," replied Caraway; "but my astral vision is, of course, independent of all such aids." Before Sir John could advise the theosophist to avoid the discomfort of glasses by always using this astral vision, that follower of Madame Blavatsky, that disciple of Gautama Buddha, had plunged into the topic of the astral plane. "You must know," said he, "that our physical eyes are incapable of seeing the marvellous spirit world which surrounds us. All about our path move and toil the inhabitants of the astral plane, the human denizens of Kâmaloka. And these wonderful beings can only be seen by those who have cultivated, after much labour, the astral vision. Consider for a single moment the imperfection of physical sight, a sight on which the mass of mankind relies so utterly and so contentedly for its business and its knowledge. Take a glass cube. On the physical plane, the further side appears to be smaller than the side nearest to the eyes, which is, of course, a delusion. On the astral plane all the sides appear equal, as they really are. To the occult student, let me tell you, the molecule and atom postulated by science are visible realities. And all objects on this plane are seen from all sides at once, the inside of a rock being as visible as the exterior. This is not wonderful, except by comparison with physical vision, which the undeveloped persist in believing is perfect and all-sufficent."

"I begin to understand," said Sir John. "This astral vision is spiritual vision; it is the way in which we shall see when we are angels?"

"Students of occultism," replied Caraway Skyler, "do not talk of angels; but let that pass. In the main you are right."

"Tell me something of the astral plane," said Sir John keenly.

"A large subject!" replied Caraway Skyler, fingering the point of his beard. "But by your aura I am able to see that you are one of the blessed to whom light will be given, and therefore I essay the difficult task." He bent forward, with one arm laid across the table, and looking deeply into Sir John's eyes, spoke as follows: "Four thousand years ago in the Egyptian papyrus of the Scribe Ani, we read, 'What manner of place is this into which I have come? It hath no water, it hath no air; it is deep, unfathomable; it is black as the blackest night, and men wander helplessly about therein; in it a man may not live in quietness of heart.' This is the seventh subdivision of the astral plane, viewed by an undeveloped mortal. From that standpoint all the beauty, glory, and spirituality are missed. But there are terrible sights to be seen on the astral plane. The Vampire ranges there seeking for blood—human blood; the Werewolf too; the Black Magician, who, without obtaining proper permission, has arrested his natural evolution, maintaining himself in Kâmaloka by acts of the most horrible nature; and then there are the degraded beings, the *incubi* and *succubae* of mediævalism, demons of thirst and gluttony, of lust and avarice, of intensified craft, wickedness and cruelty, provoking their victims to horrible crimes 'and revelling in their commission. These unfortunates are to be seen hanging round butchers' shops and public-houses. But when we ascend from the seventh subdivision of the astral plane, more beautiful sights encounter the eye of the psychic investigator. One sees the Chela——"

"I beg your pardon?" said Sir John.

"The Chela—that is to say the pupil of an occultist —one sees him, I say, waiting on the astral plane until a suitable reincarnation can be arranged for him by his master. One sees, too, the ordinary living person floating about in his astral body in a more or less unconscious condition. The Nirmânakâya — that is to say the Buddha of Compassion — who renounces Nirvâna to remain in the service of humanity until the race attains final liberation. Then there is the very large class of the ordinary person *dead*, that is to say, the soul of the ordinary person freed from its physical vehicle by death. This is an extremely interesting class, a class that may be divided and subdivided as many times as you please. For instance, there is the ordinary dissenter, who bursts into Kâmaloka, exclaiming, 'Stuff and nonsense! don't tell me I'm dead; I won't believe it. This isn't heaven, and it isn't hell. Stuff and nonsense!'"

"You surprise me!" cried Sir John.

"Oh, that is a very common experience!" replied Caraway Skyler easily. "This belief in hell is quite extraordinary. It takes some souls several centuries in Kâmaloka to shake off the idea of a place of torment; they can't believe they are dead, simply because there isn't a hell to receive them. And so you get millions of different experiences, according to the development of the ordinary person, at the time of his death. One great ecclesiastic after death was hailed mockingly by one of the succubae, and he drew himself up exclaiming, 'Are you aware that you are speaking to the Bishop of Rochester?' That was his point of development. Some go quickly from the astral plane, and pass into the devachanic condition, where alone the spiritual aspirations can find full fruition. Others function for a considerable time in their Kâmarupa, slowly adapting themselves to the altered conditions of life, till finally they can release the Triad—the three higher human principles, forming the imperishable part of men—to pass into devachan, finally merging themselves into Nirvâna. So you see the post-mortem adventures of man are of an exceedingly wide and diverse nature."

"I take it," said Sir John, passing his hand wearily across his brow, "that you have been telling me about the astral plane. Will you now—if I am not asking you too much—tell me something about theosophy itself? I don't know, but I *think* I should be able to get a better grasp of the astral plane if I first knew roughly what theosophy is. Don't you think so?"

"The only bad thing in theosophy," replied Caraway Skyler, "is the extreme difficulty it presents of explanation. But I will endeavour to give you what I may call a rough outline. To begin, then, the fundamental idea of theosophy is universal brotherhood."

"Good," said Sir John.

"Yes, that's a good idea," continued Caraway, as if it were his own. "This universal brotherhood is no sentimental or merely political idea; it is founded on another great fact of theosophy. This other great fact is this: the spirit of man, or *monad* as we call it, is a reincarnating Ego, and passes through all the stages of evolution—vegetable, mineral, and animal. In man moral responsibility is attained, and the duty immediately arises of subordinating the passional part of his nature, and of developing the spiritual. He must do this, not for fear of hell or desire of Heaven, but in order to prepare for his next reincarnation."

"That commends itself to me hugely," said Sir John. "For I hold very firmly that man's destiny is to aspire; that this aspiration is the driving force of the universe; and, for my own part, I can tell you that the craving for the most utter perfection of which I am capable is now consuming me like a fierce fire."

"Good," said Caraway.

"I wish, sir," said Sir John, "to be perfect. I will have no compromise in the matter. If it be necessary to do so I will strip myself bare of all that I possess —go naked into Kama-deve—into the astral plane."

"You delight me, but you do not surprise me," said Caraway. "For I saw all this in your auric egg. You will go far."

"As I said, sir," went on our hero, bending eagerly forward, "I wish to give up my money, my social position, the luxuries I have not already shed, and, in brief, everything I possess except my nomad—monad, I should say; and bending all my attention to the development of this soul, await calmly and confidently my next reincarnation."

"Good again," said Skyler.

"And now, I pray you," said Sir John, "to tell me a little more about theosophy, for I am perfectly charmed by what I have already heard, and am ·in a state of spiritual fever to hear more. What I have heard already convinces me that in theosophy I have touched bottom in religion."

"There can be no higher religion than the truth," said Mr. Skyler. "Theosophy, then," he went on, "is founded on the universal brotherhood of all living things; but it does not leave out of consideration the great mysteries of existence. At the back of everything we postulate Sat."

"Sat?" queried Sir John.

"Sat, sir," replied Mr. Skyler. "And Sat is Be-ness, not even Being or Existence. It is above and beyond Being; It is Be-ness. Be-ness!" he repeated loftily; "so far defeating the comprehension even of the Mahatmas and Adepts that they can express It by no other term than this one signifying Be-ness! How far grander is this than the 'God' of popular theology!"

"Quite," said Sir John.

"How infinitely more humbling to the human mind! Be-ness!"

"Quite," said Sir John.

"How immeasurably it enlarges one's conception of creation!"

"Quite," said Sir John.

"As one of our greatest writers has said," went on Caraway, "'Space is the only conception that can even faintly mirror It without preposterous distortion, but silence least offends in these high regions where the wings of thought beat faintly, and lips can only falter, not pronounce.'"

"I wonder," said Sir John reflectively, in the tone of one convinced that he is about to utter something weighty, something that has never occurred to anybody before, "I wonder if you and I will live to hear the popular oath of 'By God!' altered to 'By Sat!' We may. It is quite possible."

"No," said Caraway, "for when theosophy has advanced as far as that no one will swear."

"Of course," said Sir John. "And is that not one great proof of the failure of Christianity, that its Gods are used by the profane for the sinful and vulgar purpose of emphasising carnal and foolish utterances?"

"I agree with you," said Caraway.

"Please go on with your outline," pleaded the baronet.

"There is little more that can be put into conversation," replied Caraway; "but I may conclude by telling you that the universe is the manifestation of an aspect of Sat. Rhythmically succeeding one another are periods of activity and periods of repose—the expiration and inspiration of the Great Breath, in the beautiful Eastern phrase. The outbreathing is the manifested worlds; the inbreathing terminates the period of activity. And man, moving over these worlds, is of seven parts—physical, astral, life-principle, passional, mind, spiritual soul, spirit. Very different to the narrowing idea of the Christians that he is merely soul and body! Now there is one law for man to know, which is that as he sows, so must he infallibly reap. And it is by faith in this law that we who believe implicitly in the universal brotherhood of man can look unmoved upon all the so-called cruelty and injustice in the world."

" Oh, pray tell me more! " exclaimed Sir John, with enthusiasm. " For at present the crack of a whip, the brutal call of a mother to her child, even the sight of a workman perspiring at his toil, are all a physical torture and reproach to me."

Caraway Skyler sat back in his chair. " I can at least do you one service," said he, expecting a compliment and waiting for it.

" You have already done me a hundred," said Sir John.

" For, you see," said Caraway, taking no notice of the compliment, " theosophy is a perfect religion ; it does not, like the Christian religion, shake its head over pain and cruelty, exclaiming, ' This is a great mystery ! '"

" I am delighted to hear it," cried Sir John.

" No ; it sees in the pain of others the working of Karma, and it says to itself: ' These poor things are working out their destiny ; they must assimilate all the experience which this existence affords, and therefore they must know what pain is, what hunger is, what want is.' That is what theosophy says. I myself can look unmoved on a crippled horse pulling at a load, at a mouse being tortured to death by a cat, at a child purple in the face with convulsions. For I say to myself: ' We make our own character, we make our own strength and weakness ; we are not the sport of an arbitrary god or of a soulless destiny ; we are creators of ourselves and of our lot in life.' To conclude, let me quote the words of a great theosophist summing up the Secret Wisdom : ' Reincarnation under Karmic law, until the fruit of every experience has been gathered, every blunder rectified, every fault eradicated ; until compassion has been made perfect, strength unbreakable, tenderness complete, self-abnegation the law of life, renunciation for others the natural and joyous impulse of the whole nature.' That, sir, is theosophy."

Sir John thanked Mr. Skyler effusively for his lucid explanation of undoubtedly the only true religion, and with his arms full of pamphlets began to take his departure. But Caraway Skyler, who had been fidgeting with his papers during the outpouring of our hero's gratitude, evidently extremely loth to let the baronet go, touched Sir John on the arm as he moved towards the door, and arrested his progress.

"I should like to read you a little poem I have just composed," said he; "for though my business in life is the distribution and arrangement of vegetarian literature, I have my ambitions as a poet."

"You interest me extremely," said Sir John.

"Not, you must understand, carnal ambitions," went on Mr. Skyler. "I have no desire for the laureate's bays, or for the applause of your vulgar Tennyson readers; I am theosophist here, as in all things. My ambition is to draw men into the true religion, nothing else; and if I can find someone to pay for the publication of my verses in book form I should probably issue them to the world anonymously, so little do I care for vulgar fame."

"Pray read the poem," said Sir John.

"It is called 'Macrocosm,'" replied Mr. Caraway Skyler; and lifting a paper from the table, and holding it dramatically at arm's length, he read the following verses :—

> "When from Akasha, Kosmos sprang
>   And Dharma functioned, ruled by Sat,
> Linga Sharîra felt the pang
>   Of Monads breaking from Arhat,
> Then Kâmarupa looked to see
>   An Avatara, or Chohan,
> Attest the Atma, so that we
>   Might fearless pass to Devachan.

"O for thy strength, Fohat! to be
One moment free of Kama's chase,
To pierce the Mûlaprakriti
And look Purusha in the face!
To see the Shastra closed and shut,
Manasa Putra all complete,
No longer Kamas Manas,—but
Pure Triad at the Jiva's feet!"

"Extremely fine," said Sir John.

"You like it?"

"Immensely. My one doubt is whether it might not, perhaps, be better to write the whole poem in Hindustani. I throw that out as a suggestion."

"So few people would understand it," objected Mr. Skyler.

"True," said Sir John thoughtfully, unwilling to hurt the poet's feelings by suggesting that in the poem's present condition neither European nor Asiatic would be able to make head or tail of it. And then, seeing how unhappy and downcast the poet appeared, he remarked, "I hope you won't think me obtrusive. You won't, will you? But, do you know, I should like very much to make myself responsible for the publication of your verses. Will you let me? I should regard it as an honour."

"Well," said Mr. Skyler, "if you are going to give up all your possessions, I really don't think you could do better than throw some of the money away on my poems."

"Please don't say I should be throwing it away!" cried Sir John.

"Oh, that's very good of you!" said Mr. Skyler genially; and then he went into figures.

When our hero started out on his return journey he looked with larger eyes upon the world. A yellow fog hung level with the roofs of the houses, and under

this pendent gloom the innumerable and irregular lights
of London blinked and winked with a dull protesting
brilliance. 'Buses, vans, carts, cabs, and carriages
crawled in an inextricable tangle through the narrow
avenue of high houses, each dark house a patch of white
light at its many windows. On the footpaths thronged
and pressed that strangest of all human spectacles, the
London crowd; innumerable, dense as a swarm of
bees, overflowing the pavement, forcing its way between 'buses and vans, ebbing and flowing at the same
moment. Into this mighty current of human activity
Sir John was caught and carried forward, as a straw
blown from London Bridge is caught into the swirl
of rushing Thames. But there was no humility, no
sense of infinitesimal unimportance in the breast of
our theosophical baronet. He cocked his head on one
side and surveyed the world. The roof of human
beings on every 'bus, the growling cab-driver, the
chaffing office-boy, the swaggering clerk, the bustling
merchant, the dawdling workman, the unimpassioned
policeman, the foreigner with guide-book in hand—
each face that loomed out of the fog for an instant
and then passed from sight in the moist darkness,
deepened the conviction of the baronet's mind that
every soul was its own creator, and that every spirit must
assimilate all the experience provided by our planet.
Even the steaming, straining horses appealed to him in
a new light, and he looked calmly upon the tattered
beggars in the gutter, calling monotonously and hopelessly the foolish toys that loaded their little trays.

A new joy possessed him. It was grand to be one
in this crowd. It was glorious to be a soul in this
procession of reincarnating Egos. Ah! if all and every
pushing, panting mortal brushing past him in that
mighty tide did but recognise that they had existed

before, that they would exist again, that it was necessary for them to touch life at all its million points, how differently would they bend their backs to the burden of existence! It was also delectable to reflect that his own Ego was superior to all the others, in that it knew the truth, and that for it life now presented neither mystery nor fear.

In this strain was our hero moralising, when he felt himself violently pushed on one side, and looking up as he struggled to recover his equipoise saw his old acquaintance Mr. Spill shooting past him at a rate astounding in that great crowd. It instantly occurred to Sir John that he could practise his new religion on no one better than this distributor of tracts, and trusting to the density of the crowd to aid him, he set off to overtake the hurrying Spill. He got into the gutter, trotted under the shadow of great 'buses, darted in front of cab horses, dived behind vans, popped on to the kerb, then back into the gutter, and now walking, now trotting, finally came up with Mr. Spill, and touched him on the sleeve.

"Ah-h-h-h!" cried Mr. Spill in an agony of fear, and turned upon Sir John a face expressing the most terrible apprehension.

"Don't you remember me?" panted our hero.

Mr. Spill glanced back down the street. "I thought he'd got me!" he exclaimed nervously. "I really thought he'd got me this time."

They were pushed and jostled by the crowd.

"Let us go up this side turning," said Sir John; "it is quieter, and I want to talk to you."

"I'm safer in the crowd," replied Spill; "he can't get me in the crowd. A crowd confuses him, beats him altogether. Thank God for crowds! The Almighty God be blessed for crowds!"

o

But he suffered himself to be led out of the main current. "You must stand by me," said he, looking anxiously over his shoulder. "You mustn't leave me till we get back into the crowd. And be quick with what you've got to say. What is it? Quick!"

"You remember me?" asked Sir John.

"Faintly. Met you somewhere before."

"In the Strand. We had tea together," replied the baronet gently. "You recommended me, if you remember, to make a business of religion."

"Hush! hush!" cried Spill, jumping violently. "For God's sake whisper it. That's why he's after me. He's determined to have me too. Speak low, and keep your eyes skinned."

All the time he was speaking or listening (if, indeed, he did listen) poor Spill was turning his head on its long neck, first this way, then that, glancing up courts and alleys, peering into doorways, peeping into gratings, and behaving as one might expect a guilty person to behave who has the entire detective force of England at his heels.

"Tell me," said Sir John—"and I can promise you that no evil shall befall you while I am at your side—tell me who it is that thus harries and worries you."

"The devil!" cried Spill in a hoarse whisper, jerking his head over his shoulder. "I took you for the devil. When you touched my arm I said to myself, 'He's got me at last.' You gave me a fright, a terrible fright."

"And why is the devil after you?" asked Sir John soothingly.

"Because I found out the secret of smashing him," replied Spill in an agony. "I almost wish I hadn't. It makes life unbearable. You can't guess what a nightmare it is to have the devil chasing one all day long. It takes away one's appetite, I can tell you."

"But, my dear sir," said Sir John softly, "if you have succeeded in thus alarming the devil, surely your God will protect you from his molestations."

"He ought to," quoth Spill, "but He doesn't. I expect it's a trial of my faith. He's trying me very high. I can't stand it much longer. If it goes on I shall give the whole thing up; I shall, indeed. I shall turn atheist. It's the only way to get rid of the devil; throw the whole thing up, and turn atheist."

"I know a better way," said Sir John.

"I doubt it," replied Spill.

"But I do, for I have found the truth. My dear brother, let me tell you something that will bring unspeakable comfort to your poor wounded soul. *There is no devil.*"

"Rot!" said Spill. "How can that be when he gives me no rest night or day? Besides, I've seen him. Good gracious me! what's the use of talking nonsense like that? No devil! You might as well say there's no hell."

"I do," said Sir John.

"Then I believe you're the devil himself," cried Spill, starting away.

Sir John sought his side. "Pray listen to me. We will get into a cab, and you shall come to my chambers, and we will have a quiet talk. Will you? I'm not the devil. I'm not, really. I am Sir John Sparrow, a vegetarian and a theosophist; a believer in the great Sat, which, you must know, is Be-ness, so far does this mighty Sat exceed all our finite ideas of being. And I am just about to start a colony in England, where people may come and live without payment of any kind, save the labour of the farm which we shall all share; and you shall come and live with us, and the devil shall never worry you any more."

Spill listened to all this very attentively. "I'm all

right when I'm with people. He never attacks me then.
It's only when I'm alone. That's why I have to sleep in
common lodging-houses, so that I have company at
night. I like the idea of this farm. But you'd never
leave me there, would you? You wouldn't send me to
milk the cows all by myself?"

"There will be no cows on our farm," said Sir John
proudly. "We shall live on fruits and vegetables, chiefly
fruit."

"What! no beef or mutton?" cried Spill in disgust.

"I must explain that to you later," replied the baronet,
hailing a hansom. "And now let us get into this cab,
and when we arrive at our chambers I will tell you all
about theosophy, the glorious faith in reincarnating
Egos, and also all about vegetarianism."

On their way Spill spoke almost cheerfully of his
persecution from the devil. "If he ever does get me,"
said he, "I shall give him a warming, and so I tell him.
By George, I shan't go under without a blow! I tell
you, sir, I shall hit him, and hit him devilishly hard too.
A man who can reduce the four millions of lost souls in
London to something over the one million isn't going to
submit quietly to the devil or anyone else. As soon as
he saw that my great discovery of making a business of
religion was catching on he set about driving me out of
my wits—confound him! But I'll not go under quietly.
Trust me!"

Sir John thought it wise to say nothing of theosophy
until he had got the poor distracted creature in his
rooms, and so he listened quietly to all Spill had to
say on the subject of the devil, merely murmuring a
polite "Ah!" or a reassuring "Quite!" as the mad
reformer unfolded his tale.

On opening the front door of his lodgings Sir John
came face to face with Miss Frisby. She was waiting

to see him. Ah! but no, she would not enter his rooms; only a minute here, just one poor little minute. It would not take longer, it ;wouldn't really. Oh, would Sir John be so very kind?

The baronet said he would first conduct his friend Mr. Spill to his room, and then, if Miss Frisby would not mind waiting, he would return to her side as quickly as possible. Miss Frisby would not mind at all. She sank into a lounge in the hall while the baronet and his guest ascended the stairs.

"You will not mind sitting here by yourself for a minute," said Sir John to Spill, entering his sitting-room, and depositing his theosophical pamphlets on the table. "I won't keep you longer, I won't really. It is quite private here. No one will disturb you. Don't be frightened of the devil. Here is *Punch* to look at. I won't keep you a minute."

"Be quick," said Spill, "and if you see a dark, fierce man coming up the stairs as you go down, stop him; that's the devil. Don't let him come up."

Sir John assured him that no one should be allowed to enter the room, and hurried away to confer with Miss Frisby.

Now, there is no need to enlarge upon a lady's minute, though I could write one of the best chapters in the world on that subject. It must suffice to say that Miss Frisby had called to know whether ladies might join Sir John's colony, as both she and Miss Vince were so keen to belong to it, and she hoped that the dear, delightful, perfectly superb Captain Chivvy would join it too; and this subject occupied her for nearly twenty minutes, and was only interrupted by——

But that belongs to the other story.

You must know, then, that Mr. Spill, finding himself alone, became horribly nervous again. He got it into his poor crazy head that Sir John was in league with the devil, and that he had brought him to this room for no other purpose in the world than that the devil might seize upon him and devour him. So acutely did this supposition work upon the nerves of Mr. Spill that he began to imagine this devil of his to be actually hiding behind the curtains or under the table, waiting there for a convenient moment to spring out upon him. He could sit still no longer. Getting up from his chair, he took Sir John's malacca cane from the table, where it reposed with theosophical pamphlets and lemon-coloured gloves, and brandishing it over his head, glared about him with rolling eye in an attitude of terrible defiance. After some minutes of unbroken silence, he wheeled round and began to poke about at the window curtains, lunging out so fiercely at one moment that he drove the stick clean through a pane of glass. Then he knelt down on the floor, and peered under table and sofa; then he arose, and cut and slashed at space for several seconds, till the sweat dripped from his forehead and his breath came short and quick. Then again he dropped upon his knees, and began to peer nervously under all the articles of furniture in the room.

So intent was he on this search that he did not hear the door open quietly, nor was he aware of any presence in the room till the voice of Tiplady, loud and threatening, brought him with a shriek of terror to his feet.

"So I've caught you, have I?" said Tiplady.

The butler had entered the room cautiously, for on approaching the door to see if his master had returned he had been arrested by such queer and curious sounds from within as had convinced him that something was wrong.

"So I've caught you, have I?" said he, very fierce.

Spill faced him with white and stricken face, the sweat beading his forehead, his whole body trembling in a paroxysm of terror. For Tiplady — in close-buttoned black alpaca coat, with his wings of hair, his overflow of whiskers, his square shoulders, his resolute carriage, his dark, threatening eye—appeared to him as no other person in the world than his old enemy, the devil.

Tiplady, for his part, was not above fear, and so began to bluster. "I've had my eye on you for some time, my friend," said he. "And now I've caught you. There's no escape. The front door is locked, and the passages and staircases, front and back, all secured. So you'd better drop that stick, and submit quietly."

"Never!" gasped Spill, "never!"

"Now don't be too bold," replied Tiplady, "for you won't get over me with any such tricks. Try it on a baby, my friend, but not on old birds. I'm up to snuff, old cockalorum, I can tell you; and you can teach your grandfather to suck eggs."

"Never! never!" shouted Spill fiercely.

It struck Tiplady with a shock that burglars do not as a rule shout their defiance, however defiant they may feel. He began to feel extremely unhappy.

"You don't bounce me!" he said rather weakly. "Nobody ever bounced me yet, and I'm too old to learn."

"Devil, devil!" bawled Spill, brandishing his stick.

"Now, look here," said Tiplady, lifting an admonitory finger; "if you talk like that I shall get angry!"

"Hell, devil, fire, snakes!" shouted Spill, advancing with uplifted stick, his body quivering with the excitement of his madness.

This was too much for the nerves of the resolute Tiplady. He screwed his face into well-simulated anger, but turned his head, and looked somewhat longingly towards the door.

The sight of Tiplady's shining bald head turned away from him woke all the fury of the terrified Spill. He sprang forward with the cane in the air, and just as Tiplady made a bolt for it, brought the stick down upon his head with a resounding thwack. Tiplady dropped for a minute, but retaining his consciousness, lifted up his arms and covered his head to protect it from the blows that Spill was now raining upon him. These blows he bore with astonishing endurance, buoyed up by the delusive hope that every one must be the last, or, at any rate, the last but one. The blows, however, continuing to fall with unabated fury, and the curses of his assailant being of so terrible a nature, Tiplady determined to use his remaining strength in the stern business of retaliation, ere he lay quite helpless and broken at the mercy of this madman.

Therefore, as one of these thousand blows from the cane struck him across the arms, he suddenly unloosened their grasp about his head, darted them forward, and flinging them about the legs of his assailant brought him crashing to the ground, just as the stick descended helplessly across his own shoulders.

Then did Mr. Spill set up such a howling of " Devil ! Hell !" and then did the conquering Tiplady belabour his enemy so unmercifully—punching him in the ribs, smacking him with firm open palm across the face— that one might have expected the whole house to have rushed terrified upon the scene. But in London, so well built are the houses, you can pistol your wife in a bedroom without the lodger's wife next door stopping in her occupation of hair-curling. And so no one came to disturb these belligerents. They rolled about the floor, thumping each other's bodies, slapping each other's faces, kicking each other's shins—swearing, cursing, foaming, and perspiring, with a fury incredible to the ordinary peaceful citizen.

Chairs were dragged about with them as they tumbled on the floor, the table with its vase of flowers, theosophical pamphlets and gloves was sent crashing over, the carpet was kicked and caught up in fifty places. Blood began to flow. Mr. Spill, in a moment of inspiration, seizing upon the vase as it rolled on the floor, dealt Tiplady such a crack on the nose as lay that organ open and split the upper lip at the same time. Tiplady retaliated with his nails, scratching Mr. Spill's cheeks till they were scored like a map caged in by lines of longitude and latitude. Then their two heads came into violent collision, and for a moment they fell apart, stunned by the concussion. But Tiplady was now hungry for battle, and his head was a hard one. Losing but the fraction of a minute, he sprang to his feet, picked up the malacca cane, and set about basting the unfortunate Mr. Spill with a force and fury almost equal to that with which he himself had felt the chastisement of his master's stick. *Bang, bang, bang!* went the cane on the head of Mr. Spill, and *whop, whop, whop!* upon that unfortunate person's shoulders. You never saw such a flogging in your life! Tiplady braced all his strength to the business, opening his huge shoulders, and bringing down the cane each time with the full weight of his body behind it. Mr. Spill writhed upon the floor, yelling and kicking. Instead of curses, he took to pleading, imploring the devil—as he called Tiplady, to that honest man's unspeakable indignation—to show him a moment's mercy. But Tiplady, with the blood streaming from nose and mouth, with his ribs aching and his chest sore, was in no mood for clemency.

"Be damned to you!" says he fiercely; and this only convinced Spill the more that he was in the hands of the devil.

And so, in pure desperation, the wretched creature writhing and shrieking on the floor struggled on to his feet, and after being knocked down two or three times by Tiplady, managed at last to stand firm enough to permit of a spring towards the door. He shot past the butler, hurled himself through the doorway, and hotly pursued by Tiplady, stick in hand, dashed down the stairs seven at a time.

Such a descent as this, I believe, has never been known. I have searched through a great number of authorities, and I find that while some few desperate men have descended stairs five at a time, the average is three, the exceptional four. So that in flinging himself down the broad stairs of Sir John's chambers seven at a time Mr. Spill may congratulate himself on the establishment of a record, which even though it be equalled in the future is never likely to be surpassed.

And here let us pause and take breath, for after such a tussle neither you nor I, ladies and gentlemen, can with any comfort follow even Tiplady in his more leisurely three-stairs-at-a-time pursuit of the vanishing Mr. Spill.

Let us rest on the corridor, and when we have quite recovered our breath, with our hand upon the banisters, and one stair at a time, follow this adventure to its astounding conclusion.

CHAPTER XIII

Of the further Struggle between Mr. Spill and the Devil, with an account of the Sick-nursing shared by Sir John Sparrow and Miss Frisby, concluding with the episode of Miss Frisby's Hat

"GOOD gracious!" cried Sir John, looking up the staircase.

The hall-porter came running from his room.

"Ah! but what is it that comes so swiftly?" cried Miss Frisby, her eyes on the stairs, her hands clutching the baronet's arm.

Before answer could be returned the shrieking, bounding, rushing Something with one bewildering leap sprang from the centre of the stairs to the hall, and, as Sir John and Miss Frisby turned to escape, knocked them flat upon their faces. Down they went, without a cry, like ninepins, flat as pancakes.

Sir John, with the spirit of chivalry strong in him, was preparing to rise in order that he might assist and defend the now screaming Miss Frisby, when he felt himself suddenly beaten afresh into the floor of the hall, and heard a passionate voice at his ear, hoarsely addressing him as "Devil!" "Satan!" and "Beelzebub!" Our puzzled hero had no time to turn this mystery over in his mind before the mysterious Something on his

203

back put forth hands of flesh and bone, and so pounded him about the head and ears that he was forced to bellow with pain. This form of punishment, however, was not of long duration; for while the blows were raining upon his defenceless head, there suddenly descended plump upon his back an infinitely greater weight—imagine an elephant, sir, tumbling from the top of Snowdon on to the small of your back—and after this frightful and appalling addition to the weight of his misfortunes, the breath passed from our hero's body, and for the moment he lost consciousness.

When he was able to move, he screwed round his head, and beheld two figures locked in a fierce embrace, swinging and violently bumping about the hall in the throes of deadly conflict. When he was able to sit more or less up, he saw with horror, between the legs of one or two of his fellow-lodgers now gathered in the hall, that these two figures were those of Tiplady and Mr. Spill. He further made out, as the bodies swayed and wrestled about the hall, that the butler was beating the fiend-haunted one with his own malacca cane, crying out all the time in a voice of terrible passion—

" I'll devil you, I'll devil you; bones and all, my friend; so take that, and that, and that. Ah! would you? Then that too!"

Now there was no breath left in the body of our philosopher, so that he was unable to rise and address any orders to his servant. He could but sit painfully upon his haunches, with Miss Frisby kneeling at his side *sans pince-nez*, breathing like a spent runner, and trembling like an aspen leaf, wondering whether Kamaloka, Kamarupa, Sat, Devachan, or any other star in the theosophical heaven had lost its bearings, and, tumbling down upon his own reincarnating Ego, had broken his auric egg into a thousand pieces, and squashed his astral body out of all shape and recognition. He really could not think at all. And so there he sat, waiting for his breath to return, like nothing else I can think of at the moment than Patience on a monument. To add to his tortures, Miss Frisby at his side, grasping his arm with twitching fingers, her face agitated in every feature and every muscle, her loosened hair trembling about her ears, her crushed and broken hat whirled and torn under the labouring feet of Tiplady and Spill, continually gasped her desire for an immediate, full and detailed explanation of the frightful phenomenon.

She was comforted, poor lady, not by the breathless baronet, but by a couple of chambermaids, a fat cook, and a smutty-faced scullerymaid, who had arrived upon the scene in a twinkling of an eye. These good creatures ranging themselves about the distressed lady set up such a shrieking as nearly drowned Tiplady's devilling of Mr. Spill, and completely silenced the agonised questioning of Miss Frisby.

"Make those women shut·up!" gasped the butler to the hall-porter, who was pretending with all his might to rescue Spill from the butler's clutches. "Tell 'em to shut up! It's a burglar. He's nearly done for me, and I'll do for him quite before I hand him over to the police, see if I don't. Ah, you would, would you!" he yelled into Spill's ear, as that frantic person set about biting the plump calf of his leg.

The hall-porter joined the cook, chambermaids and scullerymaid. "It's all right," he said reassuringly; "don't make a shindy. It's all right."

"What is it? Ah! but what is it?" cried Miss Frisby, turning a face of white terror to the hall-porter.

"It's a burglar, mum," replied the porter, "and Mr. Tiplady's just giving him a warming before he hands him over. It's all right."

Sir John, too breathless to correct Tiplady's mistake by word of mouth, began waving his arms weakly.

"It's all right, Sir John," said the porter, going over to him, and stooping down to the level of our hero's ear. "It's all right, Sir John; it's only Mr. Tiplady warming a burglar. Mary," he added, turning to one of the chambermaids, "go and get a drop of brandy; the sight of the blood's upset him; he's lost his power of speech."

While Mary vowed that there were more burglars in the kitchen, and that she would no more descend to those regions without police protection than she would stoop to take a pin that didn't belong to her, Sir John waved his arms, rolled his eyes, shook his head, and continued to exhibit signs of the utmost distress.

The hall-porter, when he wasn't chuckling unconstrainedly at the delightful spectacle of Tiplady belabouring a burglar who would insist upon biting the butler's leg, assured Sir-John politely, with serious face, and with all the confidence of omniscience, that it was all right, quite all right, and that he wasn't to worry himself.

The agony of seeing Mr. Spill—his guest—flogged, kicked, and cursed by Tiplady—his servant—without having the power to utter a single word and put an instant stop to the encounter, forced our hero into the manufacture of such astounding contortions of the face as would infallibly have driven him clean out of his senses had he been able to see them himself. So astounding were these facial gymnastics that they attracted the attention of Miss Frisby and the servants, who suddenly desisted from their screaming, abandoned all interest in the fierce struggle, and gazed open-eyed at the squatting baronet. It was now only the grinning porter and the few lodgers who followed the various moves in the historic battle between Mr. Spill and the butler. All the others gazed, terrified and bewildered, into the working face of the baronet, as our hero sat upon the floor, his mouth wide open, his arms painfully sawing the air, and his eyes rolling in their sockets like two tops wobbling to their fall.

"Lor'!" cried one of the servants, "the sight of the blood's upset him, right enough! It's Mr. Tiplady's nose what has done it, mark my words if it isn't!"

"He's gone deaf and dumb!" cried another.

"Poor gentleman," said a third.

"I never could stand the sight of blood myself," said the first conversationally.

"Oh, you get used to it!" replied the cook professionally.

"*I* never could!" put in the third. "Blood always makes me feel—well, kind of creepy. You know?"

"Lord, lord! but look at him now!" cried the cook, jumping back in alarm.

"He's daft!" cried a chambermaid.

"What faces!" said her fellow. "Well, to be sure!"

And they drew further back. Only the faithful Miss Frisby remained.

The cause of this new terror on the servants' part was merely that Sir John, in a phrase of the people, had set about "fetching his wind." He was, in short, pumping out, a very painful process. His eyes started from his head, his jaws continually snapped together, and he became of a remarkably deep purple in the face. From his snapping jaws issued long-drawn grating gasps, sounds like the premonitory gurgles of a donkey preparing to lift up his voice and bray. He looked at Miss Frisby, he turned a despairing gaze on the servants, he rolled his eyes up to heaven, screwed them painfully round till they appeared to be looking for the back of his own head, and then glanced down as if straining for a sight of his collar. At last, with his hands pressing against his stomach, rocking backwards and forwards, his eyes fixed suddenly on the wall opposite, he emitted a throat-splitting gasp, sat completely still, and said—

"Spill!"

This monosyllable was uttered so faintly that the owner of the name heard it not, but the servants and Miss Frisby, who caught it with straining ears, all jumped back together and looked at each with glances of sad conviction. Clearly the baronet was mad.

Sir John, however, now had all his attention set upon the warring, bellowing couple, still bumping against the walls, pitching over the chairs, clattering against the hat-stand, and banging into the fast-closed hall-door. Rising slowly and painfully upon his feet, our gallant hero crept slowly towards the rocking wrestlers, and stretching out an arm to its fullest extent, while he dodged back to avoid collision with the fighters, he touched Tiplady in the ribs, and called him by his name.

The butler turned a proud, smiling, blood-stained face upon his master. "It's nearly done, Sir John," he gasped. "He didn't steal anything. I caught him in time. He's about half-dead already." And with that Tiplady caught the unfortunate Mr. Spill a tremendous cuff over the ear.

"Stop!" cried Sir John. "He's my friend. Stop at once!"

Tiplady did stop, but he still retained his grasp on Mr. Spill's collar. "A friend, Sir John?" he panted.

There was an awful silence.

"Why don't you leave the gentleman alone?" shouted the porter angrily.

"Well, Mr. Tiplady," said the cook, "whoever would have thought it of you?"

"What a brute he is!" cried a chambermaid.

"Leave the gentleman alone, you great bully!" screamed another.

The fainting, bleeding Mr. Spill dropped limply into Miss Frisby's arms. "Ah, but we must take him upstairs!" she cried. "Quick, oh, quick! Hot water, hot water! Get the hot water, quick!"

While Tiplady, the victorious Tiplady, fell back against the wall, exclaiming, "Well, I'm beat!" the hall-porter rescued Mr. Spill from the convulsive squeezes of Miss Frisby, and bore him through the chattering crowd of lodgers and servants up the stairs which he had descended seven at a time, down the long corridor through which he had rushed with Tiplady at his heels, and laid him at last on the sofa in Sir John's tumbled sitting-room—the first scene of this immortal struggle.

There the unconscious Mr. Spill was tenderly nursed by the baronet and Miss Frisby. His blood-stained face was sponged by the lady; our teetotal hero poured brandy down his throat. Eau-de-cologne was spread by the long, white, trembling fingers of Miss Frisby on the poor fellow's brow, upper lip, and behind his ears; his torn and twisted collar was removed by the baronet, who further humbled himself before his ill-treated guest by unlacing and removing the devil-haunted gentleman's boots. His pillows were rearranged every other minute by Miss Frisby; first a dressing-gown, then a quilt, and then a rug were laid across his legs by the unwearying baronet. In short, whispering and muttering to themselves, these two humanitarians waited so assiduously and indefatigably upon the battered warrior that in something less than half an hour he opened his eyes, looked wearily about him, sighed gratefully, and then dropped off into an easy slumber.

P

It was then that Sir John, whose heart ached for his faithful servant, stole out from the room, and sought for Tiplady. He found that valiant warrior in the hall-porter's room, with a doctor attending to his split nose, the saddest tears of repentance in his eyes, and as crestfallen an appearance on his dignified visage as one could hope to see in the face of an unfrocked bishop. A nearly finished brandy-and-soda stood at his side.

After the doctor had taken his departure, leaving Tiplady with a plastered nose, Sir John heard the history of the struggle from the butler's point of view, and with his knowledge of Spill's mania was enabled to put two and two together, thus arriving at a tolerably correct idea of the tragical misunderstanding. He comforted Tiplady with his forgiveness, and even paid a generous eulogy to the unflinching and whole-hearted valour which the butler had displayed in the course of the conflict. Then, cautioning the servant to remain in his own room—"for," said he, "'tis very certain Mr. Spill will mistake you for the devil when he sees you next time"—our worthy gentleman once more ascended the stairs, and, after a secret confabulation with a chambermaid, stole noiselessly on tiptoe into the sitting-room where Miss Frisby guarded the sleep of Mr. Spill.

"You must be famished," said Sir John, going to the sideboard. "You must let me offer you some refreshment. You must really." And thereupon he drew out of his storehouse apples, nuts, almonds, raisins, grapes, and figs, and placing them upon the table, which Miss Frisby had set once more on its legs, he drew up two chairs, and bade the lady approach. So they sat down and ate.

Whether Mr. Spill had slept his sleep out, or whether

it was the cheerful cracking of Brazil nuts that called him from the kingdom of dreams, the deponent historian does not say definitely; but it is very certain that soon after the baronet and Miss Frisby had made havoc of a dish of grapes, another of figs, and another of apples, and had set about attacking a cairn of Brazil nuts, Mr. Spill opened his eyes, yawned unrestrainedly, stretched his aching limbs, and asked for something to drink.

He was immediately provided with lemonade, Miss Frisby holding the glass while Sir John fired off a soda-water bottle, and set the lemon-juice fizzing in the tumbler. Ere he had drained the glass dry, Miss Frisby was at him with a dish of apples, while Sir John followed quickly with almonds and raisins. These delicacies somewhat petulantly refused, Miss Frisby started rearranging his pillow, while Sir John, pulling the rug off his legs, spread the quilt in its place with great delicacy of touch. Mr. Spill began to mutter angrily. Miss Frisby at once made a dive for the bottle of eau-de-cologne, and proceeded to bathe the invalid's frowning and dodging forehead, while Sir John, carefully removing the quilt, gently unbuttoned the top button of Mr. Spill's trousers, and then tenderly replaced the quilt. The invalid appearing to doze once more, the unselfish nurses returned again to the table, and took up their nut-cracking where they had left it, with a pleasing sense of duty well and conscientiously done. But they were not left long in peace—the cruel destiny of all good nurses— for hardly had they cracked half a dozen noisy nuts, when Mr. Spill opened his eyes wide, turned himself upon an elbow, and regarded them with unclouded consciousness.

Miss Frisby sprang up at once, and with eau-de-cologne in one hand and a dish of apples in the other swam to the sofa with the most praiseworthy alacrity. Sir John, no whit behind her in zeal, seized up the empty bottle of soda-water, and grabbing up a tumbler, hurried to the invalid's side.

"Are you better?" said he in his dulcet voice. "Are you really better? A little more lemonade? An apple? Let me peel you an apple. Perhaps the quilt is too warm for you. Let me try this dressing-gown; it isn't so heating—nothing like so heating."

"Ah, but you are better, Mr. Spill!" exclaimed Miss Frisby. "You look—oh, you do look so well and refreshed! It is the eau-de-cologne, Sir John's superb eau-de-cologne. And your pillows, are they comfortable? Are they soft to the head? Let me make them smooth for you, so smooth and comfortable."

Mr. Spill turned a frowning gaze from the agitated and agitating Miss Frisby, and cast an inquiring glance upon the calm though troubled countenance of the baronet.

"I can't tell you how sorry I am," said Sir John. "I wish I had never left you."

"It was my fault, all my fault!" cried Miss Frisby in distress. "Oh, my dear Sir John, why did I come at that moment? Why, why, why?"

"I pray you not to distress yourself," said the baronet. "It was really not your fault. All the blame attaches to me. I should not have left our friend alone."

Mr. Spill sat up. "What did you promise me?" he said in a good healthy voice of remonstrance. "You said you could bring unspeakable comfort to my poor wounded soul. And now I am aching in every bone of my body."

"I know, I know!" cried the baronet, greatly distressed. "My dear fellow, I am extremely upset by this accident. Believe me, my mind is as tortured as your own body; it is really. I assure you that I am most dreadfully put out about it. But are you all right now? Would you like any buttons loosened, any——?"

"I was never so treated in my life," grumbled Spill. "Every bone in my body is cracked into a hundred fractures, and my flesh is one big, aching bruise."

"Oh, some more eau-de-cologne!" cried Miss Frisby.

"Shall I send for a doctor?" asked Sir John.

"Let me alone," cried Spill. "I only ask to be let alone."

Now it struck Sir John with joyful surprise that the battering which Mr. Spill had received from Tiplady, even if it had bruised his body, had apparently brought the unspeakable comfort which he promised to his guest's soul. For the blows and the cuffs and the kicks, it seemed, had driven the devil clean out of Mr. Spill's mind; he made no reference to any spiritual conflict, nor expressed apprehension at lying in the very chamber where the devil had fallen upon him. Sir John noticed this with all the joy that his distressed mind could harbour at that moment.

"I owe you an explanation," he said tentatively.

"I think you do," replied Spill.

"Do you feel well enough to receive it now?" inquired the baronet. "Do you feel sufficiently recovered for conversation? There is no hurry, you know."

"I am as well as I am ever likely to be again," answered the ungracious Mr. Spill, groaning miserably.

"Ah, more eau-de-cologne!" cried Miss Frisby.

Mr. Spill sat up suddenly. "What has become of my boots?" he demanded sharply.

"I took them off," said Sir John.

"Ah!" sighed Spill, sinking back on the pillows. "I feel as if my feet were trodden to a pulp."

"Will you have some more lemonade?" asked Sir John tenderly.

"No!—no!—no!" grumbled Mr. Spill. "Do for pity's sake let me alone. I'm trying to think what has happened, and how it happened, and where it happened, and when it happened, and why it happened; and every time I begin to get my thoughts into something like order—for I feel as if they had been pounded into splinters—you put me clean out with your eau-de-cologne and your lemonade. Let me be." And with that he turned his head away and closed his eyes.

At that very moment there came a gentle tap at the door, and Sir John, begging Miss Frisby to excuse him for a minute, moved across the room, opened the door, and passed into the corridor. Miss Frisby heard a muttering of voices; the sharp, quick treble of a woman, the low, measured bass of the baronet; then there followed a gentle clinking of money; then the treble expressed gratitude; then——

Sir John re-entered the room with a bonnet-box.

"I took the liberty," said he, his head very much on one side, "to send for a new hat. Your own, I fear, is damaged past repair."

Miss Frisby deserted Mr. Spill's couch at a bound. Oh, how she overwhelmed Sir John with the prettiest of effusive thanks! And while she smiled, beamed, twinkled, and chattered, her quick, darting eyes took in the name of the milliner on the box, and her woman's heart (God bless their royal weaknesses) leaped in her bosom, for she knew that her head would be crowned with glory.

What perfect courtesy it was, oh, my dear, dear Sir John, to think of such a trivial thing at such a terrible moment! How superb! How magnificent! Was there ever such a man in the world? You think of everything. Ah, but this hat must never wear out; it must be kept for ever and ever. It shall mean more, oh, infinitely more, than a head covering; it is a hat for the heart. Ah, yes, it shall hang on the peg of memory in the heart's own wardrobe for ever and ever and ever.

While Miss Frisby, fluttering delightfully, poured forth her almost hysterical gratitude, Sir John, blushing a little, cut the string, opened the lid, and removed the tissue paper.

Then—with beaming diffidence—he drew forth the hat.

Now of all the presents man can make to inamorata or poor relation there is none—though it be platitudinous to say it—so fraught, woven, interwoven, bound, threaded, and lined with the possibility of failure as a hat. For women attach as much importance to their hats as to their souls—the one being there for all the world to gape at, the other being hidden and fenced about from the gaze even of their husbands; and over and above this importance of the hat in their eyes rises the supreme difficulty of feminine taste and caprice. What will suit you, madam, will no more suit your wife, sir, than the hat either lady gave to the maid last season. Every face must have its own hat! The colour or twist of a ribbon is a matter of more moment to madam than the Thirty-nine Articles; the shape of the hat a business closer to her soul than the Catechism. It is so, sir; and it has ever been so, ever will be so, world without end. And verily do I believe that even the First Epistle General of St. Peter will never put a stop to it. 'Tis true, and all men's suffrage.

Now this I say to prepare you for the behaviour of Miss Frisby at that intensely human moment, when our dapper little baronet, frowning importantly through his eyeglass, folded back the crinkling tissue-paper, peeped down into the box, and then, with elaborate care, drew forth the hat.

Miss Frisby made a step forward, her eyes sparkling,

her lips parted, her dear long hands clasped dramatically against her breast. Then she uttered a shuddering cry, covered her face with her hands, and sobbed such iron tears as Orpheus drew down Pluto's cheek.

"Good gracious!" cried Sir John, setting down the hat in a hurry, and going to Miss Frisby all anxiety.

She tore her hands away from her face, looked him for a flashing second deeply in the eyes (you could scarce have put tissue-paper between their faces), and then letting her hands fall desperately upon his shoulder, she sunk her head there and sobbed pitiably.

Sir John, with his spare hand, patted the lady's back. "What is it? What is it?" he asked, coaxing. What a pretty, slight creature it was!

"Oh, I must seem such a beast!" sobbed Miss Frisby.

"You will never seem that to me," said Sir John tenderly.

"Say that—say that again!" she pleaded.

Sir John grew a little alarmed. "Dear lady, you could never appear in an unpleasant light to me; you couldn't really. But tell me what has upset you in this way. You are so unlike your calm self. What is it? Do tell me! Do."

Miss Frisby released the baronet, and turning away, bottled her tears by the aid of a little handkerchief. "All this dreadful fighting has upset me," said she; "I am trembling now. Ah, shall I ever forget it?" Then she turned about and faced the baronet. "Don't think me ungrateful. Oh, Sir John, you must never think I could be ungrateful to you; but—that hat. Ah, it is horrid, horrid!"

You could have knocked our hero down with a feather.

"I am extremely sorry," said he. "Really, I thought the maid had done rather well. I'm so sorry you don't approve of it. Shall I send and change it? Let me do that."

But Miss Frisby had charged upon him, and was clasping one of his arms affectionately. "Oh, the hat is lovely, *lovely* as the world counts hats! Ah, do not think I find fault with your present; no, no, no! It is exquisite, sublime—as a hat. Don't think me so abominably rude as that. But as a theosophist, dear Sir John, as a fellow Monad passing through this present birth to the wider joy of Kâmaloka——"

Sir John studied the hat attentively. He looked for an auric egg and searched for some symbol of Sat, or at least Kâmarupa. "Tell me," he said at last, "what is the matter with the hat, theosophically?"

Then Miss Frisby pointed to two white feathers curled gracefully from the centre of the hat on either side of the brim.

"One of my little brothers," said she pathetically, "was slain to decorate this hat!"

"Good gracious!" cried Sir John angrily, "and I never saw it. 'Pon me soul, how unobservant I am! Yes, to be sure. Perfectly horrible!"

"Only cannibals should wear such decorations; is it not so, dear Sir John?"

"Most true, most true," replied the baronet. "I will send it back."

But Miss Frisby restrained him. "Oh, no; as a hat it is beautiful, exquisite, really exquisite. Let me try and alter it. Have you scissors, needle, thread, or thimble; have you? Do I ask too much? Ah, the maid will bring them! Oh, how good you are, how kind, how thoughtful!"

Scissors, needle, thread, and thimble were provided, and in another minute Miss Frisby was bending over the hat, while Sir John, seated close at her side, watched her white fingers flashing deftly at the intricate work of reconstruction.

Now and then he looked from the fingers to the lady's smiling eyes.

Once the lady returned his gaze.

" How clever you are ! " said he.

" 'Tis woman's work," she answered.

" But some would blunder it," he protested.

" The hat is so precious to me ! "

" Is it ? "

She looked into his eyes.

" No present ever gave donor more pleasure," said Sir John, glowing.

" How sweetly you say kind things ! "

" 'Tis easy when the heart is at the back of them."

She looked into his eyes.

" We shall see much of each other at the colony," said the baronet, with meaning.

Miss Frisby smiled. The picture of Sir John running over the meadow after his sun-bath rose then before her eyes.

" You will come, won't you ? " said he.

" I think of nothing else."

" You mean that ? "

" Indeed, and indeed I do."

" It will be a beautiful communion," said Sir John, bending forward.

" There is nothing so wonderful, so mystical, so exquisitely thrilling as the commingling of twin souls."

" Nothing," said Sir John.

" One is taken off one's feet. One doesn't know what has happened to one. It is intoxication of all the senses."

" The Triad and the Kâmarupa," sighed Sir John. " The Higher and the Lower Manas."

The lady sighed too. " One is spiritual and physical," she said resignedly.

" It is difficult to conquer Kâmarupa," said Sir John.

She looked him in the eyes. Oh, so closely, such fires in the pupils!

"How cleverly you are managing the hat," said Sir John.

"You distract my thoughts from millinery," said she, protesting.

"I am in a fever lest the needle prick your finger," he made answer.

Again she raised her gaze. They looked long into each other's eyes. Then Miss Frisby sighed, and returned to the hat.

"You will be careful, won't you?" said Sir John, bending nearer.

"Tell me," she said slowly—how strange it was to hear her speak no faster than the rest of the world!— "tell me, would .you really care—I mean, deeply and very, very sincerely—if I were to prick myself?"

Sir John summoned up all his courage to take the plunge. He bent nearer to the lady, he stretched out his arm (Miss Frisby felt its magnetism behind her back), he leant to one side in act to clasp her tenderly about the waist; he was on the utmost verge of opening. his lips—the tongue staggering there—to utter irrevocable words, when——

"He was bald-headed!" shouted Spill, sitting up with a start. Sir John and Miss Frisby jumped to their feet.

"Side-whiskers!" cried Spill excitedly.

"The eau-de-cologne!" cried Miss Frisby.

"Let me give you some lemonade," pleaded the baronet.

"I have it!" cried Spill. "It all comes back! I remember distinctly. I should know him anywhere. I can tell you what happened. Yes, I'll have some lemonade; strong, strong as you like. And when the lady's gone (no, I will *not* have any more of that eau-de-cologne), when she's gone, I say, I'll tell you the whole story."

It is to the infinite credit of Miss Frisby—whose long spinsterhood at that moment trembled in the balance—it is, I repeat—to give more emphasis to the remark—infinitely to her credit that she evinced towards the interrupting invalid the most tender and womanlike solicitude. Whatever she might think of him in the secret chambers of her Lower Manas, she displayed to him as gentle, unselfish, and compassionate an interest as ever Sister Dora bestowed upon her wounded miners. Outwardly she was a saint, and whatever she might be inwardly, let us remember that we fallible ones have nothing to do with the lady's Atmâ-Buddhi-Manas. That belongs to Sat.

When Miss Frisby, then, had smoothed Mr. Spill's cushions, sprinkled eau-de-cologne upon his pillows, and placed smelling-salts, apples, and raisins on a chair at his side, she put on the new hat, now innocent of her little brother's feathers, gave Sir John her hand, thanked him a thousand times for all his incomparable and superb kindnesses, and then, accompanied by the baronet, made her way to the hall door.

For every person loitering in the passages or climbing the broad stairs Sir John offered up a prayer of gratitude. When he returned to the sick-room he went towards Mr. Spill's couch, his face charged with crisis, and taking the invalid's hand in his own, bent upon him a most solemn and concentrated look.

"My dear brother," said he, "I thank you. I thank you. Without knowing it, you have done me an unconscionable service."

Then did Mr. Spill give the whole thing up, and turning upon his side, ask wearily whether he was dreaming or mad.

CHAPTER XIV

Of Love, and the Siege laid to Mrs. FitzGerald's Heart

IF any foolish ones have murmured that this history is without the sweet, constraining interest of love, let them now hold their peace, and for ever after laud this volume as the best book of amours in the libraries of the world. For, leaving Sir John Sparrow in the tangle of ideals that his own folly has got about him, and, as we have seen, in the peril of Miss Frisby's attractions, we flee from before the face of vegetarianism, fruitarianism, theosophy, and religious manias, and, so please your honour, get our breath wandering at great peace of mind through the cool, glimmering garden of the lovely Mrs. FitzGerald.

The widow is entertaining.

There are one or two matrons leisurely walking beside beds all a gay jumble of cottage-flowers. There is a stout old gentleman reading a novel in a hammock swaying softly under spreading boughs. There are two pretty girls in two punts moving listlessly over the lake of green shadows, with chivalrous manhood to protect them from disaster. And—oh, Sir John, see it not!—in two deep wicker-chairs under a close brotherhood of elms—elms

"Annihilating all that's made
To a green thought in a green shade";

while about them

> "All the flowers and trees do close
> To weave the garlands of Repose"

—recline the beautiful widow and Guy Drayton.

'Tis pleasant, madam, when you are in the neighbourhood of thirty, to have one-and-twenty dangling at your side—all the youth you have so lately left behind, all the carelessness which you have just begun to miss, all the inexperience for which you pine again, there prostrate in adoration at your feet. Ah, 'tis sweet, passing sweet! 'Tis the company that chases trouble from the heart, brings back something lost out of life, and drives sad-eyed reflection from the mind. 'Tis the company that gives earth its gladness, and thrusts the churchyard fifty fathoms deep in the ocean of oblivion. 'Tis the company that sets the blood coursing through the veins, the heart beating high again; that gives a tenderer greenness to the grass, a richer glory to the rose, a subtler fragrance to the breeze.

Because—because——

It leaves the brain alone!

What matters it to her that he talks of a polo match, of the regiment he adorns, of his club, of his servant, of his tobacco, even of his grandmother?

Not a pin's head, sir.

'Tis the boy's blue eyes, his fair cheeks, his burgeoning manhood, his unconscious conceit. She has got youth at her feet, a gift from the gods. The joy of existence is there before her; the carelessness, the breeziness, the recklessness of youth! Could the wisest philosopher in the world break the spell?

Nay, sir; for the lady is back again

> In that first garden of our simpleness,

dreaming such soft dreams, thinking such trembling

thoughts, plucking such tender buds as never philosopher could lay in her lap, though he had the wisdom of Plato, the persistence of Diogenes, and went searching day and night through the Garden of Eden.

Ah, had Mrs. FitzGerald cultivated her mind, had she but learned the abiding joy which comes from study of social problems, the spiritual satisfaction which springs from profound interest in animals' rights and dietetics, she might now have sent the youth to fetch *The Ethics of Diet* from the library table and put delusion out of her poor foolish heart.

But being a very silly lady, with scarce a care beyond the adornment of her person and the presenting of a smiling face to the world, she sits in the green shade of those doming trees, her face turned upon its cushion towards him, her lips trembling into delicious smiles, her eyes merry with the heart's happiness; and thus sitting, thus looking, all unlistening, she is content with her hour.

> "Ah! I remember well (and how can I
> But evermore remember well) when first
> Our flame began, when scarce we knew what was
> The flame we felt; when as we sat and sighed
> And looked upon each other, and conceived
> Not what we ailed,—yet something we did ail";

and so do you, sir; and so do you, madam; and so does all the wide, merry world of humanity, when it isn't engaged trying to hop the hurdle of our good, wholesome Finity.

And so it comes about that Guy Drayton, lieutenant of Light Horse, up to his brown ears in debt, with no more brains than one's next-door neighbour, has got the prettiest widow in England at his feet, while he talks about his ponies and his chance of the adjutancy. Is it that woman sees farther than any of us—as far as the

Knight of the Rueful Feature—and behind this front of self-satisfaction, boyish swagger, and youthful light-heartedness beholds that spirit burning into flame, which will one day hurl him glad at the head of thundering horse, through the rolling clouds of battle into the jaws of glorious death? The man of action— Don Quixote has proved it beyond the peddling reach of disputants—is first favourite in the human race. And if he does his duty, your honour who stays at home when the bugles blow, will not say he has no right there, even though he bore you to death at the dinner-table.

Now if all this be not sufficient to awaken your interest in the plot running through and dissecting the adventures of the open-minded baronet, I would bid you observe that the tall, distinguished-looking gentleman in white ducks, talking so easily and charmingly to the matrons among the flowers, does ever and anon glance under his dark eyelashes, without the wonted smile in his eyes, towards the widow and the young soldier.

This is no other than Clarence Mortimer—he whose friends are grand dukes and archduchesses; he whose anecdotes are of kings and ministers of state; he who, whenever you meet him, has always just got back from Vienna, St. Petersburg, Rome, or Cairo. This is no other than Clarence Mortimer, who has a bedroom in a London club, and lives for the most part in the castles and palaces of Europe. The wittiest raconteur, the suavest gentleman, the most polished courtier at that day ruffling it in courts and chancelleries. "At that day"—for the reign of these drawing-room favourites is scarce longer, and rests on no surer foundation, than the tyranny of a social beauty. And even now Clarence Mortimer is beginning to grow a little anxious about his future; is in the very state of mind which sends the social beauty to skin tonics, quack soaps and powders. Alas, poor Clarry!

But, prithee, regard him not as a faded butterfly. With those easy manners, that bright torrent of talk, that comprehensive knowledge of his world, he is a dangerous rival to our little rustic baronet, may even prove smiling conqueror of the inexperienced lieutenant. of horse. Though the grey twinkles in the black hair and lights the dark moustache, though the Italian complexion puts on another greyness of its own, and though there are lines round the eyes which are not the ripples of laughter—there is a strength behind it all, a long-enduring strength, which some women get to love a thousand times more recklessly than the smooth bloom of youth. With Mrs. FitzGerald's fortune for the stakes —and let us assume that he has a polite affection for the lady — Clarence would fight hard, persistently, mercilessly.

Does he not know, too, the story of that first bootless marriage, and is he not, therefore, ready with subtle sympathy? Happy is Mrs. FitzGerald when she sits at his side, and at every soft phrase of gentleness and tenderness, must not her dear woman's heart yearn for something that hitherto her life has missed? But a burned child dreads the fire. If the headstrong passion of the young soldier is to be mistrusted, so also is the careful sympathy of the experienced man of the world. Mrs. FitzGerald is besieged, but the garrison in that pretty head of hers is vigilant and alert; the gates of the heart will not be opened, we may rest assured, till the brain commands. That is Sir John's one hope— and a woman's brain!

So you see that while our hero is away, our heroine is besieged on both sides. While philosophy run mad is scattering his brains on the waste places of the earth,

Q

youth on this side and the world on that lay siege
to the simple lady's heart. Body o' me! what a plot
is here! If after this, madam, you can prove before
twelve honest men and true that you read not the
story to its end, I hereby covenant and make promise
to pay to your bankers, or to any charity you may be
gracious enough to designate, such sums or sums, not
exceeding six shillings, as you may have spent, or
caused to be spent, in the acquisition of this true,
faithful, and philosophical history.

Now while Mrs. FitzGerald dreamed beneath the
elms, and while Clarence Mortimer glanced appre-
hensively under his dark lashes at the widow and the
youth, there came over the park towards the garden
where this drama was being played that very staunch
friend and ally of our absent hero, Parson Tom Shott.

In the breast pocket of the leviathan lay a letter just
received from Tiplady, relating (to the horror and consternation of Tom Shott) the aberrations of the baronet,
and drawing as gloomy a picture of the future as a
split nose and aching body could inspire. With this
document in his pocket came the parson, to concoct
with the widow some plan for bringing the baronet
both to his senses and to the lady's feet.

In this way argued Tom Shott, reading his own
wishes into the heart of Mrs. FitzGerald: She loves
him; he, if he only knew it, loves her. God made them
for each other. The village is going to the devil without him. Life here isn't the same thing. Even the
widow has begun entertaining house - parties. Now,
if she learns how desperately her lover is situated, will
she not, being true woman, throw conventional modesty
to the winds and go seek him where he wanders, blind
and foolish, in the wilderness of fads and crotchets?
If she won't I must make her, that's all.

In this way argued Tom Shott.

But when he drew near and beheld her with Adonis at her side, his heart grew sad within him, for he knew the weaknesses of women. And when, taking advantage o his presence there, Clarence Mortimer forsook the matrons and the flower-beds, and came smiling into the· midst of the trio, with his eyes all for the widow, poor Tom Shott knitted his brows, humped his great shoulders, thrust out his red upper lip, and wished the two lovers at the devil. Here was confusion of all his plans, confusion with a vengeance.

"I have news of Sir John," said he gloomily.

The widow was delighted. How was he, when was he coming back, what was he doing, was he very well? This was charming, quite charming; the long silence broken at last!

"He's as happy as a king," said Tom Shott stoutly. "Goes everywhere, sees everyone; most popular, of course."

"Of course, of course."

"Tremendous favourite! People delighted with him." He glared at Mr. Mortimer.

"But when is he coming back?" protested she, jealous of London.

"Not a word of that. Too happy; much too happy."

"The traitor!" cried she. "Does he mean to desert us then?" She laughed mischievously.

"There is a hint in the letter," said Tom Shott, with great meaning. He did not like the lady's laugh. Clearly she was mortified by the baronet's neglect, a most dangerous mood in woman.

"A hint of return?" she asked carelessly.

The parson nodded his head.

"Tell him," said she, "please tell him that we are in sackcloth and ashes till he returns."

The parson considered that remark for several seconds. He turned it over and over—slowly, of course—and at the end of his meditation could make neither head nor tail of it. It might have been the utterance of in-difference, the careless remark of amused interest, or the unhappy challenge of pique.

"He'll be back—soon," said the parson at last. "That's as plain as butter." An answer which seemed to him at the moment the very apogee of diplomatic discretion.

Then Clarence Mortimer said something about London distractions, and Mr. Drayton came in with a full-blooded testimony to the joys of the country. Mrs. FitzGerald danced away to the midst of the battle, smiling, rippling, applauding, controverting—now for London, now for Arcadia, now for society, now for seclusion. And outside the battle, glum, and without a stroke for this side or that, stood the parson, thinking of the vegetarian.

'Twas black, mighty black for Sparrow.

He had said farewell and was lunging away, when he turned slowly round and retraced his steps thoughtfully. He must do something more for Sparrow. Women are weak and—kittle cattle. Mrs. FitzGerald came out of the shadow of the trees and met him. That was a good sign.

"You want to speak to me?" she said, opening her parasol.

He stood considering, looking down gloomily into her eyes.

"There's no bad news in the village, is there?" she asked, no smile in her eyes.

"I am thinking about Sparrow," said he.

"Oh!" The smile came twinkling back.

"I wanted to tell you that I may possibly go to

town next week to see him. A matter of great importance."

"Yes?" said she, waiting.

"And in the meantime," he said slowly; "and in the meantime——" He stopped and half turned away.

"Yes?" said she.

He came slowly round and faced her. "Promise me not to do anything!" he said, and with that shot fired, bungled off before she could answer him.

"Now what does that dear, sweet old creature mean?" cried she. "*Promise not to do anything!* What in the world can——"

"Come and play croquet," cried Mr. Drayton at her side. "You and I against Thingmebob and Miss Campbell. Do!"

"Thingmebob," watching them under his dark lashes beneath the elms, his hand gently smoothing the cushion where the widow's face had rested, was considering whether her mind was yet ready for his profession.

"If he loses her," muttered the parson, stumbling towards the village, "'twill be his own fault. Never before did I go so near telling a lie for another man; I won't do it again. Jack must fight his own battles. 'Tis no affair of mine. And a vegetarian! The Lord help us!"

CHAPTER XV

Of the fierce and futile Colloquy which passed between
Sir John Sparrow and Mr. Spill

WE have now left the reader in a state of fine sus-
pense concerning the fate of Mrs. FitzGerald,
bagging him, so to speak, for the rest of the story; and
now we proceed to follow the errant Sir John in those
adventures of his which show, if they do nothing else,
how dangerous it is for anyone to strive to be perfect.

Before, however, taking the reader to the famous
Nature Colony, established by the joint labours of the
baronet and Alexander Fontey (we shall arrive there in
the next chapter, if Mrs. FitzGerald doesn't precipitate
matters in the meantime), we must relate a conversation
between Sir John and the battered Mr. Spill which was
held during the latter's convalescence.

"So you see," said Sir John, winding up an exordium
on theosophy, "that this religion explains all the phe-
nomena in the world, that it disestablishes the devil,
explains the reason for man's existence, and removes
from the mind of good people the uncomfortable reflection that the very large majority of their fellow-
mortals are destined for a place of torment."

"That may be," said Mr. Spill, "but it won't work."

"Won't work!" cried the baronet. "My dear sir, are
you aware, can you possibly be aware, that this is the

religion of the teeming millions of the East? Why, it is working now, and has been working ever since the creation of the world."

"Very possibly, but it won't do," answered Mr. Spill imperturbably. "It may suit the people of India, for they're a lazy, dreamy, happy-go-lucky sort of people, they are; but here, we're business-like, go-ahead, and practical. Practical! We must have a business-like religion. When I knocked your butler down for the devil I stood typical for England. I was wrong in detail, right in intent. I may have been a bit touched in the upper story at the moment; that doesn't matter. When I met what I thought was the devil, I knocked him down. That's English, and that's business."

"But can you comfortably—tell me honestly and sincerely—contemplate, without misgiving of any kind, a place or state of eternal torment?"

"Why, that's the hang of the whole thing," quoth Mr. Spill, smiling at the baronet's ignorance. "That's business! You must have profit and loss in a matter of this kind, and if you don't have loss, how the deuce are you going to expect any profit?"

"But hell, eternal hell!" cried Sir John in a hollow voice. "It is a monstrous thought!"

Mr. Spill laughed quickly.

"It doesn't do to be too squeamish in matters of this kind," said he. "Remember that outside this little world of ours *everything* is on a big scale. Size is nothing, time is nothing. Eternal hell, sir?—a mere nothing."

"I am puzzled how to appeal to you," said Sir John, most troubled. "For hitherto I have only met Christians who shudder at the thought of eternal punishment, and are therefore glad to contemplate any possible and reverent explanation of scriptural allusions to such a thing. But you—well, 'pon me soul, Spill, **you seem** to take a positive delight in the thought."

Mr. Spill smiled good-temperedly as though he had been congratulated on the accomplishment of some bold feat. "I don't know that I take a delight in it," said he; "I don't think I should quite say that; but I'll tell you what I don't do. I don't funk it! If it's got to be, it's got to be. Your squeamish people are so confoundedly narrow; they judge everything from their own little standpoint. Don't you see? Can't you really see? Now do just try if you can't see it in this way, that hell mustn't be judged from a *human* point of view. It's a divine institution. When we get out of this body of death we shan't think anything about it. It won't strike us as anything extraordinary. We shall be too big, much too big."

"Isn't it a more reasonable faith——?" began Sir John.

"There you go!" quoth Spill, flinging up his hands. "Reason! reason! What the dickens has reason got to do with it?"

"We are given our reason to use, not to despise," replied Sir John.

"You might as well say we are given our lusts to employ, not to curb," answered Spill. "Rot, sir, rot."

"I see what you mean," said Sir John slowly. "You regard reason as a dangerous gift?"

"Now, look here," said Spill, "the reason can't comprehend eternity, can it? It can't comprehend a self-existing God, can it? It can't comprehend space without a brick wall at either end of it, can it? So what's the good of reason? Now, come!"

"To me," replied Sir John, "none of these presents any difficulty. I find no trouble whatever in contemplating be-ness, that is to say absoluteness. I find no difficulty in postulating a beginning that had no beginning, a creation that had no creation, an ego that has been incarnating and reincarnating ever since the beginning that had no beginning begun. These things I accept and can believe, merely because they couldn't be otherwise."

"Then what's the matter with Christianity?" demanded Mr. Spill, with great force.

"I have no quarrel with the spirit of your religion," replied Sir John, warming to his work. "Its aims are my aims; its *raison d'être* is my *raison d'être;* for I seek the perfection of the human race. But according to those Christians who by placing a literal meaning upon every word in the gospels that suits their theory, and a rhetorical meaning upon every word that challenges their compromise between God and Mammon—according to them this perfection of man, which they seek and I seek, is to be reached in one incarnation between the narrow points of a single birth and a single death. That, I say, is monstrous. The perfection of man must be the labour of æons. And you will see, if you join my colony, that the first step in this direction—a step which your Christians, in despite of their desperate hurry, dare not take—is the complete, perfect, and utter renunciation of all those things which the world counts good and to be desired."

"A religion like that won't work," said Mr. Spill.

"But it is the Christianity of the gospels," retorted Sir John.

"What's to become of trade?" demanded Mr. Spill.

"Perish trade!" cried the baronet hotly.

"There you go!" laughed Mr. Spill, smiting his knee. "Perish trade! Why, that's part of Christianity! 'Blessed are the poor'; why? A person isn't blest because he's pinched for money. He's blest because, being poor, he has to work. Work's the salvation of the world. If a man isn't working he's doing something he oughtn't to do, and thinking thoughts he oughtn't to think, and that's why a camel can go easier through the eye of a needle, et cætera! Christianity, don't you see, is a practical, common-sense, business-like religion."

"I do not contemplate a time when all the world will be peopled by idlers," rejoined Sir John, growing calm again. "But between consecrated labour and the hurrying struggle to get rich that is ruining men to-day there is all the difference in the world."

"Now let's fight this matter out," said Spill, sitting on the edge of his chair. "What do you give more than Christianity gives?"

"We explain the sorrow and suffering of creation," said Sir John.

"We say, 'Don't bother about 'em,'" replied Spill.

"We give a wider conception of the Creator."

"Too wide to get inside the earth; we give a Father. Go on."

"But you don't seem to——"

"Go on," said Spill; "name your points; never mind about argument."

"We embrace the whole world," cried the baronet, waving a rhetorical arm.

"Niggers mostly," said Spill.

"I mean, we do not shut out from our heaven any race, nationality, or creed."

"Neither do we."

"But you do! You say that only such-and-such will enter into the kingdom of heaven?"

"They shut themselves out; we don't."

"But how narrow, how cramping, how petty!"

"How many more hows?" laughed Spill, lying back at ease. "Now, let's get to business; business is my strong point, and in business I'll match my religion against yours. Come, now. We tell men the object of this life is to save their souls. So do you. We tell them not to do evil, but to do good—so do you. We tell them that if they do good they'll go to heaven. You tell 'em the same thing in a more roundabout fashion. We tell them if they do evil they'll go to hell. You tell 'em it will all come right in the end. That's the rock where we split. Now, which of these two is going to do most good to the drunken, swearing, idle vagabonds that illtreat their wives, starve their children, and cheat their masters? Which of these two is going to do most good to the little, miserable, swindling tradesman; to the painted, powdered, flouncing woman of fashion; the gambling clerk, the lying solicitor, the dirty - minded puppies of smoke-rooms and taverns?"

"I see your point," said Sir John; "but what merit would there be in abstention from evil on the part of these poor creatures springing merely from fear of punishment in another world? Would there be any merit in it? Do you think there would, now?"

"Business, business!" said Spill, striking his knee with his fist. "We're not talking philosophy, we're doing a bit of business; don't let's have any high-falutin' in this deal; human souls are the merchandise and eternity the contract. Now, look here. Is it better for a boy to learn his lesson for fear of the cane; or, because he doesn't like lessons, and because it's immoral to fear the cane, is it better for him to spend his time flinging stones at cats and sucking his thumb in front of a tuck-shop?"

"There's something in what you say," said the baronet thoughtfully.

"Only business, common-sense business," laughed Spill.

"But the great rock on which we split, of course, is not the doctrine of hell," said the baronet, pulling down his shirt-cuffs. "We deny that the Absolute required, or could tolerate, any vicarious atonement for the sins of men and women. We cannot accept, though we reverence the Being, the divinity of Christ. And we most seriously reject and denounce the dogma, that it is only by accepting the divinity of Christ that men are received into the kingdom of heaven."

"Oh, then, you're damned!" said Spill easily; "and that's all about it. I didn't know you were quite such a fool as that. I thought you were only playing about with theosophy, and trying to fit it in with Christianity. I see. You're an atheist."

"No, sir, I am not!" cried Sir John, rising up very angry.

"There you are!" laughed Spill. "You deny every jack thing! First you deny God, and then you deny that you deny God. And now I suppose you'll deny that. Where's the end of all this denying?"

"The God in whom I believe——" began Sir John.

Spill interrupted. "You deny Christ."

"Well?"

"He is the one and only God."

"He is not!"

"He is."

Then Spill laughed, and reached out for his hat. "At the end of all our arguments we get to that: 'He is'—'He isn't.' That's how it's always been, that's how it always will be; and that's how it was meant to be! Men fiddle with arguments about the Miracles, about the Birth, about the Resurrection; but in the end it all comes back to the oldest of all sceptical questions, Is He God? Well, my friend, my answer to that is, By their fruits ye shall know them! You say He isn't; well, that's your look-out. You do just as you please, and don't bother about me. I shan't be able to get to you in the next world to say, 'I told you so'; but you'll know right enough when you get there that you were wrong and I was right. If you'll take a friend's advice—I don't force it on you—you'll give up all your Kâmarupa-fiddlesticks, and take what Heaven has been good enough to provide for you. Christianity, sir, didn't get into Great Britain by accident. Take my word for it. If you had been born with a turban on your head and a cummerbund round your stomach there might be some excuse for your Kâmarupa; but as it is, why, it won't work. It's not English; it's not common-sense; it's not downright; it's not business; and if it is anything at all it's Kâmaruparish—which damns it at once."

Now, the devil, with a plastered nose, entering the apartment at that moment, Mr. Spill beat a hasty retreat, and left the baronet in possession of the field.

CHAPTER XVI

Wherein Sir John Sparrow Bids Farewell to the World from the top of a packing-case

ON a certain blustering day in August a train steamed out of a North London terminus with a saloon carriage attached to it, bearing the label "Sir John Sparrow's party." This was the first exodus from civilisation to the Nature Colony.

Among the company in the saloon were Simon, Priscilla, and Izzie Peace; Jane Vince and Eleanor Frisby; Spill and Tiplady; Richard Sparrow and Captain Chivvy. These were the invited guests of Sir John. But the advertisement which the hero of these pages had caused to appear in the *Vegetarian Herald*, inviting people to be present at the opening ceremony, had brought into the party some dozen or more guests with whom the reader is no more acquainted than was Sir John Sparrow at the moment of their appearance. Included among these strangers to the baronet—though, with one exception, all the party had some knowledge of each other—were a handsome couple, brother and sister, by name John and Mary Hessey, a certain Thomas Pugh, and a Mr. Gabriel Pick. The one person in the company, of whom nobody knew anything at all, was a thin, under-sized man, with a long, red, inflamed face, large, cod-like eyes, hair plastered with grease, upon whose lips sat a perpetual grin, and in whose eyes one perceived scorn of a sort ambushed behind weak laughter. He sat by himself, listened slyly to the talk about him, and studied the rest of the party with an amused interest.

Whether Captain Chivvy, who was fully determined, poor fellow, to blow his brains out on the following morning, had depressed our hero on their walk to the station, or whether some doubt as to the wisdom of the step he was taking tortured and distracted Sir John's mind, we know not; but on the authority of so close an observer of his master as Tiplady, we have it that never before had the baronet appeared so utterly spiritless, so sunk in abstraction, so dead to the things about him.

Spill, however, was in fine form, and kept the saloon in a hubbub by his brisk and cheery championing of Christianity, a religion which he defended with astonishing alacrity and point against the attacks of atheists, deists, agnostics, Swedenborgians, Buddhists, and positivists. Captain Chivvy, who had been asked by the baronet to protect him from Eleanor Frisby, but who was sitting as near to the beautiful Miss Hessey as the Peace family would let him, joined in this animated discussion of comparative religions, and observed of every single creed as it was championed by its follower that he had always thought there was a great deal to be said for it.

In the midst of this discussion Mrs. Peace informed Captain Chivvy that her dear daughter Izzie had taken to authorship.

Chivvy looked up, as polite and interested as possible, and asked Miss Peace if she were writing a novel.

Izzie's eyebrows shot up, a hopeless smile got entangled in her eyes and she looked helplessly up to

Simon, against whose side she was nestling with over-whelming affection.

"My daughter," said Simon, the Adam's apple palpitating, "does not write novels. I hope she never may write novels. For a novel is the lowest form of composition, scarcely removed from the story wherewith foolish nurses beguile the tedium of infants. It has improved somewhat of late years, since the importation by novelists of psychology and philosophy into their plots; but the novel, *per se*, must ever remain incomparably below all other forms of composition."

"It takes a thundering clever fellow to write a good one," objected Chivvy.

"You surprise me," said Simon sarcastically. "I had always imagined that the only quality required for story-telling was an unnatural and unphilosophical fertility of imagination."

"Take Dumas!" cried Chivvy.

"I must refuse to take Dumas," laughed Simon. "That is a medicine my mind does not stand in need of at the present moment. I don't know, of course, what it may come to; but for the present I must refuse to take Dumas. I am sorry to disappoint you, but I really cannot take Dumas!"

Before Chivvy could reply—he was getting a little angry—Priscilla Peace intervened. "Izzie," said she, "is dreadfully in earnest; she is writing a most portentous volume, frightfully deep, you know. It is called—what's the book called, Izzie?"

Simon made answer: "My daughter's work, the first pages of which I have been privileged to read warm from her brain, and for which I venture to prophesy an enduring reputation when it leaves the press, is called *The Larger God.* It sweeps away all the legends that have grown round religion, it strips faith of all its parasitical difficulties, and in a really masterly fashion presents the founder of Christianity in an entirely new light."

"A very ambitious book," said Chivvy, glancing at the smiling Miss Hessey.

"That is a quality of all great works, I understand," replied Simon.

John Hessey broke in: "I always thought that for a book of such a kind one had to be the master of all classical languages, had to know the history of nearly all the ancient races of mankind, besides having an acquaintance with Oriental tongues, and a working knowledge of the science of religious evolution."

"No, sir," replied Simon, "all that is unnecessary. What is required is not a knowledge of grammar-books, but the seeing eye, the open mind, the understanding heart. These three my daughter possesses in what I venture to describe as a remarkable degree."

After this Captain Chivvy, wisely enough, devoted himself to Miss Hessey.

At the other end of the saloon Sir John sat with Mr. Gabriel Pick, a prickly-faced youth, with the hard concentrated expression of the fanatic.

"I've brought my meal with me," said he, holding up two little paper bags.

"A very small quantity, surely?" said the baronet, coming out from the shadow of his gloom.

"It lasts me twenty-four hours," replied Gabriel Pick. "I'm a one-meal-a-day man, and I never drink a drop of liquid. My object is to put down the eating part of life to its lowest point. Vegetarians make the mis_ take, and a very fatal mistake it is, of thinking far too much of eating. That's why people call them faddists. In reality, of course, vegetarianism is a religion, not a diet."

R

"And what do you eat, may I ask?" quoth the baronet.

Mr. Gabriel Pick untwisted the grubby mouth of one little bag and disclosed to Sir John's view some uncooked grains of oatmeal. He then served the other bag in the same fashion, and showed a small quantity of apple-pips.

"You astound me," said Sir John.

Mr. Pick smiled easily. "Has it never struck you," said he, "that the vital force in all fruits is to be found in the seed? When one eats the flesh of an apple, one is swallowing a large quantity of water and a very small quantity of useless pulp. It is in the pip of the apple, as in the germ of the oat grain, that the real strength resides. Think," he added, taking a single pip from his bag and holding it upon the palm of his extended hand, "think what this little seed contains! In it there lie compact the roots, the trunk, the boughs, the leaves, the innumerable fruitage of a whole apple tree! Within this little seed is all the rest lying dormant; but behind it, to quicken the rest into blooming existence, is that marvellous vitalising force—the germ of life. It is that which I eat."

"You interest me amazingly," answered Sir John. "It never struck me before that the flesh of fruit is the least useful part about it. Reflection, of course, tells me that it is. I like your theory hugely. It is the theory of common sense. And—you find yourself well upon it?"

"Never better in my life."

"Good, good!" exclaimed Sir John; "I must certainly try it. It seems to me that such a diet is a distinct advance upon the more clumsy form of fruitarianism which I have hitherto practised."

In this way the journey was passed, and after some

three-quarters of an hour in the train the party got out at a small wind-blown station, where an old man in corduroys was doing the office of station-master, ticket-collector, and several porters.

Outside the station two long, dusty, and ramshackle brakes were drawn up for the baronet's party, and after the porter had despatched the train, scratched his head over the luggage, and examined the papers thrust by the guard into his horny hand, he unbolted the gate, collected the tickets, and left our folk free to scramble into these carriages.

It was an interminable drive, a drive during which the horses walked more than a half of the journey. The wind blew great towering waves of dust from the road, and hurled the gritty powder into the eyes and teeth of our passengers. The sun having got behind a vast continent of leaden cloud, the scenery on either side of the hedges presented a cold and cheerless aspect. Neither house nor mortal, not even a beast, was to be seen on the blue-grey landscape. Nothing was there but swaying trees, reeling hedges, and a sad earth.

After an hour of this the party was set down before a small, flat-faced flint house, and when the cloud of dust which welcomed them at their destination had blown away, Alexander Fontey, in his Nature costume, was seen with an axe on his shoulder coming forward to greet the travellers. It was arranged that the horses should be put up in the barns (for the stables had been turned into bedrooms by the ingenious Mr. Fontey), and that the drivers should eat their lunch there in company with the horses. The party not remaining at the Colony would return at five o'clock.

"Rather a long way from the station," said Sir John to Alexander Fontey, as the guests moved towards the house.

"Just what we want," spluttered Fontey. "The further we are from trains, shops, people, and houses, the nearer we are to Nature."

"Yes, that is true," said Sir John, looking a little sorrowfully towards Captain Chivvy at the side of Miss Hessey.

"By-the-by, Fontey, can you tell me who that individual is there—the little man in the brown hat?" asked Sir John.

"Probably a Press representative," answered Pontey. "I'll go and ask him. We must make a fuss over him if he's a journalist. I sent an invitation to all the papers." And with that he hurried away to the red-faced man, who had sat silent during the journey.

When he returned he looked unhappy. "No; he's only a vegetarian. His name is Snape. It seems that there are no pressmen here, not one. Beastly nuisance. I wanted to get my speech into the papers."

"Perhaps it is better to be private just at first," answered the baronet, who was feeling somewhat unhappy.

"I wanted to have lunch under that tree," went on Fontey, "but it's too blowy. We shall have to have it in the kitchen. It's the best we can do. Shall we make our speeches in the kitchen or under this tree? I'm rather in favour of the tree myself; it looks to me a kind of historical tree. It might be very famous one day. It's young, too; it will last a good time. Just what one wants when one's making history."

"I think perhaps the kitchen would be better," said Sir John. "The wind is rather against speaking, isn't it?"

"Just as you like," answered Pontey carelessly. "The kitchen's not likely to last, though. There's a crack in one of the walls big enough to put one's arm in; it's only stucco, you know. But I don't know that that need matter. We can hold all our future discussions under the tree, and so future generations will not care so much about the first gathering."

"Where can we wash?" asked the baronet, entering the house. "Some of the ladies would certainly like to get rid of the dust and dirt of the journey."

"Wash! Oh, I never thought of that. I always bathe in the river. We don't want to start with wash-stands and basins. If you once get the thin end of the wedge in, you never know where it will end. We might even get to armchairs and sofas, and then it would be all U.P. with Nature. I shouldn't suggest washing if I were you."

Sir John did not.

Lunch was served in the kitchen, the gentlemen leaning against the walls and doors, the ladies being accommodated with a small deal table and long benches. The meal consisted entirely of uncooked food—biscuits, cakes, plums, dates, prunes, apples, oranges, almonds and raisins, dried walnuts, and brown bread.

"What are we going to drink, uncle?" asked Richard Sparrow cheerfully, a piece of cake in his hand. He had been laughing very merrily with Mr. Spill.

Sir John looked dolefully at Fontey.

"Drink! Oh, I never thought of that," replied Alexander. "I always go to the river myself; it's the natural way of drinking, and the water's as cold as ice. But there's a pump somewhere; I'll go and see."

He returned presently with a pailful of water, staggering under the load, and splashing the liquid down his bare legs and over the stone floor. A few cups were discovered, and having been filled by Richard Sparrow, were passed down the table.

Captain Chivvy distinguished himself during this part

of the festivities by stuffing the sporting newspaper **he** had brought with him into the huge, windy crack in the wall, so that Miss Hessey might be relieved from holding her handkerchief against her ear.

Mr. Snape, by himself in a corner, ate a great deal, and smiled sweetly upon the company.

Alexander Fontey approached Sir John. "As soon as you've had enough to eat," he whispered, "you'd better go and get into your Nature dress. I've shoved it into your hammock in the stables. Your opening speech ought to be made in the proper dress."

Sir John, meek as a lamb, consented to this arrangement, and when Fontey had pointed through a cracked window to the stables where he was to sleep, the baronet slipped out of the kitchen, and made his way thither with as heavy a heart as he had ever known in all his life.

Somehow the Colony did not appeal to him. It was not what his fancy had painted. There was an absence of beauty, an absence of peace, an absence of enthusiasm. It was too real, too solid, too brick and mortar. The ideal was in his mind; this sad reality could find no lodgment there. As he went to his stable the merriment of the coachmen over their meal in the barn smote unpleasantly on his ear.

He found several hammocks strung up in the stable, one in every stall, and a few benches without backs placed against the whitewashed walls. All the hammocks were swinging in the wind, which whistled through the windows and came sharply from the loft above.

He went to the hammock loaded with a bundle, found it to contain a Nature dress, and having examined it pathetically (he felt very lonely), he took off his clothes, arrayed himself in the new costume, and feeling a little awkward in his sandals, emerged from his stable and shuffled towards the house.

As he crossed the yard the coachmen burst into a hearty laugh, and crowded clatteringly to the doorway of the barn, chattering and chuckling as unrestrainedly as if Sir John had dressed himself in this fashion expressly for their amusement. The baronet certainly did present a very comical appearance, for the gown was loose and full, his legs were extremely thin, and his well-brushed hair, his eyeglass, and his general appearance of breeding struck incongruously with the savage oddity of the costume. Then the cold wind caused him to walk shrinkingly, and scraps of whirling paper were blown against his shins, plastering themselves there. So the coachmen held their sides in excess of merriment.

When he entered the kitchen the first eyes he encountered were those of the mysterious Mr. Snape, and the steady grin in those cod-like orbs discomposed Sir John infinitely more than the laughter of the coachmen. Here he was wounded in the house of his friends.

Miss Frisby, too, harassed and distressed him by exclaiming, with a thousand passionate gestures, and with all the emphasis of which that good lady was capable, that never before had she seen Sir John look one quarter so well. Richard Sparrow said that his uncle looked like a Frenchman going to bathe, and Tiplady set about arranging the folds of the garment in something like order.

All this struck Sir John in an unhappy light. He felt that everybody regarded the whole thing as unreal —a farce, a comedy. But when Spill exclaimed cheerfully and confidently from the end of the room, "Now, how is this sort of rot going to upset Christianity?" our hero experienced such a wave of depression as very nearly swept vegetarianism, theosophy, and communism clean out of his mind.

The remark of Mr. Spill, however, raised a storm of debate, and distracted the attention of the company, save in the case of the ladies, from our hero and his dress. It was in the midst of this clamour that Alexander Fontey, who had a speech of his own to deliver, banged upon the table with his axe, and called out for silence.

"Brother John Sparrow," said he, "will now make the opening speech."

In the clapping that followed our hero inquired of Pontey where he should stand. "Oh, on the end of one of those benches!" said Alexander carelessly, pointing to the table.

"I don't think that would quite do," said Sir John anxiously. "You see, standing on any such height, with——" He waved his hand about his thighs.

"Just as you please," answered the cheerful Fontey, and plunged away to the scullery. Ere the murmur of conversation had risen again to its full tide of cheerfulness Alexander returned, bearing in his hands a small packing-case. This box he set down on the stone floor· at the head of the table, and then, as if he had done his part, with eyebrows raised and arms swinging, stalked to the other end of the kitchen.

Sir John mounted the packing-case gingerly.

The garment he wore immediately began to flap against his legs; a cold wind tickled his shrinking calves. He looked sadly at the window on his right hand.

Miss Frisby jumped from the bench, loosened her cloak as she went, and dragging two bonnet-pins from her hat, transfixed the cloak across the window in the twinkling of an eye.

"Thank you very much," said Sir John.

A deep silence followed, and our hero had nothing to do but deliver himself of his speech.

Now, 'tis easy to sit at home rounding periods, or 'tis easy to stand before an audience of a thousand and paint one's political opponents in Cimmerian shades; but to stand upon a wobbling packing-case in a little whitewashed kitchen, with the wind howling outside, and, moreover, in a dress admirably adapted for sea-bathing, and thus to address some twenty grinning people on the brotherhood of humanity—Lord, sir, 'tis a task to tie the tongue of a Gaelic orator.

Sir John stroked his nose, then inserted his fingers in his girdle, then looked perplexedly at his sandals, then fixed an appealing gaze upon a dish of apples in the centre of the table, and then—

"Life is real, life is earnest," said he very sadly.

He would have proceeded, but at that moment he chanced to catch the cod-like eyes of Mr. Snape fixed amusingly upon him, and so he stopped dead.

"Fire away!" cried Spill cheerfully.

"Permit me to collect my thoughts," answered the baronet politely.

"Let 'em come from the heart," answered Spill briskly. "Don't stop to think; let 'em flow, let 'em flow. Turn on the tap, shut your eyes, and kick out. Kick hard, man, hard! Now, then, off you go!"

The little audience laughed, while Sir John, on top of the packing-case, stroked the back of his head with a deliberate hand.

"Now then!" cried Spill encouragingly.

Sir John glanced down at Miss Frisby. "There is no hurry," whispered that sweet lady. "Choose your own time, dear Sir John. Don't be hurried. We shall remember every word you say to us, every word!"

He looked at Captain Chivvy. The friend of his Oxford days was gazing disconsolately upon the pretty Miss Hessey.

"Off you go!" cried Spill, rubbing his hands like a tradesman.

Mr. Snape took a step forward to the table, helped himself to a couple of bananas, and stripping the fruit of its skin, returned, grinning, to his corner.

Sir John pulled himself together.

"As I was saying," quoth he, "life is real, life is earnest; at least it is to me. And I find that the founder of Christianity, Buddha, and indeed all the great spirits of the world, held the same opinion. This colony, then, is a refuge for those who believe that life is real, life is earnest, a refuge from the world, a refuge from dishonest compromise between God and Mammon, a refuge from an industrial system in which no one can participate without rendering himself responsible for what is termed 'sweating' and the moral degradation of his brother man. We do not shut ourselves up in monasteries. We take this farm, we cultivate the land with our hands, we have all our goods in common, and we devote ourselves spiritually to the development of our eternal souls."

"And you wear bathing-gowns," laughed Spill cheerfully.

"We wear a Nature costume," retorted Sir John. "For one of our main beliefs is that sin and wickedness, misery and cruelty, are not works of the devil, but simply the results of departure from the laws of nature. Speaking for myself, I hold that opinion very strongly. I do really. I believe that the flesh foods eaten by mankind and the stuffy clothes worn by mankind are responsible for a very great deal of our present misery and wretchedness, and so in this colony we shall eat pure and natural food, and we shall wear clothes that will afford the body as much air as is compatible with the prejudices of decency. But this is by the way."

The packing-case shook a little at this point, and Sir John stooped down, the tips of his fingers resting on the table, and paused till the box quieted down. Then he continued his discourse, saying—

"The main topic on which I would speak, however, is the larger one of life itself. Ladies and gentlemen, I conceive that there can be but two opinions on this question. Either life has a serious purpose, or it is a jest. If a jest, we cannot laugh too heartily at it; we cannot struggle hard enough to overreach our fellows. We must eat, drink, and be merry, for to-morrow we die. But if serious, how serious! Ladies and gentlemen, can we possibly be too much in earnest if life is real, and the grave is not our goal? Can we? I trow not. Sincerely, I trow not. There can be no fanaticism, no zeal too fierce in such a cause. There can be no isolation from the miserable compromise of the world severe enough in such a matter. And for my own part, though I have a horror of appearing Pharisaical, I must really say that it is inconceivable to me, utterly inconceivable, how Christians who believe that this single life-experience determines either for eternal bliss or for eternal misery the immortal soul of man, can bring themselves to violate every day of their lives that great and fundamental injunction of their Master—'Ye cannot serve God and Mammon.' There is no question here of 'must not.' It is simply a statement of fact, a statement of impossibility. Ye cannot! And yet that is what the Church and the State and the nation are doing. They are serving Mammon six days in the week, and God on the seventh. Ladies and gentlemen, a little thought on our present industrial system makes the world unen-

durable to the sensitive mind. Think of the unutterable
agony of child-labour in the slums and alleys of London!
Think of the spiritual degradation of those poor wretches
who in our slaughterhouses stand ankle-deep in blood
through the long hours of the day! Think, on the
one hand, of the filth, squalor, and hideousness of the
east end of London, and, on the other, of the ease,
luxury, and voluptuousness of the west end of London!
Is it Christian? How little real Christianity there is in
the world may be seen, I think, in the state of the
Church itself, which gives to one minister in a small
parish some two thousand pounds a year, and to another
in a fierce and teeming parish a beggarly fifty! Ladies
and gentlemen, does that strike you that the Church is
sincere in this matter; is sincere in that religion which
says, 'Let him that hath give to him that hath not, and
he who seeth his brother in need and shutteth up the
bowels of his compassion, how dwelleth the love of God
in him?'"

Sir John was warming to his work. He spoke in his
low, undulated voice, as if he were pleading in the ear
of a friend; but a fire was burning in his eyes, and his
arms had begun to swing with rhetorical emphasis.

"Such a world," he went on, "strikes me as a dishonest world, or a mad world. Therefore I withdraw
from it. Though not a Christian, I seek to obey the
injunction of Christ, that I should strive to be perfect;
I wash my hands of the world's compromise; I turn my
back upon its hypocrisy; I give up all my possessions;
I will not eat unless I toil; I serve God, and God only.
Though my religion is not the Christian religion, I take
it that my future life (if so led) will be more in the
spirit of Christianity than the life of the bishop in his
palace, who preaches an eternal heaven and an eternal
hell after the gates of death are passed. And so, ladies

and gentlemen, I say farewell to the world. I know full well that while I wear the livery of mortality I can but touch the hem of the garment of spiritual progression; yet that hem I will touch with my two hands. And so—

"To the flesh-eating, wine-drinking world I bid farewell.

" To the tobacco-poisoned world I bid farewell.

"To the money-getting world I bid farewell.

"To the world of coarseness and vulgarity I bid farewell.

" To the world of idleness and luxury I bid farewell.

" To the world of——"

Now with each of these farewells, ladies and gentlemen, Sir John Sparrow gave a great sweep with his right arm, signifying a very palpable and a very dramatic *Retro me Sathana!* With the first sweep the packing-case on which he stood gave a jerk, with the second a tilt, with the third a lurch, with the fourth a swing, and with the fifth the momentum of the swing had so far increased that with the beginning of the sixth sweep over went the box, over went Sir John, and the people at the end of the room saw, instead of the baronet's earnest face and swinging arms, two little thin white legs sticking pathetically in the air.

For our gentleman, by his rhetoric, had brought the box over on its bottom, and in slipping from his perch, he had landed plump in the case itself, with his head on the edge, his hands grasping the sides, and his legs, as we have said, pointing pathetically towards the ceiling.

Never did impassioned oratory end so disastrously before. For in this dénouement there was so little of tragedy and so large a portion of comedy that the most sympathetic could not prevent laughter from leaping out of wide lips to riot above the discomfiture of the abashed and terrified gentleman in the packing-case.

Miss Hessey laughed. Captain Chivvy laughed. Miss Frisby laughed. Even Simon Peace smiled. Everybody, in fact, if we omit Mr. Snape, laughed over Sir John's misfortune; and Mr. Snape, we may mention, took advantage of the universal distraction to pocket a few apples, bananas, and raisins.

"There!" cried Spill, bringing the fist of his right hand with a terrible crack into the palm of his left; "there, what did I tell you? Directly you stop gassing all your arguments fall to the ground!"

This pleasantry had the effect of making Sir John's audience laugh all the more, and it was in a veritable storm of merriment that our hero was rescued from his uncomfortable position and set upon his feet by the faithful, if disgusted, Tiplady.

"Now, look here!" cried Spill in a loud voice, banging on the table with a spoon; "I can prove in about two twos that every word uttered by our Jack-in-the box is rot, pure rot. Listen to me. I say that——"

But Alexander Fontey rushing towards Spill with an axe caused that gentleman to cease abruptly.

"Stop it!" cried Fontey. "This isn't a debate, it's an opening ceremony, and heckling isn't allowed. You speak when you're asked to, and don't poke your nose in where it isn't wanted." And with that he banged with his axe on the table till the laughter and chatting ceased.

Then said he, springing upon a bench axe in hand, "Brothers and sisters, we have just heard Brother Sparrow's views on this Nature Colony, and now you shall have mine. I'm a man with no religion. I don't believe in anything outside Nature. Nature's good enough for me. I can see it, touch it, hear it, understand it. What's beyond the clouds doesn't bother my head a penny-piece. And why I believe in this colony is just this—it's Nature. I don't bid farewell to the world; I don't care a twopenny hang about bishops, industrial systems, or the Stock Exchange. But I do care about Nature. What I say is—follow Nature and you can't go wrong. Now in this colony we shall be natural; we shall work with our hands, sleep in the trees when weather permits, eat natural food, bathe in the river, and let the sun get at our bodies, front and back, both sides, top and bottom. And we're not going to have any laws here; no laws, rules, or regulations of any kind. All rules are against Nature. Anybody may come here, may share our food, share our house, and work or not just as he pleases. That's socialism, the socialism of Nature, and no stupid blabber of the hustings. That's socialism, and that's my religion, Nature religion. You who stay here can do what you like—dig, plant trees, wash the plates, scrub the floor, anything you like; or you can do nothing at all. Just whatever you please. While there is food you shall eat it. While there's a roof over our heads you shall share it. And you who go back to London, who prefer civilisation to nature, tell your friends, tell all the world that here in this spot there are men and women living the life Nature intended them to lead, and that, there-fore, they are the only happy people under the sun. That's all I've got to say, and now I'll show you over the farm."

This speech was fired off at a rate incredible, and hardly had the last word died away before Fontey jumped from the bench, reached the door, flung it wide, and stalked out into the windy yard, his axe on his shoulder, as nonchalantly as a mediæval headsman going home to dinner.

The party followed.

Sir John was drawn on one side by his nephew.

"You hinted, Uncle Jack, that you were giving up all your money; I hope that was only said in a Pickwickian sense?" The two coachmen, stamping their feet to keep warm, came grinning to the barn door.

"Every penny, Richard, is at the disposal of the Colony. I renounce ownership."

"But what is your poor unfortunate heir to do?" laughed that young gentleman, something unhappy.

"You are a Christian Socialist yourself!" countered Sir John.

"You take things so dreadfully in earnest."

"Life is real, life is earnest. Surely if one honestly desires perfection one must give up everything! My dear Richard, is our present social and industrial system an honest aim at perfection? Is it, now? And besides, you may regard my theosophy as my bride and the Colony as my heir. I am entitled to marry."

But they were interrupted by Alexander Fontey, who dragged Sir John forward among the company to admire innumerable bundles of spindly fruit trees lying prone upon the ground. He had to shout, because of the wind: "We shall start planting these as soon as possible; capital work for the muscles; the spades are up in the barn—a gross of 'em—grand work early in the morning." Then the energetic Alexander led the shivering knot of blue-nosed people towards another field, where a great quantity of pink-coloured woodwork was piled together, with endless stacks of glass on every side of it. "Here I propose raising the glass-houses," shouted Alexander. "Difficult job putting these frames together, but healthy; four or five of us at it early every morning, and it will soon be done!"

Sir John looked anxiously at the company. Mr. Snape was grinning at the back, his coat collar about his ears. "Would it not be wiser," ventured Sir John, "to employ a responsible person to put up these houses?"

Alexander smiled impatiently. "When once you begin that sort of thing you may as well chuck up the whole idea. What have we come out of the world for? Not to sit idle, not to employ work-people, not to live on the skill or the toil of another; we have come out in order to live naturally, to do for ourselves, to be independent, to be free!"

"Quite, quite," said Sir John, as the shrieking wind fluttered the skirt of his garment, and he staggered a pace or two back.

"Better let me fetch you an overcoat, Sir John," whispered Tiplady. But the baronet shook his bare head.

They went forward again. Field after field was passed through, and in every one Mr. Alexander Fontey had dumped down either trees, boxes of seeds, or timber for building; it was a world in embryo, and mightily depressing on a grey, whistling afternoon. Perhaps if a June sun had been shining on a neat homestead, fewer people would have pulled out watches and told each other that it was time to be getting back. As it was, with the exception of our hero, Tiplady, Alexander Fontey, Thomas Pugh, the mysterious Mr. Snape, and Gabriel Pick, the rest of the company elected to return to the evils of civilisation.

Sir John took Chivvy on one side. "You think I am doing the right thing?" he asked. He stood, with his hands on his hips, his bare arms very white—a lonely, anxious, pathetic little figure.

"Anything's better than London," answered the dapper Chivvy. "What is London, after all? What is our life there? My dear old fellow, there's no more

S

narrowing and vulgarising existence in the world than the life of the Londoner. As for myself—why, I am tied to it; I can't break away from it; I'm too old to change now; I've lived the life too long and too deeply. But I can see perfectly well what the end will be. Racing, my dear old chap, is leading me on to the inevitable. I know it, but I can't help it."

Sir John interrupted. "I've made over my money to the Colony," he explained confidentially, "all except a small sum which will provide Tiplady with an annuity. But there is my house and the furniture in Yorkshire. I am sending instructions for the selling of both. If the little money they bring in would be of any service in clearing you with the bookmakers——"

But Captain Chivvy stopped him. "By George, what a good fellow you are, Sparrow! No, my dear old chap, I wouldn't touch a penny of it. I'll go to the devil at my own expense. A thousand thanks all the same. I shall never forget your offer—never, as long as I live. It isn't often one makes a real friend in this life, and, by gad, your offer has touched me to the heart—it has really."

And so they shook hands very earnestly, very affectionately; and then Captain Chivvy clambered into one of the waggonettes, and Sir John, with his hands on his hips, turned sadly away towards the farmhouse.

Miss Vince and Miss Frisby had promised to come later on if the Colony proved a success. The good-looking John and Mary Hessey had expressed their regret, and explained that the Colony, in point of situation, was not their ideal; they sought for more beauty and homeliness. The Peace family had sniffed, and retired without a good wish or an explanation of their withdrawal. Sir John had neglected them, and Mr. Peace had not been asked to speak. Spill—the earnest, energetic, and mocking Spill—had made such fun of the whole undertaking that Sir John's heart was sore for the success of the enterprise. It is depressing to have one's highest ideal treated as the greatest good joke in the world.

Pontey was left, the seed-eating Pick was left, the theosophical Pugh was left, and the mysterious Mr. Snape was left.

Above all, Tiplady was left—treasurer of the Colony's fortunes.

CHAPTER XVII

Which introduces Sir John Sparrow as Author

ON the first page of a manuscript book which Sir John Sparrow brought new with him to the Nature Colony we find the following interesting note on the Sparrovian theory of existence:—

"When will a groaning and miserable creation realise that salvation lies in a studious and sustained effort at perfection? It is not enough to master our tempers and give doles to the poor. The sick world has tried this quack medicine for long æons, and is still bed-ridden. The truly spiritual man must hunger and thirst after utter and supreme perfection. The virtues must be acquired one by one, not accepted negatively and indifferently in the lump. Each virtue is a step in the Jacob's ladder that leads to heaven, and one virtue is higher than another. It is not enough to acquire vege-tarianism; we must go on to fruitarianism. Nor must we stop here, for, still higher, the seed and pip theory beckons us upward still. There is no stopping-place on the road of perfection, for perfection is eternal. But we must begin humbly, shackled as we are by mortality. The first step is abnegation of self. We must give up what the body most cherishes. Animal food and spiritu-ous liquors are enemies of the soul. Know, too, that Civilisation is an impediment to the development of originality. We must return to Nature, we must live simply, and, above all, we must give up much time to the silent contemplation of spiritual things. All property and personal ownership must be discarded, for how can a man burdened with such responsibilities present an open and a flexible mind to the inspiration of the Almighty Creator of men and worlds?

"How dangerous is civilisation may be seen in the pride men take in their native land. Could anything be meaner than patriotism? Shall I, who profess that God is the Father of all men, rejoice that my country is richer or more powerful than the country of my neighbour? Shall I not rather regard all men as my brothers, and labour to advance them, even to my own great detriment? This I must do if I would be perfect. But it is difficult, so deep-rooted are our prejudices.

"Concerning the soul, is it not plain that a religion whose pastors and bishops are at enmity one with another, whose wrangles are inspired by words in a book, whose priests and deacons feed upon the murdered bodies of animals like savages—is it not plain that such a religion can never advance the struggling, storm-swept soul of man on the road to perfection? The soul must be free of religion. It must be an open book for the pen of God to write within; it must be convinced that it has lived before, and will live again. The soul of man is an arrow shot from the bow of God; it is for ever piercing the darkness of the worlds, and must go on till it has traversed the circle of existences and returned to Him who sent it forth. I have lived in the jelly-fish and in the mole, in the egg and the fowl, in the dog and in the horse; I have inhabited a hundred human shapes; I am eternal, and my destiny is eternal. The more perfect I am the nearer I approach to God. How can that man desire perfection who has property

which his brother may not share, who wears a warm
coat while his neighbour is in rags, who eats the flesh
of tortured animals, who supports a system which
separates humanity into classes called Rich and Poor?
Is he not palpably and preposterously selfish, and
wholly without the love of God? Is he not most
blind?

"In this Colony which I have founded is the germ of
the new world. Anarchy is the method of God. All
laws are selfish and opposed to God. Here a man is
free of law and responsibility, free of nationality and
popular opinion. No one may compel him to work.
Our food, Nature's food, we will share with whomsoever
cometh. The labour of tilling the earth will be a communion with God, an act of sacrifice and devotion.
When the world beholds our happiness, will it not
straightway fling off the burden of its weariness, and,
crushing ambition, selfishness, greed, vanity, and miserable egotism, accept the beautiful freedom we offer and
live closer to Nature?

"What is the wealth of the millionaire to my peace
of mind?

"Is there a king who knows my freedom?

"I am living as God would have me live. I am at
peace with all the world. I have not a shilling that
I can call my own.

"He is surely a madman who toils to amass silver
and gold, with eternity drawing daily nearer.

"Oh, foolish, miserable, and weary world, the stones of
your cities are splashed with blood and tears; your
streets echo with the groans of a toil that is profitless;
your temples resound with praises to a God you cannot
understand! How narrow are your streets, how dark
are your ways!

"Here the sun shines upon green fields; the lark

carols in the blue; the river sings to the
we are gathering our daily bread with glad
brotherhood of man is begun in earnest."

The remaining pages of the manuscrip
historian's eternal regret, **are** innocent c
reflection.

CHAPTER XVIII

Which contains an account of Tom Shott's hurried Breakfast with Mrs. FitzGerald

"I 'M so sorry to have kept you; but I never rise with the lark, and I haven't had breakfast yet!" Among the letters in her hand was one from York Barracks.

"Nor I," grumped the parson, both hands in the pockets of his cutaway coat.

Mrs. FitzGerald laughed. "Then come and have breakfast with me."

"Servants there?" asked Tom Shott.

"None."

"Umph! lead the way; very kind of you."

At the table, when the parson had lumbered from the sideboard with a full plate, and while Mrs. FitzGerald, smiling quietly to her dimples, was pouring out the coffee, looking, ladies and gentlemen, like an angel on a fine Sunday morning, Tom Shott, eating hard, pulled out a letter from his pocket, dragging it forth from among other papers with a trembling, fumbling hand, and a little unceremoniously pitched it over for her to see.

"What's this?" she asked, setting down the coffee-pot.

"Read it," said he, filling his mouth with brawn.

She handed him a brimming cup of coffee, and picked up the paper. "From Tiplady," she murmured, opening the letter.

"Yes," said the parson, going with empty plate to the sideboard.

"Good heavens!" cried the widow, ere the parson had cut a third slice of ham. "Oh, but this is absurd! What is it for? Why should he do it?"

Tom Shott came to the table, set down his plate, took an egg from the stand, and chopped off the top of the shell. "He's a splendid fellow—splendid," he said.

"But what does this mean? Tiplady says: 'You will be grieved to hear that Sir John gets more extravagant every hour of his life, and now he has just sent up to Yorkshire to have the old home sold, furniture and all, which is like to break my heart. If, Reverend Mr. Shott, you could come and stop him and persuade him to return, you would be rendering humanity a service worthy of your cloth and heart.' Is he living extravagantly, is he throwing his money away? And what is this address—the Nature Colony?"

"Generous heart; splendid fellow—splendid."

She watched the little silver spoon loaded with orange yolk go up to the lobster face, and then turned her eyes to the letter. "I confess I don't understand. I can't think of Sir John living foolishly and extravagantly, any more than I can imagine him living wickedly or dashingly." She began to laugh.

"He's touched by the sorrow in London; that's what it means," explained Tom Shott.

"Oh, is he giving his money away in charity?"

"Every farthing."

"And now he is selling his cottage?"

"Um."

"But what will he have left for himself?"

"Nothing."

"Poor Sir John! But how very foolish of him,

isn't it? One admires charity so much up to a certain point. But—but what will he do? Will the Nature Colony keep him? He can't possibly go to the work-house. Fancy those dear little fingers picking oakum! Let me give you some more coffee."

"Listen."

"Yes?"

Tom Shott masticated for several moments, his huge hands resting arm's length on the edge of the table, his blue eyes fixed frowningly upon the widow. Then he spoke. "Buy his cottage."

"What?"

"You buy his cottage. I'll get him back." He took the full cup from her hands. "And keep it dark. Between you and me—a secret."

"But why should I buy his cottage?"

If he could have dared to unfold his great scheme at this stage, the parson would have said, Because now that he is penniless I can bring him home; and when he is home you will see each other constantly again, and the love-making interrupted by a madness inspired by my own foolish opposition will renew itself, and then you will marry him, and the old days will come back. As it was, he said bluntly—

"You don't want to see him homeless?"

"No."

"Very well, then."

"And you are going to London?"

"Yes."

"To bring him back?"

He nodded his head.

"How devoted you are!" she exclaimed, pushing him marmalade, and wondering greatly how the old man would find the money for his long journey

"He's a good little chap."

"The village hasn't been the same since he left, has it?"

"Not the least." He took the last piece of toast.

"As you suggest that I should buy his cottage, you had better let me act as financier in your mission of mercy." She laughed lightly, fearing to offend this old, tender-hearted bear.

But Parson Shott said, No. Certainly not. If she saved the cottage, he would undertake to save the man. 'Twas parson's work.

So she contented herself by asking details about the buying of the cottage, and teasing Parson Tom with the possibility of his failing to bring back the errant baronet. Thus they talked and laughed.

Finally, "I'm glad your house is empty again," said the parson nervously, getting up to go, napkin in hand, his jaws still masticating.

"But why?"

"Two of those fellows were dangerous."

Mrs. FitzGerald, pushing back her chair, stopped, and looked at the parson.

"Dangerous!"

"They were after you."

"What!" She burst into a merry laugh.

"They were. Nice fellows, but no good. Most serious step for you to take when you know quite well that—that other things are expected of you. Good-bye."

And without another word, but with just one hurried and awkward look to see how she took the hint, Tom Shott lumbered out of the room and was gone.

Then Mrs. FitzGerald, puzzling for one moment over the parson's dark saying, looked over her letters once again.

If she accepted a certain invitation among them, so

Mr. Drayton told her, she would have the joy of seeing him. And in the letter of invitation itself, the hostess mentioned that among her guests she hoped to have that charming and delightful Mr. Mortimer.

She felt the crisis was at hand : that to one of these lovers she must now yield. Vain was it to go on with her life hoping for the divine companionship of love, and yet for ever checking the impulse of her heart with the chilling reflections of experience. It was not easy to keep a smiling face to the world while her heart was sick for sympathy.

No, she must decide.

The boy with the light laugh and the open eye——

The man with the soft voice and the tender sympathy——

Which?

CHAPTER XIX

Concerning the Disasters which overtook the Nature Colony

SIR JOHN became greatly enamoured of Mr. Gabriel Pick's seed theory of life, and he practised it with admirable ardour, though he grew daily weaker and paler, and an uncomfortable soreness threatening a boil manifested itself on the side of his nose; but what captivated him more than anything else—certainly more than planting fruit trees on a cold and windy morning —were the theosophical ambitions of Mr. Thomas Pugh.

"The reason, brother, why you and I do not see the astral world as clearly as the devotees of the East is because we have never tried," said Mr. Pugh, drawing a chair to the fire.

"But how should we try, brother?" replied Sir John, crossing his naked legs, and smoothing the folds of his garment over his knees.

"The first thing we must do, brother, is to practise concentration of thought."

"That sounds very excellent advice, brother."

Mr. Pugh leant forward in his chair. "Have you never heard it said that not one person in a million can say the Lord's Prayer without the mind once wandering from the words? Such, brother, is the untrained human mind. But we can cultivate our minds, and we can acquire concentration of thought."

"I beg you to say how."

"By patient practice, brother. Take a pebble from the brook, or a piece of straw from the barn, lay it in the palm of your left hand, and then, sitting down at your ease, gaze hard and wholly at the little object for fifteen minutes by the clock. Do this day after day, checking your mind every time it wanders from the object, and in a week or two's time you will be able to enlarge the fifteen minutes to half an hour, presently to an hour, after that to a whole day. So, slowly and laboriously, you will acquire sovereignty over your mind; every thought will become your slave; and presently you will see with astral eyes the spiritual world about us."

"A glorious gospel!" cried Sir John. "Let us begin at once."

They went out to fetch a stick of straw from the barn, and as they reached the door they became suddenly aware of a strong smell of tobacco.

On entering they discovered Mr. Snape reclining full length on a heap of dirty straw with a pipe in his mouth.

"You are a smoker?" queried Sir John.

Mr. Snape grinned. "I'm fighting against it."

"On your back," put in Mr. Pugh.

"If a man can't fight against a weakness on his back," answered Snape, "he's no man worth speaking of."

"There's something in that," said Sir John.

"Brother Fontey would be glad of your services," said Pugh; "he's planting apple-trees in the second field."

"I'll join him when I've done wrestling with the devil," replied Brother Snape, resuming his pipe.

"There is nothing wicked in smoking," quoth Sir

John, "but in my philosophy, which Brother Pugh is good enough to call the Sparrovian theory of life, the open mind aiming at utter perfection must of necessity as the first step evident, conquer all those appetites of the body which do not contribute to the development of spiritual selflessness. Therefore, when we give up meat and tobacco, we give up, not actual sins, but impediments on the path of spiritual evolution. Look at it in this light, for I am sure you desire perfection, and you will find it easy to put down your pipe."

But, alas! for the fortunes of the brotherhood, the Sparrovian theory of life was not Mr. Pontey's idea of working a Nature Colony, and very soon strife and dissension arose in the midst of the brotherhood. To practise concentration of thought by gazing for hours at a pebble or a waistcoat button was a mere foolishness to the iconoclastic Fontey. He himself called it blazing rot, being a man of quick words. He cried loudly for help in his orchard, but only the prickly-faced Gabriel Pick responded. Sir John was developing his astral vision, so was Brother Pugh; Treasurer Tiplady was keeping the house habitable; and, as we have seen, Mr. Snape was busy fighting the devil. So the innumerable fruit trees lay prone and pitiable on the grass, while Fontey and Pick struggled like martyrs to dig unyielding ground with sandalled feet. Pontey complained. He faced Brother Sparrow with boldness, reprehended him for indifference to the brotherhood, and threatened to abandon the whole enterprise. Sir John, on his part, replied that digging was too much for his strength, and counselled Fontey to employ skilful labourers for work so arduous and difficult.

Then came a great shock to the little brotherhood with the painful discovery that one of their number, to wit the mysterious Mr. Snape, was a secret drinker of spirituous liquors. For one night as they sat at supper, Sir John and Gabriel Pick munching apple-pips and bird-seed, Fontey cracking nuts at surprising speed, and Thomas Pugh sharing with Tiplady a dish of haricot-stew, there came a thundering knock on the door, and the next minute the latch was lifted, the door swung open, and Mr. Snape lurched into the room.

"Goo' evenin'!" he cried, stumbling to the table.

No one answered.

"Goo' evenin', I said!" he exclaimed angrily.

And still no one replied.

Mr. Snape dashed his hat upon the ground. "I'll fight the man who doesn't wish me goo' evenin'."

Tiplady rose, but Sir John restrained him.

"Brother Snape," quoth the worthy baronet, "you pain me. I beg you to go quietly to your hammock. To - morrow we will discuss the matter quietly and soberly."

Mr. Snape demanded to know what matter Sir John referred to. Nothing was the matter with *him!* He'd fight the man who said there was. And as for going to bed, how on earth was he to get into a hammock suffering as he was with pins and needles in both feet? Besides, he wanted his supper.

"Supper! Tiplady, old cock, get my supper! A bit o' beefsteak and ripe stilton, ripe as you can get it— the more mites the merrier."

"You ugly little cod-eyed guttersnipe!" cried the outraged Tiplady, advancing on him, but once again the baronet restrained his servant.

Then he went forward to Brother Snape. "My friend," said he, "let me lead you to your hammock."

Brother Snape glared at him. "You dare t' insult me?" he demanded, swaying fiercely.

"You will be better when you have slept."

" I'm not to have any supper ? " His head shot forward, and he tottered to Sir John.

" You are not in a fit state."

" You mean to say I'm 'toshicated ? "

" I do ; I regret to say that I do."

Snape closed his right fist, drew it slowly but jerkily to his shoulder, extended it quietly towards the baronet's nose with one eye closed, the other squinting down the length of the arm to take aim, and then drawing it back once more to his shoulder, he warned Sir John to prepare for an instant and a painful death.

But before the victim could reply or make supplication for mercy, the fist shot out, landed plump upon the baronet's nose, and Mr. Snape, whose strength was spent with the blow, sprawled helplessly upon the stone floor.

Sir John stood where he was struck, the incipient boil a deeper purple. "Leave him alone, Tiplady," he cried, in a voice shaking with emotion; "I am fighting, fighting, fighting !" The blood trickled from his nose.

" Fighting, Sir John ?" cried Tiplady, who was burning to break every limb in Mr. Snape's body.

"Yes," gulped Sir John, "fighting my pride." Then he added in a tremulous voice, " I hope he will hit me again."

Mr. Snape struggled to his feet. "Where's man who insulted me ?" he demanded. "Where's imp'dent blackguard who dared t' say I was 'toshicated ? "

He caught sight of Sir John.

"Oh, there you are ! There you are ! I say *there you are !* D'yon und'stand ? "

" Leave him alone, Tiplady," cried Sir John. "Leave him alone, I say." Then after a pause, " I wish to see if I have conquered the natural man. My soul is on trial. Stand away."

He hurried out into the fields, calling aloud to Fontey, Pugh, and Gabriel Pick, waving his hands and summoning the toilers to his side. Fontey rested on his spade. Pugh alone came forward.

"Sir John's ill!" cried the puffing Tiplady. "If we aren't nippy we'll lose him. Run for the doctor and bring him back with you. Don't waste a minute."

Without pausing for reply—for did not Tiplady think that the whole world loved his little master?—the butler hurried on towards Fontey and Gabriel Pick.

"Why didn't you come when I called?" he panted. "Sir John's ill, probably dying——"

He stopped.

"God love me, Mr. Pontey, but what are you smiling at?"

"Smiling, smiling!" snapped Fontey; "how dare you say I am smiling?"

"Your face lit up! I saw it! When I said Sir John was a dying man your face lit like a gas-lamp!" He paused. "You don't mean to tell me——"

Tiplady stopped again. "God bless my soul, to think of it!" he cried, and straightway turned away and hurried back towards the farm. But Fontey followed.

"A word with you, Mr. Tiplady——"

The butler wheeled round. "Get you to hell!" he cried vehemently, flourishing his arms. "If you come nigh me I'll crack your skull for 'ee."

Fontey held back.

"You, wishing for my master's death—ah, yes, you do!—and daring to come near me! Keep away from me, Fontey; night and day, man, from this time forth, keep away from me, lest I do you such a harm as you'll carry to the grave with you!"

So said Tiplady, standing baldheaded under the blue

heaven, with his little black eyes flashing, his mouth pursed up under his pudgy nose, and his great shoulders squared before the shrinking Fontey. Then he wheeled round and trotted back to the farm, careless of his dignity.

"Damn it," he puffed, "but I meant to send that Pick for some milk! Dare I go myself? Oh, Lord, if only that little Snape had been left!"

But as he reached the farm a fly drove up at the gate, and out of the fly lumbered no less a person than Tom Shott—very red in the face, with petulance in his light blue eyes, and sullenness in his out-thrust lips.

"Here!" cried he, catching sight of Tiplady, and the butler made haste to his side.

"What's the proper fare?" he asked.

But Tiplady had caught the cabman by the arm. "Drive down to Brickett's farm and bring back a gallon of milk; I'll give you five shillings," he gasped, panting very hard.

"First of all I want my fare," argued the cabman, "which is seven shillings, as I've told the gentleman twice already."

Tom Shott's red face was high in the air, the blue eyes searching the hills as if for sympathy, his left hand was slowly and reluctantly dragging a purse from his trouser pocket, while his right grasped the head of an umbrella under his arm.

"Seven shillings," he muttered, half to himself, while the cabman wagged his head and said, yes, it was seven shillings, and cheap too.

No one ever knew what this long journey cost the poor parson.

Tiplady turned to Tom Shott. "Sir John's ill, sir, very ill."

Tom Shott jumped, wheeling round upon the butler. "Ill!" That was all, but his face was bruised by the news.

"Quick, sir, quick," went on Tiplady; "pay the fare and follow me; he's mortal bad, sir; I fear it may be the last. And you hurry up with that milk, d'you hear?"

The parson unstrapped his purse, emptied the coins into his hand, picked out the man's fare, paid it to him, and walked off strapping up his depleted purse. He lumbered along, his head a little thrust forward, his eyes very dull and fixed, and his great shoulders humped about his ears. Tiplady waited for him at the door.

"He's in my bed, sir. Been sleeping in a hammock! Living on pips and given up drinking even water! Wasted to a shadow. Living on pips, sir! And there was a man who did the same thing, eating wheat and oats and all manner of corn as raw as could be, and one day he went into a Turkish bath and exploded on the spot. Combustion. And Sir John knows it!"

Tom Shott only stared. Then he thrust one of his huge hands into Tiplady's back, and pushed him forward. "This way, sir," said the butler, and climbed the narrow stairs of the farmhouse to the upper floor.

Sir John, white as the paper whereon these words are printed, save for the flaming boil on the side of his nose, lay with closed eyes in Tiplady's bed, his head on one side, his brows drawn sharply together. There was no sign of life in the white face; the arms lay rigid at his side, and the bed-clothes were unfluttered by respiration. It was all very still, and white, and unearthly.

"He's going!" cried Tiplady. "Lord of mercy and love, he's going!" Then he looked up at the parson and started, holding his peace. Never before had Tiplady beheld mortal agony face to face.

Tom Shott, fumbling at his breast-pocket and treading laboriously on the tips of his toes, moved slowly towards the bed. From the breast-pocket came a huge silver flask, and as he unscrewed the stopper with trembling fingers he went down on one knee at the bedside, so that by stooping his stricken face was on a level with the deathlike countenance of Sir John.

Tiplady was at his side. "I gave him brandy ten minutes ago, sir," he whispered reverently.

The parson paused.

"And I've sent for the doctor," he added, under his breath.

The parson looked at the flask. After much thinking he bent over Sir John and poured brandy between the close-set teeth, slowly and deliberately. The patient fought against it, murmured, choked, and jerked his eyes open; then he tried to sit up, but fell back gasping, his eyes staring fearfully at the parson.

After a little while the eyes closed again, and he relapsed into his old deathlike swoon.

Tom Shott remained kneeling at the bedside, his strained eyes fixed upon the boil on the baronet's nose until the doctor arrived.

CHAPTER XX

*Wherein it is recounted how Tom Shott broke up
the Nature Colony without uttering a word*

NOW it was a wondrous weight off the mind of
Tom Shott when Doctor Peter, with much
verbiage, informed him that Sir John, in spite of
extreme poorness of blood and the very ugly boil
upon his nose, would eventually recover; but there
remained the almost deeper anxiety, certainly the more
puzzling problem, of getting our hero away from his
fads and crotchets. How could this Herculean labour
be accomplished? He loaded his pipe, our reverend
Hercules, and paced to and fro in the farmyard, blowing
blue clouds of tobacco about his scarlet face, and rack-
ing his brain for strategic suggestions. It was in a
moment of deep despair that Tiplady issued from the
house and joined him; for the parson had just then
reached the conclusion that, with convalescence, Sir
John's pig-headedness would have a disastrous palin-
genesis, and that if he clung to his pips and seeds now,
the more would he stick to that monstrous diet when he
rose up well and strong from a bed of sickness.

Then came Tiplady, voluble and indignant. "Vegetarians!" said he; "they're a lot of white-livered
Hottentots. It's my belief they make a virtue of
their fruit and nuts just because they haven't got no
stomach for honest meat. A lot of quarrelsome, crack-

brained old maids, that's what they are. It's like a girls' school being here—such fighting and whispering and slandering you never heard in all your life." And then he related how Sir John had fallen foul of Alexander Fontey, how the face of Fontey had lighted up at the suggestion that the baronet lay a-dying, and much more to the effect that jealousy and malice and all uncharitableness were even now disintegrating forces in the body politic of this crack-brained brotherhood.

Tom Shott listened with dull eyes, walking to and fro, pipe in mouth, with his hands deep in his coat pockets; then, of a sudden, he whipped out his right hand, smote Tiplady over the shoulder, and burst out with—

"I've got it."

Tiplady, recovering equipoise, asked politely for explanation.

"I'll smoke 'em out!" cried the parson.

Tiplady did not quite follow.

"We'll make it too hot for them."

"How, sir?"

"We'll roast beef and mutton day and night; fill the house with the smell of it. We'll turn their stomachs!" He stopped, panting from much speech.

Tiplady chuckled. "I see, sir. Break up the Colony before Sir John recovers? That's a first-class bit of generalship, sir. If I may make so bold, it's an idea worthy of a statesman."

Tom Shott had begun to chuckle; his solemn face was lighted by the merest shadow of a smile, but his shoulders were shaking, and a weird, whistling sound issued staccato from his lips. He was amused. "Chops and steaks," he chuckled to himself. "I'll dose 'em with chops and steaks!"

"Capital!" cried Tiplady.

"I'll smoke day and night, in every room."

"Excellent, sir!"

"I'll leave the cork out of the whisky bottle!"

"Ha, that'll give 'em the jumps!"

"The house shall reek like a tavern."

"And like a cook-shop. I'll see to that. Lord! but I could make a sirloin of beef smell through Buckingham Palace!"

"The spit shall be always turning."

"I'll spill gravy on the table. Ha! ha! that'll make 'em wish they'd never been born!"

"We'll hang the kitchen with joints."

"We'll make a butcher's shop of the parlour."

"We must have strings of sausages."

"A sucking-pig would drive 'em crazy. That's the trick, sir, a sucking-pig. Did you never notice, sir, that a little sucking-pig is the dead spit of a human baby?" Tiplady rubbed his hands.

"Got any money?" demanded the parson, growing suddenly solemn.

"Yes, sir."

"Begin at once. Go off immediately. Bring back meat, cigars, whisky, and—strings of sausages. Go sharp."

When the butler had departed Tom Shott went into the house and sat down in the kitchen, the chamber wherein the colonists took their meals. Thomas Pugh was above stairs, sitting with the slumbering baronet; the doctor was expected back in an hour with trained nurse, medicines, and nourishing food.

Tom Shott drew to the fire the least uncomfortable chair he could discover, and, resting his feet upon the fender, gave himself up to the quiet enjoyment of his pipe. In a few minutes the door opened, and Alexander Fontey, with Gabriel Pick at his heels, entered the room.

"Phew!" said Pontey.

"Great Scott!" cried Gabriel.

Tom Shott never turned his head. With his face to the fire he went on quietly with his pipe.

Fontey was puzzled. Before him he saw a huge, red-faced, white-haired parson, resting immense feet on the colonial fender, and filling the kitchen of the brotherhood with the poisonous fumes of tobacco. For a minute he was tongue-tied. Then Gabriel Pick whispering in his ear, he strode forward, and looked at the parson sideways.

"Who are you, sir?" he demanded.

Tom Shott looked round, pipe in mouth, blinked his eyes a moment, and then turned to the fire again.

"Are you deaf, sir?" cried Fontey.

But the parson puffed placidly at his pipe.

"Let me inform you, sir," shouted Fontey, "that you are smoking in the room in which we take our meals, and that we object to tobacco in this room and in all others."

Tom Shott swung one leg across the other, and went on smoking.

"Well, of all the cheek!" exclaimed Brother Gabriel Pick.

"I'll put a stop to this!" cried Fontey, approaching nearer to the parson. "Sir," he exclaimed passionately, "I request you to put your pipe out!"

He got no response.

"Sir, I order you to put your pipe out!"

Tom Shott leaned quietly and leisurely forward, and knocked out the grey ashes of his pipe on the top of the fireplace.

"Ah, that's politeness!" cried the mollified Fontey.

But ere he could go further in his exultation, the parson quietly drew a tobacco pouch from one of his capacious coat pockets, and very slowly—his eyes fixed

dreamily on the fire—proceeded to reload the offending
pipe. There was nothing aggressive in the action.

"Well, I'm jiggered!" cried Mr. Gabriel Pick.

Fontey forced himself against the mantelpiece, so
that he was facing the parson. He stooped down and
glared into his face. "A word with you!" he cried.
"This house is consecrated to Nature. It belongs to a
brotherhood. We live natural lives, abhorring flesh-food
and tobacco; we will not have our constitution shattered
by an interloper who comes without invitation into our
midst. And let me tell you that I detest and despise
all ministers of religion. I have seen through their
humbug; I have exposed their sophistries." And then,
in a passionate tumble of words, the excitable Fontey
poured out all the arguments of Strauss, Renan, Buckle,
and Mill. It was such a tirade as you shall hear any
fine Sunday afternoon in Victoria Park, and through it
all the parson sat quietly in his chair, fingering the
threads of tobacco at the top of his pipe, and looking at
the raving Fontey as a wondering boy may look at a
wriggling centipede. There was no resentment in his
gaze, only a kind of dull interest, the sort of interest
manifested by a bursting turkey-cock towards the
dairymaid who occasionally feeds him.

When Fontey paused for breath the parson drew from
his pocket a fat box of wooden matches and quietly
struck a light. But hardly had the flame spluttered
into existence before Fontey blew it furiously out.
Tom Shott looked at the smoking match a moment,
then pitched it quietly into the fire; after that he
lighted a second. But again Fontey blew it out; and
again the parson after a moment's pause threw the dead
match into the flames of the fire. As the third match
was produced and struck, and as Fontey leaned forward
to blow it out again, Tom Shott let it fall from his

fingers, and with his empty hand boxed Fontey smartly across the ear. Then, as the worshipper of Nature staggered backward, bumping his head badly against the mantelpiece, Tom Shott quietly struck a fourth match and lighted his pipe.

"You have assaulted me!" cried Pontey, nursing his flaming cheek.

Tom Shott slipped the matchbox into his side pocket, crossed his legs, and gazed placidly into the fire. The wreathing smoke clung lovingly about his big face.

"You have assaulted me!" repeated Fontey. "You witnessed the assault, Brother Pick? You will be prepared to swear in a court of justice that this clergyman struck me across the face?"

Brother Pick looked a little unhappy. "Our constitution is against going to law," he whispered; "let us go out and talk things over. Something's up. Don't give yourself away."

So they went out, and for the nonce Tom Shott was left in possession of his pipe and the brotherhood's kitchen.

By the time these two valiant defenders of the vegetarian faith had mustered courage sufficient to return to the charge, Tiplady, who had borrowed a farmer's horse and cart, had got back from his marketing, and was as busy as any restaurant cook in the lamp-lighted kitchen. Therefore, when Fontey, followed by his prickly-faced henchman, burst open the door, and strode masterfully in, his nostrils were not only saluted by the smell of tobacco—though that odour was strong enough to have bowled over a less vigorous fruitarian—but in addition they were assaulted by the rich and pungent savour of roasting flesh. For in front of the fire, smoking a pipe, stood Tiplady in shirt-sleeves, watching with lambent eyes a huge sirloin of beef turning royally on the jack; while on a chair by the table, a glass of whisky in his hand, the bottle at his side, sat the mighty red-faced parson who had boxed Brother Pontey's ears. And on the table there was something more than a bottle of Scotch whisky; pounds of sausages were stacked together in little pinky-white heaps, a dish of uncooked beef-steak shone redly in their midst, and a pompous ham, a humble gammon of bacon, and a plate of pathetic-looking sprats helped to complete the picture of a carnivorous diet in course of preparation for barbarian tables.

Before Fontey could find voice for his horror Brother Pugh, who had just given place at Sir John's bedside to the doctor and a trained nurse, came panting breathless with the painful tidings that the baronet was actually being dosed with beef-tea. But the horrid message was only half delivered, for Brother Pugh's theosophical soul was sent reeling into a very wilderness of amazement at sight of the brotherhood's kitchen table.

"Great heaven!" he cried, having no theosophical exclamation at hand, and fell back on Fontey and the terrified Gabriel Pick.

The imperturbable Tiplady reached up his hand to the mantelpiece, took down a glass of whisky, and held it up to the astonished vegetarians. "Good health, gentlemen!" he exclaimed, and moistened his lips. Tom Shott, whose eyes never wandered from Tiplady, as though by force of example lifted his glass and drained it to the dregs.

"What's the meaning of this?" demanded Fontey.

"Horrible!" exclaimed Gabriel Pick.

"Sausages!" gurgled Brother Pugh.

"D'you hear, Tiplady? What's the meaning of this?" cried the trembling Fontey.

"Meaning?" said Tiplady. "Why, it's plain enough.

A little surprise dinner for the brotherhood. Come in at about half-past seven, and you'll find it served. In the meantime you might fetch me a few vegetables; I've forgotten 'em." He turned to the spluttering joint.

"How dare you bring flesh into the Colony?" shouted Pontey.

"Dare!" cried Tiplady, wheeling round. "Why, it's a free brotherhood, isn't it? Didn't you say at the very foundation that there was to be no law in this little institution? Of course you did, Fontey, and I'm as free to eat beef as Pick there to eat seed like a blooming parrot. There's no *dare* about it, my boy; none at all. It's just glorious freedom." Then reaching down his glass again he winked one of his little black eyes, and added, "I drink to freedom; heaven bless her ladyship!"

"Look!" cried Fontey fiercely. "I'll chuck the whole thing up if this tomfoolery goes on!"

Tiplady turned a terrified face to him. "Don't say that now, Fontey; no, you mustn't say that."

"But I do," cried Fontey, striding forward. "I'll leave this confounded place to-morrow morning by the first train; I won't stay another minute. You shall plant the trees yourself, you shall put up the glass houses yourself, you shall dig the garden yourself, you—you —you shall go to the devil yourself; I won't stay; I swear I won't."

"Now listen, Fontey," pleaded Tiplady very solemnly, while Tom Shott poured himself out a fresh dose of whisky. "I've got in this little supply of meat, which is purely temporary—for all flesh is grass, and goes before you can look round, so to speak—because, Fontey, my boy, I've seen that you aren't equal to planting something like ten thousand trees on fruit and nuts. You aren't up to it. You want stamina, Pontey.

Your muscles want building up. If you don't eat this dinner, and another to-morrow, and another the day after, you won't ever get those fruit trees into the ground; and if you don't ever get those fruit trees into the ground, how is the brotherhood going to feed itself, Fontey, my boy? It isn't everybody who can boast a parrot's stomach like Brother Pick. Can we live on meadow grass? Of course we can't, therefore you see it isn't selfishness on my part getting this dinner ready. It's for you, Fontey; for you and Brother Pick and Brother Pugh—three green P's, as I may call you—and if I don't see you all sitting round the festive board to-night it will break my heart, honour bright it will; for vegetarianism has weakened that tough old organ past all belief. Half-past seven; don't forget."

I think, brother," said Pugh, turning to Fontey, "that this matter is very simply decided. We have only to meet and put it to the vote whether disgusting flesh shall be permitted in the brotherhood to demonstrate to Brother Tiplady that the majority of the brotherhood is against him."

"Certainly," said Fontey; "we'll meet at once."

"But, dearly beloved brethren!" cried Tiplady, "you are but three, and I shall have something like six-and-thirty meat-eating Colonists arriving at the end of the week, all of 'em entitled to the franchise and bursting for Nature."

"It's a conspiracy to drive us out!" cried Fontey.

Tiplady raised shocked hands. "Now, Fontey, that's ungentlemanlike. You know as well as I do that you're simply fishing about for a good excuse for chucking a dead failure. You're sick of tree-planting, Fontey, and well you know it. You've spent Sir John's money in buying rubbishy land and thousands of trees that are half dead by this time, and boxes of seeds that you may as well give to Pick for his supper as plant in the ground — for they're all dead as pippins — and now you're wanting to desert. It isn't honest, and it isn't brotherly."

"Look!" cried Fontey. "You're a humbug and a rogue; you're——"

"What!" cried Tiplady, drawing up his shirt-sleeves.

"Don't you dare to strike me!" shouted Fontey, backing behind Brother Pick, who seemed to resent the prominence into which his leader had so suddenly thrust him.

Tiplady stood over them, very big and relentless, his fists doubled, his lips working, and his shoulders squared for battle. "Unsay those words!" he said very sharply.

"Mr. Tiplady," cried Fontey, "you're breaking the spirit of our law. If Sir John Sparrow was here you daren't violate the sacred understanding of the brotherhood."

"Unsay those words, brother," repeated Tiplady.

Brother Pugh came forward. "Your master stood here in this very kitchen and was struck by a drunkard. He forbade you then to lay hand on any man."

"Fighting is contemptible," spluttered Fontey from behind Pick.

"I beg you, Brother Tiplady," cried Pugh, "to put away your anger. It is unbrotherly and unseemly. I appeal to the clergyman at the table."

But Tom Shott was lighting his pipe, and took no notice of this appeal. He might have been the deity to whom Nero's slaughtered babes prayed for succour. His indifference was Olympian, god-like.

"Fontey," said Tiplady, speaking very quickly, "if you don't unsay those words, I'll tap you over the nose for ten minutes."

"Ten minutes!" gasped Pontey.

U

"And I'll add a minute for every minute you keep me waiting. Now then, brother, look alive."

"Unsay them," counselled Pugh. "This scene is horrible and brutal."

"Unsay them," echoed Pick; "I really think you ought to, Fontey."

"If he don't," cried Tiplady, shooting out a sudden arm and grabbing the neck of Pontey's nature-costume; "if he don't, I'll flay him!"

"I do, I do, I do!" shrieked the wretched Pontey, writhing in Tiplady's grasp. His legs were slipping about in every direction, and his arms were waving like a semaphore.

Tiplady gave him a violent twist, and threw him backwards against the wall. "And after that I hope you'll have the grace to say no more about deserting the brotherhood," he cried scornfully, turning majestically to the roasting sirloin.

Fontey gathered himself together, panting very hard, and stood, with Pick on one side, Pugh on the other, glaring at Tiplady.

"Listen!" he gasped. "I can't stand meat here. I'm going away. It's against Nature, and therefore it's against my religion. I'm going away. But I've got no money. You're the treasurer. Give me enough for my railway fare. I can't stand this."

Tiplady sat down on a chair, scratching his head. "Now that's a nice point for an argument," he said slowly. "Am I justified in spending the brotherhood's money—which belonged first of all to my master, who is now too ill to be consulted—on paying the railway fare of a deserter? Am I? That's the point; am I?"

"I wish to withdraw too," put in Pugh.

"Same here," murmured Gabriel Pick.

"Three of you!" cried Tiplady, aghast.

"I'm sure Brother Sparrow would not object to our receiving sufficient money to take us back to London," said Pugh.

"That's the point," said Tiplady magisterially. For several minutes he remained in deep thought, only breaking the monotony of his silence by muttering to himself, "That's the point," at long intervals. At last he rose from his chair, thrusting a hand into his pocket, and exclaiming, "I'll risk it"; and calling upon Tom Shott to witness the transaction, he there and then paid into the hand of Alexander Fontey the exact sum of money required to pay the third-class fare of himself, Pick, and Pugh back to the centre of civilisation.

"To think," he said sadly, "of all the money you've made my master spend on this beautiful idea, and then to chuck it! Ingratitude, thy name is fruit and nuts!"

But the rebellious vegetarians were already out of earshot.

CHAPTER XXI

Wherein Dr. Peter prescribes for the mind of Sir John Sparrow, and Tom Shott plays his trump card; with a glimpse of Mrs. FitzGerald on horseback.

THERE now remained to Tom Shott the most difficult of all his labours, the wheedling of Sir John Sparrow from his deserted colony. The parson shuddered at the prospect. Here was a man (lying helpless on his bed, with a large boil on his nose) who had discarded meat-eating to take up with vegetarianism, who had flung over vegetarianism for fruitarianism, who had abandoned fruitarianism for the seed and pip theory; a man, moreover, who had bartered a practical religion for the elusive imaginings of theosophy, who had lost all sense of patriotism, who had espoused communism, and who had even put off the venerable trappings of modern civilisation; and yet a man to be saved and made whole at all costs. But was it not clear that such a man would go from madness to madness, that with convalescence and renewed vigour he could never return to the long, hard road of uneventful sanity?

How should Tom Shott, thought Tom — and no one was more conscious of his limitations—hope to mould or control this fictile, wandering mind? He shuddered at the task. His soul cried out to its

Creator, "I am unfit, unfit!" But the tactics he employed, as your honours shall now judge for yourselves, were masterly beyond praise.

He began by consulting Doctor Peter, a thin, loose-limbed gentleman, with fluffy whiskers, weak eyes, and gold spectacles.

"This is a singularly interesting case," said the physician, drawing his gloves through his hands, "a case, Mr. Shott, which possesses for the medical man considerable charm and bewitchment. For here we have a beautiful example of the mind playing upon the body, we see under our very eyes the whole physical man tortured and racked by the lightest caprices of the brain. Now, in such cases as this we must proceed with great delicacy; I cannot sufficiently impress upon you the need of great tact and discretion, Mr. Shott. It is obvious we must not decide upon a course of action which will harden the brain in its delusions. No, Mr. Shott, that would be most impolitic; it would display an utter lack of tact and discretion, and unfit us to cope with any case of a similar nature which should come under our notice in the future."

He paused, cocking his head on one side, and glancing smilingly through his gold-rimmed spectacles at the troubled face of Tom Shott. He was evidently waiting for the parson to express unbounded admiration for the wisdom of these remarks, but as he had only repeated Tom Shott's own insistence for need of caution, the honest parson did not even grunt approval.

"We must go gingerly, Mr. Shott—gingerly," said Doctor Peter. "That is a very useful and expressive word—gingerly. Our distinguished friend upstairs is renewing his strength; he will soon be ready to match his mind against ours, the least thoughtless word may undo us; therefore, let us proceed gingerly."

"What do you propose?" asked the parson, shuffling with his boots on the stone floor.

Doctor Peter nursed a knee, stooping well forward in his chair, while his head rolled languorously to one side, and a thin smile played about his mobile lips. "Diamond cuts diamond, Mr. Shott. Poison destroys poison. Ergo, fad will kill fad. That is my theory. But, as I just said, we must go gingerly; there must be no rushing at it, we must use tact and discretion. The question is, what fad shall we employ? Now, a fad that has lately come under my notice, and it is a comparatively new one, Mr. Shott, is the fad called Christian Science. Now it seems to me, Mr. Shott, that if we can make our distinguished friend upstairs a Christian Scientist (hateful word, sir, *scientist*—no word at all, in fact), we should not only be destroying his interest in vegetarianism, but we should return him safe and sound to the Christian fold, a consummation (if you will permit me to quote) devoutly to be wished."

Doctor Peter smoothed his glossy hair with his right hand, and sat back beaming in his chair.

"Now, Mr. Shott," he went on, leaning suddenly forward till his head was well over the parson's knees, "the question is, How are we to make our distinguished friend upstairs a Christian scienter? That is the point. Now, might we not—always proceeding gingerly—make use of the boil on the baronet's nose? I don't force the idea; I submit it as a working hypothesis. Might we not utilise for this purpose the boil on Sir John's nose? May we not, Mr. Shott, even regard the boil on the nose of Sir John as a merciful act of Providence, pointing us, like the star in the East, to a great and glorious occurrence? I say, may we not? It isn't for me to decide a theological question of this kind, but I venture to put it to you."

Tom Shott nodded his head. His eyebrows were high up in the troubled forehead, the eyes were lustreless, the upper lip thrust despondently forward. But he was beginning to see light.

The smiling doctor struck his folded gloves several times in the palm of his very white left hand, and exclaimed : " I think, Mr. Shott, we have got upon the right road. I think so, sir; it is early yet to prophesy, but I venture to say that I think we may justly suppose that we are travelling at any rate in the right direction. That is your own idea, I take it? Very well, then ; now let us proceed with our method." He rose suddenly from his chair and paced up and down the little room. At one moment his two hands were in the small of his back, at the next they were on his hips, at the next they were fiddling his tie, at the next they were smoothing his hair, and at the next they were laid dramatically upon his breast. And while his hands were so employed, the worthy doctor's head was now turned upwards to the ceiling, now bent down to a level with his stomach, now hanging slackly on the right shoulder, and now inclined knowingly to the left. At one moment he was taking gigantic strides, at the next he was mincing his steps, and at the next he would pull suddenly up and plant a neatly gaitered boot upon the seat of a chair.

"It seems to me, Mr. Shott," he went on, during these dizzying extension motions, "that if I were to tell our distinguished friend upstairs that his boil was incurable—a tarradiddle which I am content to think the Recording Angel will blot out with a tear —and if, sir, the nurse in attendance—a thoroughly capable woman, Mr. Shott — having been previously prompted by me, sir, were to comfort the mourning and lamenting baronet with the assurance that Christian

Science could easily remove the pimple defying **the** faculty, we might, sir—I venture to think we might, I say—hope that we had *suggested* to Sir John's mind a new, interesting, and intensely powerful delusion. Please note the delicacy of the idea—*suggestion*, sir, nothing more than that. No clumsy force, no vulgar bullying; *suggestion*, hypnotic suggestion, sir."

The parson nodded lugubriously.

"It seems to me," said the doctor, glancing a little disappointedly at Tom Shott's imperturbable countenance, "that the extreme beauty and delicacy of this case has escaped you, Mr. Shott. You seem to have quite missed the extraordinary interest attaching to the providential boil on the proboscis of our distinguished friend upstairs. I presume it is your theological training which is responsible; to a medical mind, sir—a scientific mind, I should say—the case is one of quite engrossing fascination. I cannot tell you when I have felt my intellect so quickened, my sympathies so thoroughly aroused. If you will permit me, I will speak to the nurse immediately, and prepare her for her rôle. Permit me, Mr. Shott, to wish you a very good morning." And with a profound bow the slippery physician took up his hat, smoothed the polished silk with one of his white hands, and disappeared like an eel.

On the following day Tom Shott went to sit for half an hour with his distinguished friend upstairs. The nurse withdrew.

"My dear Tom," said the baronet, "I have an immense load weighing on my mind. I am in grievous need of spiritual consolation." He was very weak, and his soft voice came with difficulty.

"Don't worry yourself," said the parson, striving to keep his eyes away from the boil.

"I would with all my soul that I could follow that prescription," sighed the baronet; "but, my dear Tom, it is a terrible thought for a man that he has neglected, even attacked the true religion, and taken up with strange gods."

"It is," said the parson decisively.

"And that is what I have done. My consolation is that I did it honestly and with pure motives; but this consolation is but a slight medicament for my distracted soul, and I am now torn, Tom, torn by the pangs of mocking contrition. I am, really. You cannot tell, Tom, how I am suffering at this moment."

Tom Shott lay one of his huge hands on the baronet's arm, and pressed it gently.

"Thank you, my dear fellow, thank you," sighed the unhappy invalid.

"It's never too late to mend," said the parson.

"Ah, that is a great gospel!" cried Sir John in stronger voice. "My comfort is that I may recover from this bed of sickness to devote the remainder of my days to a resuscitation of primitive Christianity, by this means making atonement for my digression from the path of faith. For, Tom, this excellent woman who is nursing me has placed into my hands a pamphlet on Christian Science, and she has assured me that the boil upon my nose, which Doctor Peter confesses is beyond the skill of medicine to remove, will be obliterated by means of Christian Science, if I have but sufficient faith to follow its blessed teachings. This you must keep secret from the doctor, for the bigotry of physicians is so great that he would of a surety dismiss the nurse if he had any suspicion of her dealings with this wonderful revival of primitive Christianity."

"I'll be silent as the grave," said the parson.

"Thank you, Tom, thank you," answered the baronet;

"and if you will glance over this pamphlet I should be so glad, my dear fellow; for the cases of recovery from incurable illnesses are so many and so wonderful that I am quite sure you have only to read the paper to become, as I am, a convinced believer in the power of Christian Science, a power which demonstrates to my mind, with a forcefulness impossible to Butler and Paley, the truth of the narrative of the four evangelists."

The worthy gentleman then quoted several miraculous cases from the pamphlet, and expressed his firm conviction that the incurable boil upon his nose would be dissipated by the action of Christian Science. At the end of the half-hour the nurse returned to find her patient in a greatly excited condition, and turning the parson out, devoted the remainder of the day to soothing our hero's nerves.

It was some three days after this, when the angry boil was showing unmistakable signs of subsidence, that Tom Shott played his master card. He had listened for many moments to the baronet's exhortations over this wonderful testimony to the truth of Christian Science, and then laying a hand upon the bed, and looking steadily into our hero's eyes, said he—

"It's never too late to mend, Jack!"

"Thank God for it!" cried the baronet.

"You've done more wrong than wandering from the faith of your fathers, Jack."

"I fear so."

"One wrong in particular, Jack."

"Tell me what it is, that I may make amends."

"That *beautiful* woman," with deep emotion.

"That beautiful woman? I don't understand."

"Mrs. FitzGerald, Jack."

"Mrs. FitzGerald! My dear Tom, what on earth are you driving at?"

"She is pining away."

Sir John raised himself in the bed. "You perplex me. What do you mean? I can't follow you, Tom."

The parson sat back in his chair. "You've treated her cruelly," he said, with great firmness.

"I!"

"You've broke her heart, Jack."

"But how? When? You mystify me."

"You led her on."

"I!"

"You encouraged her to hope."

"Good heavens! what have I done?"

"You suddenly threw her over."

"I never realised!"

"You left her to weep her heart out."

"But I had no idea."

"And she's drooping till you return."

There was a pause, and then the parson added, "Jack, you must marry her."

Sir John's eyes searched the heavy countenance of Tom Shott for some token of wavering, some sign of mercy, but there was none.

"My dear Tom," said he, speaking very low, "on my word of honour as a gentleman I had no notion that Mrs. FitzGerald took my little attentions seriously. If I had ever thought *that*, as truly as I lie here, I would have instantly ceased all intercourse with her. But as it is, willingly as I would sacrifice myself to make amends for an unconscious sin, it is now impossible. My money is gone, my home is gone; I have nothing left but this Colony, to whose interests I must devote myself body and soul in the hope of making it, in God's good time, the great centre of Christian Science. It is impossible for me to offer marriage to a lady; I am homeless and a beggar."

"The Colony, Jack, is broken up. They've all gone," quoth the parson.

"Gone!"

"Every one of them. It's a dead failure."

"Pontey ruined it," sighed Sir John. "He was too pushing."

"Vegetarianism is opposed to the gospel," went on the parson. "I hope you'll fight it tooth and nail for the rest of your life. You must, Jack."

This was a mistake on the part of the parson, for it set Sir John talking for twenty minutes on the perplexing problem of vegetarianism regarded in the light of the gospel. It was an interesting homily, for it showed plainly enough that the worthy baronet was seeking some way to break gently and honourably with his recent notions on the subject of food. But it interrupted the parson's effort to get Sir John back to the village, and at the end of the disquisition the nurse arrived upon the scene to cut short the colloquy. On the following day, however, it was renewed, and the baronet began it.

"I have been thinking, Tom," said he, "of what you told me yesterday concerning poor Mrs. FitzGerald. It has distressed me beyond words. One never knows what amount of sorrow and agony one may cause by a word or a glance; it only shows how careful we should be to curb the natural desire for displaying our attractions. We should not think so much of ourselves; we should think more of the effect of ourselves upon others. Isn't it so, my dear fellow?"

The parson nodded.

"But what can I do? I am, to all intents and purposes, moneyless. My home is gone, my——"

"Your home is yours still."

"No, my dear fellow, you are mistaken. I received

a cheque for the sale of lease and furniture only a week ago. A very handsome cheque too—more than I expected, a great deal."

"Your home is yours still, Jack; it was bought for you."

"Bought for me!"

"By an admirer, Jack."

"Is it possible?"

"Such is true love, Jack."

"How wonderful!"

"Nay, Jack, how beautiful!"

"Wonderful, beautiful, and—humiliating," sighed Sir John, proud as a peacock.

"Such is her love, Jack, that she won't wait for you to propose. She'll beg you to do her the honour of marrying her; I know she will, poor thing—poor thing!"

Sir John smoothed his hair, and looked with great self-importance at the counterpane on his bed. Never before had his vanity been so ministered to; never before had he realised how irresistible were his attractions for the fair sex. And as he thought of himself and his manifold fascinations he began to think of Mrs. FitzGerald, of the beautiful manor-house that slumbered to the cawing of rooks in the green embrace of comfortable trees, of the river brawling through her land, of the village world that had loved and reverenced him, of those pleasant dinners with Tom Shott, of the cigar smoked over the coffee, of the tea-tables at which his conversation had been the delight of so many gentle ladies; and then he dwelt for a moment on the fragrant beauty of the merry Mrs. FitzGerald, and his conscience smote him that he had driven the laughter from those entrancing eyes.

But while the baronet lay in this dream Mrs. Fitz-

Gerald herself was riding a bay mare, with Clarence Mortimer on a mighty hunter at her side. They were walking back from a day's cub-hunting, and the midland world was filled with a soft radiance that suggested tender thoughts and heart's confidence; you could feel the throbbing of the sunset. They had been talkative, but now were grown suddenly silent, dangerously silent. He had been for many days her close attendant, her charming slave (as often as Guy Drayton would allow), and she had found pleasure in his devotion. Yet her heart, so far as she knew it herself, inclined to the handsome youth, though her judgment leaned, she thought, to the side of the stronger nature, the maturer man. On this run he had managed to keep his heavy horse at the side of her wonderful little mare almost from start to finish, and now they were walking home together, side by side, through the bewitchment of an autumn twilight.

"Think of the hot cakes at the fire!" said she suddenly.

"I am thinking of something less transitory—something a thousand times more appetising!" quoth he.

Her little mare tossed its head and pretended to trot. She leant forward, stroking its neck. "Betty is thinking of crushed oats and a rack full of hay. Bless her little heart!" said the lady, clenching her teeth; "I love every wrinkle in her neck!"

His horse walked soberly, its head dropping a little, its motion inelastic.

"And to-morrow," said he, "you go away?"

"Back to my dale; yes. There! did you see Betty prick her ears? Oh, the pretty, pretty!" she cried, leaning forward; "she loves the very sound of the word!"

She was not too far ahead to catch his sigh.

They were on the grass under the trees of a wide avenue, and Betty tripped like a ballet girl, flinging up her little head and setting the curb chain a-jingling. Clarence jogged his horse to Mrs. FitzGerald's side.

"Will you let me speak to you after dinner to-night?" he asked very solemnly.

She turned and looked at him. "Speak to me?"

"I want to ask you a question."

She smiled. "Don't you hate answering questions? But of course you shall speak to me, and if your question isn't a very hard one I will give you an answer; only—only—it mustn't be a serious question."

"It is a most serious question for me," he pleaded.

"Don't ask it," she cried, looking at him half solemnly, and brushing a loose tress from her brow.

"I have no choice."

She looked at him searchingly. Then she turned away, gazing on Betty's twitching ears.

"No, don't ask it, because, don't you see, it's so much nicer for people to be bright and merry; and serious questions kill merriment, and when merriment goes, friendship goes, and friendship is the pleasantest thing in all the world—there is nothing half so honest and strong and comfortable as friendship."

"There are emotions infinitely deeper."

"They can all be devoted to friendship, every one of them. I love making friends. Wherever I go, I try to make new friends, people who will tell me about their bothers and scrapes, their worries and anxieties, and to whom I can talk about the gossip of the world, about my dogs, and my horses, and my dear old women in the village. (By the way, you've never once asked after Budge and Toddy!) It's so pleasant to have heaps of people like that. And then one can write to them, and they can come and see one and writing letters to real honest friends is one of the best labours of the day, and as for a house-party of true, tried friends, why, there's nothing half so good in all the world."

"But surely there is something that goes deeper, something that preserves all that is best in friendship, and yet gives the heart finer satisfaction?"

"In our dreams and our story books," she replied, rubbing Betty's flank with her whip.

"No; in common, humdrum existence," he insisted.

"For the lucky ones."

"Yes, for the lucky ones."

"And Fate never tells us whether we are lucky ones till it is too late."

Then she touched Betty with her heel. "Think of those hot cakes!" she cried, and sailed away from him, smiling back with frank eyes.

"Think of my confounded bills!" he muttered to himself, and spurred after her.

CHAPTER XXII

Which tells how the two Rivals slew each other

MR. DRAYTON hated Mr. Mortimer, and Mr. Mortimer hated Mr. Drayton, as deeply as "two hinds quarrelling for the river-right." Rivals were they, as stern in their rivalry as fiercest lovers of transpontine melodrama, yet they dined peaceably at the same table, smoked cigarettes together, played pool in company, and even got so far as chaffing each other with a polite grace.

Oh, Civil Progress, great the debt we owe, since Romeo and Country Paris now may meet with smiling mask of amity, and never dagger flash forth from its sheath in furious rivalry of clashing love!

But we are not yet passionless, and jealousy forges weapons from the armoury of civilisation as easily as old-world rivals laid hand on sword and dagger. So Mr. Drayton made plans for getting Mr. Mortimer out of the thoughts of the lady, and Mr. Mortimer schemed diligently for ridding himself of a continual menace to the success of his passion in the person of Mr. Drayton. Civilisation in this case is merely a horror of blood-shedding.

. "Poor old Clarry!" sighed the soldier, sitting at the widow's side, radiant with happiness, and filled with a giant determination to win this lovely dame at all costs.

x   305

"Why so compassionate?" she added, looking suddenly towards Mr. Mortimer, coldly handsome in the distance.

"Oh, I don't know!" exclaimed Guy lightly and triumphantly. "It's only that one knows the poor beggar must have a struggle to keep going. He lives too high."

She turned quickly. "You mean he is poor?"

"Not that quite; but he is so recklessly extravagant." To do Mr. Drayton justice, he faltered. Then in a rush, he went on: "People say if he doesn't marry a rich old dowager soon he'll go under. I don't believe it. Anyway, he won't marry while he can borrow, that's certain! Such a good chap."

There was a pang at the widow's heart.

"What a world!" she exclaimed sadly.

"Why?"

"All so sordid, isn't it?"

He laughed. "Well, one would hardly look for romance in old Clarry. Hang it all, he's old enough to be the father of both of us! You couldn't expect him to marry for love. What?"

She looked at him suddenly and for a moment fixedly.

"I don't like it—I don't like it!" she said, smiling uneasily and looking away. "Oh, what a hard, cruel, sordid, selfish little world it is! What a gossiping, money-getting, self-seeking Vanity Fair! But to-morrow I shall be back in my dale, in my Cranford, and Miss Matty and Miss Pole shall come to tea with me——"

"I didn't meet them, did I?" he asked, interrupting.

She laughed. "No, you didn't meet them."

"I like to know all your friends. But why do you laugh?"

"Because I am glad to be going back."

She looked into his eyes, trying to renew the old, plentiful delight she had once found in his pleasant face. But it was gone now. The boyhood was stripped away: the petty schemer was revealed. The little word that had stabbed at Clarry had effectually slain the hopes of his rival.

"Don't be glad to be going back," he said gently, leaning forward. "That is selfish, frightfully selfish. I shall miss you like anything. You know that; you must."

Again the brave woman laughed. "I am part of the selfish little world," she said lightly; "and like your friend Mr. Mortimer, I am—what shall we say?—*blasé.*"

"You!" he cried. "You! Why, you're utterly unspoilt. Everybody says you're the freshest woman anywhere. You're quite different to the ordinary woman; you're so awfully gentle, and sweet, and sympathetic. I never can talk to anyone as I can talk to you; I can't really. Do believe that of me." He came to a full stop, for she was watching him critically.

"Well, I am not *blasé,*" she said brightly. "Of course I believe that there are kind and gentle and true people in our little corner of Vanity Fair. Do you know, even if Mr. Mortimer is running after a rich dowager, I somehow like him, and I certainly feel very sorry for him. He is always so nice and kind, and always so—tactful."

Guy realised that he had put his foot in it. Poor dear boy, with his child's heart full of green love, he felt at that moment as though death in its most hideous shapes was preferable to life. His world broke up about him; his heavens crashed above his head. Good Lord, he had lost her—lost this woman he loved with all his soul!

He protested the liveliest affection for Clarence

vowed he would be glad to lend him every single
penny he could possibly afford, and then straightway
went on to urge his own suit at the full gallop of panic.
Never had lover adored so devotedly as he; never,
of course, had lover been so blessed with mistress; and,
finally, before the goddess of his heaven withdrew herself
from him, she must—in justice, in mercy, in very pity—
tell him at least if she were not indifferent to him.

It was the most difficult protestation of love our
young gallant had ever made, though it was possibly
the sincerest; for the beautiful goddess watched him
throughout it all with calm and critical eyes, studying
him with steady penetration, and never helping him
by the droop of an eyelid or the soft, surging sympathy
of a blush from beginning to end. So that Mr. Drayton
had constantly to look down, constantly to raise or
draw down his eyebrows, constantly to shift and fidget
in his chair.

And at the end of it all, suddenly to their little alcove
came the hostess with Mr. Mortimer, and in the next
minute—he was almost glad of deliverance—Guy
Drayton was at the other end of the room in a circle
of chatterers, wounded unto death.

Clarence Mortimer, cool and collected, took possession
of Mr. Drayton's chair. He remembered afterwards
that he congratulated himself at this moment on the
steadiness of his pulse, the obedience of his nerves,
and the steely determination of his brain.

He did not know that never had his hopes been
brighter. He did not know that the beautiful widow
was at this very moment possessed by a tender sympathy for one who had all the tastes and capacity
for the enjoyments of a gentleman, and was yet so
cruelly cursed by penury. She admired him for dis-
sembling his troubles, and applauded him in her heart

for preserving a calm and gentle disposition in the face
of petty and pestering worries. Never before, perhaps,
had she looked so sympathetically on this quiet lover.

All Clarence knew was this: that Guy Drayton had
got the start, and that his own time was exceeding
short; but even in his anxiety he did not fail to observe
that Mrs. FitzGerald was radiantly lovely to-night.
"Really," said Clarry to himself, "she is a very distinguished-looking woman; quite pretty—really quite
pretty."

He began by disposing of his rival—easily, as two
captains may discuss the juvenilities of their subalterns
before they talk of their own august affairs.

"When poets profess to sigh for the golden days of
youth, they forget the pangs of youthful affections.
I doubt if the pleasures of three-and-twenty are worth
the nuisance of falling in love every other day. Poor
Mr. Drayton, he is as deep in love with you as he was
with little Lady Marjorie at the Grahams' last week.
I hope he will forgive me for turning him away. It
is cruel, but I was promised, wasn't I?"

Mrs. FitzGerald almost gasped. She stared at
Clarence as though he had demanded (as she well
might have thought) her money or her life. Was
he, too, a stabbing lover? Was all modern affection
a miserable intrigue? And was that first terrible
marriage of hers typical of all unions in Vanity Fair?

Sympathy with the troubles of Mr. Mortimer deserted
the widow's heart. She knew then that he was a
schemer, that he was seeking his own ends; but after
the first moment of revulsion she was struck only by
the drollery of the situation. These two lovers, these
two rivals, fighting each other with stabbing words!
She determined to make use of the situation. The
Irish blood in her veins throbbed delightedly. These

two lovers, each maligning the other—or telling the truth of each other—deserved to be punished. She would punish them.

So she smiled and jested and played with words, and Clarence grew more and more sure of his prize, while he became for the first time supremely conscious that the rich widow was a really charming and entrancing creature. That was the unfortunate part assigned to Clarence in this little comedy—it gave him love at the end of the play, when it was too late.

Mrs. FitzGerald, driven to bay for an answer, fell to blushing, and turning away her head and begging so prettily for time,'till at last, so sure did he feel of his prize, Clarence Mortimer let her go with the promise that he should receive his answer in the morning before her departure.

"She is mine," said Clarence, "all mine. I wonder if she is as rich as they say."

Now, as our dear widow went into the hall she was met by Guy Drayton, greatly excited and greatly miserable, who implored her in a whisper to give him at least some scrap of hope before she went away. And so she promised him that with the morning he should receive her answer, and smiling as mischievously as a child, she glided away and betook herself to her room.

There, for a moment, she was disposed to cry. But the peace of the dale, and all the simple joys of the village world, came flooding into her heart, and she felt hungry for her people and her home. Her Cranford! The love she had dreamed of was not to be hers—if it existed at all. Perhaps there was no such thing in the world as true love; could a thing so celestial exist in the midst of all the vanities of this transitory life? Why should she break her heart for a vain thing? There were other things in life—little things, no doubt, but occupations for time and a satisfaction in some measure for the heart's desires. Oh, a hundred little things!

She wanted to cry now, but as the tears gathered in her eyes she smiled to herself at the memory of those weeping heroines who distressed her so much in the pages of her best-loved books. No, she would not cry. Cry! Nay, she would laugh and be merry.

Her punishment for these modern rivals! Here at least was rest from teasing thought and the mockery of disillusion. Oh, yes, she must make sport with these lovers, even if modern life forbade a buck-basket and the garments of the Fat Woman of Brentford.

So she sat down, even in the midst of the ruin of her dreams, at the very moment of illusion's death-throes, and wrote, with laughter and smiles, two little notes— the one to Clarence and the other to Guy.

Then, when her maid came to her, she presented the old sweet smiling face to the world, laughed and chatted, discussed the morning's arrangements with eagerness, and talked of the dale with an enthusiasm that surprised even the north-bred maid.

In the morning, ready dressed to descend, she stood at the window of her room and looked from behind a curtain at the lawn below. Yes, her plan was working well. Guy Drayton was already out. Fresh from his morning's ablutions and dumb-bells, rosy and good to look upon, he walked to and fro on the green grass, playing with the little lap-dog of his hostess, ever and anon looking up to exchange a word with another of the guests. And now from the terrace to the lawn, very calm and self-possessed, marched Clarence Mortimer. She held her breath. They were both together—close, close together. Now was the moment; another second, and it might be too late.

As she trembled for the success of her plan a servant approached the two men, carrying two little notes on a salver. Her maid had done her work well. Good maid, good maid! She clapped her hands with delight, and watched the rivals with overflowing eyes. As the servant approached they both started and looked at each other. Mortimer received his note first, examined it for a second, and then turned his back, breaking the envelope. Guy was not a moment behind him. Mrs. FitzGerald from her window could have persuaded herself that she heard the tearing of the envelopes—both at the same moment.

Suddenly they both looked from the letters to the envelopes, and then, as though commanded by an invisible drill-sergeant to turn about, they swung round simultaneously, and half proffered the other the missive in his hand. But at the very moment of this common impulse, they checked, glared at each other, pocketed the letters, and then struck off by different paths in the direction of the house.

Now the explanation of this pantomime—the drollery of which moved our pretty widow to uncontrollable laughter—is to be sought merely in the naughtiness of Mrs. FitzGerald. She had written on the previous night two sweet little notes, the one to Clarence and the other to Guy; but when it came to putting these tender missives in their envelopes, she had most reprehensibly addressed Clarence's letter to Guy and Guy's letter to Clarence—truly, a most serious slip of the pen. Imagine the feelings of Clarence when he opened a letter addressed to his own proud person, and read :—

"DEAR MR. DRAYTON,—I am so very sorry I cannot possibly marry you. The only person I have really loved just recently is Mr. Mortimer, and now that you have convinced me he is a mere gold-seeker I am determined to remain in my present state. When we meet at breakfast, behave as if nothing had happened. If you offer to get me some scrambled eggs, or a little brawn, or something of that sort, I shall know I am forgiven.

" Sincerely yours,
" BEATRICE FITZGERALD."

And imagine the feelings of poor Guy when he opened his letter, and read, with Clarence almost at his very side :—

"DEAR MR. MORTIMER,—I should be only too pleased to accept your kind invitation to marry you if it were not for a previous engagement of my affections. To be frank with you, I have been head over heels in love with Mr. Drayton for the last four-and-twenty hours. But I begin to realise at last that what you say of him is perfectly true— he is young, immature, and a little too prone to the infection of love ever to make a good husband. I could never marry an easy victim of pretty faces. In this heart-broken condition you will not expect me to dwell upon your very pretty offer of marriage. Let us meet at breakfast as though nothing had happened. Offer to get me some scrambled eggs, or a little brawn, or something of that wholesome nature, and I shall know we are to remain good friends.

" Sincerely yours,
" BEATRICE FITZGERALD."

In this way the brave little widow opposed herself to the shafts of disillusion, and in this way the two rivals slew each other. How effectually may be guessed, when it is recorded that each in a high state of indignation returned to the other his own letter, and learned that a woman's wit had converted their tragedy into farce.

And yet the element of tragedy remained for them— they realised that they had lost what was greatly worth **winning.**

CHAPTER XXIII

Of how Tom Shott concluded his Herculean Labour

NOW it came to pass, as your honours may very well believe, that Sir John Sparrow recovered from the boil upon his nose, and by the same token rose from his bed of sickness a stout-hearted believer in the efficacy of Christian Science. His vegetarianism now seemed a slight thing to him, and his communism a foolishness; the dominating idea in his mind was to spread the light of this merciful discovery, whereby not only would the sick be healed, but all the world be made righteous and acceptable to the Lord. Finding him in this frame of mind, Tom Shott argued with admirable subtlety that Sir John would best be able to effect his beneficent purpose as an author, and that he could not be in a better position for practising authorship than as the husband of Mrs. FitzGerald, living in comfortable affluence, with an excellent library at his disposal.

It therefore fell out that Sir John Sparrow, protesting that he was sacrificing himself for a quixotic notion of chivalry, and blessing heaven for his open mind, set out one fine wintry morning to return to the old dull life, and to bind up the broken heart of the widow FitzGerald.

Mrs. FitzGerald, as fate would have it, was pondering a reply to a long and earnest letter from Guy Drayton, which she had received that very morning, when Parson Tom Shott all unexpectedly presented himself before her. She tumbled her pen into its tray, banged up her blotting-book, and turned a smiling face over her shoulder.

"Why, it's weeks since we've seen you!" she exclaimed, getting up from the davenport.

"I've got him back," said the parson, taking and dropping her hand. Then he sat down with a sigh of relief, feeling that his task was over. Oh, the many sore-needed pounds it had cost the old fellow to bring his scheme to this fine point.

"Sir John has come back?" she questioned.

"I brought him—last night."

"And how is he, poor dear?"

"Still shaky. Great care will be necessary. But you'll see to that."

"I'll see to it!—see to nursing Sir John!" She began to laugh.

"The thing is," said the parson, very serious, "you'll have to propose."

. Mrs. FitzGerald's eyes opened wide, and her lips parted. She gazed dumbstricken at the parson.

"He's too crushed," said Tom Shott. "Feels his position; no money, no home—couldn't possibly propose himself."

"But—but—but!"

She began to laugh.

"Poor fellow's very broken," said Tom Shott, wondering why in the world she was laughing. "Magnificent sight to see him fighting on that death-bed. Splendid pluck."

Mrs. FitzGerald was still staring with wide eyes, her lips twitching. "But why in the world have I got to propose to him?"

"He's given almost every shilling away. Been trying to make the world better."

"Yes, that was very good and very stupid of him."

"And now, in his poverty, he hasn't the heart to propose to you."

"Hasn't the heart!"

"Looks as if he was after your fortune. Surely that's obvious, isn't it?"

"It is, indeed!" She laughed gaily. "When he's squandered all his money, the dear little creature sends you to say that he loves me with his last penny, and will I make him the happiest man that ever lived? Was ever woman's heart besieged in this fashion? And I am to believe that he has loved me all these long years, and that he was only waiting to declare his passion till he thought I could bear the tidings!"

Tom Shott was puzzled. "He loves you; you love him. Everyone's known that for years. Talk of the dale. Plain as a pikestaff." He paused, puffing. "He loves you; you love him; that's how things stand," he said bluntly. No man saw an open gate quicker than Tom Shott.

Mrs. FitzGerald's beautiful eyes were wide again. "My very dear Mr. Shott," said she, "are you the arch-enchanter of enchanters, and am I under some strange, wonderful, and potent spell, or is this indeed real life, and are you a real live, sane, human person? I must pinch myself to see if I am awake. Oh, I am!"

"What's the matter?"

"You come to me and tell me that I am in love with Sir John Sparrow quite calmly, as if you were telling me Mrs. Gathercole had the gout. What has led you to imagine such an utterly ridiculous thing?"

Tom Shott got up from his chair. His chin had dropped, his eyes were gaping wildly out of his head. "God bless my soul!" he gasped; "is it possible?"

He had never dreamed of this, never contemplated the possibility that she would reject him. His brain had been drilled to believe that she was deeply in love with Jack Sparrow. All the world loved Jack Sparrow. All the gossip of the dale had said that these two would inevitably marry. And now—now. Why, the ground was gone from under him, and it is a very dark moment for slow-witted gentlemen when that happens. "God bless my soul!" he repeated, and shook like a leaf, the whole of him.

She had never seen the old man so moved. She went to him, laid a hand on his great arm, and looked into those staring blue eyes of his.

"Tell me," she said, "what all this means. I will listen quietly, and I won't joke any more."

"You were joking?" he cried in a rush, catching at a straw.

She looked at him for a long moment, and then nodded her head. "Yes," said she.

"Thank God!" cried the parson, shaking off her hand, and beginning to stump about the room. Then, half chuckling and half talking to himself, he went muttering to and fro, "For the moment I thought you meant it! It would have spoilt everything. I'd built on you. Never doubted for a moment but you'd jump at him. Thought I was doing you both a turn. Most suitable match, everybody says so—said so for years. But you frightened me badly. Great Heaven, I'm glad you were joking!" He came up to where she stood wondering, and touched her confidentially on the arm. "A quiet wedding will be best," said he; "something simple; no show, no fashions. Perhaps you'll see him in the morning and talk things over?"

"Hasn't he sent patterns for the bridesmaids' dresses?" she asked, smiling.

"No, he wants something quite simple. The only thing he asks for is to have a Captain Chivvy up for his best man."

"Has he ordered the cake?"

Tom Shott was just going to utter a "No," when he caught sight of her face and stopped. "You're joking again?" he asked. "You mustn't with me, I can't see 'em. Jack will; Jack's nimble-witted. Save 'em till you're married, my dear."

She grew serious. "Now, listen!" she said. "I won't joke at all, and I'll be very, very solemn, I promise. Now, answer these questions like a dear soul. Sir John is penniless?"

"Nearly so—a few hundreds left."

"He has come back specially to marry me?"

"Yes."

"Did you tell him I wanted him to marry me?"

"Hinted it." Heaven forgave him.

"Why?"

"Nothing else would have brought him; everybody's said it for years; it's an ideal match."

"I see. And you think he wants to marry me?"

"Always has."

"And he thinks I want to marry him?"

He nodded.

"And as he's so poor, and as I love him so distractedly, he wants me to go down to the cottage to-morrow and say, 'Please, sir, will you marry me?'"

The parson pursed his lips. "You can put it differently from that. Make a perfectly friendly thing of it. No ceremony. You're old friends; it's a most suitable match."

She bundled him out of the room, laughing gaily, and when he was gone, his honest old heart beating proudly at the smooth working of his great plan, she came back into the room and went to the davenport with the laughter still in her eyes.

"Now this," she said to herself, "is an ideal marriage. There can be no fears of unhappiness. He is the dearest little soft-voiced dandy that ever went a-wooing, and he'll make the best squire in the world. By marrying him I shall please him, please that dear old lumbering bull, and please all the village. Perhaps I shall even please myself. Really, when I think and think and think it over, I don't believe Parson Tom could have found me a caretaker more to my satisfaction. The only person I shall not please will be poor dear Guy Drayton. Oh, dear! oh, dear! What shall I say to him? How difficult these letters are! I can't say now that I am averse from marriage; I can't even say that I love somebody else."

But at this point the door burst open, and Budge and Toddy, radiant from the bath-tub, came suddenly into the room, charging at lightning speed into the skirts of their mistress. She wheeled round on her chair, her face lit up with joy, and welcomed them with petting and patting as they sprang tail-wagging upon her knee. Then, with her face in the air—for they were both struggling, scrambling with all four paws, to kiss her chin—the pretty lady gave herself up to dog worship.

"Bother the letter," said she, with her arms round the excited dogs, "bother everything in the world except my lovely Budge—you white darling, you!—and my perfectly beautiful little Toddy, in your nice, clean coat!"

And a servant entered the room with sugar that she might feed her pets and make a fuss over them after their tub. So the letter to Guy Drayton was not written till the morrow.

CHAPTER XXIV

Of the Last State of Sir John's Mind

IT is now evident·to the meanest intelligence among your honours that Sir John Sparrow, our worthy and notable hero, having run through the gamut of modern crotchets, is in a fit state of mind to settle down to comfortable normality. But we must inform you, for the glory of Parson Shott, that there remained one abominable fad to Sir John, and that it was by the inspiration of the parson that this last demon was exorcised from the baronet's mind.

Of all the miserable delusions that festered in Sir John's soul, the madness of cosmopolitanism was the strongest. The excellent little gentleman having returned to meat, wine and tobacco, spared no opportunity for expressing his great admiration of foreigners to the detriment of our own insulars. It was the last rag of his madness, to which he clung desperately as though to shield himself from the charge of being turncoat, apostate, Judas, or any of those coarse terms we apply to gentlemen who grow in knowledge. It seemed to afford him the liveliest satisfaction to uphold the part of our opponents wherever Great Britain's interests conflicted with the scheming designs of the foreigner. He held that in art, literature, and science the whole world was in advance of England, and he professed himself very sure that in no country was there greater

ignorance, more appalling destitution, or wider drunkenness than was to be found in every town of the United
Kingdom.

When Sir John mentioned these views of his to Tom
Shott they did no harm, but so soon as he began bruit-
ing them about the neighbourhood they became mis-
chievous, and by the same token extremely dangerous
to his reputation of popular hero. Therefore did Tom
Shott rack those slow brains of his for a remedy, and
some ten days before the wedding—by the mercy of
Providence—he came upon a cure for the baronet.

One of Sir John's neat little dinners was just finished
in the cottage, and Tiplady, having set the cigar-box
and cigarettes before his little master, was bustling over
the coffee-tray in his pantry. On the right of Sir John
sat Captain Chivvy, very spruce and extremely sorrowful, and at the end of the table—in his old place—sat
the parson loading his pipe.

"One more glass," cried Sir John, passing the decanter, "and let us drink a toast to the days of my
freedom!" He held the glass to the candles, and then
glanced, love-lorn, to the pictures of fair ladies adorning
his walls.

"It's no light wrench, parting from one's bachelorhood," sighed he; "and I can promise you that to
desert my public work for the amelioration of mankind
is no slight sacrifice to me. The world will never know
what I have given up. But let us be merry. Shott!
Chivvy! I drink with you! Good fellows both; God
bless us all." He emptied his glass. "I rejoice that
I have preserved an open mind through all the vicissi-
tudes of my philanthropical career—a mind open
enough to return immediately to my old habits when
I realised the illogical bases of some of those movements with which it was my great happiness to become

Y

associated. Where should I be now but for my open mind? That is what we must all aim at, in sickness and in health, in poverty and in riches, as bachelors and as married men, the preservation of an open mind."

Tom Shott struck a match, and Tiplady entered with coffee.

In another moment he was attacking England. England was a doomed country. Look at her Parliament House! Look at her shrieking Press! Look at her playhouses! Look at Margate Sands! Look at Hampstead Heath on an Easter Monday! Was there any sign that the England of to-day was the England of Elizabeth? In a word, we were living on our past.

Tom Shott puffed slowly at his pipe, and Captain Chivvy admitted that there was a great deal in what Sparrow said, a very great deal indeed. "By Jove! yes, England was played out! Look at the War Office——!" Whereupon followed this conversation—

"Always back your own side," said the parson.

"Even when they are going to the devil?" asked the baronet.

"Certainly," replied the parson.

"My dear fellow——"

"I'd sooner," said the parson, with vehemence—"I'd sooner see you one of these crack-brained British-Israelites than a miserable anti-Englander."

"A British-Israelite! What is that?" asked Sir John.

"It sounds like a Rothschild," put in Chivvy.

"I've never heard the phrase before," said Sir John.

"People," said the parson, "who say we're the lost tribes, seed of Abraham, and all that. Cranks!"

"The lost tribes!" said the baronet, beginning to think. "Dear me, it never struck me before. The lost tribes! Good gracious, how stupid of me! Dear me yes; the lost tribes of Israel—Dan and Beersheba, wasn't it? Now, what *has* happened to those lost tribes? When one begins to think about it the question becomes exceedingly interesting. I don't say for a moment, of course, that *we* represent the lost tribes, but I do say that they must be somewhere on the earth at this present moment, working out their salvation and fulfilling the destiny prepared for them before the foundation of the world. I say that most emphatically. Now, where are they?"

"Not in Jerusalem," said Captain Chivvy. "Probably on the Stock Exchange."

"You mustn't confound the Jews with the Israelites," said Sir John.

"Nor," said the parson, "the British with either of 'em."

"I don't say that," said the baronet.

"Humph!" said the parson.

"Now let us pause to consider," went on the baronet, pushing his chair further from the table and crossing his legs—"let us pause to consider that the Almighty made certain promises to the Israelites, certain glorious and definite promises. They were, among other things, if I remember right, to inherit the earth. Now, which of the nations possesses the largest superficial area of the globe's surface? Which is the greatest colonising force among the nations? From a strictly *à posteriori* point of view the answer to the question, 'Which nation represents the seed of Abraham?' would undoubtedly be, 'The British.' But, of course, there are other considerations, and before offering any definite opinion on the subject one must make himself acquainted with the literature of the subject. At the present time I am deeply concerned in the absorbing topic of Christian Science. I am struggling to impress upon my genera-

tion that our Lord bade His disciples not only preach
the Gospel, but *heal the sick.* Not by medicines, not by
the use of the scalpel, but by means of mind-science—
faith. When I have made some progress in my book
I shall most certainly look into the question of the lost
tribes. The lost tribes, yes; dear me, it never struck
me before. A very interesting question, very."

"Don't forget you've got to captain the cricket club,"
said the parson.

"There is a time for all things, my dear Tom."

"And they want you as chairman for the first council."

"Most certainly."

"And we want you to organise a sports' day—running
jumping, donkey races, tug-o'-war, and all that."

"I shall be delighted."

"And you must do something about preserving. I
want to shoot with you again this autumn—good
shooting."

"We will look into it, with pleasure—certainly,
certainly."

But the fascinating idea that the lost tribes of Israel,
blessed so splendidly by the God of Abraham, the God
of Isaac, the God of Jacob, must of necessity be still
habitants of the earth, did bite so closely upon the
baronet's mind that he could think of no other subject
under heaven. Straightway did he send for books and
pamphlets on the subject, shut himself up for the next
two or three days to the great scandal of the neighbourhood—everybody in the place declaring that he was
about to jilt Mrs. FitzGerald—and finally he emerged
from his study a confirmed and inveterate British-
Israelite.

Your honour has only got to read one British-Israel
pamphlet to feel convinced that this realm, this England,
cannot by any possible manner of means be anything

else but the home of Abraham's seed. There is something so plausible in the theory, something so sweetly complimentary to the national character, that to refuse to believe it is to admit oneself ungracious and even traitorous.

I am convinced that if all the nations of the world get bitten by the idea, the next great war will be a struggle to maintain one's right to this proud title Now it is territory and goldfields; then it will be the banner of British-Israel. He will be a supreme statesman who patents the idea for England.

Sir John, of course, with that open mind of his, was the very easiest convert in the world. He at once became an enthusiastic and active British-Israelite, to the very great detriment of his work on Christian Science. He talked of nothing else; he read no other literature; and in twenty-four hours after the arrival of the pamphlets he had determined to annotate the Books of Genesis, Exodus, and Numbers for immediate publication.

But note the beneficent influence of the British-Israel theory in the case of our hero. Was not your honour trembling lest I should dismiss the baronet from your presence a miserable Anglophobe, a wretched and contemptible traitor? Nay, did not that appeal to your sense of realism as the inevitable end of a faddist's career? Behold how the accidental word of that good friend of his, Tom Shott, has converted our baronet into the most glowing patriot within the zones of the British Empire! Not only is he ready to back his own side in whatever trouble may befall, but he is prepared to avouch before the whole world that his nation is the blessed of God, the very elect of heaven, that it will one day possess the gates of its enemies, and ultimately reign supreme arbiter of the world.

What a glorious conclusion to the aberrations of our faddist!

Behold him, an eater of meat—
A drinker of wine—
A wearer of clothes, and
Shoe leather—
A smoker of tobacco—
A bridegroom—
A patriot, and—
A British-Israelite!

And this new creed gave a sudden zest to his life. England grew more and more to him; the little village world about him became a sacred shrine over whose tender greenness brooded eternally the gracious blessing of God. He loved the world; he loved the continuity, which linked for him English history with the great books of the Old Testament, making life one and whole. He talked as sympathetically of Moses as John Richard Green talked of Freeman and Stubbs. On one occasion, it is believed, he even said very solemnly, " Moses and I are certainly opposed to the majority of modern historians." Moses and I! He was quite happy.

This zest produced a marvellous effect upon his everyday life. He shook off his old boredom, became a dashing young lover, and so enchanted the widow by his high spirits and the sweetness of his temper that she very nearly fell in love with him. He certainly got back to his old position of universal favourite—the life and soul of the village.

And when the wedding bells rang, and every cottage hung out a flag, and set jam-pots filled with flowers on every window-sill in the village; when Tom Shott actually went twice over his red face with his old blunt razor, and when all the ladies were admiring themselves in the most wonderful new bonnets and dresses; when the children with nosegays formed up on either side of the church path, and when farmers and labourers and tradesmen from all quarters of the dale came driving or trudging in Sunday best to the foot of the old grey tower, rocking with the merriest carillons ever heard in that part of the world—why, then Sir John, with Chivvy in attendance, came forth to the world radiant with happiness, and marched into the church with as fine a dash and swagger as though he had been the youngest subaltern of dragoons.

Here we might well leave him—and for the life of me I cannot bring myself to tell of Mrs. FitzGerald at this particular moment—God bless her!—but for one little incident at the end of the service which is often talked of with much relish in the village.

You must know that Tom Shott had got almost to the end of the exhortation, and was beginning to puff and blow sorely, while all the ladies were sniffing scent-bottles and looking sentimental, when of a sudden from the open doors of the church there came upon the stilly church the strident crowing of a cock. ·

At the first crow Sir John started, at the second he wheeled round, and at the third, with beaming face, he started off down the aisle—almost with open arms—as fast as he could go.

"Come in, come in!" he said, reaching the door. "I'm being married; it's nearly over, and you're in plenty of time for the breakfast and the fête. Come in; you must—you really must. Let me take your hat."

And then the congregation saw Sir John returning up the aisle, leading old Josey, the hedge-preacher, to a place of honour at the altar, and heard him, moreover, apologising to Tom Shott for the interruption of the service, begging him to continue his really most interesting address.

After that, with a scowl at Josey, Tom Shott continued his reading, and the service went on to its beautiful conclusion.

Your honours are now at peace. Sir John departs out of your sight—but, I pray, not out of your memories —a civilised English gentleman, an eater of meat, a drinker of wine, a smoker of tobacco; and, above all things, a great patriot, one, indeed, who holds his own nation to be the very elect of Heaven. For he fell a victim to the accidental word of Tom Shott, clave passionately to this new idea, and to the great diversion of my Lady Sparrow spent the entire honeymoon in reading up the literature of " British Israel."

And so, farewell. While there are fads in this restless world, so long will there be Sparrows, and while there are Sparrows there will be fads, and you and I shall not lack for amusement. But for the sake of the Sparrows—for we cannot wish them harm—God grant there never be a failure in the supply of Shotts, or a dearth of Tipladys.

" Tom! Tiplady! I drink to you. Good fellows both; God bless us all! "

And so, farewell.

W. BRENDON AND SON, LIMITED, PLYMOUTH

A SELECTION OF BOOKS
PUBLISHED BY METHUEN
AND COMPANY LIMITED
36 ESSEX STREET
LONDON W.C.

CONTENTS

FEBRUARY 1911

A SELECTION OF

MESSRS. METHUEN'S

PUBLICATIONS

Addleshaw (Percy). SIR PHILIP SIDNEY. Illustrated. *Second Edition.* *Demy 8vo.* 10s. 6d. net.

Adeney (W. F.), M.A. See Bennett (W. H.).

Ady (Cecilia M.). A HISTORY OF MILAN UNDER THE SFORZA. Illustrated. *Demy 8vo.* 10s. 6d. net.

Aldis (Janet). THE QUEEN OF LETTER WRITERS, MARQUISE DE SÉVIGNÉ, DAME DE BOURBILLY, 1626-96. Illustrated. *Second Edition. Demy 8vo.* 12s. 6d. net.

Allen (M.). A HISTORY OF VERONA. Illustrated. *Demy 8vo.* 12s. 6d. net.

Amherst (Lady). A SKETCH OF EGYPTIAN HISTORY FROM THE EARLIEST TIMES TO THE PRESENT DAY. Illustrated. *A New and Cheaper Issue. Demy 8vo.* 7s. 6d. net.

Andrewes (Amy G.). THE STORY OF BAYARD. Edited by A. G. ANDREWES. *Cr. 8vo.* 2s. 6d.

Andrewes (Bishop). PRECES PRIVATAE. Translated and edited, with Notes, by F. E. BRIGHTMAN, M.A., of Pusey House, Oxford. *Cr. 8vo.* 6s.

Anon. THE WESTMINSTER PROBLEMS BOOK. Prose and Verse. Compiled from *The Saturday Westminster Gazette* Competitions, 1904-1907. *Cr. 8vo.* 3s. 6d. net.

VENICE AND HER TREASURES. Illustrated. *Round corners. Fcap. 8vo.* 5s. net.

Aristotle. THE ETHICS OF. Edited, with an Introduction and Notes, by JOHN BURNET, M.A. *Cheaper issue. Demy 8vo.* 10s. 6d. net.

Atkinson (C. T.), M.A., Fellow of Exeter College, Oxford, sometime Demy of Magdalen College. A HISTORY OF GERMANY, from 1715-1815. Illustrated. *Demy 8vo.* 12s. 6d. net.

Atkinson (T. D.). ENGLISH ARCHITECTURE. Illustrated. *Fcap. 8vo.* 3s. 6d. net.

A GLOSSARY OF TERMS USED IN ENGLISH ARCHITECTURE. Illustrated. *Second Edition. Fcap. 8vo.* 3s. 6d. net.

Atteridge (A. H.). NAPOLEON'S BROTHERS. Illustrated. *Demy 8vo.* 18s. net.

Aves (Ernest). CO-OPERATIVE INDUSTRY. *Cr. 8vo.* 5s. net.

Bagot (Richard). THE LAKES OF NORTHERN ITALY. Illustrated. *Fcap. 8vo.* 5s. net.

Bain (R. Nisbet). THE LAST KING OF POLAND AND HIS CONTEMPORARIES. Illustrated. *Demy 8vo.* 10s. 6d. net.

Balfour (Graham). THE LIFE OF ROBERT LOUIS STEVENSON. Illustrated. *Fifth Edition in one Volume. Cr. 8vo. Buckram,* 6s.

Baring (The Hon. Maurice). A YEAR IN RUSSIA. *Second Edition. Demy 8vo.* 10s. 6d. net.
RUSSIAN ESSAYS AND STORIES. *Second Edition. Cr. 8vo.* 5s. net.
LANDMARKS IN RUSSIAN LITERATURE. *Cr. 8vo.* 6s. net.

Baring-Gould (S.). THE LIFE OF NAPOLEON BONAPARTE. Illustrated. *Second Edition. Wide Royal 8vo.* 10s. 6d. net.
THE TRAGEDY OF THE CÆSARS: A STUDY OF THE CHARACTERS OF THE CÆSARS OF THE JULIAN AND CLAUDIAN HOUSES. Illustrated. *Seventh Edition. Royal 8vo.* 10s. 6d. net.
A BOOK OF FAIRY TALES. Illustrated. *Second Edition. Cr. 8vo. Buckram.* 6s. Also *Medium 8vo.* 6d.
OLD ENGLISH FAIRY TALES. Illustrated. *Third Edition. Cr. 8vo. Buckram.* 6s.
THE VICAR OF MORWENSTOW. Revised Edition. With a Portrait. *Third Edition. Cr. 8vo.* 3s. 6d.
OLD COUNTRY LIFE. Illustrated. *Fifth Edition. Large Cr. 8vo.* 6s.
A GARLAND OF COUNTRY SONG: English Folk Songs with their Traditional Melodies. Collected and arranged by S. BARING-GOULD and H. F. SHEPPARD. *Demy 4to.* 6s.
SONGS OF THE WEST: Folk Songs of Devon and Cornwall. Collected from the Mouths of the People. By S. BARING-GOULD, M.A., and H. FLEETWOOD SHEPPARD, M.A. New and Revised Edition, under the musical editorship of CECIL J. SHARP. *Large Imperial 8vo.* 5s. net.
STRANGE SURVIVALS : SOME CHAPTERS IN THE HISTORY OF MAN. Illustrated. *Third Edition. Cr. 8vo.* 2s. 6d. net.
YORKSHIRE ODDITIES : INCIDENTS AND STRANGE EVENTS. *Fifth Edition. Cr. 8vo.* 2s. 6d. net.
A BOOK OF CORNWALL. Illustrated. *Second Edition. Cr. 8vo.* 6s.
A BOOK OF DARTMOOR. Illustrated. *Second Edition. Cr. 8vo.* 6s.
A BOOK OF DEVON. Illustrated. *Third Edition. Cr. 8vo.* 6s.
A BOOK OF NORTH WALES. Illustrated. *Cr. 8vo.* 6s.
A BOOK OF SOUTH WALES. Illustrated. *Cr. 8vo.* 6s.
A BOOK OF BRITTANY. Illustrated. *Second Edition. Cr. 8vo.* 6s.

A BOOK OF THE RHINE : From Cleve to Mainz. Illustrated. *Second Edition. Cr. 8vo.* 6s.
A BOOK OF THE RIVIERA. Illustrated. *Second Edition. Cr. 8vo.* 6s.
A BOOK OF THE PYRENEES. Illustrated. *Cr. 8vo.* 6s.

Barker (E.), M.A., (Late) Fellow of Merton College, Oxford. THE POLITICAL THOUGHT OF PLATO AND ARISTOTLE. *Demy 8vo.* 10s. 6d. net.

Baron (R. R. N.), M.A. FRENCH PROSE COMPOSITION. *Fourth Edition. Cr. 8vo.* 2s. 6d. *Key,* 3s. net.

Bartholomew (J. G.), F.R.S.E. See Robertson (C. G.).

Bastable (C. F.), LL.D. THE COMMERCE OF NATIONS. *Fourth Edition. Cr. 8vo.* 2s. 6d.

Bastian (H. Charlton), M.A., M.D., F.R.S. THE EVOLUTION OF LIFE. Illustrated. *Demy 8vo.* 7s. 6d. net.

Batson (Mrs. Stephen). A CONCISE HANDBOOK OF GARDEN FLOWERS. *Fcap. 8vo.* 3s. 6d. net.
THE SUMMER GARDEN OF PLEASURE. Illustrated. *Wide Demy 8vo.* 15s. net.

Beckett (Arthur). THE SPIRIT OF THE DOWNS: Impressions and Reminiscences of the Sussex Downs. Illustrated. *Second Edition. Demy 8vo.* 10s. 6d. net.

Beckford (Peter). THOUGHTS ON HUNTING. Edited by J. OTHO PAGET. Illustrated. *Second Edition. Demy 8vo.* 6s.

Begbie (Harold). MASTER WORKERS. Illustrated. *Demy 8vo.* 7s. 6d. net.

Behmen (Jacob). DIALOGUES ON THE SUPERSENSUAL LIFE. Edited by BERNARD HOLLAND. *Fcap. 8vo.* 3s. 6d.

Bell (Mrs. Arthur G.). THE SKIRTS OF THE GREAT CITY. Illustrated. *Second Edition. Cr. 8vo.* 6s.

Belloc (H.), M.P. PARIS. Illustrated. *Second Edition, Revised. Cr. 8vo.* 6s.
HILLS AND THE SEA. *Third Edition. Fcap. 8vo.* 5s.
ON NOTHING AND KINDRED SUBJECTS. *Third Edition. Fcap. 8vo.* 5s.
ON EVERYTHING. *Second Edition. Fcap. 8vo.* 5s.
MARIE ANTOINETTE. Illustrated. *Third Edition. Demy 8vo.* 15s. net.
THE PYRENEES. Illustrated. *Second Edition. Demy 8vo.* 7s. 6d. net.

Bellot (H. H. L.), M.A. See Jones (L. A. A).

Bennett (Joseph). FORTY YEARS OF MUSIC, 1865-1905. Illustrated. *Demy 8vo.* 16s. net.

Bennett (W. H.), M.A. A PRIMER OF THE BIBLE. *Fifth Edition.* *Cr. 8vo.* 2s. 6d.

Bennett (W. H.) and Adeney, (W. F.). A BIBLICAL INTRODUCTION. With a concise Bibliography. *Fifth Edition.* *Cr. 8vo.* 7s. 6d.

Benson (Archbishop). GOD'S BOARD. Communion Addresses. *Second Edition.* *Fcap. 8vo.* 3s. 6d. net.

Benson (R. M.). THE WAY OF HOLINESS. An Exposition of Psalm cxix. Analytical and Devotional. *Cr. 8vo.* 5s.

*Bensusan (Samuel L.). HOME LIFE IN SPAIN. Illustrated. *Demy 8vo.* 10s. 6d. net.

Berry (W. Grinton), M.A. FRANCE SINCE WATERLOO. Illustrated. *Cr. 8vo.* 6s.

Betham-Edwards (Miss). HOME LIFE IN FRANCE. Illustrated. *Fifth Edition.* *Cr. 8vo.* 6s.

Bindley (T. Herbert), B.D. THE OECUMENICAL DOCUMENTS OF THE FAITH. With Introductions and Notes. *Second Edition.* *Cr. 8vo.* 6s. net.

Binyon (Laurence). See Blake (William).

Blake (William). ILLUSTRATIONS OF THE BOOK OF JOB. With General Introduction by LAURENCE BINYON. Illustrated. *Quarto.* 21s. net.

Body (George), D.D. THE SOUL'S PILGRIMAGE: Devotional Readings from the Published and Unpublished writings of George Body, D.D. Selected and arranged by J. H. BURN, D.D., F.R.S.E. *Demy 16mo.* 2s. 6d.

Boulting (W.). TASSO AND HIS TIMES. Illustrated. *Demy 8vo.* 10s. 6d. net.

Bovill (W. B. Forster). HUNGARY AND THE HUNGARIANS. Illustrated. *Demy 8vo.* 7s. 6d. net.

Bowden (E. M.). THE IMITATION OF BUDDHA: Being Quotations from Buddhist Literature for each Day in the Year. *Fifth Edition.* *Cr. 16mo.* 2s. 6d.

Brabant (F. G.), M.A. RAMBLES IN SUSSEX. Illustrated. *Cr. 8vo.* 6s.

Bradley (A. G.). ROUND ABOUT WILTSHIRE. Illustrated. *Second Edition.* *Cr. 8vo.* 6s.
THE ROMANCE OF NORTHUMBERLAND. Illustrated. *Second Edition. Demy 8vo.* 7s. 6d. net.

Braid (James), Open Champion, 1901, 1905 and 1906. ADVANGED GOLF. Illustrated. *Fifth Edition.* *Demy 8vo.* 10s. 6d. net.

Braid (James) and Others. GREAT GOLFERS IN THE MAKING. Edited by HENRY LEACH. Illustrated. *Second Edition.* *Demy 8vo.* 7s. 6d. net.

Brailsford (H. N.). MACEDONIA: Its RACES AND THEIR FUTURE. Illustrated. *Demy 8vo.* 12s. 6d. net.

Brodrick (Mary) and Morton (A. Anderson). A CONCISE DICTIONARY OF EGYPTIAN ARCHÆOLOGY. A Handbook for Students and Travellers. Illustrated. *Cr. 8vo.* 3s. 6d.

Brown (J. Wood), M.A. THE BUILDERS OF FLORENCE. Illustrated. *Demy 4to.* 18s. net.

Browning (Robert). PARACELSUS. Edited with Introduction, Notes, and Bibliography by MARGARET L. LEE and KATHARINE B. LOCOCK. *Fcap. 8vo.* 3s. 6d. net.

Buckton (A. M.). EAGER HEART: A Mystery Play. *Ninth Edition.* *Cr. 8vo.* 1s. net.

Budge (E. A. Wallis). THE GODS OF THE EGYPTIANS. Illustrated. *Two Volumes. Royal 8vo.* £3 3s. net.

Bull (Paul), Army Chaplain. GOD AND OUR SOLDIERS. *Second Edition.* *Cr. 8vo.* 6s.

Bulley (Miss). See Dilke (Lady).

Burns (Robert), THE POEMS. Edited by ANDREW LANG and W. A. CRAIGIE. With Portrait. *Third Edition. Wide Demy 8vo, gilt top.* 6s.

Bussell (F. W.), D.D. CHRISTIAN THEOLOGY AND SOCIAL PROGRESS (The Bampton Lectures of 1905). *Demy 8vo.* 10s. 6d. net.

Butler (Sir William), Lieut.-General, G.C.B. THE LIGHT OF THE WEST. With some other Wayside Thoughts, 1865-1908. *Cr. 8vo.* 5s. net.

Butlin (F. M.). AMONG THE DANES. Illustrated. *Demy 8vo.* 7s. 6d. net.

Cain (Georges), Curator of the Carnavalet Museum, Paris. WALKS IN PARIS. Translated by A. R. ALLINSON, M.A. Illustrated. *Demy 8vo.* 7s. 6d. net.

Cameron (Mary Lovett). OLD ETRURIA AND MODERN TUSCANY. Illustrated. *Second Edition.* *Cr. 8vo.* 6s. net.

Carden (Robert W.). THE CITY OF GENOA. Illustrated. *Demy 8vo.* 10s. 6d. net.

Carlyle (Thomas). THE FRENCH REVOLUTION. Edited by C. R. L. FLETCHER, Fellow of Magdalen College, Oxford. *Three Volumes. Cr. 8vo.* 18s.
THE LETTERS AND SPEECHES OF OLIVER CROMWELL. With an Introduction by C. H. FIRTH, M.A., and Notes and Appendices by Mrs. S. C. LOMAS. *Three Volumes. Demy 8vo.* 18s. *net.*

Celano (Brother Thomas of). THE LIVES OF FRANCIS OF ASSISI. Translated by A. G. FERRERS HOWELL. Illustrated. *Cr. 8vo.* 5s. *net.*

Chambers (Mrs. Lambert). Lawn Tennis for Ladies. Illustrated. *Crown 8vo.* 2s. 6d. *net.*

Chandler (Arthur), Bishop of Bloemfontein. ARA CŒLI: AN ESSAY IN MYSTICAL THEOLOGY. *Fourth Edition. Cr. 8vo.* 3s. 6d. *net.*

Chesterfield (Lord). THE LETTERS OF THE EARL OF CHESTERFIELD TO HIS SON. Edited, with an Introduction by C. STRACHEY, with Notes by A. CALTHROP. *Two Volumes. Cr. 8vo.* 12s.

Chesterton (G.K.). CHARLES DICKENS. With two Portraits in Photogravure. *Sixth Edition. Cr. 8vo.* 6s.
ALL THINGS CONSIDERED. *Sixth Edition. Fcap. 8vo.* 5s.
TREMENDOUS TRIFLES. *Fourth Edition. Fcap. 8vo.* 5s.

Clausen (George), A.R.A., R.W.S. SIX LECTURES ON PAINTING. Illustrated. *Third Edition. Large Post. 8vo.* 3s. 6d. *net.*
AIMS AND IDEALS IN ART. Eight Lectures delivered to the Students of the Royal Academy of Arts. Illustrated. *Second Edition. Large Post 8vo.* 5s. *net.*

Clutton-Brock (A.) SHELLEY: THE MAN AND THE POET. Illustrated. *Demy 8vo.* 7s. 6d. *net.*

Cobb (W. F.), M.A. THE BOOK OF PSALMS: with an Introduction and Notes. *Demy 8vo.* 10s. 6d. *net.*

Cockshott (Winifred), St. Hilda's Hall, Oxford. THE PILGRIM FATHERS, THEIR CHURCH AND COLONY. Illustrated. *Demy 8vo.* 7s. 6d. *net.*

Collingwood (W. G.), M.A. THE LIFE OF JOHN RUSKIN. With Portrait. *Sixth Edition. Cr. 8vo.* 2s. 6d. *net.*

Colvill (Helen H.). ST. TERESA OF SPAIN. Illustrated. *Second Edition. Demy 8vo.* 7s. 6d. *net.*

*Condamine (Robert de la). THE UPPER GARDEN. *Fcap. 8vo.* 5s. *net.*

Conrad (Joseph). THE MIRROR OF THE SEA: Memories and Impressions. *Third Edition. Cr. 8vo.* 6s.

Coolidge (W. A. B.), M.A. THE ALPS. Illustrated. *Demy 8vo.* 7s. 6d. *net.*

Cooper (C. S.), F.R.H.S. See Westell (W.P.)

Coulton (G. G.). CHAUCER AND HIS ENGLAND. Illustrated. *Second Edition. Demy 8vo.* 10s. 6d. *net.*

Cowper (William). THE POEMS. Edited with an Introduction and Notes by J. C. BAILEY, M.A. Illustrated. *Demy 8vo.* 10s. 6d. *net.*

Crane (Walter), R.W.S. AN ARTIST'S REMINISCENCES. Illustrated. *Second Edition. Demy 8vo.* 18s. *net.*
INDIA IMPRESSIONS. Illustrated. *Second Edition. Demy 8vo.* 7s. 6d. *net.*

Crispe (T. E.). REMINISCENCES OF A K.C. With 2 Portraits. *Second Edition. Demy 8vo.* 10s. 6d. *net.*

Crowley (Ralph H.). THE HYGIENE OF SCHOOL LIFE. Illustrated. *Cr. 8vo.* 3s. 6d. *net.*

Dante (Alighieri). LA COMMEDIA DI DANTE. The Italian Text edited by PAGET TOYNBEE, M.A., D.Litt. *Cr. 8vo.* 6s.

Davey (Richard). THE PAGEANT OF LONDON. Illustrated. *In Two Volumes. Demy 8vo.* 15s. *net.*

Davis (H. W. C.), M.A., Fellow and Tutor of Balliol College. ENGLAND UNDER THE NORMANS AND ANGEVINS: 1066-1272. Illustrated. *Demy 8vo.* 10s. 6d. *net.*

Deans (R. Storry). THE TRIALS OF FIVE QUEENS: KATHARINE OF ARAGON, ANNE BOLEYN, MARY QUEEN OF SCOTS, MARIE ANTOINETTE and CAROLINE OF BRUNSWICK. Illustrated. *Second Edition. Demy 8vo.* 10s. 6d. *net.*

Dearmer (Mabel). A CHILD'S LIFE OF CHRIST. Illustrated. *Large Cr. 8vo.* 6s.

D'Este (Margaret). IN THE CANARIES WITH A CAMERA. Illustrated. *Cr. 8vo.* 7s. 6d. *net.*

Dickinson (G. L.), M.A., Fellow of King's College, Cambridge. THE GREEK VIEW OF LIFE. *Seventh and Revised Edition. Crown 8vo.* 2s. 6d. *net.*

Ditchfield (P. H.), M.A., F.S.A. THE PARISH CLERK. Illustrated. *Third Edition. Demy 8vo.* 7s. 6d. *net.*
THE OLD-TIME PARSON. Illustrated. *Second Edition. Demy 8vo.* 7s. 6d. *net.*

Douglas (Hugh A.). VENICE ON FOOT. With the Itinerary of the Grand Canal. Illustrated. *Second Edition. Fcap. 8vo.* 5s. *net.*

Douglas (James). THE MAN IN THE PULPIT. *Cr. 8vo. 2s. 6d. net.*

Dowden (J.), D.D., Late Lord Bishop of Edinburgh. FURTHER STUDIES IN THE PRAYER BOOK. *Cr. 8vo. 6s.*

Driver (S. R.), D.D., D.C.L., Regius Professor of Hebrew in the University of Oxford. SERMONS ON SUBJECTS CONNECTED WITH THE OLD TESTAMENT. *Cr. 8vo. 6s.*

Duff (Nora). MATILDA OF TUSCANY. Illustrated. *Demy 8vo. 10s. 6d. net.*

Dumas (Alexandre). THE CRIMES OF THE BORGIAS AND OTHERS. With an Introduction by R. S. GARNETT. Illustrated. *Cr. 8vo. 6s.*
THE CRIMES OF URBAIN GRANDIER AND OTHERS. Illustrated. *Cr. 8vo. 6s.*
THE CRIMES OE THE MARQUISE DE BRINVILLIERS AND OTHERS. Illustrated. *Cr. 8vo. 6s.*
THE CRIMES OF ALI PACHA AND OTHERS. Illustrated. *Cr. 8vo. 6s.*
MY MEMOIRS. Translated by E. M. WALLER. With an Introduction by ANDREW LANG. With Frontispieces in Photogravure. In six Volumes. *Cr. 8vo. 6s. each volume.*
VOL. I. 1802–1821. VOL. IV. 1830–1831.
VOL. II. 1822–1825. VOL. V. 1831–1832.
VOL. III. 1826–1830. VOL. VI. 1832–1833.
MY PETS. Newly translated by A. R. ALLINSON, M.A. Illustrated. *Cr. 8vo. 6s.*

Duncan (David), D.Sc., LL.D. THE LIFE AND LETTERS OF HERBERT SPENCER. Illustrated. *Demy 8vo. 15s.*

Dunn-Pattison (R. P.). NAPOLEON'S MARSHALS. Illustrated. *Demy 8vo. Second Edition. 12s. 6d. net.*
THE BLACK PRINCE. Illustrated. *Second Edition. Demy 8vo. 7s. 6d. net.*

Durham (The Earl of). A REPORT ON CANADA. With an Introductory Note. *Demy 8vo. 4s. 6d. net.*

Dutt (W. A.). THE NORFOLK BROADS. Illustrated. *Second Edition. Cr. 8vo. 6s.*
WILD LIFE IN EAST ANGLIA. Illustrated. *Second Edition. Demy 8vo. 7s. 6d. net.*
SOME LITERARY ASSOCIATIONS OF EAST ANGLIA. Illustrated. *Demy 8vo. 10s. 6d. net.*

Edmonds (Major J. E.), R.E.; D. A. Q.-M, G. See Wood (W. Birkbeck).

Edwardes (Tickner). THE LORE OF THE HONEY BEE. Illustrated. *Cr. 8vo. 6s.*
LIFT-LUCK ON SOUTHERN ROADS. Illustrated. *Cr. 8vo. 6s.*

Egerton (H. E.), M.A. A HISTORY OF BRITISH COLONIAL POLICY. *Third Edition. Demy 8vo. 7s. 6d. net.*

Everett-Green (Mary Anne). ELIZABETH; ELECTRESS PALATINE AND QUEEN OF BOHEMIA. Revised by her Niece S. C. LOMAS. With a Prefatory Note by A. W. WARD, Litt.D. *Demy 8vo. 10s. 6d. net.*

Fairbrother (W. H.), M.A. THE PHILOSOPHY OF T. H. GREEN. *Second Edition. Cr. 8vo. 3s. 6d.*

Fea (Allan). THE FLIGHT OF THE KING. Illustrated. *New and Revised Edition. Demy 8vo. 7s. 6d. net.*
SECRET CHAMBERS AND HIDING-PLACES. Illustrated. *New and Revised Edition. Demy 8vo. 7s. 6d. net.*
JAMES II. AND HIS WIVES. Illustrated. *Demy 8vo. 10s. 6d. net.*

Fell (E. F. B.). THE FOUNDATIONS OF LIBERTY. *Cr. 8vo. 5s. net.*

Firth (C. H.), M.A., Regius Professor of Modern History at Oxford. CROMWELL'S ARMY: A History of the English Soldier during the Civil Wars, the Commonwealth, and the Protectorate. *Cr. 8vo. 6s.*

FitzGerald (Edward). THE RUBÁIYÁT OF OMAR KHAYYÁM. Printed from the Fifth and last Edition. With a Commentary by Mrs. STEPHEN BATSON, and a Biography of Omar by E. D. ROSS. *Cr. 8vo. 6s.*

*****Fletcher (B. F. and H. P.).** THE ENGLISH HOME. Illustrated. *Second Edition. Demy 8vo. 12s. 6d. net.*

Fletcher (J. S.). A BOOK OF YORKSHIRE. Illustrated. *Demy 8vo. 7s. 6d. net.*

Flux (A. W.), M.A., William Dow Professor of Political Economy in M'Gill University, Montreal. ECONOMIC PRINCIPLES. *Demy 8vo. 7s. 6d. net.*

Foot (Constance M.). INSECT WONDERLAND. Illustrated. *Second Edition. Cr. 8vo. 3s. 6d. net.*

Forel (A.). THE SENSES OF INSECTS. Translated by MACLEOD YEARSLEY. Illustrated. *Demy 8vo. 10s. 6d. net.*

Fouqué (La Motte). SINTRAM AND HIS COMPANIONS. Translated by A. C. FARQUHARSON. Illustrated. *Demy 8vo. 7s. 6d. net. Half White Vellum, 10s. 6d. net.*

Fraser (J. F.). ROUND THE WORLD ON A WHEEL. Illustrated. *Fifth Edition. Cr. 8vo. 6s.*

Galton (Sir Francis), F.R.S.; D.C.L., Oxf.; Hon. Sc.D., Camb.; Hon. Fellow Trinity College, Cambridge. MEMORIES OF MY LIFE. Illustrated. *Third Edition.* *Demy 8vo.* 10s. 6d. net.

Garnett (Lucy M. J.). THE TURKISH PEOPLE; THEIR SOCIAL LIFE, RELIGIOUS BELIEFS AND INSTITUTIONS, AND DOMESTIC LIFE. Illustrated. *Demy 8vo.* 10s. 6d. net.

Gibbins (H. de B.), Litt.D., M.A. INDUSTRY IN ENGLAND: HISTORICAL OUTLINES. With 5 Maps. *Fifth Edition. Demy 8vo.* 10s. 6d.
THE INDUSTRIAL HISTORY OF ENGLAND. Illustrated. *Sixteenth Edition. Cr. 8vo.* 3s.
ENGLISH SOCIAL REFORMERS. *Second Edition. Cr. 8vo.* 2s. 6d.
See also Hadfield, R.A.

Gibbon (Edward). MEMOIRS OF THE LIFE OF EDWARD GIBBON. Edited by G. BIRKBECK HILL, LL.D. *Cr. 8vo.* 6s.
THE DECLINE AND FALL OF THE ROMAN EMPIRE. Edited, with Notes, Appendices, and Maps, by J. B. BURY, M.A., Litt.D., Regius Professor of Modern History at Cambridge. Illustrated. *In Seven Volumes. Demy 8vo. Gilt Top.* Each 10s. 6d. net.

Gibbs (Phillip.) THE ROMANCE OF GEORGE VILLIERS: FIRST DUKE OF BUCKINGHAM, AND SOME MEN AND WOMEN OF THE STUART COURT. Illustrated. *Second Edition. Demy 8vo.* 15s. net.

Gloag (M. R.) and Wyatt (Kate M.). A BOOK OF ENGLISH GARDENS. Illustrated. *Demy 8vo.* 10s. 6d. net.

Glover (T. R.), M.A., Fellow and Classical Lecturer of St. John's College, Cambridge. THE CONFLICT OF RELIGIONS IN THE EARLY ROMAN EMPIRE. *Fourth Edition. Demy 8vo.* 7s. 6d. net.

Godfrey (Elizabeth). A BOOK OF REMEMBRANCE. Being Lyrical Selections for every day in the Year. Arranged by E. Godfrey. *Second Edition. Fcap. 8vo.* 2s. 6d. net.
ENGLISH CHILDREN IN THE OLDEN TIME. Illustrated. *Second Edition. Demy 8vo.* 7s. 6d. net.

Godley (A. D.), M.A., Fellow of Magdalen College, Oxford. OXFORD IN THE EIGHTEENTH CENTURY. Illustrated. *Second Edition. Demy 8vo.* 7s. 6d. net.
LYRA FRIVOLA. *Fourth Edition. Fcap. 8vo.* 2s. 6d.
VERSES TO ORDER. *Second Edition. Fcap. 8vo.* 2s. 6d.
SECOND STRINGS. *Fcap. 8vo.* 2s. 6d.

Goll (August). CRIMINAL TYPES IN SHAKESPEARE. Authorised Translation from the Danish by Mrs. CHARLES WEEKES. *Cr. 8vo.* 5s. net.

Gordon (Lina Duff) (Mrs. Aubrey Waterfield). HOME LIFE IN ITALY: LETTERS FROM THE APENNINES. Illustrated. *Second Edition. Demy 8vo.* 10s. 6d. net.

Gostling (Frances M.). THE BRETONS AT HOME. Illustrated. *Second Edition. Demy 8vo.* 10s. 6d. net.

Graham (Harry). A GROUP OF SCOTTISH WOMEN. Illustrated. *Second Edition. Demy 8vo.* 10s. 6d. net.

Grahame (Kenneth). THE WIND IN THE WILLOWS. Illustrated. *Fifth Edition. Cr. 8vo.* 6s.

Gwynn (Stephen), M.P. A HOLIDAY IN CONNEMARA. Illustrated. *Demy 8vo.* 10s 6d. net.

Hall (Cyril). THE YOUNG CARPENTER. Illustrated. *Cr. 8vo.* 5s.

Hall (Hammond). THE YOUNG ENGINEER: or MODERN ENGINES AND THEIR MODELS. Illustrated. *Second Edition. Cr. 8vo.* 5s.

Hall (Mary). A WOMAN'S TREK FROM THE CAPE TO CAIRO. Illustrated. *Second Edition. Demy 8vo.* 16s. net.

Hamel (Frank). FAMOUS FRENCH SALONS. Illustrated. *Third Edition. Demy 8vo.* 12s. 6d. net.

Hannay (D.). A SHORT HISTORY OF THE ROYAL NAVY. Vol. I., 1217–1688. Vol. II., 1689–1815. *Demy 8vo.* Each 7s. 6d. net.

Hannay (James O.), M.A. THE SPIRIT AND ORIGIN OF CHRISTIAN MONASTICISM. *Cr. 8vo.* 6s.
THE WISDOM OF THE DESERT. *Fcap. 8vo.* 3s. 6d. net.

Harper (Charles G.). THE AUTOCAR ROAD-BOOK. Four Volumes with Maps. *Cr. 8vo.* Each 7s. 6d. net.
Vol. I.—SOUTH OF THE THAMES.
Vol. II.—NORTH AND SOUTH WALES AND WEST MIDLANDS.

Headley (F. W.). DARWINISM AND MODERN SOCIALISM. *Second Edition. Cr. 8vo.* 5s. net.

Henderson (B. W.), Fellow of Exeter College, Oxford. THE LIFE AND PRINCIPATE OF THE EMPEROR NERO. Illustrated. *New and cheaper issue. Demy 8vo.* 7s. 6d. net.

Henderson (M. Sturge). GEORGE MEREDITH: NOVELIST, POET, REFORMER. Illustrated. *Second Edition. Cr. 8vo.* 6s.

Henderson (T. F.) and Watt (Francis). SCOTLAND OF TO-DAY. Illustrated. *Second Edition. Cr. 8vo. 6s.*

Henley (W. E.). ENGLISH LYRICS. CHAUCER TO POE, 1340-1849. *Second Edition. Cr. 8vo. 2s. 6d. net.*

Heywood (W.). A HISTORY OF PERUGIA. Illustrated. *Demy 8vo. 12s. 6d. net.*

Hill (George Francis). ONE HUNDRED MASTERPIECES OF SCULPTURE. Illustrated. *Demy 8vo. 10s. 6d. net.*

Hind (C. Lewis). DAYS IN CORNWALL. Illustrated. *Second Edition. Cr. 8vo. 6s.*

Hobhouse (L. T.), late Fellow of C.C.C., Oxford. THE THEORY OF KNOWLEDGE. *Demy 8vo. 10s. 6d. net.*

Hodgetts (E. A. Brayley). THE COURT OF RUSSIA IN THE NINETEENTH CENTURY. Illustrated. *Two volumes. Demy 8vo. 24s. net.*

Hodgson (Mrs. W.). HOW TO IDENTIFY OLD CHINESE PORCELAIN. Illustrated. *Second Edition. Post 8vo. 6s.*

Holdich (Sir T. H.), K.C.I.E., C.B., F.S.A. THE INDIAN BORDERLAND, 1880-1900. Illustrated. *Second Edition. Demy 8vo. 10s. 6d. net.*

Holdsworth (W. S.), D.C.L. A HISTORY OF ENGLISH LAW. *In Four Volumes. Vols. I., II., III. Demy 8vo. Each 10s. 6d. net.*

Holland (Clive). TYROL AND ITS PEOPLE. Illustrated. *Demy 8vo. 10s. 6d. net.*

Hollway-Calthrop (H. C.), late of Balliol College, Oxford; Bursar of Eton College. PETRARCH: HIS LIFE, WORK, AND TIMES. Illustrated. *Demy 8vo. 12s. 6d. net.*

Horsburgh (E. L. S.), M.A. LORENZO THE MAGNIFICENT: AND FLORENCE IN HER GOLDEN AGE. Illustrated. *Second Edition. Demy 8vo. 15s. net.* WATERLOO: with Plans. *Second Edition. Cr. 8vo. 5s.*

Hosie (Alexander). MANCHURIA. Illustrated. *Second Edition. Demy 8vo. 7s. 6d. net.*

Hulton (Samuel F.). THE CLERK OF OXFORD IN FICTION. Illustrated. *Demy 8vo. 10s. 6d. net.*

Humphreys (John H.). PROPORTIONAL REPRESENTATION. Cr. 8vo. 3s. 6d. net.

Hutchinson (Horace G.). THE NEW FOREST. Illustrated. *Fourth Edition. Cr. 8vo. 6s.*

Hutton (Edward). THE CITIES OF UMBRIA. Illustrated. *Fourth Edition. Cr. 8vo. 6s.* THE CITIES OF SPAIN. Illustrated. *Third Edition. Cr. 8vo. 6s.* FLORENCE AND THE CITIES OF NORTHERN TUSCANY, WITH GENOA. Illustrated. *Second Edition. Crown 8vo. 6s.* ENGLISH LOVE POEMS. Edited with an Introduction. *Fcap. 8vo. 3s. 6d. net.* COUNTRY WALKS ABOUT FLORENCE. Illustrated. *Fcap. 8vo. 5s. net.* IN UNKNOWN TUSCANY With an Appendix by WILLIAM HEYWOOD. Illustrated. *Second Edition. Demy 8vo. 7s. 6d. net.* ROME. Illustrated. *Second Edition. Cr. 8vo. 6s.*

Hyett (F. A.) FLORENCE: HER HISTORY AND ART TO THE FALL OF THE REPUBLIC. *Demy 8vo. 7s. 6d. net.*

Ibsen (Henrik). BRAND. A Drama. Translated by WILLIAM WILSON. *Fourth Edition. Cr. 8vo. 3s. 6d.*

Inge (W. R.), M.A., Fellow and Tutor of Hertford College, Oxford. CHRISTIAN MYSTICISM. (The Bampton Lectures of 1899.) *Demy 8vo. 12s. 6d. net.*

Innes (A. D.), M.A. A HISTORY OF THE BRITISH IN INDIA. With Maps and Plans. *Cr. 8vo. 6s.* ENGLAND UNDER THE TUDORS. With Maps. *Third Edition. Demy 8vo. 10s. 6d. net.*

Innes (Mary). SCHOOLS OF PAINTING. Illustrated. *Cr. 8vo. 5s. net.*

James (Norman G. B.). THE CHARM OF SWITZERLAND. *Cr. 8vo. 5s. net.*

Jebb (Camilla). A STAR OF THE SALONS: JULIE DE LESPINASSE. Illustrated. *Demy 8vo. 10s. 6d. net.*

Jeffery (Reginald W.), M.A. THE HISTORY OF THE THIRTEEN COLONIES OF NORTH AMERICA, 1497-1763. Illustrated. *Demy 8vo. 7s. 6d. net.*

Jenks (E.), M.A., B.C.L. AN OUTLINE OF ENGLISH LOCAL GOVERNMENT. *Second Edition. Revised by R. C. K. ENSOR, M.A. Cr. 8vo. 2s. 6d.*

Jennings (Oscar), M.D. EARLY WOODCUT INITIALS. Illustrated. *Demy 4to. 21s. net.*

Jerningham (Charles Edward). THE MAXIMS OF MARMADUKE. *Second Edition. Cr. 8vo. 5s.*

Johnston (Sir H. H.), K.C.B. BRITISH CENTRAL AFRICA. Illustrated. *Third Edition. Cr. 4to. 18s. net.*

*THE NEGRO IN THE NEW WORLD. Illustrated. *Demy 8vo.* 16s. net.

Jones (R. Crompton), M.A. POEMS OF THE INNER LIFE. Selected by R. C. JONES. *Thirteenth Edition.* *Fcap 8vo.* 2s. 6d. net.

Julian (Lady) of Norwich. REVELA-TIONS OF DIVINE LOVE. Edited by GRACE WARRACK. *Third Edition. Cr. 8vo.* 3s. 6d.

'Kappa.' LET YOUTH BUT KNOW: A Plea for Reason in Education. Second Edition. *Cr. 8vo.* 3s. 6d. net.

Keats (John). THE POEMS. Edited with Introduction and Notes by E. de SÉLINCOURT, M.A. With a Frontispiece in Photogravure. *Second Edition Revised. Demy 8vo.* 7s. 6d. net.

Keble (John). THE CHRISTIAN YEAR. With an Introduction and Notes by W. LOCK, D.D., Warden of Keble College. Illustrated. *Third Edition. Fcap. 8vo.* 3s. 6d.; *padded morocco.* 5s.

Kempis (Thomas à). THE IMITATION OF CHRIST. With an Introduction by DEAN FARRAR. Illustrated. *Third Edition. Fcap. 8vo.* 3s. 6d.; *padded morocco,* 5s.
Also translated by C. BIGG, D.D. *Cr. 8vo.* 3s. 6d.

Kerr (S. Parnell). GEORGE SELWYN AND THE WITS. Illustrated. *Demy 8vo.* 12s. 6d. net.

Kipling (Rudyard). BARRACK-ROOM BALLADS. *96th Thousand. Twenty-eighth Edition. Cr. 8vo.* 6s. Also *Fcap. 8vo, Leather.* 5s. net.
THE SEVEN SEAS. *81st Thousand. Sixteenth Edition. Cr. 8vo.* 6s. Also *Fcap. 8vo, Leather.* 5s. net.
THE FIVE NATIONS. *69th Thousand. Seventh Edition. Cr. 8vo.* 6s. Also *Fcap. 8vo, Leather.* 5s. net.
DEPARTMENTAL DITTIES. *Eighteenth Edition. Cr. 8vo.* 6s. Also *Fcap. 8vo, Leather.* 5s. net.

Knox (Winifred F.). THE COURT OF A SAINT. Illustrated. *Demy 8vo.* 10s. 6d. net.

Lamb (Charles and Mary), THE WORKS. Edited by E. V. LUCAS. Illustrated. *In Seven Volumes. Demy 8vo.* 7s. 6d. each.

Lane-Poole (Stanley). A HISTORY OF EGYPT IN THE MIDDLE AGES. Illustrated. *Cr. 8vo.* 6s.

Lankester (Sir Ray), K.C.B., F.R.S. SCIENCE FROM AN EASY CHAIR. Illustrated. *Fifth Edition. Cr. 8vo.* 6s.

Leach (Henry). THE SPIRIT OF THE LINKS. *Cr. 8vo.* 6s.

Le Braz (Anatole). THE LAND OF PARDONS. Translated by FRANCES M. GOSTLING. Illustrated. *Third Edition. Cr. 8vo.* 6s.

Lees (Frederick). A SUMMER IN TOURAINE. Illustrated. *Second Edition. Demy 8vo.* 10s. 6d. net.

Lindsay (Lady Mabel). ANNI DOMINI: A GOSPEL STUDY. With Maps. *Two Volumes. Super Royal 8vo.* 10s. net.

Llewellyn (Owen) and Raven-Hill (L.). THE SOUTH-BOUND CAR. Illustrated. *Cr. 8vo.* 6s.

Lock (Walter), D.D., Warden of Keble College. ST. PAUL, THE MASTER-BUILDER. *Third Edition. Cr. 8vo.* 3s. 6d.
THE BIBLE AND CHRISTIAN LIFE. *Cr. 8vo.* 6s.

Lodge (Sir Oliver), F.R.S. THE SUBSTANCE OF FAITH, ALLIED WITH SCIENCE: A Catechism for Parents and Teachers. *Tenth Edition. Cr. 8vo.* 2s. net.
MAN AND THE UNIVERSE: A STUDY OF THE INFLUENCE OF THE ADVANCE IN SCIENTIFIC KNOWLEDGE UPON OUR UNDER-STANDING OF CHRISTIANITY. *Ninth Edition. Demy 8vo.* 5s. net.
THE SURVIVAL OF MAN. A STUDY IN UNRECOGNISED HUMAN FACULTY. *Fourth Edition. Demy 8vo.* 7s. 6d. net.

Lofthouse (W. F.), M.A. ETHICS AND ATONEMENT. With a Frontispiece. *Demy 8vo.* 5s. net.

Lorimer (George Horace). LETTERS FROM A SELF-MADE MERCHANT TO HIS SON. Illustrated. *Eighteenth Edition. Cr. 8vo.* 3s. 6d.
OLD GORGON GRAHAM. Illustrated. *Second Edition. Cr. 8vo.* 6s.

Lorimer (Norma). BY THE WATERS OF EGYPT. Illustrated. *Demy 8vo.* 16s. net.

Lucas (E. V.). THE LIFE OF CHARLES LAMB. Illustrated. *Fifth and Revised Edition in One Volume. Demy 8vo.* 7s. 6d. net.
A WANDERER IN HOLLAND. Illustrated. *Twelfth Edition. Cr. 8vo.* 6s.
A WANDERER IN LONDON. Illustrated. *Tenth Edition. Cr. 8vo.* 6s.
A WANDERER IN PARIS. Illustrated. *Sixth Edition. Cr. 8vo.* 6s.

THE OPEN ROAD: A Little Book for Wayfarers. *Seventeenth Edition. Fcp. 8vo.* 5s.; *India Paper,* 7s. 6d.

THE FRIENDLY TOWN: a Little Book for the Urbane. *Sixth Edition. Fcap. 8vo.* 5s.; *India Paper,* 7s. 6d.

FIRESIDE AND SUNSHINE. *Sixth Edition. Fcap. 8vo.* 5s.

CHARACTER AND COMEDY. *Sixth Edition. Fcap. 8vo.* 5s.

THE GENTLEST ART. A Choice of Letters by Entertaining Hands. *Sixth Edition. Fcap 8vo.* 5s.

A SWAN AND HER FRIENDS. Illustrated. *Demy 8vo.* 12s. 6d. net.

HER INFINITE VARIETY: A FEMININE PORTRAIT GALLERY. *Fifth Edition. Fcap. 8vo.* 5s.

LISTENER'S LURE: AN OBLIQUE NARRATION. *Eighth Edition. Fcap. 8vo.* 5s.

GOOD COMPANY: A RALLY OF MEN. *Second Edition. Fcap. 8vo.* 5s.

ONE DAY AND ANOTHER. *Fourth Edition. Fcap. 8vo.* 5s.

OVER BEMERTON'S: AN EASY-GOING CHRONICLE. *Eighth Edition. Fcap. 8vo.* 5s.

M. (R.). THE THOUGHTS OF LUCIA HALLIDAY. With some of her Letters. Edited by R. M. *Fcap. 8vo.* 2s. 6d. net.

Macaulay (Lord). CRITICAL AND HISTORICAL ESSAYS. Edited by F. C. MONTAGUE, M.A. *Three Volumes. Cr. 8vo.* 18s.

McCabe (Joseph) (formerly Very Rev. F. ANTONY, O.S.F.). THE DECAY OF THE CHURCH OF ROME. *Second Edition. Demy 8vo.* 7s. 6d. net.

McCullagh (Francis). The Fall of Abd-ul-Hamid. Illustrated. *Demy 8vo.* 10s. 6d. net.

MacCunn (Florence A.). MARY STUART. Illustrated. *New and Cheaper Edition. Large Cr. 8vo.* 6s.

McDougall (William), M.A. (Oxon., M.B. (Cantab.). AN INTRODUCTION TO SOCIAL PSYCHOLOGY. *Third Edition. Cr. 8vo.* 5s. net.

'Mdlle. Mori' (Author of). ST. CATHERINE OF SIENA AND HER TIMES. Illustrated. *Second Edition. Demy 8vo.* 7s. 6d. net.

Maeterlinck (Maurice). THE BLUE BIRD: A FAIRY PLAY IN SIX ACTS. Translated by ALEXANDER TEIXEIRA DE MATTOS. *Eighteenth Edition. Fcap. 8vo. Deckle Edges.* 3s. 6d. net. *Also Fcap. 8vo. Paper covers,* 1s. net.

Mahaffy (J. P.), Litt.D. A HISTORY OF THE EGYPT OF THE PTOLEMIES. Illustrated. *Cr. 8vo.* 6s.

Maitland (F. W.), M.A., LL.D. ROMAN CANON LAW IN THE CHURCH OF ENGLAND. *Royal 8vo.* 7s. 6d.

Marett (R. R.), M.A., Fellow and Tutor of Exeter College, Oxford. THE THRESHOLD OF RELIGION. *Cr. 8vo.* 3s. 6d. net.

Marriott (Charles). A SPANISH HOLIDAY. Illustrated. *Demy 8vo.* 7s. 6d. net.

Marriott (J. A. R.), M.A. THE LIFE AND TIMES OF LORD FALKLAND. Illustrated. *Second Edition. Demy 8vo.* 7s. 6d. net.

Masefield (John). SEA LIFE IN NELSON'S TIME. Illustrated. *Cr. 8vo.* 3s. 6d. net.

A SAILOR'S GARLAND. Selected and Edited. *Second Edition. Cr. 8vo.* 3s. 6d. net.

AN ENGLISH PROSE MISCELLANY. Selected and Edited. *Cr. 8vo.* 6s.

Masterman (C. F. G.), M.A., M.P. TENNYSON AS A RELIGIOUS TEACHER. *Second Edition. Cr. 8vo.* 6s.

THE CONDITION OF ENGLAND. *Fourth Edition. Cr. 8vo.* 6s.

Mayne (Ethel Colburn). ENCHANTER OF MEN. Illustrated. *Demy 8vo.* 10s. 6d. net.

Meakin (Annette M. B.), Fellow of the Anthropological Institute. WOMAN IN TRANSITION. *Cr. 8vo.* 6s.

GALICIA: THE SWITZERLAND OF SPAIN. Illustrated. *Demy 8vo.* 12s. 6d. net.

Medley (D. J.), M.A., Professor of History in the University of Glasgow. ORIGINAL ILLUSTRATIONS OF ENGLISH CONSTITUTIONAL HISTORY, COMPRISING A SELECTED NUMBER OF THE CHIEF CHARTERS AND STATUTES. *Cr. 8vo.* 7s. 6d. net.

Methuen (A. M. S.), M.A. THE TRAGEDY OF SOUTH AFRICA. *Cr. 8vo.* 2s. net.

ENGLAND'S RUIN: DISCUSSED IN FOURTEEN LETTERS TO A PROTECTIONIST. *Ninth Edition. Cr. 8vo.* 3d. net.

Meynell (Everard). COROT AND HIS FRIENDS. Illustrated. *Demy 8vo.* 10s. 6d. net.

Miles (Eustace), M.A. LIFE AFTER LIFE: OR, THE THEORY OF REINCARNATION. *Cr. 8vo.* 2s. 6d. net.

THE POWER OF CONCENTRATION: HOW TO ACQUIRE IT. *Third Edition. Cr. 8vo.* 3s. 6d. net.

Millais (J. G.). THE LIFE AND LETTERS OF SIR JOHN EVERETT MILLAIS, President of the Royal Academy. Illustrated. *New Edition. Demy 8vo.* 7s. 6d. net.

Milne (J. G.), M.A. A HISTORY OF EGYPT UNDER ROMAN RULE. Illustrated. *Cr. 8vo.* 6s.

Mitton (G. E.). JANE AUSTEN AND HER TIMES. Illustrated. *Second and Cheaper Edition. Large Cr. 8vo. 6s.*

Moffat (Mary M.). QUEEN LOUISA OF PRUSSIA. Illustrated. *Fourth Edition. Cr. 8vo. 6s.*

Money (L. G. Chiozza). RICHES AND POVERTY. *Ninth Edition. Cr. 8vo. 1s. net.* Also *Demy 8vo. 5s. net.*
MONEY'S FISCAL DICTIONARY, 1910. *Demy 8vo. Second Edition. 5s. net.*

Moore (T. Sturge). ART AND LIFE. Illustrated. *Cr. 8vo. 5s. net.*

Moorhouse (E. Hallam). NELSON'S LADY HAMILTON. Illustrated. *Second Edition. Demy 8vo. 7s. 6d. net.*

Morgan (J. H.), M.A. THE HOUSE OF LORDS AND THE CONSTITUTION. With an Introduction by the LORD CHANCELLOR. *Cr. 8vo. 1s. net.*

Morton (A. Anderson). See Brodrick (M.).

Norway (A. H.). NAPLES. PAST AND PRESENT. Illustrated. *Third Edition. Cr. 8vo. 6s.*

Oman (C. W. C.), M.A., Fellow of All Souls', Oxford. A HISTORY OF THE ART OF WAR IN THE MIDDLE AGES. Illustrated. *Demy 8vo. 10s. 6d. net.*
ENGLAND BEFORE THE NORMAN CONQUEST. With Maps. *Second Edition. Demy 8vo. 10s. 6d. net.*

Oxford (M. N.), of Guy's Hospital. A HANDBOOK OF NURSING. *Fifth Edition. Cr. 8vo. 3s. 6d.*

Pakes (W. C. C.). THE SCIENCE OF HYGIENE. Illustrated. *Demy 8vo. 15s.*

Parker (Eric). THE BOOK OF THE ZOO; BY DAY AND NIGHT. Illustrated. *Second Edition. Cr. 8vo. 6s.*

Parsons (Mrs. C.). THE INCOMPARABLE SIDDONS. Illustrated. *Demy 8vo. 12s. 6d. net.*

Patmore (K. A.). THE COURT OF LOUIS XIII. Illustrated. *Third Edition. Demy 8vo. 10s. 6d. net.*

Patterson (A. H.). MAN AND NATURE ON TIDAL WATERS. Illustrated. *Cr. 8vo. 6s.*

Petrie (W. M. Flinders), D.C.L., LL.D., Professor of Egyptology at University College. A HISTORY OF EGYPT. Illustrated. *In Six Volumes. Cr. 8vo. 6s. each.*

VOL. I. FROM THE EARLIEST KINGS TO XVITH DYNASTY. *Sixth Edition.*
VOL. II. THE XVIITH AND XVIIITH DYNASTIES. *Fourth Edition.*
VOL. III. XIXTH TO XXXTH DYNASTIES.
VOL. IV. EGYPT UNDER THE PTOLEMAIC DYNASTY. J. P. MAHAFFY, Litt.D.
VOL. V. EGYPT UNDER ROMAN RULE. J. G. MILNE, M.A.
VOL. VI. EGYPT IN THE MIDDLE AGES. STANLEY LANE-POOLE, M.A.
RELIGION AND CONSCIENCE IN ANCIENT EGYPT. Lectures delivered at University College, London. Illustrated. *Cr. 8vo. 2s. 6d.*
SYRIA AND EGYPT, FROM THE TELL EL AMARNA LETTERS. *Cr. 8vo. 2s. 6d.*
EGYPTIAN TALES. Translated from the Papyri. First Series, ivth to xiith Dynasty. Edited by W. M. FLINDERS PETRIE. Illustrated. *Second Edition. Cr. 8vo. 3s. 6d.*
EGYPTIAN TALES. Translated from the Papyri. Second Series, xviiith to xixth Dynasty. Illustrated. *Cr. 8vo. 3s. 6d.*
EGYPTIAN DECORATIVE ART. A Course of Lectures delivered at the Royal Institution. Illustrated. *Cr. 8vo. 3s. 6d.*

Phelps (Ruth S.). SKIES ITALIAN: A LITTLE BREVIARY FOR TRAVELLERS IN ITALY. *Fcap. 8vo. 5s. net.*

Phythian (J. Ernest). TREES IN NATURE, MYTH, AND ART. Illustrated. *Cr. 8vo. 6s.*

Podmore (Frank). MODERN SPIRITUALISM. *Two Volumes. Demy 8vo. 21s. net.*
MESMERISM AND CHRISTIAN SCIENCE: A Short History of Mental Healing. *Second Edition. Demy 8vo. 10s. 6d. net.*

Pollard (Alfred W.). SHAKESPEARE FOLIOS AND QUARTOS. A Study in the Bibliography of Shakespeare's Plays, 1594-1685. Illustrated. *Folio. 21s. net.*

Powell (Arthur E.). FOOD AND HEALTH. *Cr. 8vo. 3s. 6d. net.*

Power (J. O'Connor). THE A G OF AN ORATOR. *Cr. 8vo. 6M KIN*

Price (L. L.), M.A., Fellow of Oriel College, Oxon. A HISTORY OF ENGLISH POLITICAL ECONOMY FROM ADAM SMITH TO ARNOLD TOYNBEE. *Sixth Edition. Cr. 8vo. 2s. 6d.*

Pullen-Burry (B.). IN A GERMAN COLONY; or, FOUR WEEKS IN NEW BRITAIN. Illustrated. *Cr. 8vo. 5s. net.*

Pycraft (W. P.). BIRD LIFE. Illustrated. *Demy 8vo. 10s. 6d. net.*

Ragg (Lonsdale), B.D. Oxon. DANTE AND HIS ITALY. Illustrated. *Demy 8vo.* 12s. 6d. net.

*Rappoport (Angelo S.). HOME LIFE IN RUSSIA. Illustrated. *Demy 8vo.* 10s. 6d. net.

Raven-Hill (L.). See Llewellyn (Owen).

Rawlings (Gertrude). COINS AND HOW TO KNOW THEM. Illustrated. *Third Edition. Cr. 8vo.* 5s. net.

Rea (Lilian). THE LIFE AND TIMES OF MARIE MADELEINE COUNTESS OF LA FAYETTE. Illustrated, *Demy 8vo.* 10s. 6d. net.

Read (C. Stanford), M.B. (Lond.), M.R.C.S., L.R.C.P. FADS AND FEEDING. *Cr. 8vo.* 2s. 6d. net.

Rees (J. D.), C.I.E., M.P. THE REAL INDIA. *Second Edition. Demy 8vo.* 10s. 6d. net.

Reich (Emil), Doctor Juris. WOMAN THROUGH THE AGES. Illustrated. *Two Volumes. Demy 8vo.* 21s. net.

Reid (Archdall), M.B. THE LAWS OF HEREDITY. *Second Edition. Demy 8vo.* 21s. net.

Richmond (Wilfrid), Chaplain of Lincoln's Inn. THE CREED IN THE EPISTLES. *Cr. 8vo.* 2s. 6d. net.

Roberts (M. E.). See Channer (C.C.).

Robertson (A.), D.D., Lord Bishop of Exeter. REGNUM DEI. (The Bampton Lectures of 1901.) *A New and Cheaper Edition. Demy 8vo.* 7s. 6d. net.

Robertson (C. Grant), M.A., Fellow of All Souls' College, Oxford. SELECT STATUTES, CASES, AND CONSTITUTIONAL DOCUMENTS, 1660-1832. *Demy 8vo.* 10s. 6d. net.

Robertson (Sir G. S.), K.C.S.I. CHITRAL: THE STORY OF A MINOR SIEGE. Illustrated. *Third Edition. Demy 8vo.* 10s. 6d. net.

Roe (Fred). OLD OAK FURNITURE. Illustrated. *Second Edition. Demy 8vo.* 10s. 6d. net.

Royde-Smith (N. G.). THE PILLOW BOOK: A GARNER OF MANY MOODS. Collected. *Second Edition. Cr. 8vo.* 4s. 6d. net.
POETS OF OUR DAY. Selected, with an Introduction. *Fcap. 8vo.* 5s.

Rumbold (The Right Hon. Sir Horace), Bart., G.C.B., G.C.M.G. THE AUSTRIAN COURT IN THE NINETEENTH CENTURY. Illustrated. *Second Edition. Demy 8vo.* 18s. net.

Russell (W. Clark). THE LIFE OF ADMIRAL LORD COLLINGWOOD. Illustrated. *Fourth Edition. Cr. 8vo.* 6s.

St. Francis of Assisi. THE LITTLE FLOWERS OF THE GLORIOUS MESSER, AND OF HIS FRIARS. Done into English, with Notes by WILLIAM HEYWOOD. Illustrated. *Demy 8vo.* 5s. net.

'Saki' (H. Munro). REGINALD. *Second Edition. Fcap. 8vo.* 2s. 6d. net.
REGINALD IN RUSSIA. *Fcap. 8vo.* 2s. 6d. net.

Sanders (Lloyd). THE HOLLAND HOUSE CIRCLE. Illustrated. *Second Edition. Demy 8vo.* 12s. 6d. net.

*Scott (Ernest). TERRE NAPOLÉON, AND THE EXPEDITION OF DISCOVERY DESPATCHED TO AUSTRALIA BY ORDER OF BONAPARTE, 1800-1804. Illustrated. *Demy 8vo.* 10s. 6d. net.

Sélincourt (Hugh de). GREAT RALEGH. Illustrated. *Demy 8vo.* 10s. 6d. net.

Selous (Edmund). TOMMY SMITH'S ANIMALS. Illustrated. *Eleventh Edition. Fcap. 8vo.* 2s. 6d.
TOMMY SMITH'S OTHER ANIMALS. Illustrated. *Fifth Edition. Fcap. 8vo.* 2s. 6d.

*Shafer (Sara A.). A WHITE PAPER GARDEN. Illustrated. *Demy 8vo.* 7s. 6d. net.

Shakespeare (William).
THE FOUR FOLIOS, 1623; 1632; 1664; 1685. Each £4 4s. net, or a complete set, £12 12s. net.
Folios 2, 3 and 4 are ready.
THE POEMS OF WILLIAM SHAKESPEARE. With an Introduction and Note by GEORGE WYNDHAM. *Demy 8vo. Buckram, gilt top.* 10s. 6d.

Sharp (A.). VICTORIAN POETS. *Cr. 8vo.* 2s. 6d.

Sidgwick (Mrs. Alfred). HOME LIFE IN GERMANY. Illustrated. *Second Edition. Demy 8vo.* 10s. 6d. net.

Sime (John). See Little Books on Art.

Sladen (Douglas). SICILY: The New Winter Resort. Illustrated. *Second Edition. Cr. 8vo.* 5s. net.

Smith (Adam). THE WEALTH OF NATIONS. Edited with an Introduction and numerous Notes by EDWIN CANNAN, M.A. *Two Volumes. Demy 8vo.* 21s. net.

Smith (Sophia S.). DEAN SWIFT. Illustrated. *Demy 8vo.* 10s. 6d. net.

Snell (F. J.). A BOOK OF EXMOOR. Illustrated. *Cr. 8vo.* 6s.

'Stancliffe.' GOLF DO'S AND DON'TS. *Second Edition. Fcap. 8vo.* 1s.

Stead (Francis H.), M.A. HOW OLD AGE PENSIONS BEGAN TO BE. Illustrated. *Demy 8vo.* 2s. 6d. net.

Stevenson (R. L.). THE LETTERS OF ROBERT LOUIS STEVENSON TO HIS FAMILY AND FRIENDS. Selected and Edited by Sir SIDNEY COLVIN. *Ninth Edition. Two Volumes. Cr. 8vo.* 12s.
VAILIMA LETTERS. With an Etched Portrait by WILLIAM STRANG. *Eighth Edition. Cr. 8vo. Buckram.* 6s.
THE LIFE OF R. L. STEVENSON. See Balfour (G.).

Stevenson (M. I.). FROM SARANAC TO THE MARQUESAS. Being Letters written by Mrs. M. I. STEVENSON during 1887–88. *Cr. 8vo.* 6s. net.
LETTERS FROM SAMOA, 1891-95. Edited and arranged by M. C. BALFOUR. Illustrated. *Second Edition. Cr. 8vo.* 6s. net.

Storr (Vernon F.), M.A., Canon of Winchester. DEVELOPMENT AND DIVINE PURPOSE. *Cr. 8vo.* 5s. net.

Streatfeild (R. A.). MODERN MUSIC AND MUSICIANS. Illustrated. *Second Edition. Demy 8vo.* 7s. 6d. net.

Swanton (E. W.). FUNGI AND HOW TO KNOW THEM. Illustrated. *Cr. 8vo.* 6s. net.

*Sykes (Ella C.). PERSIA AND ITS PEOPLE. Illustrated. *Demy 8vo.* 10s. 6d. net.

Symes (J. E.), M.A. THE FRENCH REVOLUTION. *Second Edition. Cr. 8vo.* 2s. 6d.

Tabor (Margaret E.). THE SAINTS IN ART. Illustrated. *Fcap. 8vo.* 3s. 6d. net.

Taylor (A. E.). THE ELEMENTS OF METAPHYSICS. *Second Edition. Demy 8vo.* 10s. 6d. net.

Taylor (John W.). THE COMING OF THE SAINTS. Illustrated. *Demy 8vo.* 7s. 6d. net.

Thibaudeau (A. C.). BONAPARTE AND THE CONSULATE. Translated and Edited by G. K. FORTESCUE, LL.D. Illustrated. *Demy 8vo.* 10s. 6d. net.

Thompson (Francis). SELECTED POEMS OF FRANCIS THOMPSON. With a Biographical Note by WILFRID MEYNELL. With a Portrait in Photogravure. *Second Edition. Fcap. 8vo.* 5s. net.

Tileston (Mary W.). DAILY STRENGTH FOR DAILY NEEDS. *Seventeenth Edition. Medium 16mo.* 2s. 6d. net. Also an edition in superior binding, 6s.

Toynbee (Paget), M.A., D. Litt. DANTE IN ENGLISH LITERATURE: FROM CHAUCER TO CARY. *Two Volumes. Demy 8vo.* 21s. net.
See also Oxford Biographies.

Tozer (Basil). THE HORSE IN HISTORY. Illustrated. *Cr. 8vo.* 6s.

Trench (Herbert). DEIRDRE WEDDED, AND OTHER POEMS. *Second and Revised Edition. Large Post 8vo.* 6s.
NEW POEMS. *Second Edition. Large Post 8vo.* 6s.
APOLLO AND THE SEAMAN. *Large Post 8vo. Paper,* 1s. 6d. net; *cloth,* 2s. 6d. net.

Trevelyan (G. M.), Fellow of Trinity College, Cambridge. ENGLAND UNDER THE STUARTS. With Maps and Plans. *Fourth Edition. Demy 8vo.* 10s. 6d. net.

Triggs (Inigo H.), A.R.I.B.A. TOWN PLANNING: PAST, PRESENT, AND POSSIBLE. Illustrated. *Second Edition. Wide Royal 8vo.* 15s. net.

Vaughan (Herbert M.), B.A. (Oxon), F.S.A. THE LAST OF THE ROYAL STUARTS, HENRY STUART, CARDINAL, DUKE OF YORK. Illustrated. *Second Edition. Demy 8vo.* 10s. 6d. net.
THE MEDICI POPES (LEO X. AND CLEMENT VII.). Illustrated. *Demy 8vo.* 15s. net.
THE NAPLES RIVIERA. Illustrated. *Second Edition. Cr. 8vo.* 6s.
*FLORENCE AND HER TREASURES. Illustrated. *Fcap. 8vo.* 5s. net.

Vernon (Hon. W. Warren), M.A. READINGS ON THE INFERNO OF DANTE. With an Introduction by the REV. DR. MOORE. *Two Volumes. Second Edition. Cr. 8vo.* 15s. net.
READINGS ON THE PURGATORIO OF DANTE. With an Introduction by the late DEAN CHURCH. *Two Volumes. Third Edition. Cr. 8vo.* 15s. net.
READINGS ON THE PARADISO OF DANTE. With an Introduction by the BISHOP OF RIPON. *Two Volumes. Second Edition. Cr. 8vo.* 15s. net.

Vincent (J. E.). THROUGH EAST ANGLIA IN A MOTOR CAR. Illustrated. *Cr. 8vo.* 6s.

Waddell (Col. L. A.), LL.D., C.B. LHASA AND ITS MYSTERIES. With a Record of the Expedition of 1903-1904. Illustrated. *Third and Cheaper Edition. Medium 8vo.* 7s. 6d. net.

Wagner (Richard). RICHARD WAGNER'S MUSIC DRAMAS: Interpretations, embodying Wagner's own explanations. By ALICE LEIGHTON CLEATHER and BASIL CRUMP. *In Three Volumes. Fcap. 8vo.* 2s. 6d. each.
VOL. I.—THE RING OF THE NIBELUNG. *Third Edition.*
VOL. III.—TRISTAN AND ISOLDE.

Walneman (Pau). A SUMMER TOUR IN FINLAND. Illustrated. *Demy 8vo.* 10s. 6d. net.

Walkley (A. B.). DRAMA AND LIFE. *Cr. 8vo.* 6s.

Waterhouse (Elizabeth). WITH THE SIMPLE-HEARTED: Little Homilies to Women in Country Places. *Second Edition. Small Pott 8vo.* 2s. net.
COMPANIONS OF THE WAY. Being Selections for Morning and Evening Reading. Chosen and arranged by ELIZABETH WATERHOUSE. *Large Cr. 8vo.* 5s. net.
THOUGHTS OF A TERTIARY. *Second Edition. Small Pott 8vo.* 1s. net.

Watt (Francis). See Henderson (T. F.).

Weigall (Arthur E. P.). A GUIDE TO THE ANTIQUITIES OF UPPER EGYPT: From Abydos to the Sudan Frontier. Illustrated. *Cr. 8vo.* 7s. 6d. net.

Welch (Catharine). THE LITTLE DAUPHIN. Illustrated. *Cr. 8vo.* 6s.

Wells (J.), M.A., Fellow and Tutor of Wadham College. OXFORD AND OXFORD LIFE. *Third Edition. Cr. 8vo.* 3s. 6d.
A SHORT HISTORY OF ROME. *Tenth Edition.* With 3 Maps. *Cr. 8vo.* 3s. 6d.

Westell (W. Percival). THE YOUNG NATURALIST. Illustrated. *Cr. 8vo.* 6s.

Westell (W. Percival), F.L.S., M.B.O.U., and Cooper (C. S.), F.R.H.S. THE YOUNG BOTANIST. Illustrated. *Cr. 8vo.* 3s. 6d. net.

*Wheeler (Ethel R.). FAMOUS BLUE STOCKINGS. Illustrated. *Demy 8vo.* 10s. 6d. net.

Whibley (C.). See Henley (W. E.).

White (George F.), Lieut.-Col. A CENTURY OF SPAIN AND PORTUGAL, 1788-1898. *Demy 8vo.* 12s. 6d. net.

Whitley (Miss). See Dilke (Lady).

Wilde (Oscar). DE PROFUNDIS. *Twelfth Edition. Cr. 8vo.* 5s. net.

THE WORKS OF OSCAR WILDE. *In Twelve Volumes. Fcap. 8vo.* 5s. net each volume.
I. LORD ARTHUR SAVILE'S CRIME AND THE PORTRAIT OF MR. W. H. II. THE DUCHESS OF PADUA. III. POEMS. IV. LADY WINDERMERE'S FAN. V. A WOMAN OF NO IMPORTANCE. VI. AN IDEAL HUSBAND. VII. THE IMPORTANCE OF BEING EARNEST. VIII. A HOUSE OF POMEGRANATES. IX. INTENTIONS. X. DE PROFUNDIS AND PRISON LETTERS. XI. ESSAYS. XII. SALOMÉ, A FLORENTINE TRAGEDY, and LA SAINTE COURTISANE.

Williams (H. Noel). THE WOMEN BONAPARTES. The Mother and three Sisters of Napoleon. Illustrated. *In Two Volumes. Demy 8vo.* 24s. net.
A ROSE OF SAVOY: MARIE ADELAIDE OF SAVOY, DUCHESSE DE BOURGOGNE, MOTHER OF LOUIS XV. Illustrated. *Second Edition. Demy 8vo.* 15s. net.
*THE FASCINATING DUC DE RICHELIEU: LOUIS FRANÇOIS ARMAND DU PLESSIS, MARÉCHAL DUC DE RICHELIEU. Illustrated. *Demy 8vo.* 15s. net.

Wood (Sir Evelyn), F.M., V.C., G.C.B., G.C.M.G. FROM MIDSHIPMAN TO FIELD-MARSHAL. Illustrated. *Fifth and Cheaper Edition. Demy 8vo.* 7s. 6d. net.
THE REVOLT IN HINDUSTAN. 1857-59. Illustrated. *Second Edition. Cr. 8vo.* 6s

Wood (W. Birkbeck), M.A., late Scholar of Worcester College, Oxford, and Edmond (Major J. E.), R.E., D.A.Q.-M.G. HISTORY OF THE CIVIL WAR IN THE UNITED STATES. With a Introduction by H. SPENSER WILKINSON. With 24 Maps and Plans. *Third Edition. Demy 8vo.* 12s. 6d. net.

Wordsworth (W.). THE POEMS. With an Introduction and Notes by NOWELL C. SMITH, late Fellow of New College, Oxford. *In Three Volumes. Demy 8vo.* 15s. net.
POEMS BY WILLIAM WORDSWORTH Selected with an Introduction by STOPFORD A. BROOKE. Illustrated. *Cr. 8vo.* 7s. 6d. net.

Wyatt (Kate M.). See Gloag (M. R.).

Wyllie (M. A.). NORWAY AND ITS FJORDS. Illustrated. *Second Edition. Cr. 8vo.* 6s.

Yeats (W. B.). A BOOK OF IRISH VERSE. *Revised and Enlarged Edition. Cr. 8vo.* 3s. 6d.

Young (Filson). See The Complete Series.

PART II.—A SELECTION OF SERIES.

Ancient Cities.

General Editor, B. C. A. WINDLE, D.Sc., F.R.S.

Cr. 8vo. 4s. 6d. net.

With Illustrations by E. H. NEW, and other Artists.

BRISTOL. By Alfred Harvey, M.B.
CANTERBURY. By J. C. Cox, LL.D., F.S.A.
CHESTER. By B. C. A. Windle, D.Sc., F.R.S.
DUBLIN. By S. A. O. Fitzpatrick.

EDINBURGH. By M. G. Williamson, M.A.
LINCOLN. By E. Mansel Sympson, M.A.
SHREWSBURY. By T. Auden, M.A., F.S.A.
WELLS and GLASTONBURY. By T. S. Holmes.

The Antiquary's Books.

General Editor, J. CHARLES COX, LL.D., F.S.A.

Demy 8vo. 7s. 6d. net.

With Numerous Illustrations.

ARCHÆOLOGY AND FALSE ANTIQUITIES. By R. Munro.
BELLS OF ENGLAND, THE. By Canon J. J. Raven. *Second Edition.*
BRASSES OF ENGLAND, THE. By Herbert W. Macklin. *Second Edition.*
CELTIC ART IN PAGAN AND CHRISTIAN TIMES. By J. Romilly Allen.
DOMESDAY INQUEST, THE. By Adolphus Ballard.
ENGLISH CHURCH FURNITURE. By J. C. Cox and A. Harvey. *Second Edition.*
ENGLISH COSTUME. From Prehistoric Times to the End of the Eighteenth Century. By George Clinch.
ENGLISH MONASTIC LIFE. By the Right Rev. Abbot Gasquet. *Fourth Edition.*
ENGLISH SEALS. By J. Harvey Bloom.
FOLK-LORE AS AN HISTORICAL SCIENCE. By Sir G. L. Gomme.

GILDS AND COMPANIES OF LONDON, THE. By George Unwin.
MANOR AND MANORIAL RECORDS, THE. By Nathaniel J. Hone.
MEDIÆVAL HOSPITALS OF ENGLAND, THE. By Rotha Mary Clay.
OLD SERVICE BOOKS OF THE ENGLISH CHURCH. By Christopher Wordsworth, M.A., and Henry Littlehales. *Second Edition.*
PARISH LIFE IN MEDIÆVAL ENGLAND. By the Right Rev. Abbot Gasquet. *Second Edition.*
*PARISH REGISTERS OF ENGLAND, THE. By J. C. Cox.
REMAINS OF THE PREHISTORIC AGE IN ENGLAND. By B. C. A. Windle. *Second Edition.*
ROYAL FORESTS OF ENGLAND, THE. By J. C. Cox, LL.D.
SHRINES OF BRITISH SAINTS. By J. C. Wall.

The Arden Shakespeare.

Demy 8vo. 2s. 6d. net each volume.

An edition of Shakespeare in single Plays. Edited with a full Introduction, Textual Notes, and a Commentary at the foot of the page.

ALL'S WELL THAT ENDS WELL.
ANTONY AND CLEOPATRA.
CYMBELINE.
COMEDY OF ERRORS, THE.
HAMLET. *Second Edition.*
JULIUS CÆSAR.
KING HENRY V.
KING HENRY VI. PT. I.
KING HENRY VI. PT. II.
KING HENRY VI. PT. III.
KING LEAR.
KING RICHARD III.
LIFE AND DEATH OF KING JOHN, THE.
LOVE'S LABOUR'S LOST.
MACBETH.

MEASURE FOR MEASURE.
MERCHANT OF VENICE, THE.
MERRY WIVES OF WINDSOR, THE.
MIDSUMMER NIGHT'S DREAM, A.
OTHELLO.
PERICLES.
ROMEO AND JULIET.
TAMING OF THE SHREW, THE.
TEMPEST, THE.
TIMON OF ATHENS.
TITUS ANDRONICUS.
TROILUS AND CRESSIDA.
TWO GENTLEMEN OF VERONA, THE.
TWELFTH NIGHT.

Classics of Art.

Edited by Dr. J. H. W. LAING.

With numerous Illustrations. Wide Royal 8vo. Gilt top.

THE ART OF THE GREEKS. By H. B. Walters. 12s. 6d. net.

FLORENTINE SCULPTORS OF THE RENAIS-SANCE. Wilhelm Bode, Ph.D. Translated by Jessie Haynes. 12s. 6d. net.

*GEORGE ROMNEY. By Arthur B. Chamberlain. 12s. 6d. net.

GHIRLANDAIO. Gerald S. Davies. *Second Edition.* 10s. 6d.

MICHELANGELO. By Gerald S. Davies 12s. 6d. net.

RUBENS. By Edward Dillon, M.A. 25s. net

RAPHAEL. By A. P. Oppé. 12s. 6d. net.

*TITIAN. By Charles Ricketts. 12s. 6d. net

*TURNER'S SKETCHES AND DRAWINGS. B A. J. Finberg. 12s. 6d. net. *Secon Edition.*

VELAZQUEZ. By A. de Beruete. 10s. 6d. net

The "Complete" Series.

Fully Illustrated. Demy 8vo.

THE COMPLETE COOK. By Lilian Whitling. 7s. 6d. net.

THE COMPLETE CRICKETER. By Albert E. Knight. 7s. 6d. net.

THE COMPLETE FOXHUNTER. By Charles Richardson. 12s. 6d. net. *Second Edition.*

THE COMPLETE GOLFER. By Harry Vardon. 10s. 6d. net. *Tenth Edition.*

THE COMPLETE HOCKEY-PLAYER. By Eustace E. White. 5s. net. *Second Edition.*

THE COMPLETE LAWN TENNIS PLAYER. By A. Wallis Myers. 10s. 6d. net. *Second Edition.*

THE COMPLETE MOTORIST. By Filso Young. 12s. 6d. net. *New Editio (Seventh).*

THE COMPLETE MOUNTAINEER. By G. D Abraham. 15s. net. *Second Edition.*

THE COMPLETE OARSMAN. By R. C. Lehmann, M.P. 10s. 6d. net.

THE COMPLETE PHOTOGRAPHER. By R Child Bayley. 10s. 6d. net. *Fourt Edition.*

THE COMPLETE RUGBY FOOTBALLER, ON TH NEW ZEALAND SYSTEM. By D. Gallahe and W. J. Stead. 10s. 6d. net. *Secon Edition.*

THE COMPLETE SHOT. By G. T. Teasdal Buckell. 12s. 6d. net. *Third Edition.*

The Connoisseur's Library.

With numerous Illustrations. Wide Royal 8vo. Gilt top. 25s. net.

ENGLISH FURNITURE. By F. S. Robinson.

ENGLISH COLOURED BOOKS. By Martin Hardie.

EUROPEAN ENAMELS. By Henry H. Cunynghame, C.B.

GLASS. By Edward Dillon.

GOLDSMITHS' AND SILVERSMITHS' WORK. By Nelson Dawson. *Second Edition.*

*ILLUMINATED MANUSCRIPTS. By J. Herbert.

IVORIES. By A. Maskell.

JEWELLERY. By H. Clifford Smith. *Secon Edition.*

MEZZOTINTS. By Cyril Davenport.

MINIATURES. By Dudley Heath.

PORCELAIN. By Edward Dillon.

SEALS. By Walter de Gray Birch.

Handbooks of English Church History.

Edited by J. H. BURN, B.D. *Crown 8vo. 2s. 6d. net.*

THE FOUNDATIONS OF THE ENGLISH CHURCH. By J. H. Maude.

THE SAXON CHURCH AND THE NORMAN CONQUEST. By C. T. Cruttwell.

THE MEDIÆVAL CHURCH AND THE PAPACY. By A. C. Jennings.

THE REFORMATION PERIOD. By Henry Gee.

THE STRUGGLE WITH PURITANISM. By Bruce Blaxland.

THE CHURCH OF ENGLAND IN THE EIGHTEENTH CENTURY. By Alfred Plummer.

The Illustrated Pocket Library of Plain and Coloured Books.

Fcap. 8vo. 3s. 6d. net each volume.

WITH COLOURED ILLUSTRATIONS.

OLD COLOURED BOOKS. By George Paston. 2s. net.

THE LIFE AND DEATH OF JOHN MYTTON, ESQ. By Nimrod. *Fifth Edition.*

THE LIFE OF A SPORTSMAN. By Nimrod.

HANDLEY CROSS. By R. S. Surtees. *Third Edition.*

MR. SPONGE'S SPORTING TOUR. By R. S. Surtees.

JORROCKS' JAUNTS AND JOLLITIES. By R. S. Surtees. *Third Edition.*

ASK MAMMA. By R. S. Surtees.

THE ANALYSIS OF THE HUNTING FIELD. By R. S. Surtees.

THE TOUR OF DR. SYNTAX IN SEARCH OF THE PICTURESQUE. By William Combe.

THE TOUR OF DR. SYNTAX IN SEARCH OF CONSOLATION. By William Combe.

THE THIRD TOUR OF DR. SYNTAX IN SEARCH OF A WIFE. By William Combe.

THE HISTORY OF JOHNNY QUAE GENUS. By the Author of 'The Three Tours.'

THE ENGLISH DANCE OF DEATH, from the Designs of T. Rowlandson, with Metrical Illustrations by the Author of 'Doctor Syntax.' *Two Volumes.*

THE DANCE OF LIFE: A Poem. By the Author of 'Dr. Syntax.'

LIFE IN LONDON. By Pierce Egan.

REAL LIFE IN LONDON. By an Amateur (Pierce Egan). *Two Volumes.*

THE LIFE OF AN ACTOR. By Pierce Egan.

THE VICAR OF WAKEFIELD. By Oliver Goldsmith.

THE MILITARY ADVENTURES OF JOHNNY NEWCOMBE. By an Officer.

THE NATIONAL SPORTS OF GREAT BRITAIN. With Descriptions and 50 Coloured Plates by Henry Alken.

THE ADVENTURES OF A POST CAPTAIN. By a Naval Officer.

GAMONIA. By Lawrence Rawstone, Esq.

AN ACADEMY FOR GROWN HORSEMEN. By Geoffrey Gambado, Esq.

REAL LIFE IN IRELAND. By a Real Paddy.

THE ADVENTURES OF JOHNNY NEWCOMBE IN THE NAVY. By Alfred Burton.

THE OLD ENGLISH SQUIRE. By John Careless, Esq.

THE ENGLISH SPY. By Bernard Blackmantle. *Two Volumes. 7s. net.*

WITH PLAIN ILLUSTRATIONS.

THE GRAVE: A Poem. By Robert Blair.

ILLUSTRATIONS OF THE BOOK OF JOB. Invented and engraved by William Blake.

WINDSOR CASTLE. By W. Harrison Ainsworth.

THE TOWER OF LONDON. By W. Harrison Ainsworth.

FRANK FAIRLEGH. By F. E. Smedley.

HANDY ANDY. By Samuel Lover.

THE COMPLEAT ANGLER. By Izaak Walton and Charles Cotton.

THE PICKWICK PAPERS. By Charles Dickens.

Leaders of Religion.

Edited by H. C. BEECHING, M.A., Canon of Westminster. *With Portraits.*
Crown 8vo.   2s. net.

CARDINAL NEWMAN. By R. H. Hutton.

JOHN WESLEY. By J. H. Overton, M.A.

BISHOP WILBERFORCE. By G. W. Daniell, M.A.

CARDINAL MANNING. By A. W. Hutton, M.A.

CHARLES SIMEON. By H. C. G. Moule, D.D.

JOHN KNOX. By F. MacCunn. *Second Edition.*

JOHN HOWE. By R. F. Horton, D.D.

THOMAS KEN. By F. A. Clarke, M.A.

GEORGE FOX, THE QUAKER. By T. Hodgkin, D.C.L. *Third Edition.*

JOHN KEBLE. By Walter Lock, D.D.

THOMAS CHALMERS. By Mrs. Oliphant.

LANCELOT ANDREWES. By R. L. Ottley D.D. *Second Edition.*

AUGUSTINE OF CANTERBURY. By E. L Cutts, D.D.

WILLIAM LAUD. By W. H. Hutton, M.A. *Third Edition.*

JOHN DONNE. By Augustus Jessop, D.D.

THOMAS CRANMER. By A. J. Mason, D.D.

BISHOP LATIMER. By R. M. Carlyle an A. J. Carlyle, M.A.

BISHOP BUTLER. By W. A. Spooner, M.A.

The Library of Devotion.

With Introductions and (where necessary) Notes.

Small Pott 8vo, gilt top, cloth, 2s. ; leather, 2s. 6d. net.

THE CONFESSIONS OF ST. AUGUSTINE. *Seventh Edition.*

THE IMITATION OF CHRIST. *Sixth Edition.*

THE CHRISTIAN YEAR. *Fourth Edition.*

LYRA INNOCENTIUM. *Second Edition.*

THE TEMPLE. *Second Edition.*

A BOOK OF DEVOTIONS. *Second Edition.*

A SERIOUS CALL TO A DEVOUT AND HOLY LIFE. *Fourth Edition.*

A GUIDE TO ETERNITY.

THE INNER WAY. *Second Edition.*

ON THE LOVE OF GOD.

THE PSALMS OF DAVID.

LYRA APOSTOLICA.

THE SONG OF SONGS.

THE THOUGHTS OF PASCAL. *Second Edition.*

A MANUAL OF CONSOLATION FROM THE SAINTS AND FATHERS.

DEVOTIONS FROM THE APOCRYPHA.

THE SPIRITUAL COMBAT.

THE DEVOTIONS OF ST. ANSELM.

BISHOP WILSON'S SACRA PRIVATA.

GRACE ABOUNDING TO THE CHIEF OF SINNERS.

LYRA SACRA : A Book of Sacred Verse *Second Edition.*

A DAY BOOK FROM THE SAINTS AN FATHERS.

A LITTLE BOOK OF HEAVENLY WISDOM. Selection from the English Mystics.

LIGHT, LIFE, and LOVE. A Selection fro the German Mystics.

AN INTRODUCTION TO THE DEVOUT LIFE

THE LITTLE FLOWERS OF THE GLORIOU MESSER ST. FRANCIS AND OF HIS FRIARS.

DEATH AND IMMORTALITY.

THE SPIRITUAL GUIDE.

DEVOTIONS FOR EVERY DAY IN THE WEE AND THE GREAT FESTIVALS.

PRECES PRIVATÆ.

HORÆ MYSTICÆ : A Day Book from th Writings of Mystics of Many Nations.

Little Books on Art.

With many Illustrations. Demy 16mo. Gilt top. 2s. 6d. net.

Each volume consists of about 200 pages, and contains from 30 to 40 Illustrations, including a Frontispiece in Photogravure.

ALBRECHT DÜRER. J. Allen.

ARTS OF JAPAN, THE. E. Dillon.

BOOKPLATES. E. Almack.

BOTTICELLI. Mary L. Bonnor.

BURNE-JONES. F. de Lisle.

*CHRISTIAN SYMBOLISM. Mrs. H. Jenner.

CHRIST IN ART. Mrs. H. Jenner.

CLAUDE. E. Dillon.

CONSTABLE. H. W. Tompkins.

COROT. A. Pollard and E. Birnstingl.

ENAMELS. Mrs. N. Dawson.

FREDERIC LEIGHTON. A. Corkran.

GEORGE ROMNEY. G. Paston.

GREEK ART. H. B. Walters.

GREUZE AND BOUCHER. E. F. Pollard.

HOLBEIN. Mrs. G. Fortescue.

ILLUMINATED MANUSCRIPTS. J. W. Bradley.

JEWELLERY. C. Davenport.

JOHN HOPPNER. H. P. K. Skipton.

SIR JOSHUA REYNOLDS. J. Sime.

MILLET. N. Peacock.

MINIATURES. C. Davenport.

OUR LADY IN ART. Mrs. H. Jenner.

RAPHAEL. A. R. Dryhurst. *Second Edition.*

REMBRANDT. Mrs. E. A. Sharp.

TURNER. F. Tyrrell-Gill.

VANDYCK. M. G. Smallwood.

VELASQUEZ. W. Wilberforce and A. R. Gilbert.

WATTS. R. E. D. Sketchley.

The Little Galleries.

Demy 16mo. 2s. 6d. net.

Each volume contains 20 plates in Photogravure, together with a short outline of the life and work of the master to whom the book is devoted.

A LITTLE GALLERY OF REYNOLDS.

A LITTLE GALLERY OF ROMNEY.

A LITTLE GALLERY OF HOPPNER.

A LITTLE GALLERY OF MILLAIS.

A LITTLE GALLERY OF ENGLISH POETS.

The Little Guides.

With many Illustrations by E. H. NEW and other artists, and from photographs.

Small Pott 8vo, gilt top, cloth, 2s. 6d. net; leather, 3s. 6d. net.

The main features of these Guides are (1) a handy and charming form; (2) illustrations from photographs and by well-known artists; (3) good plans and maps; (4) an adequate but compact presentation of everything that is interesting in the natural features, history, archaeology, and architecture of the town or district treated.

CAMBRIDGE AND ITS COLLEGES. A. H. Thompson. *Third Edition, Revised.*

ENGLISH LAKES, THE. F. G. Brabant.

ISLE OF WIGHT, THE. G. Clinch.

MALVERN COUNTRY, THE. B. C. A. Windle.

NORTH WALES. A. T. Story.

OXFORD AND ITS COLLEGES. J. Wells. *Ninth Edition.*

SHAKESPEARE'S COUNTRY. B. C. A. Windle. *Third Edition.*

ST. PAUL'S CATHEDRAL. G. Clinch.

WESTMINSTER ABBEY. G. E. Troutbeck. *Second Edition.*

———

BUCKINGHAMSHIRE. E. S. Roscoe.

CHESHIRE. W. M. Gallichan.

THE LITTLE GUIDES—*continued.*

CORNWALL. A. L. Salmon.
DERBYSHIRE. J. C. Cox.
DEVON. S. Baring-Gould. *Second Edition.*
DORSET. F. R. Heath. *Second Edition.*
ESSEX. J. C. Cox.
HAMPSHIRE. J. C. Cox.
HERTFORDSHIRE. H. W. Tompkins.
KENT. G. Clinch.
KERRY. C. P. Crane.
MIDDLESEX. J. B. Firth.
MONMOUTHSHIRE. G. W. Wade and J. H. Wade.
NORFOLK. W. A. Dutt. *Second Edition, Revised.*
NORTHAMPTONSHIRE. W. Dry.
*NORTHUMBERLAND. J. E. Morris.
NOTTINGHAMSHIRE. L. Guilford.

OXFORDSHIRE. F. G. Brabant.
SOMERSET. G. W. and J. H. Wade.
*STAFFORDSHIRE. C. E. Masefield.
SUFFOLK. W. A. Dutt.
SURREY. F. A. H. Lambert.
SUSSEX. F. G. Brabant. *Third Edition.*
*WILTSHIRE. F. R. Heath.
YORKSHIRE, THE EAST RIDING. J. E. Morris.
YORKSHIRE, THE NORTH RIDING. J. Morris.

BRITTANY. S. Baring-Gould.
NORMANDY. C. Scudamore.
ROME. C. G. Ellaby.
SICILY. F. H. Jackson.

The Little Library.

With Introductions, Notes, and Photogravure Frontispieces.

Small Pott 8vo. Gilt top. Each Volume, cloth, 1s. 6d. *net ; leather,* 2s. 6d. *net.*

Anon. A LITTLE BOOK OF ENGLISH LYRICS. *Second Edition.*

Austen (Jane). PRIDE AND PREJUDICE. *Two Volumes.*
NORTHANGER ABBEY.

Bacon (Francis). THE ESSAYS OF LORD BACON.

Barham (R. H.). THE INGOLDSBY LEGENDS. *Two Volumes.*

Barnet (Mrs. P. A.). A LITTLE BOOK OF ENGLISH PROSE.

Beckford (William). THE HISTORY OF THE CALIPH VATHEK.

Blake (William). SELECTIONS FROM WILLIAM BLAKE.

Borrow (George). LAVENGRO. *Two Volumes.*
THE ROMANY RYE.

Browning (Robert). SELECTIONS FROM THE EARLY POEMS OF ROBERT BROWNING.

Canning (George). SELECTIONS FROM THE ANTI-JACOBIN : with GEORGE CANNING'S additional Poems.

Cowley (Abraham). THE ESSAYS OF ABRAHAM COWLEY.

Crabbe (George). SELECTIONS FROM GEORGE CRABBE.

Craik (Mrs.). JOHN HALIFAX, GENTLEMAN. *Two Volumes.*

Crashaw (Richard). THE ENGLIS POEMS OF RICHARD CRASHAW.

Dante (Alighieri). THE INFERNO O DANTE. Translated by H. F. CARY.
THE PURGATORIO OF DANTE. Tran lated by H. F. CARY.
THE PARADISO OF DANTE. Tran lated by H. F. CARY.

Darley (George). SELECTIONS FROM THE POEMS OF GEORGE DARLEY

Deane (A. C.). A LITTLE BOOK O LIGHT VERSE.

Dickens (Charles). CHRISTMAS BOOK *Two Volumes.*

Ferrier (Susan). MARRIAGE. *Tw Volumes.*
THE INHERITANCE. *Two Volumes.*

Gaskell (Mrs.). CRANFORD.

Hawthorne (Nathaniel). THE SCARLE LETTER.

Henderson (T. F.). A LITTLE BOO OF SCOTTISH VERSE.

Keats (John). POEMS.

Kinglake (A. W.). EOTHEN. *Seco Edition.*

Lamb (Charles). ELIA, AND THE LAS ESSAYS OF ELIA.

Locker (F.). LONDON LYRICS.

Longfellow (H. W.). SELECTION FROM LONGFELLOW.

THE LITTLE LIBRARY—*continued.*

Marvell (Andrew). THE POEMS OF ANDREW MARVELL.

Milton (John). THE MINOR POEMS OF JOHN MILTON.

Moir (D. M.). MANSIE WAUCH.

Nichols (J. B. B.). A 'LITTLE BOOK OF ENGLISH SONNETS.

Rochefoucauld (La). THE MAXIMS OF LA ROCHEFOUCAULD.

Smith (Horace and James). REJECTED ADDRESSES.

Sterne (Laurence). A SENTIMENTAL JOURNEY.

Tennyson (Alfred, Lord). THE EARLY POEMS OF ALFRED, LORD TENNYSON.
IN MEMORIAM.
THE PRINCESS.
MAUD.

Thackeray (W. M.). VANITY FAIR. *Three Volumes.*
PENDENNIS. *Three Volumes.*
ESMOND.
CHRISTMAS BOOKS.

Vaughan (Henry). THE POEMS OF HENRY VAUGHAN.

Walton (Izaak). THE COMPLEAT ANGLER.

Waterhouse (Elizabeth). A LITTLE BOOK OF LIFE AND DEATH. *Thirteenth Edition.*

Wordsworth (W.). SELECTIONS FROM WORDSWORTH.

Wordsworth (W.) and Coleridge (S. T.) LYRICAL BALLADS.

The Little Quarto Shakespeare.

Edited by W. J. CRAIG. With Introductions and Notes.

Pott 16mo. In 40 Volumes. Gilt top. Leather, price 1s. net each volume.

Mahogany Revolving Book Case. 10s. net.

Miniature Library.

Gilt top.

EUPHRANOR: A Dialogue on Youth. By Edward FitzGerald. *Demy 32mo. Leather,* 2s. net.

THE LIFE OF EDWARD, LORD HERBERT OF CHERBURY. Written by himself. *Demy 32mo. Leather, 2s. net.*

POLONIUS: or Wise Saws and Modern Instances. By Edward FitzGerald. *Demy 32mo. Leather, 2s. net.*

THE RUBÁIYÁT OF OMAR KHAYYÁM. By Edward FitzGerald. *Fourth Edition. Leather, 1s. net.*

The New Library of Medicine.

Edited by C. W. SALEEBY, M.D.; F.R.S. Edin. *Demy 8vo.*

CARE OF THE BODY, THE. By F. Cavanagh. *Second Edition.* 7s. 6d. net.

CHILDREN OF THE NATION, THE. By the Right Hon. Sir John Gorst. *Second Edition.* 7s. 6d. net.

CONTROL OF A SCOURGE, THE: or, How Cancer is Curable. By Chas. P. Childe. 7s. 6d. net.

DISEASES OF OCCUPATION. By Sir Thomas Oliver. 10s. 6d. net.

DRINK PROBLEM, THE, in its Medico-Sociological Aspects. Edited by T. N. Kelynack. 7s. 6d. net.

DRUGS AND THE DRUG HABIT. By H. Sainsbury.

FUNCTIONAL NERVE DISEASES. By A. T. Schofield. 7s. 6d. net.

*HEREDITY, THE LAWS OF. By Archdall Reid. 21s. net.

HYGIENE OF MIND, THE. By T. S. Clouston. *Fifth Edition.* 7s. 6d. net.

INFANT MORTALITY. By Sir George Newman. 7s. 6d. net.

PREVENTION OF TUBERCULOSIS (CONSUMPTION), THE. By Arthur Newsholme. 10s. 6d. net.

AIR AND HEALTH. By Ronald C. Macfie. 7s. 6d. net. *Second Edition.*

The New Library of Music.

Edited by ERNEST NEWMAN. *Illustrated. Demy 8vo. 7s. 6d. net.*

HUGO WOLF. By Ernest Newman. Illustrated.

HANDEL. By R. A. Streatfeild. Illustrated. *Second Edition.*

Oxford Biographies.

Illustrated. Fcap. 8vo. Gilt top. Each volume, cloth, 2s. 6d. net; leather, 3s. 6d. net.

DANTE ALIGHIERI. By Paget Toynbee, M.A., D. Litt. *Third Edition.*

GIROLAMO SAVONAROLA By E. L. S. Horsburgh, M.A. *Second Edition.*

JOHN HOWARD. By E. C. S. Gibson, D.D., Bishop of Gloucester.

ALFRED TENNYSON. By A. C. Benson, M.A. *Second Edition.*

SIR WALTER RALEIGH. By I. A Taylor.

ERASMUS. By E. F. H. Capey.

THE YOUNG PRETENDER. By C. S. Terry.

ROBERT BURNS. By T. F. Henderson.

CHATHAM. By A. S. M'Dowall.

FRANCIS OF ASSISI. By Anna M. Stoddart.

CANNING. By W. Alison Phillips.

BEACONSFIELD. By Walter Sichel.

JOHANN WOLFGANG GOETHE. By H. Atkins.

FRANÇOIS FENELON. By Viscount St. Cyres

Romantic History.

Edited by MARTIN HUME, M.A. *Illustrated. Demy 8vo.*

A series of attractive volumes in which the periods and personalities selected ar such as afford romantic human interest, in addition to their historical importance.

THE FIRST GOVERNESS OF THE NETHERLANDS, MARGARET OF AUSTRIA. Eleanor E. Tremayne. 10s. 6d. net.

TWO ENGLISH QUEENS AND PHILIP. Martin

Hume, M.A. 15s. net.

THE NINE DAYS' QUEEN. Richard Dave With a Preface by Martin Hume, M. *Second Edition.* 10s. 6d. net.

Handbooks of Theology.

THE DOCTRINE OF THE INCARNATION. By R. L. Ottley, D.D. *Fifth Edition revised.* Demy 8vo. 12s. 6d.

A HISTORY OF EARLY CHRISTIAN DOCTRINE. By J. F. Bethune-Baker, M.A. *Demy 8vo.* 10s. 6d.

AN INTRODUCTION TO THE HISTORY OF RELIGION. By F. B. Jevons. M.A. Litt. D. *Fourth Edition. Demy 8vo.* 10s. 6d.

AN INTRODUCTION TO THE HISTORY OF T CREEDS. By A. E. Burn, D.D. *Den 8vo.* 10s. 6d.

THE PHILOSOPHY OF RELIGION IN ENGLA AND AMERICA. By Alfred Caldecott. D. *Demy 8vo.* 10s. 6d.

THE XXXIX. ARTICLES OF THE CHURCH ENGLAND. Edited by E. C. S. Gibsc D.D. *Seventh Edition. Demy 8vo.* 12s.

The Westminster Commentaries.

General Editor, WALTER LOCK, D.D., Warden of Keble College.

Dean Ireland's Professor of Exegesis in the University of Oxford.

THE ACTS OF THE APOSTLES. Edited by R. B. Rackham, M.A. *Demy 8vo.* *Fifth Edition.* 10s. 6d.

THE FIRST EPISTLE OF PAUL THE APOSTLE TO THE CORINTHIANS. Edited by H. L. Goudge, M.A. *Second Ed.* *Demy 8vo.* 6s.

THE BOOK OF EXODUS. Edited by A. H. M'Neile, B.D. With a Map and 3 Plans. *Demy 8vo.* 10s. 6d.

THE BOOK OF EZEKIEL. Edited by H. A. Redpath, M.A., D.Litt. *Demy 8vo.* 10s. 6d.

THE BOOK OF GENESIS. Edited with Introduction and Notes by S. R. Driver, D.D. *Eighth Edition.* *Demy 8vo.* 10s. 6d.

ADDITIONS AND CORRECTIONS IN THE SEVENTH EDITION OF THE BOOK OF GENESIS. By S. R. Driver, D.D. *Demy 8vo.* 1s.

THE BOOK OF JOB. Edited by E. C. S. Gibson, D.D. *Second Edition.* *Demy 8vo.* 6s.

THE EPISTLE OF ST. JAMES. Edited with Introduction and Notes by R. J. Knowling, D.D. *Second Edition.* *Demy 8vo.* 6s.

PART III.—A SELECTION OF WORKS OF FICTION

Albanesi (E. Maria). SUSANNAH AND ONE OTHER. *Fourth Edition.* Cr. 8vo. 6s.
LOVE AND LOUISA. *Second Edition.* Cr. 8vo. 6s.
THE BROWN EYES OF MARY. *Third Edition.* Cr. 8vo. 6s.
I KNOW A MAIDEN. *Third Edition.* Cr. 8vo. 6s.
THE INVINCIBLE AMELIA: OR, THE POLITE ADVENTURESS. *Third Edition.* Cr. 8vo. 3s. 6d.
THE GLAD HEART. *Fifth Edition.* Cr. 8vo. 6s.

Allerton (Mark). SUCH AND SUCH THINGS. Cr. 8vo. 6s.

Annesley (Maude). THIS DAY'S MADNESS. *Second Edition.* Cr. 8vo. 6s.

Bagot (Richard). A ROMAN MYSTERY. *Third Edition.* Cr. 8vo. 6s.
THE PASSPORT. *Fourth Edition.* Cr. 8vo. 6s.
TEMPTATION. *Fifth Edition.* Cr. 8vo. 6s.
ANTHONY CUTHBERT. *Fourth Edition.* Cr. 8vo. 6s.
LOVE'S PROXY. Cr. 8vo. 6s.
DONNA DIANA. *Second Edition.* Cr. 8vo. 6s.
CASTING OF NETS. *Twelfth Edition.* Cr. 8vo. 6s.

Bailey (H. C.). STORM AND TREASURE. *Second Edition.* Cr. 8vo. 6s.

Ball (Oona H.) (Barbara Burke). THEIR OXFORD YEAR. Illustrated. Cr. 8vo. 6s.

BARBARA GOES TO OXFORD. Illustrated. *Third Edition.* Cr. 8vo. 6s.

Baring-Gould (S.). ARMINELL. *Fifth Edition.* Cr. 8vo. 6s.
IN THE ROAR OF THE SEA. *Seventh Edition.* Cr. 8vo. 6s.
MARGERY OF QUETHER. *Third Edition.* Cr. 8vo. 6s.
THE QUEEN OF LOVE. *Fifth Edition.* Cr. 8vo. 6s.
JACQUETTA. *Third Edition.* Cr. 8vo. 6s.
KITTY ALONE. *Fifth Edition.* Cr. 8vo. 6s.
NOEMI. Illustrated. *Fourth Edition.* Cr. 8vo. 6s.
THE BROOM - SQUIRE. Illustrated. *Fifth Edition.* Cr. 8vo. 6s.
DARTMOOR IDYLLS. Cr. 8vo. 6s.
GUAVAS THE TINNER. Illustrated. *Second Edition.* Cr. 8vo. 6s.
BLADYS OF THE STEWPONEY. Illustrated. *Second Edition.* Cr. 8vo. 6s.
PABO THE PRIEST. Cr. 8vo. 6s.
WINEFRED. Illustrated. *Second Edition.* Cr. 8vo. 6s.
ROYAL GEORGIE. Illustrated. Cr. 8vo. 6s.
CHRIS OF ALL SORTS. Cr. 8vo. 6s.
IN DEWISLAND. *Second Edition.* Cr. 8vo. 6s.
THE FROBISHERS. Cr. 8vo. 6s.
DOMITIA. Illustrated. *Second Edition.* Cr. 8vo. 6s.
MRS. CURGENVEN OF CURGENVEN. Cr. 8vo. 6s.

Barr (Robert). IN THE MIDST OF ALARMS. *Third Edition.* Cr. 8vo. 6s.
THE COUNTESS TEKLA. *Fifth Edition.* Cr. 8vo. 6s.

THE MUTABLE MANY. *Third Edition.*
Cr. 8vo. 6s.

Begbie (Harold). THE CURIOUS AND
DIVERTING ADVENTURES OF SIR
JOHN SPARROW; or, THE PROGRESS
OF AN OPEN MIND. *Second Edition. Cr.
8vo. 6s.*

Belloc (H.). EMMANUEL BURDEN,
MERCHANT. Illustrated. *Second Edition.
Cr. 8vo. 6s.*
A CHANGE IN THE CABINET. *Third
Edition. Cr. 8vo. 6s.*

Benson (E. F.). DODO: A DETAIL OF THE
DAY. *Sixteenth Edition. Cr. 8vo. 6s.*

Birmingham (George A.). THE BAD
TIMES. *Second Edition. Cr. 8vo. 6s.*
SPANISH GOLD. *Fifth Edition. Cr.
8vo. 6s.*
THE SEARCH PARTY. *Fourth Edition.
Cr. 8vo. 6s.*

Bowen (Marjorie). I WILL MAIN-
TAIN. *Fourth Edition. Cr. 8vo. 6s.*

Bretherton (Ralph Harold). AN HONEST
MAN. *Second Edition. Cr. 8vo. 6s.*

Capes (Bernard). WHY DID HE DO
IT? *Third Edition. Cr. 8vo. 6s.*

Castle (Agnes and Egerton). FLOWER
O' THE ORANGE, and Other Tales.
Third Edition. Cr. 8vo. 6s.

Clifford (Mrs. W. K.). THE GETTING
WELL OF DOROTHY. Illustrated.
Second Edition. Cr. 8vo. 3s. 6d.

Conrad (Joseph). THE SECRET AGENT:
A Simple Tale. *Fourth Ed. Cr. 8vo. 6s.*
A SET OF SIX. *Fourth Edition. Cr. 8vo. 6s.*

Corelli (Marie). A ROMANCE OF TWO
WORLDS. *Thirtieth Ed. Cr. 8vo. 6s.*
VENDETTA. *Twenty-Eighth Edition. Cr.
8vo. 6s.*
THELMA. *Forty-first Ed. Cr. 8vo. 6s.*
ARDATH: THE STORY OF A DEAD
SELF. *Nineteenth Edition. Cr. 8vo. 6s.*
THE SOUL OF LILITH. *Sixteenth Edi-
tion. Cr. 8vo. 6s.*
WORMWOOD. *Seventeenth Ed. Cr. 8vo. 6s.*
BARABBAS: A DREAM OF THE
WORLD'S TRAGEDY. *Forty-Fourth
Edition. Cr. 8vo. 6s.*
THE SORROWS OF SATAN. *Fifty-Sixth
Edition. Cr. 8vo. 6s.*
THE MASTER CHRISTIAN. *Twelfth
Edition. 177th Thousand. Cr. 8vo. 6s.*
TEMPORAL POWER: A STUDY IN
SUPREMACY. *Second Edition. 150th
Thousand. Cr. 8vo. 6s.*
GOD'S GOOD MAN; A SIMPLE LOVE
STORY. *Fourteenth Edition. 152nd Thou-
sand. Cr. 8vo. 6s.*
HOLY ORDERS: THE TRAGEDY OF A
QUIET LIFE. *Second Edition. 120th
Thousand. Crown 8vo. 6s.*
THE MIGHTY ATOM. *Twenty-eighth
Edition. Cr. 8vo. 6s.*

BOY: a Sketch. *Twelfth Edition. Cr. 8vo
6s.*
CAMEOS. *Thirteenth Edition. Cr. 8vo. 6s*

Cotes (Mrs. Everard). See Duncan (Sara
Jeannette). I

Crockett (S. R.). LOCHINVAR. Illus-
trated. *Third Edition. Cr. 8vo. 6s.*
THE STANDARD BEARER. *Second
Edition. Cr. 8vo. 6s.*

Croker (Mrs. B. M.). THE OLD CAN-
TONMENT. *Cr. 8vo. 6s.*
JOHANNA. *Second Edition. Cr. 8vo. 6s*
THE HAPPY VALLEY. *Fourth Edition
Cr. 8vo. 6s.*
A NINE DAYS' WONDER. *Fourth
Edition. Cr. 8vo. 6s.*
PEGGY OF THE BARTONS. *Seventh
Edition. Cr. 8vo. 6s.*
ANGEL. *Fifth Edition. Cr. 8vo. 6s.*
KATHERINE THE ARROGANT. *Sixth
Edition. Cr. 8vo. 6s.*

Cuthell (Edith E.). ONLY A GUARD
ROOM DOG. Illustrated. *Cr. 8vo. 3s. 6d*

Dawson (Warrington). THE SCAR.
Second Edition. Cr. 8vo. 6s.
THE SCOURGE. *Cr. 8vo. 6s.*

Douglas (Theo.). COUSIN HUGH.
Second Edition. Cr. 8vo. 6s.

Doyle (A. Conan). ROUND THE RED
LAMP. *Eleventh Edition. Cr. 8vo. 6s.*

Duncan (Sara Jeannette) (Mrs. Everard
Cotes).
A VOYAGE OF CONSOLATION. Illus-
trated. *Third Edition. Cr. 8vo. 6s.*
COUSIN CINDERELLA. *Second Edition
Cr. 8vo. 6s.*
THE BURNT OFFERING. *Second
Edition. Cr. 8vo. 6s.*

*Elliot (Robert). THE IMMORTAL
CHARLATAN. *Second Edition. Crown
8vo. 6s.*

Fenn (G. Manville). SYD BELTON; or
The Boy who would not go to Sea. Illustrated. *Second Ed. Cr. 8vo. 3s. 6d.*

Findlater (J. H.). THE GREEN GRAVES
OF BALGOWRIE. *Fifth Edition. Cr.
8vo. 6s.*
THE LADDER TO THE STARS. *Second
Edition. Cr. 8vo. 6s.*

Findlater (Mary). A NARROW WAY.
Third Edition. Cr. 8vo. 6s.
OVER THE HILLS. *Second Edition. Cr.
8vo. 6s.*
THE ROSE OF JOY. *Third Edition
Cr. 8vo. 6s.*
A BLIND BIRD'S NEST. Illustrated
Second Edition. Cr. 8vo. 6s.

Francis (M. E.). (Mrs. Francis Blundell).
STEPPING WESTWARD. *Second Edition. Cr. 8vo. 6s.*

MARGERY O' THE MILL. *Third Edition*. *Cr. 8vo*. 6s.

HARDY-ON-THE-HILL. *Third Edition*. *Cr. 8vo*. 6s.

GALATEA OF THE WHEATFIELD. *Second Edition*. *Cr. 8vo*. 6s.

Fraser (Mrs. Hugh). THE SLAKING OF THE SWORD. *Second Edition*. *Cr. 8vo*. 6s.

GIANNELLA. *Second Edition*. *Cr. 8vo*. 6s.

IN THE SHADOW OF THE LORD. *A Third Edition*. *Cr. 8vo*. 6s.

Fry (B. and C. B.). A MOTHER'S SON. *Fifth Edition*. *Cr. 8vo*. 6s.

Gerard (Louise). THE GOLDEN CENTIPEDE. *Third Edition*. *Cr. 8vo*. 6s.

Gibbs (Philip). THE SPIRIT OF REVOLT. *Second Edition*. *Cr. 8vo*. 6s.

Gissing (George). THE CROWN OF LIFE. *Cr. 8vo*. 6s.

Glendon (George). THE EMPEROR OF THE AIR. Illustrated. *Cr. 8vo*. 6s.

Hamilton (Cosmo). MRS. SKEFFINGTON. *Second Edition*. *Cr. 8vo*. 6s.

Harraden (Beatrice). IN VARYING MOODS. *Fourteenth Edition*. *Cr. 8vo*. 6s.

THE SCHOLAR'S DAUGHTER. *Fourth Edition*. *Cr. 8vo*. 6s.

HILDA STRAFFORD and THE REMITTANCE MAN. *Twelfth Ed*. *Cr. 8vo*. 6s.

INTERPLAY. *Fifth Edition*. *Cr. 8vo*. 6s.

Hichens (Robert). THE PROPHET OF BERKELEY SQUARE. *Second Edition*. *Cr. 8vo*. 6s.

TONGUES OF CONSCIENCE. *Third Edition*. *Cr. 8vo*. 6s.

FELIX. *Seventh Edition*. *Cr. 8vo*. 6s.

THE WOMAN WITH THE FAN. *Eighth Edition*. *Cr. 8vo*. 6s.

BYEWAYS. *Cr. 8vo*. 6s.

THE GARDEN OF ALLAH. *Nineteenth Edition*. *Cr. 8vo*. 6s.

THE BLACK SPANIEL. *Cr. 8vo*. 6s.

THE CALL OF THE BLOOD. *Seventh Edition*. *Cr. 8vo*. 6s.

BARBARY SHEEP. *Second Edition*. *Cr. 8vo*. 6s.

Hillers (Ashton). THE MASTER-GIRL. Illustrated. *Second Edition*. *Cr. 8vo*. 6s.

Hope (Anthony). THE GOD IN THE CAR. *Eleventh Edition*. *Cr. 8vo*. 6s.

A CHANGE OF AIR. *Sixth Edition*. *Cr. 8vo*. 6s.

A MAN OF MARK. *Seventh Ed*. *Cr. 8vo*. 6s.

THE CHRONICLES OF COUNT ANTONIO. *Sixth Edition*. *Cr. 8vo*. 6s.

PHROSO. Illustrated. *Eighth Edition*. *Cr. 8vo*. 6s.

SIMON DALE. Illustrated. *Eighth Edition*. *Cr. 8vo*. 6s.

THE KING'S MIRROR. *Fifth Edition*. *Cr. 8vo*. 6s.

QUISANTE. *Fourth Edition*. *Cr. 8vo*. 6s.

THE DOLLY DIALOGUES. *Cr. 8vo*. 6s.

A SERVANT OF THE PUBLIC. Illustrated. *Fourth Edition*. *Cr. 8vo*. 6s.

TALES OF TWO PEOPLE. *Third Edition*. *Cr. 8vo*. 6s.

THE GREAT MISS DRIVER. *Fourth Edition*. *Cr. 8vo*. 6s.

Hueffer (Ford Maddox). AN ENGLISH GIRL: A ROMANCE. *Second Edition*. *Cr. 8vo*. 6s.

MR. APOLLO: A JUST POSSIBLE STORY. *Second Edition*. *Cr. 8vo*. 6s.

Hutten (Baroness von). THE HALO. *Fifth Edition*. *Cr. 8vo*. 6s.

Hyne (C. J. Cutcliffe). MR. HORROCKS, PURSER. *Fifth Edition*. *Cr. 8vo*. 6s.

PRINCE RUPERT, THE BUCCANEER. Illustrated. *Third Edition*. *Cr. 8vo*. 6s.

Jacobs (W. W.). MANY CARGOES. *Thirty-second Edition*. *Cr. 8vo*. 3s. 6d.

SEA URCHINS. *Sixteenth Edition*. *Cr. 8vo*. 3s. 6d.

A MASTER OF CRAFT. Illustrated. *Ninth Edition*. *Cr. 8vo*. 3s. 6d.

LIGHT FREIGHTS. Illustrated. *Eighth Edition*. *Cr. 8vo*. 3s. 6d.

THE SKIPPER'S WOOING. *Ninth Edition*. *Cr. 8vo*. 3s. 6d.

AT SUNWICH PORT. Illustrated. *Tenth Edition*. *Cr. 8vo*. 3s. 6d.

DIALSTONE LANE. Illustrated. *Seventh Edition*. *Cr. 8vo*. 3s. 6d.

ODD CRAFT. Illustrated. *Fourth Edition*. *Cr. 8vo*. 3s. 6d.

THE LADY OF THE BARGE. Illustrated. *Eighth Edition*. *Cr. 8vo*. 3s. 6d.

SALTHAVEN. Illustrated. *Second Edition*. *Cr. 8vo*. 3s. 6d.

SAILORS' KNOTS. Illustrated. *Fifth Edition*. *Cr. 8vo*. 3s. 6d.

James (Henry). THE SOFT SIDE. *Second Edition*. *Cr. 8vo*. 6s.

THE BETTER SORT. *Cr. 8vo*. 6s.

THE GOLDEN BOWL. *Third Edition*. *Cr. 8vo*. 6s.

Le Queux (William). THE HUNCHBACK OF WESTMINSTER. *Third Edition*. *Cr. 8vo*. 6s.

THE CLOSED BOOK. *Third Edition*. *Cr. 8vo*. 6s.

THE VALLEY OF THE SHADOW. Illustrated. *Third Edition*. *Cr. 8vo*. 6s.

BEHIND THE THRONE. *Third Edition*. *Cr. 8vo*. 6s.

THE CROOKED WAY. *Second Edition*. *Cr. 8vo*. 6s.

Lindsey (William). THE SEVERED MANTLE. *Cr. 8vo*. 6s.

London (Jack). WHITE FANG. *Seventh Edition*. *Cr. 8vo*. 6s.

Lubbock (Basil). DEEP SEA WAR-RIORS. Illustrated. *Third Edition. Cr. 8vo. 6s.*

Lucas (St John). THE FIRST ROUND. *Cr. 8vo. 6s.*

Lyall (Edna). DERRICK VAUGHAN, NOVELIST. *44th Thousand. Cr. 8vo. 3s. 6d.*

Maartens (Maarten). THE NEW RELI-GION: A MODERN NOVEL. *Third Edition. Cr. 8vo. 6s.*
BROTHERS ALL; MORE STORIES OF DUTCH PEASANT LIFE. *Third Edition. Cr. 8vo. 6s.*
THE PRICE OF LIS DORIS. *Second Edition. Cr. 8vo. 6s.*

M'Carthy (Justin H.). THE DUKE'S MOTTO. *Fourth Edition. Cr. 8vo. 6s.*

Macnaughtan (S.). THE FORTUNE OF CHRISTINA M'NAB. *Fifth Edition. Cr. 8vo. 6s.*

Malet (Lucas). COLONEL ENDERBY'S WIFE. *Fourth Edition. Cr. 8vo. 6s.*
A COUNSEL OF PERFECTION. *Second Edition. Cr. 8vo. 6s.*
THE WAGES OF SIN. *Sixteenth Edition. Cr. 8vo. 6s.*
THE CARISSIMA. *Fifth Ed., Cr. 8vo. 6s.*
THE GATELESS BARRIER. *Fifth Edition. Cr. 8vo. 6s.*
THE HISTORY OF SIR RICHARD CALMADY. *Seventh Edition. Cr. 8vo. 6s.*

Mann (Mrs. M. E.). THE PARISH NURSE. *Fourth Edition. Cr. 8vo. 6s.*
A SHEAF OF CORN. *Second Edition. Cr. 8vo. 6s.*
THE HEART-SMITER. *Second Edition. Cr. 8vo. 6s.*
AVENGING CHILDREN. *Second Edition. Cr. 8vo. 6s.*

Marsh (Richard). THE COWARD BE-HIND THE CURTAIN. *Cr. 8vo. 6s.*
THE SURPRISING HUSBAND. *Second Edition. Cr. 8vo. 6s.*
A ROYAL INDISCRETION. *Second Edition. Cr. 8vo. 6s.*
LIVE MEN'S SHOES. *Second Edition. Cr. 8vo. 6s.*

Marshall (Archibald). MANY JUNES. *Second Edition. Cr. 8vo. 6s.*
THE SQUIRE'S DAUGHTER. *Third Edition. Cr. 8vo. 6s.*

Mason (A. E. W.). CLEMENTINA. Illustrated. *Third Edition. Cr. 8vo. 6s.*

Maud (Constance). A DAUGHTER OF FRANCE. *Third Edition. Cr. 8vo. 6s.*

Maxwell (W. B.). VIVIEN. *Ninth Edition. Cr. 8vo. 6s.*
THE RAGGED MESSENGER. *Third Edition. Cr. 8vo. 6s.*
FABULOUS FANCIES. *Cr. 8vo. 6s.*

THE GUARDED FLAME. *Seventh Edition. Cr. 8vo. 6s.*
ODD LENGTHS. *Second Ed. Cr. 8vo. 6s.*
HILL RISE. *Fourth Edition. Cr. 8vo. 6s.*
THE COUNTESS OF MAYBURY: BE-TWEEN YOU AND I. *Fourth Edition. Cr. 8vo. 6s.*

Meade (L. T.). DRIFT. *Second Edition. Cr. 8vo. 6s.*
RESURGAM. *Second Edition. Cr. 8vo. 6s.*
VICTORY. *Cr. 8vo. 6s.*
A GIRL OF THE PEOPLE. Illustrated *Fourth Edition. Cr. 8vo. 3s. 6d.*
HEPSY GIPSY. Illustrated. *Cr. 8vo. 2s. 6d.*
THE HONOURABLE MISS: A STORY OF AN OLD-FASHIONED TOWN. Illustrated *Second Edition. Cr. 8vo. 3s. 6d.*

Mitford (Bertram). THE SIGN OF TH SPIDER. Illustrated. *Seventh Edition Cr. 8vo. 3s. 6d.*

Molesworth (Mrs.). THE RED GRANGE Illustrated. *Second Edition. Cr. 8vo 3s. 6d.*

Montague (C. E.). A HIND LE LOOSE. *Third Edition. Cr. 8vo. 6s.*

Montgomery (K. L.). COLONEL KATE *Second Edition. Cr. 8vo. 6s.*

Morrison (Arthur). TALES OF MEA STREETS. *Seventh Edition. Cr. 8vo. 6s.*
A CHILD OF THE JAGO. *Fifth Edition Cr. 8vo. 6s.*
THE HOLE IN THE WALL. *Fourth Edi tion. Cr. 8vo. 6s.*
DIVERS VANITIES. *Cr. 8vo. 6s.*

Nesbit (E.), (Mrs. H. Bland). THE RE HOUSE. Illustrated. *Fifth Edition Cr. 8vo. 6s.*

Noble (Edward). LORDS OF THE SEA *Third Edition. Cr. 8vo. 6s.*

Ollivant (Alfred). OWD BOB, TH GREY DOG OF KENMUIR. With Frontispiece. *Eleventh Ed. Cr. 8vo. 6s.*

Oppenheim (E. Phillips). MASTER O MEN. *Fourth Edition. Cr. 8vo. 6s.*

Oxenham (John). A WEAVER O WEBS. Illustrated. *Fourth Ed. Cr. 8vo. 6s.*
THE GATE OF THE DESERT. *Fourt Edition. Cr. 8vo. 6s.*
PROFIT AND LOSS. *Fourth Edition Cr. 8vo. 6s.*
THE LONG ROAD. *Fourth Edition. C 8vo. 6s.*
THE SONG OF HYACINTH, AN OTHER STORIES. *Second Edition Cr. 8vo. 6s.*
MY LADY OF SHADOWS. *Fourth Edi tion. Cr. 8vo. 6s.*

Pain (Barry). THE EXILES OF FALOO *Second Edition. Crown 8vo. 6s.*

Parker (Gilbert). PIERRE AND HI. PEOPLE. *Sixth Edition. Cr. 8vo. 6s.*

MRS. FALCHION. *Fifth Edition.* *Cr.* 8*vo.* 6*s.*

THE TRANSLATION OF A SAVAGE. *Fourth Edition.* *Cr.* 8*vo.* 6*s.*

THE TRAIL OF THE SWORD. Illustrated. *Tenth Edition.* *Cr.* 8*vo.* 6*s.*

WHEN VALMOND CAME TO PONTIAC: The Story of a Lost Napoleon. *Sixth Edition.* *Cr.* 8*vo.* 6*s.*

AN ADVENTURER OF THE NORTH. The Last Adventures of 'Pretty Pierre.' *Fourth Edition.* *Cr.* 8*vo.* 6*s.*

THE SEATS OF THE MIGHTY. Illustrated. *Seventeenth Edition.* *Cr.* 8*vo.* 6*s.*

THE BATTLE OF THE STRONG: a Romance of Two Kingdoms. Illustrated. *Sixth Edition.* *Cr.* 8*vo.* 6*s.*

THE POMP OF THE LAVILETTES. *Third Edition.* *Cr.* 8*vo.* 3*s.* 6*d.*

NORTHERN LIGHTS. *Fourth Edition.* *Cr.* 8*vo.* 6*s.*

Pasture (Mrs. Henry de la). THE TYRANT. *Fourth Edition.* *Cr.* 8*vo.* 6*s.*

Patterson (J. E.). WATCHERS BY THE SHORE. *Third Edition.* *Cr.* 8*vo.* 6*s.*

Pemberton (Max). THE FOOTSTEPS OF A THRONE. Illustrated. *Fourth Edition.* *Cr.* 8*vo.* 6*s.*

I CROWN THEE KING. Illustrated. *Cr.* 8*vo.* 6*s.*

LOVE THE HARVESTER: A STORY OF THE SHIRES. Illustrated. *Third Edition.* *Cr.* 8*vo.* 3*s.* 6*d.*

THE MYSTERY OF THE GREEN HEART. *Third Edition.* *Cr.* 8*vo.* 6*s.*

Phillpotts (Eden). LYING PROPHETS. *Third Edition.* *Cr.* 8*vo.* 6*s.*

CHILDREN OF THE MIST. *Fifth Edition.* *Cr.* 8*vo.* 6*s.*

THE HUMAN BOY. With a Frontispiece. *Seventh Edition.* *Cr.* 8*vo.* 6*s.*

SONS OF THE MORNING. *Second Edition.* *Cr.* 8*vo.* 6*s.*

THE RIVER. *Third Edition.* *Cr.* 8*vo.* 6*s.*

THE AMERICAN PRISONER. *Fourth Edition.* *Cr.* 8*vo.* 6*s.*

THE SECRET WOMAN. *Fourth Edition.* *Cr.* 8*vo.* 6*s.*

KNOCK AT A VENTURE. *Third Edition.* *Cr.* 8*vo.* 6*s.*

THE PORTREEVE. *Fourth Edition.* *Cr.* 8*vo.* 6*s.*

THE POACHER'S WIFE. *Second Edition.* *Cr.* 8*vo.* 6*s.*

THE STRIKING HOURS. *Second Edition.* *Cr.* 8*vo.* 6*s.*

THE FOLK AFIELD. *Crown* 8*vo.* 6*s.*

Pickthall (Marmaduke). SAÏD THE FISHERMAN. *Eighth Edition.* *Cr.* 8*vo.* 6*s.*

'Q' (A. T. Quiller Couch). THE WHITE WOLF. *Second Edition.* *Cr.* 8*vo.* 6*s.*

THE MAYOR OF TROY. *Fourth Edition.* *Cr.* 8*vo.* 6*s.*

MERRY-GARDEN AND OTHER STORIES. *Cr.* 8*vo.* 6*s.*

MAJOR VIGOUREUX. *Third Edition.* *Cr.* 8*vo.* 6*s.*

Querido (Israel). TOIL OF MEN. Translated by F. S. ARNOLD. *Cr.* 8*vo.* 6*s.*

Rawson (Maud Stepney). THE ENCHANTED GARDEN. *Fourth Edition.* *Cr.* 8*vo.* 6*s.*

THE EASY GO LUCKIES: OR, ONE WAY OF LIVING. *Second Edition.* *Cr.* 8*vo.* 6*s.*

HAPPINESS. *Second Edition.* *Cr.* 8*vo.* 6*s.*

Rhys (Grace). THE BRIDE. *Second Edition.* *Cr.* 8*vo.* 6*s.*

Ridge (W. Pett). ERB. *Second Edition.* *Cr.* 8*vo.* 6*s.*

A SON OF THE STATE. *Third Edition.* *Cr.* 8*vo.* 3*s.* 6*d.*

A BREAKER OF LAWS. *Cr.* 8*vo.* 3*s.* 6*d.*

MRS. GALER'S BUSINESS. Illustrated. *Second Edition.* *Cr.* 8*vo.* 6*s.*

THE WICKHAMSES. *Fourth Edition.* *Cr.* 8*vo.* 6*s.*

NAME OF GARLAND. *Third Edition.* *Cr.* 8*vo.* 6*s.*

SPLENDID BROTHER. *Fourth Edition.* *Cr.* 8*vo.* 6*s.*

Ritchie (Mrs. David G.). MAN AND THE CASSOCK. *Second Edition.* *Cr.* 8*vo.* 6*s.*

Roberts (C. G. D.). THE HEART OF THE ANCIENT WOOD. *Cr.* 8*vo.* 3*s.* 6*d.*

Robins (Elizabeth). THE CONVERT. *Third Edition.* *Cr.* 8*vo.* 6*s.*

Rosenkrantz (Baron Palle). THE MAGISTRATE'S OWN CASE. *Cr.* 8*vo.* 6*s.*

Russell (W. Clark). MY DANISH SWEETHEART. Illustrated. *Fifth Edition.* *Cr.* 8*vo.* 6*s.*

HIS ISLAND PRINCESS. Illustrated. *Second Edition.* *Cr.* 8*vo.* 6*s.*

ABANDONED. *Second Edition.* *Cr.* 8*vo.* 6*s.*

MASTER ROCKAFELLAR'S VOYAGE. Illustrated. *Fourth Edition.* *Cr.* 8*vo.* 3*s.* 6*d.*

Sandys (Sydney). JACK CARSTAIRS OF THE POWER HOUSE. Illustrated. *Second Edition.* *Cr.* 8*vo.* 6*s.*

Sergeant (Adeline). THE PASSION OF PAUL MARILLIER. *Cr.* 8*vo.* 6*s.*

Shakespear (Olivia). UNCLE HILARY. *Cr.* 8*vo.* 6*s.*

Sidgwick (Mrs. Alfred). THE KINSMAN. Illustrated. *Third Edition.* *Cr.* 8*vo.* 6*s.*

THE SEVERINS. *Fourth Edition.* *Cr.* 8*vo.* 6*s.*

Stewart (Newton V.). A SON OF THE EMPEROR: BEING PASSAGES FROM THE LIFE OF ENZIO, KING OF SARDINIA AND CORSICA. *Cr.* 8*vo.* 6*s.*

Swayne (Martin Lutrell). THE BISHOP AND THE LADY. *Second Edition.* *Cr.* 8*vo.* 6*s.*

Thurston (E. Temple). MIRAGE. *Fourth Edition.* *Cr. 8vo. 6s.*

Underhill (Evelyn). THE COLUMN OF DUST. *Cr. 8vo. 6s.*

Vorst (Marie Van). THE SENTIMENTAL ADVENTURES OF JIMMY BULSTRODE. *Cr. 8vo. 6s.*
IN AMBUSH. *Second Edition. Cr. 8vo. 6s.*

Waineman (Paul). THE WIFE OF NICHOLAS FLEMING. *Cr. 8vo. 6s.*

Watson (H. B. Marriott). TWISTED EGLANTINE. us ra . *Third Edition. Cr. 8vo. 6s.*Ill t ted
THE HIGH TOBY. *Third Edition. Cr. 8vo. 6s.*
A MIDSUMMER DAY'S DREAM. *Third Edition. Cr. 8vo. 6s.*
THE CASTLE BY THE SEA. *Third Edition. Cr. 8vo. 6s.*
THE PRIVATEERS. Illustrated. *Second Edition. Cr. 8vo. 6s.*
A POPPY SHOW: BEING VE S AND DIVERSE TALES. *Cr. 8vo.* 6s.DI R
THE FLOWER OF THE HEART. *Third Edition. Cr. 8vo. 6s.*

Webling (Peggy). THE STORY OF VIRGINIA PERFECT. *Third Edition. Cr. 8vo. 6s.*
*THE SPIRIT OF MIRTH. *Cr. 8vo. 6s.*

Wells (H. G.). THE SEA LADY. *Cr. 8vo. 6s.*, Also *Medium 8vo. 6d.*

Weyman (Stanley). UNDER THE RED ROBE. Illustrated. *Twenty-third Edition. Cr. 8vo. 6s.*

Whitby (Beatrice). THE RESULT O AN ACCIDENT. *Second Edition. C 8vo. 6s.*

White (Edmund). THE HEART O HINDUSTAN. *Cr. 8vo. 6s.*

White (Percy). LOVE AND THE WIS MEN. *Third Edition. Cr. 8vo. 6s.*

Williamson (Mrs. C. N.). THE ADVEN TURE OF PRINCESS SYLVIA. *Secon Edition. Cr. 8vo. 6s.*
THE CASTLE OF THE SHADOWS *Third Edition. Cr. 8vo. 6s.*

Williamson (C. N. and A. M.). TH LIGHTNING CONDUCTOR: Th Strange Adventures of a Motor Car. Illus trated. *Seventeenth Edition. Cr. 8v 6s.* Also *Cr. 8vo. 1s. net.*
THE PRINCESS PASSES : A Romance a Motor. Illustrated. *Ninth Edition Cr. 8vo. 6s.*
MY FRIEND THE CHAUFFEUR. Illus trated. *Tenth Edition. Cr. 8vo. 6s.*
LADY BETTY ACROSS THE WATER *Eleventh Edition. Cr. 8vo. 6s.*
THE CAR OF DESTINY AND IT ERRAND IN . Illustrated. *Fourt Edition. Cr. 8vo.*SPAIN.
THE BOTOR CHAPERON. Illustrate *Sixth Edition. Cr. 8vo. 6s.*
SCARLET RUNNER. Illustrated. *Thir Edition. Cr. 8vo. 6s.*
SET IN SILVER. Illustrated. *Secon Edition. Cr. 8vo. 6s.*
LORD LOVELAND DISCOVER AMERICA. *Second Edition. Cr. 8vo. 6*

Wyllarde (Dolf). THE PATHWAY O THE PIONEER (Nous Autres). *Four Edition. Cr. 8vo. 6s.*

Books for Boys and Girls.

Illustrated. Crown 8vo. 3s. 6d.

THE GETTING WELL OF DOROTHY. By Mrs. W. K. Clifford. *Second Edition.*
ONLY A GUARD-ROOM DOG. By Edith E. Cuthell.
MASTER ROCKAFELLAR'S VOYAGE. By W. Clark Russell. *Fourth Edition.*
SYD BELTON : Or, the Boy who would not go to Sea. By G. Manville Fenn. *Second Edition.*
THE RED GRANGE. By Mrs. Molesworth. *Second Edition.*

A GIRL OF THE PEOPLE. By L. T. Mead *Fourth Edition.*
HEPSY GIPSY. By L. T. Meade. *2s. 6d.*
THE HONOURABLE MISS. By L. T. Mead *Second Edition.*
THERE WAS ONCE A PRINCE. By Mrs. M. Mann.
WHEN ARNOLD COMES HOME. By Mrs. M. Mann.

The Novels of Alexandre Dumas.

Medium 8vo. Price 6d. Double Volumes, 1s.

ACTÉ.
THE ADVENTURES OF CAPTAIN PAMPHILE.
AMAURY.
THE BIRD OF FATE.
THE BLACK TULIP.
THE CASTLE OF EPPSTEIN.
CATHERINE BLUM.
CÉCILE.
THE CHATELET.
THE CHEVALIER D'HARMENTAL. (Double volume.)
CHICOT THE JESTER.
THE COMTE DE MONTGOMERY.
CONSCIENCE.
THE CONVICT'S SON.
THE CORSICAN BROTHERS; and OTHO THE ARCHER.
CROP-EARED JACQUOT.
DOM GORENFLOT.
THE FATAL COMBAT.
THE FENCING MASTER.
FERNANDE.
GABRIEL LAMBERT.
GEORGES.
THE GREAT MASSACRE.
HENRI DE NAVARRE.
HÉLÈNE DE CHAVERNY.

THE HOROSCOPE.
LOUISE DE LA VALLIÈRE. (Double volume.
THE MAN IN THE IRON MASK. (Double volume.)
MAÎTRE ADAM.
THE MOUTH OF HELL.
NANON. (Double volume.)
OLYMPIA.
PAULINE; PASCAL BRUNO; and BONTEKOE.
PÈRE LA RUINE.
THE PRINCE OF THIEVES.
THE REMINISCENCES OF ANTONY.
ROBIN HOOD.
SAMUEL GELB.
THE SNOWBALL and THE SULTANETTA.
SYLVANDIRE.
THE TAKING OF CALAIS.
TALES OF THE SUPERNATURAL.
TALES OF STRANGE ADVENTURE.
TALES OF TERROR.
THE THREE MUSKETEERS. (Double volume.)
THE TRAGEDY OF NANTES.
TWENTY YEARS AFTER. (Double volume.)
THE WILD-DUCK SHOOTER.
THE WOLF-LEADER.

Methuen's Sixpenny Books.

Medium 8vo.

Albanesi (E. Maria). LOVE AND LOUISA.
I KNOW A MAIDEN.
Anstey (F.). A BAYARD OF BENGAL.
Austen (J.). PRIDE AND PREJUDICE.
Bagot (Richard). A ROMAN MYSTERY.
CASTING OF NETS.
DONNA DIANA.
Balfour (Andrew). BY STROKE OF SWORD.

Baring-Gould (S.). FURZE BLOOM.
CHEAP JACK ZITA.
KITTY ALONE.
URITH.
THE BROOM SQUIRE.
IN THE ROAR OF THE SEA.
NOÉMI.
A BOOK OF FAIRY TALES. Illustrated.
LITTLE TU'PENNY.
WINEFRED.
THE FROBISHERS.
THE QUEEN OF LOVE.

ARMINELL.
BLADYS OF THE STEWPONEY.

Barr (Robert). JENNIE BAXTER.
IN THE MIDST OF ALARMS.
THE COUNTESS TEKLA.
THE MUTABLE MANY.

Benson (E. F.). DODO.
THE VINTAGE.

Brontë (Charlotte). SHIRLEY.

Brownell (C. L.). THE HEART OF
JAPAN.

Burton (J. Bloundelle). ACROSS · THE
SALT SEAS.

Caffyn (Mrs.). ANNE MAULEVERER.

Capes (Bernard). THE LAKE, OF
WINE.

Clifford (Mrs. W. K.). A. FLASH OF
SUMMER.
MRS. KEITH'S CRIME.

Corbett (Julian). A BUSINESS IN
GREAT WATERS.

Croker (Mrs. B. M.). ANGEL.
A STATE SECRET.
PEGGY OF THE BARTONS.
JOHANNA.

Dante (Alighieri). THE DIVINE
COMEDY (Cary).

Doyle (A. Conan). ROUND THE RED
LAMP.

Duncan (Sara Jeannette). A VOYAGE
OF CONSOLATION.
THOSE DELIGHTFUL AMERICANS.

Eliot (George). THE MILL ON THE
FLOSS.

Findlater (Jane H.). THE GREEN
GRAVES OF BALGOWRIE.

Gallon (Tom). RICKERBY'S FOLLY.

Gaskell (Mrs.). CRANFORD.
MARY BARTON.
NORTH AND SOUTH.

Gerard (Dorothea). HOLY MATRI-
MONY.
THE CONQUEST OF LONDON.
MADE OF MONEY.

Gissing (G.). THE TOWN TRAVELLER.
THE CROWN OF LIFE.

Glanville (Ernest). THE INCA'S
TREASURE.
THE KLOOF BRIDE.

Gleig (Charles). BUNTER'S CRUISE.

Grimm (The Brothers). GRIMM'
FAIRY TALES.

Hope (Anthony). A MAN OF MARK.
A CHANGE OF AIR.
THE CHRONICLES OF COUN
ANTONIO.
PHROSO.
THE DOLLY DIALOGUES.

Hornung (E. W.). DEAD MEN TEL
NO TALES.

Ingraham (J. H.). THE THRONE O
DAVID.

Le Queux (W.). THE HUNCHBAC
OF WESTMINSTER.

Levett-Yeats (S. K.). THE TRAITOR'
WAY.
ORRAIN.

Linton (E. Lynn). THE TRUE HI
TORY OF JOSHUA DAVIDSON.

Lyall (Edna). DERRICK VAUGHAN.

Malet (Lucas). THE CARISSIMA.
A COUNSEL OF PERFECTION.

Mann (Mrs. M. E.). MRS. PETEF
HOWARD.
A LOST ESTATE.
THE CEDAR STAR.
ONE ANOTHER'S BURDENS.
THE PATTEN EXPERIMENT.
A WINTER'S TALE.

Marchmont (A. W.). MISER HOAD
LEY'S SECRET.
A MOMENT'S ERROR.

Marryat (Captain). PETER SIMPLE.
JACOB FAITHFUL.

March (Richard). A METAMORPHOSIS.
THE TWICKENHAM PEERAGE.
THE GODDESS.
THE JOSS.

Mason (A. E. W.). CLEMENTINA.

Mathers (Helen). HONEY.
GRIFF OF GRIFFITHSCOURT.
SAM'S SWEETHEART.
THE FERRYMAN.

Meade (Mrs. L. T.). DRIFT.
Miller (Esther). LIVING LIES.
Mitford (Bertram). THE SIGN OF THE
SPIDER.
Montresor (F. F.). THE ALIEN.

Morrison (Arthur). THE HOLE IN THE WALL.

Nesbit (E.). THE RED HOUSE.

Norris (W. E.). HIS GRACE.
GILES INGILBY.
THE CREDIT OF THE COUNTY.
LORD LEONARD THE LUCKLESS.
MATTHEW AUSTEN.
CLARISSA FURIOSA.

Oliphant (Mrs.). THE LADY'S WALK.
SIR ROBERT'S FORTUNE.
THE PRODIGALS.
THE TWO MARYS.

Oppenheim (E. P.). MASTER OF MEN.

Parker (Gilbert). THE POMP OF THE LAVILETTES.
WHEN VALMOND CAME TO PONTIAC.
THE TRAIL OF THE SWORD.

Pemberton (Max). THE FOOTSTEPS OF A THRONE.
I CROWN THEE KING.

Phillpotts (Eden). THE HUMAN BOY.
CHILDREN OF THE MIST.
THE POACHER'S WIFE.
THE RIVER.

'Q' (A. T. Quiller Couch). THE WHITE WOLF.

Ridge (W. Pett). A SON OF THE STATE.
LOST PROPERTY.
GEORGE and THE GENERAL.

ERB.

Russell (W. Clark). ABANDONED.
A MARRIAGE AT SEA.
MY DANISH SWEETHEART.
HIS ISLAND PRINCESS.

Sergeant (Adeline). THE MASTER OF BEECHWOOD.
BALBARA'S MONEY.
THE YELLOW DIAMOND.
THE LOVE THAT OVERCAME.

Sidgwick (Mrs. Alfred). THE KINSMAN.

Surtees (R. S.). HANDLEY CROSS.
MR. SPONGE'S SPORTING TOUR.
ASK MAMMA.

Walford (Mrs. L. B.). MR. SMITH.
COUSINS.
THE BABY'S GRANDMOTHER.
TROUBLESOME DAUGHTERS.

Wallace (General Lew). BEN-HUR.
THE FAIR GOD.

Watson (H. B. Marriott). THE ADVENTURERS.
*CAPTAIN FORTUNE.

Weekes (A. B.). PRISONERS OF WAR.

Wells (H. G.). THE SEA LADY.

White (Percy). A PASSIONATE PILGRIM.

PRINTED BY
WILLIAM CLOWES AND SONS, LIMITED,
LONDON AND BECCLES.